NEW STORIES
FROM THE SOUTH

The Year's Best, 1986

edited by
Shannon Ravenel

NEW STORIES
FROM THE SOUTH

The Year's Best, 1986

Algonquin Books of Chapel Hill
1986

published by
Algonquin Books of Chapel Hill
Post Office Box 2225, Chapel Hill, North Carolina 27515–2225
in association with Taylor Publishing Company
1550 West Mockingbird Lane, Dallas, Texas 75235

Library of Congress Cataloging-in-Publication Data
New stories from the South.
1. Short stories, American—Southern States. 2. Southern States—Fiction. 3. American fiction—20th century. I. Ravenel, Shannon.
PS551.N49   1986   813'.01'08975   86–7971
ISBN 0–912867–40–7 cloth
ISBN 0–912697–49–0 paper

CONTENTS

PREFACE

Each of the stories in this book first appeared in an American magazine, review, journal, or quarterly. And all of them appeared there within the year preceding selection for this book. So truly, they *are* all "new."

None of these short stories is, as far as I can know, part of a larger piece. None is an excerpt. Each was written to stand alone. And so they are all truly "stories."

But are they all truly "from the South"?

Twenty years ago, John Corrington White and Miller Williams edited a collection of stories they called *Southern Writing in the Sixties* (LSU Press, 1966). They gave their criteria for selection as follows: "The fiction included here has been selected from the works of . . . writers who were raised in the South . . ." So far so good, clear and simple. They went on to finish the sentence, ". . . or, having reached the age of responsibility, came to the South and became Southerners." That's not as simple.

It's getting harder all the time to draw the borders to the South. People move—both geographically and spiritually—a lot more than they used to. Do we still believe in the Mason-Dixon Line? Does being a Southern place still require one-time membership in the Confederacy? Does being a Southern writer still mean being particularly and peculiarly shaped by history, the past more than the present, nostalgia, defeat, poverty, color, guilt?

I call myself a Southerner. I was born and raised in South Carolina. So were my parents, and their parents, and theirs. I have an accent that doesn't fade completely even though I have lived far away from the Low Country for more than 25 years. In thinking about whether and how to judge what is and what isn't Southern writing, I find that my notion of it hasn't so much to do with geography or a personal relationship with history. What it does have to do with is belonging, something related to my having hung on to my accent. Corrington and Williams said it well: "The Southerner is not the only person who knows where his home is. But he is one of the few to whom it matters very much."

When I chose the stories for this book, I was, in many cases, unaware of the individual authors' origins. I didn't know whether Max Apple had been "raised" Southern, for instance, or whether Ron Carlson had ever "become" Southern, or indeed, anything at all about Doug Crowell. But "Bridging" seemed to me to nearly perfectly celebrate that Southern thing—how much home matters. I didn't know whether Suzanne Brown or Wallace Whatley were raised Southern either, but their stories have the same safe-at-home feeling, if in more explicitly Southern settings than Apple's. Ron Carlson's young male characters, swaying on that chain-link fence, reflect a relationship to a hometown that matters to the writer and his vision as much as the patently Southern hometown does in Sylvia Wilkinson's "Chicken Simon." Velma's voice speaks volumes about *her* home, wherever it is, and does it just as plainly as does Ginnie's Southern bad seed behavior in Mary Hood's story. The grit and determination to make a place for herself of Elizabeth Harris's Texas divorcee is no less true than that of Kurt Rheinheimer's Appalachian umpire or Gloria Norris's Mississippi restauranteur. And loss of the innocent belief in the inviolate security of the home place is painful no matter where it happens—on a pig farm known to Madison Smartt Bell, in David Huddle's Rosemary, Va., in James Lee Burke's field, Mary Ward Brown's evangelical church hall, Luke Whisnant's North St. Louis tenement, or W. A. Smith's Charleston operating room. Love and the commitment to it are, of course, the basis of this Southern home business. See "Martha Jean" for Leon V. Driskell's version of home-in-the-making.

The reader will notice that all but one of the stories here were first published in the so-called "little magazines." Most, but not all, of the journals represented here are issued from Southern locations—Louisiana, Georgia, Mississippi, North Carolina, Texas, Tennessee. The other ones are from such far-flung parts as California, Ohio, New Mexico, Nebraska, Utah. Only one lists New York City as home. The point of all this is to emphasize that wonderful short stories are being first brought to light by "little magazines." Year after year, decade after decade, this country's finest fiction is consistently to be found in the pages of these publications with their consistently tiny circulations. Whatever your favorite American home place, you will find near it a literary journal supporting, on a shoe string, our remarkable outpouring of creative writing. That all but one of the stories here came from the literary journals is not due to any effort on my part to help the literary journals. It is simply because the best short stories are to be found there.

And so here are my favorite new stories from the South. In each of them I find startling evidence of the meaning of "home" to the writer—home of past, of present, and of future; home in the form of place and of person; and, most Southern of all, the discovery of why one speaks with an accent and where one really belongs.

Shannon Ravenel

NEW STORIES
FROM THE SOUTH

The Year's Best, 1986

Max Apple

BRIDGING

(from *The Atlantic*)

At the Astrodome, Nolan Ryan is shaving the corners. He's going through the Giants in order. The radio announcer is not even mentioning that, through the sixth, the Giants haven't had a hit. The Ks mount. Tonight, Nolan passes the Big Train and becomes the all-time strikeout king. Ryan is almost as old as I am, and he still throws nothing but smoke. His fast ball is an aspirin; batters seem to tear their tendons lunging for his curve.

My daughter, Jessica, and I have season tickets, but tonight she's home listening and I'm in the basement of St. Anne's Church, watching Kay Randall's fingertips. Kay is holding her hands out from her chest, her fingertips touching. Her fingers move a little as she talks, and I can hear her nails click when they meet. That's how close I'm sitting.

Kay is talking about "bridging"; that's what her arched fingers represent.

"Bridging," she says, "is the way Brownies become Girl Scouts. It's a slow, steady process. It's not easy, but we allow a whole year for bridging."

Eleven girls in brown jumpers, with orange ties at their necks, are imitating Kay as she talks. They hold their stumpy, chewed fingertips out and bridge them; so do I.

I brought the paste tonight, and the stick-on gold stars, and the thread for sewing buttonholes.

"I feel a little awkward," Kay Randall said on the phone, "asking a man to do these errands . . . but that's my problem, not yours. Just bring the supplies and try to be at the church meeting room a few minutes before seven."

I arrived a half hour early.

"You're off your rocker," Jessica said. She begged me to drop her at the Astrodome on my way to the Girl Scout meeting. "After the game, I'll meet you at the main souvenir stand on the first level. They stay open an hour after the game. I'll be all right. There are cops and ushers every five yards."

She can't believe that I am missing this game to perform my functions as an assistant Girl Scout leader. Our Girl Scout battle has been going on for two months.

"Girl Scouts is stupid," Jessica says. "Who wants to sell cookies and sew buttons and walk around wearing stupid old badges."

When she agreed to go to the first meeting, I was so happy that I volunteered to become an assistant leader. After the meeting, Jessica went directly to the car, the way she does after school, after a birthday party, after a ball game, after anything. A straight line to the car. No jabbering with girlfriends, no smiles, no dallying, just right to the car. She slid into the back seat, belted in, and braced herself for destruction.

I shrugged aside a thousand years of stereotypes and accepted my assistant leader's packet and credentials.

"I'm sure there have been other men in the movement," Kay said. "We just haven't had any in our district. It will be good for the girls."

Not for my Jessica. She won't bridge, she won't budge.

"I know why you're doing this," she said. "You think that because I don't have a mother, Kay Randall and the Girl Scouts will help me. That's crazy. And I know that Sharon is supposed to be like a mother, too. Why don't you just leave me alone."

Sharon is Jessica's therapist. Jessica sees her twice a week. Sharon and I have a meeting once a month.

"We have a lot of shy girls," Kay Randall told me. "Scouting brings them out. Believe me, it's hard to stay shy when you're nine years old and you're sharing a tent with four other girls. You have to count on each other, you have to communicate."

I imagined Jessica zipping up her sleeping bag, mumbling good night to anyone who said it to her first, and then closing her eyes and hating me for sending her out among the happy.

"She likes all sports, especially baseball," I told my leader.

"There's room for baseball in scouting," Kay said. "Once a year, the whole district goes to a game. They mention us on the big scoreboard."

"Jessica and I go to all the home games. We're real fans."

Kay smiled.

"That's why I want her in Girl Scouts. You know, I want her to go to things with her girlfriends, instead of always hanging around with me at ball games."

"I understand," Kay said; "it's part of bridging."

With Sharon, the word is "separation anxiety." That's the fast ball; "bridging" is the curve. Amid all their magic words, I feel as if Jessica and I were standing at home plate blindfolded.

While I await Kay and the members of Troop III, District 6, I eye Saint Anne in her grotto and Saint Gregory and Saint Thomas. Their hands are folded as if they started out bridging and ended up praying.

In October, the principal sent Jessica home from school because Mrs. Simmons caught her in spelling class listening to the World Series through an earphone.

"It's against the school policy," Mrs. Simmons said. "Jessica understands school policy. We confiscate radios and send the child home."

"I'm glad," Jessica said. "It was a cheap-o radio. Now I can watch TV with you."

They sent her home in the middle of the sixth game. I let her stay home for the seventh, too.

The Brewers are her favorite American League team. She likes Rollie Fingers, and especially Robin Yount.

"Does Yount go in the hole better than Harvey Kuenn used to?"

"You bet," I told her. "Kuenn was never a great fielder, but he could hit .300 with his eyes closed."

Kuenn was the Brewers' manager. He has an artificial leg and could barely make it up the dugout steps, but when I was Jessica's age and the Tigers were my team, Kuenn used to stand at the plate, tap the corners with his bat, spit some tobacco juice, and knock liners up the alley.

She took it hard when the Brewers lost.

"If Fingers hadn't been hurt, they would have squashed the Cards, wouldn't they?"

I agreed.

"But, I'm glad for Andujar."

We had Andujar's autograph. Once, we met him at a McDonald's. He was a relief pitcher then, and an erratic right-hander, though in St. Louis he improved. I was happy to get his name on a napkin. Jessica shook his hand.

One night, after I had read her a story, she said, "Daddy, if we were rich, could we go to the away games, too? I mean, if you didn't have to be at work every day?"

"Probably we could," I said, "but wouldn't it get boring? We'd have to stay at hotels and eat in restaurants. Even the players get sick of it."

"Are you kidding?" she said. "I'd never get sick of it."

"Jessica has fantasies of being with you forever, following baseball or whatever," Sharon says. "All she's trying to do is please you. Since she lost her mother, she feels that you and she are alone in the world. She doesn't want to let anyone or anything else into that unit, the two of you. She's afraid of any more losses. And, of course, her greatest worry is about losing you."

"You know," I tell Sharon, "that's pretty much how I feel, too."

"Of course it is," she says. "I'm glad to hear you say it."

Sharon is glad to hear me say almost anything. When I complain that her $100-a-week fee would buy a lot of peanut-butter sandwiches, she says she is "glad to hear" me expressing my anger.

"Sharon's not fooling me," Jessica says. "I know that she thinks drawing those pictures is supposed to make me feel better or something. You're just wasting your money. There's nothing wrong with me."

"It's a long, difficult, expensive process," Sharon says. "You and Jessica have lost a lot. Jessica is going to have to learn to trust the world again. It would help if you could do it, too."

So I decide to trust Girl Scouts. First Girl Scouts, then the world. I make my stand at the meeting of Kay Randall's fingertips. While Nolan Ryan breaks Walter Johnson's strikeout record and pitches a two-hit shutout, I hand paste and thread to nine-year-olds who are sticking and sewing their lives together in ways Jessica and I can't.

Scouting is not altogether new to me. I was a Cub Scout. I owned a blue beanie, and I remember my den mother, Mrs. Clark, very well. A den mother made perfect sense to me then, and still does. Maybe that's why I don't feel uncomfortable being a Girl Scout assistant leader.

We had no den father. Mr. Clark was only a photograph on a wall in the tiny living room where we held our weekly meetings. Mr. Clark had been killed in the Korean War. His son, John, was in the troop. John was stocky, but Mrs. Clark was huge. She couldn't sit on a regular chair, only on a couch or a stool without sides. She was the cashier in the convenience store beneath their apartment. The story we heard was that Walt, the old man who owned the store, felt sorry for her and gave her the job. He was her landlord, too. She sat on a swivel stool and rang up the purchases.

We met at the store and watched while she locked the door; then we followed her up the steep staircase to her three-room apartment. She carried two wet glass bottles of milk. Her body took up the entire width of the staircase. She passed the banisters the way trucks pass each other on a narrow highway.

We were ten years old, a time when everything is funny, especially fat people. But I don't remember ever laughing about Mrs. Clark. She had great dignity and character, and so did John. I didn't know what to call it then, but I knew John was someone you could always trust.

She passed out milk and cookies; then John collected the cups and washed them. They didn't have a television set. The only decoration in the room that barely held all of us was Mr. Clark's picture on the wall. We saw him in his uniform, and we knew he had died in Korea defending his country. We were little boys in blue beanies, drinking milk in the apartment of a hero. Through that aura I came to scouting. I wanted Kay Randall to have all of Mrs. Clark's dignity.

When she takes a deep breath and then bridges, Kay Randall has noticeable armpits. Her wide shoulders narrow into a tiny rib cage. Her armpits are like bridges. She says "bridging" as if it were a mantra, holding her hands before her for about thirty seconds at the start of each meeting.

"A promise is a promise," I told Jessica. "I signed up to be a leader and I'm going to do it, with you or without you."

"But you didn't even ask me if I liked it. You just signed up without talking it over."

"That's true. That's why I'm not going to force you to go along. It was my choice."

"What can you like about it? I hate Melissa Randall. She always has a cold."

"Her mother is a good leader."

"How do you know?"

"She's my boss. I have to like her, don't I?"

I hugged Jessica. "C'mon, honey, give it a chance. What do you have to lose?"

"If you make me go I'll do it, but if I have a choice I won't."

Every other Tuesday, Maria, the fifteen-year-old Greek girl who lives on the corner, babysits Jessica while I go to the Scout meetings. We talk about field trips and about how to earn merit badges. The girls giggle when Kay pins a "Ready Helpers" badge on me, my first merit award.

Jessica thinks it's hilarious. She tells me to wear it to work.

Sometimes, when I watch Jessica brush her hair and tie her ponytail and make her lunch, I start to think that maybe I should just relax and stop the therapy and the scouting and all my not-so-subtle attempts to get her to invite friends over. I start to think that, in spite of everything, she's a good student and she's got a sense of humor. She's barely nine years old; she'll grow up, just as everyone does. John Clark did it without a father; she'll do it without a mother. I start to wonder if Jessica seems to the girls in her class what John Clark seemed to me: dignified, serious, almost an adult, even while we were playing. I admired him; maybe the girls in her class admire her. But John had that hero on the wall, his father in a uniform, dead for reasons John and all the rest of us understood. My Jessica had to explain a neurological disease that she couldn't even pronounce. "I hate it when people ask me about Mom," she said. "I just tell them she fell off the Empire State Building."

* * *

Before our first field trip, I go to Kay's house for a planning session. We're going to collect wildflowers in East Texas. It's a one-day trip; I arranged to rent the school bus.

I told Jessica that she could go on the trip even though she wasn't a member, but she refused.

We sit on colonial furniture in Kay's den. She brings in coffee and we go over the list of sachet supplies. Another troop is joining ours, so there will be a busload among the bluebonnets—twenty-two girls, three women, and me.

"We have to be sure the girls understand that the bluebonnets they pick are on private land and that we have permission to pick them. Otherwise, they might go pick them from along the road-side, which is against the law."

I imagine all twenty-two of them behind bars for picking blue-bonnets, and Jessica laughing while I scramble for bail money.

I keep noticing Kay's hands. I notice them as she pours coffee, as she checks off the items on the list, as she gestures. I keep ex-pecting her to bridge. She has large, solid, confident hands. When she finishes bridging, I sometimes feel like clapping, the way people do after the national anthem.

"I admire you," she tells me. "I admire you for going ahead with Scouts even though your daughter rejects it. She'll get a lot out of it indirectly, from you."

Kay is thirty-three, divorced, and has two daughters. One is a Blue Bird; the older, Melissa, is one of the stubby-fingered girls. Jessica is right; Melissa always has a cold.

Kay teaches fifth grade and has been divorced for three years. I am the first assistant she's ever had.

"My husband, Bill, never helped with Scouts," Kay says. "He was pretty much turned off to everything except his business and drinking. When we separated, I can't honestly say I missed him; he'd never been there. I don't think the girls miss him, either. He only sees them about once a month. He has girlfriends, and his business is doing very well. I guess he has what he wants."

"And you?"

She uses one of those wonderful hands to move the hair away from her eyes, a gesture that makes her seem very young.

"I guess I do, too. I've got the girls and my job. I'm lonesome, though."

We both think about what might have been as we sit beside her glass coffee pot with our lists of supplies that the girls will need to make sachets with their flowers. If she were Barbra Streisand and I were Robert Redford, and the music started playing in the background to give us a clue, and there were a long close-up of our lips, we might just fade into middle age together. But Melissa calls for Mom because her mosquito bite is bleeding where she has scratched it. And I have an angry daughter waiting at home for me. All Kay and I have in common is Girl Scouts. We are both smart enough to know it. When Kay looks at me before going to put alcohol on the mosquito bite, our mutual sadness drips from us like the last drops of coffee through the grounds.

"You really missed something tonight," Jessica tells me. "The Astros did a double steal. I've never seen one before. In the fourth, they sent both Thon and Moreno, and Moreno stole home." She knows batting averages and won-lost percentages, too, just like the older boys. But they go out to play; Jessica stays in and waits for me.

During the field trip, while the girls pick the flowers, I think about Jessica at home, probably beside the radio. Juana, our once-a-week cleaning lady, agreed to work on Saturday so that she could stay with Jessica while I took the all-day field trip.

It was no small event. In the eight months since Vicki had died, I had not yet gone away for an entire day.

I made waffles in the waffle iron for Jessica before I left, but she hardly ate. "If you want anything, just ask Juana."

"Juana doesn't speak English."

"She understands; that's enough."

"Maybe for you it's enough."

"Honey, I told you, you can come. There's plenty of room on the bus. It's not too late for you to change your mind."

"It's not too late for you, either. There's going to be plenty of other leaders there. You don't have to go. You're just doing this to be mean to me."

I was ready for this. I had spent an hour with Sharon steeling myself. "Before she can leave you," Sharon said, "you'll have to show her that you can leave. Nothing's going to happen to her. And don't let her be sick that day."

Jessica is too smart to pull the "I don't feel good" routine. Instead, she became more silent and more unhappy-looking than usual. She stayed in her pajamas while I washed the dishes and got ready to leave.

I hadn't noticed the sadness as it was coming upon Jessica. It must have happened gradually, in the years of Vicki's decline, the years when I paid so little attention to my daughter. At times, Jessica seemed to recognize the truth more than I did.

As my Scouts picked their wildflowers, I remembered the last outing I had planned for Jessica, Vicki, and me. It was to have been a Fourth of July picnic with some friends in Austin. I stopped at the bank and withdrew $150 in cash for the long weekend. But when I came home, Vicki was too sick to move and the air-conditioner had broken. I called our friends to cancel the picnic; then I took Jessica with me to the mall to buy a fan. I bought the biggest one they had, a fifty-eight-inch model that sounded like a hurricane. It could cool 10,000 square feet, but it wasn't enough. Vicki was home sitting blankly in front of the TV set. The fan could move eight tons of air an hour, but I wanted it to save my wife. I wanted a fan that would blow the whole earth out of its orbit.

I had $50 left. I gave it to Jessica and told her to buy anything she wanted.

"Whenever you're sad, Daddy, you want to buy me things." She put the money back in my pocket. "It won't help." She was seven years old, holding my hand tightly in the appliance department at J. C. Penney's.

I watched Melissa sniffle among the wildflowers, and I identified various flowers for Carol and JoAnn and Sue and Linda and Rebecca, who were by now used to me and treated me pretty much as they treated Kay. I noticed that the flower book they were using had very accurate photographs, making it easy to identify the bluebonnets and buttercups and poppies. The Scouts also found several varieties of wild grasses.

We were only seventy miles from home, on some land a wealthy rancher had long ago donated to the Girl Scouts. The girls, bending among the flowers, seemed to have been quickly transformed by the colorful meadow. The gigglers and monotonous singers on the bus were now, like the bees, sucking strength from the beauty around them. Kay was in the midst of them, and so, I realized, was I, not watching and keeping score and admiring from a distance, but participating, becoming a player.

JoAnn and Carol sneaked up from behind me and dropped some dandelions down my back. I chased them; then I helped the other leaders pour the Kool-Aid and distribute the Baggies and the name tags for each girl's flowers.

My daughter is home listening to a ball game, I thought, and I'm out here having fun with nine-year-olds. My life is upside down.

When I came home, with dandelion fragments still on my back, Juana had cleaned the house and I could smell taco sauce in the kitchen. Jessica was in her room. I suspected that she had spent the day listless and tearful, although I had urged her to invite a friend over.

"I had a lot of fun, honey, but I missed you."

She hugged me and cried against my shoulder. I felt like holding her the way I used to when she was an infant, the way I had rocked her to sleep. But she was a big girl now, and she needed not sleep but wakefulness.

"I heard on the news that the Rockets signed Ralph Sampson," she sobbed, "and you hardly ever take me to any pro basketball games."

"But if they have a new center, things will be different. With Sampson, we'll be contenders. Sure, I'll take you."

"Promise?"

"Promise." I promise to take you everywhere, my lovely child, and then to leave you. I'm learning to be a leader.

Madison Smartt Bell

TRIPTYCH 2

(from *The Crescent Review*)

I

The tree line at the top of the ridge was stirred by wind so that
the light snow fell off the branches and scattered down the ragged
slope. The snow parted in grains before the wind and settled in
the low places. Not enough had fallen to coat the long gulley that
ran down the hillside and the gulley lay bare, a reddish slash in the
pale skein of snow. No snow stuck to the old disc-harrow or to the
pump at the bottom of the gulley and these dark forms were outlined sharply, like the dark trees against the sky. Their iron was so
cold it would burn skin at the touch. The iron latch of the gate
near the foot of the hill was cold too, so that no one wanted to
put his bare hand to it. The wind swept down around the grey
board house and carried the smoke from the chimney down to the
ground. The men working in the yard all ducked their heads away
from it. The wind blew across Lisa's face, disturbing her pale hair
and bringing water into her eyes. In a moment it was calm again.

Lisa was well wrapped against any kind of cold, with her cor-
duroy coat down to her knees and her jeans stuffed into red rubber
boots. She sat cross-legged on top of a wash-tub by the table where
some women were cleaning chitlins. The sharp smell didn't bother
her; it was alien and exciting. She was five years old and without
prejudice. Her hair and skin were white enough to make her an

albino, but her eyes were ordinary grey. The hog-killing animated her and she couldn't sit still for long.

Jack Lee and Luther were working over the hog in the long scalding trough. The steam from the water mingled with the smoke of the fire under it, and there was thin vapor coming from the mouths of the two men, who were holding the carcass half out of the water with a length of iron chain. They turned the hog over with the chain to scald it evenly and pulled large clumps of bristles off with their hands. Hair and patches of scum floated on the surface of the cloudy water. When the bristles began to come away easily they raised the hog out of the water and rolled its body onto a bare board platform that was against one side of the trough. Then they scraped and shaved the hair away with big knives, occasionally rinsing the skin with hot water.

The hog's eyes were clenched shut and his jaws were locked together. Lisa scratched a white line along his flank with a scraping disc. It amused her to see the hair coming off in the wide places, but when they had to work closely around the joints and the head the job became difficult and boring. Lisa set her scraper down on the platform and ran off to the shed where the women were trimming scraps for sausage.

Amelia Tyler and Elizabeth were chopping the meat under the shelter. Their black hands moved rapidly across the planks, slicing some of the fat away from the lean meat so the sausage wouldn't turn out too greasy. From time to time they wiped their hands on the fronts of their aprons, and the aprons were blotched brown. Amelia had on a thick coat with the stuffing coming out in places, and her hair was pulled back from her forehead under a bandanna. There was a dent in the front of her head that a small hen's egg could have fit into and she had once told Lisa that something bad had been growing in there and they had cut it out in the hospital. They had talked about it all one evening when Amelia was Lisa's baby-sitter.

Amelia pushed some of the extra fat over to Lisa and gave her a knife to cut it with. Lisa sliced the strips of fat into small square chunks, and Amelia said for her to take it out and put it in the crackling pot. There was a big iron kettle in a frame over a fire outside and Lisa dropped the little squares of fat into it to boil and make the cracklings. Some of them were already done and she dipped one from the surface of the water. It was crisp and golden but it had very little taste at all, and she didn't really want to eat another one.

Over near the scalding trough there was a thick pole lashed into the forks of two trees and four of the seven hogs were hanging from it waiting to be cleaned. The hogs were suspended from pointed sticks which were thrust over the pole and through the tendons of their hind legs, so that the hogs hung head down. Their heads aimed blindly at the frozen ground, and the slashes in their throats were bloodless now and white. They had been scalded and scraped and their bare skin was blue and grey, the color of a bruise. All seven of them belonged to Mrs. Denmark, who was Lisa's mother, but two of them would go to Amelia and Ben Tyler to help pay for all the work they did. They would take the heads and chitlins of all seven hogs too, because white people didn't eat those things.

Ben Tyler was up on the road where the cars were, with Luther. They were sharing bootleg whiskey from a flat unmarked bottle. Looking up there, Lisa could only see their feet under Luther's truck and their hands passing the bottle, through the windows of the cab. Ben was short and stooping and very dark. His face looked almost Chinese and he had a little beard around his mouth and chin. He was still strong, although he was starting to like to talk about how old he was getting. Amelia or Mrs. Denmark would be angry at him most times for drinking but hog killing was a big party for everybody. He told Lisa once that there was nothing like a drink for a cough and then he told her not to tell her mama. She knew that what he said was true because her mother would give her a spoon of whisky with sugar in it if she was coughing and sick.

Robert and Jack Lee were blocking out a hog that had already been gutted. Jack cut off the head with a chopping axe, and then used the axe to separate the backbone out from the ribs. The spine came out in one piece, with the stiff little tail still at the end of it. The men began to section up the sides of meat with their knives.

Ben Tyler came down from the parked cars and went over to where the hogs were hanging. He had a foot tub with him, which he set under the nose of one of the hogs. From the back pocket of his overalls he took a long butcher knife, and he threw down the cigarette that was in his mouth. Lisa was watching attentively, standing near the scalding trough.

Ben stood up straight and pushed the round hat he always wore to the back of his head. He put the point of the knife in between the hog's hind legs and pulled it straight down, almost to the big cut on the throat. Then he laid the knife on the scuffed snow beside the tub and parted the opening he had made. A great knot of blue entrails began to roll out of the hog's chest. Ben guided the tangled guts into the tub with his veiny hands. When they were all detached he took out the liver and began to slosh water into the cavity.

Lisa was backing up, watching Ben closely, and without knowing it she touched her thighs to the rim of the scalding trough. When she tried to take the next step she flipped over the edge and into the water. She was so heavily dressed that very little water got to her skin, but it wasn't easy for her to get out. She hadn't opened her mouth, but Ben and Amelia both came running at the sound of the splash.

Ben grabbed her hands and pulled her scrambling over the lip of the trough. Amelia began to yell at him before she stopped running.

"Why you can't keep an eye on her? Miz Denmark gone skin us alive over this."

"Reckon I better care her back down to her mama's house."

"I'm gone take her right inside here before she freeze to death." Amelia led Lisa to the cutting table and rubbed some fat on her hands and face. The child didn't seem to be badly burned. Amelia picked her up and carried her over the broken steps of the porch and into the house.

There was no light in the room they entered except for a red glow from an opening in the large cylindrical woodstove which heated the house. The windows were blinded and the room was dark and close. They walked across vague lumps of cloth and invisible clutter; nothing could be seen clearly. Amelia took Lisa's outer clothes off and hung them by the stove to dry. She put Lisa down on a sofa and covered her with some blanket.

Lisa lay quietly and looked at the orange eye of the stove. It was hot in the room and there was a heavy smell of wood smoke and human musk. She imagined being swallowed by an animal. The patch of light shimmered and expanded in her eyes, and Lisa went to sleep.

She woke up again in her bed at home without knowing surely how she had come there. There was moonlight out the window and her mother was sitting at the edge of the bed.

"Mama," she said, "I know how come Benjamin's so black. It's cause he works so hard in the dirt and he put his arms up in the pig's belly."

Mrs. Denmark touched her forehead and felt that it was cool.

"Don't say that," she said. "It's not polite to Ben, and it isn't true."

Lisa closed her mouth and turned her eyes to the window. She could see the beginning of the road that ran from her house to the hill where the hog-killing had been. Now she remembered being carried out of the house in the twilight, when the stars were starting to show. Out in the yard there were dark stains and footprints in the snow, which had been melted by the people's walking and had frozen again. The heads of seven hogs rested on the railing of the porch, all the hair scraped from the dull skin except for the toughest bristles. Their eyes were narrowed or entirely closed, and their jaws were shut in jagged smiles. In the vague December light each face seemed to possess some secret.

II

Ben Tyler felt like some piece of scorching wood, walking under the August sun, thinking how the heat might drive him out of his mind. From old habit he wore old clothes that covered everything but his hands and face, and now his body could not breathe. The air was still and heavy and it took effort to penetrate it. He had to keep moving though, to get on with the extra work the drought made for him to do.

All along the barn lot the dirt had hardened and cracked into small octagons and trapezoids. Ben ground powder with his feet, walking on the packed earth. Near an old bathtub which was used as a watering trough a sweaty horse stood, moving only to twitch flies away. Ben passed the tub on his way up the little grade to the barn, and turned the faucet on to refill it. It had not rained for weeks. The pasture was yellowing in the dry heat and the grass seed he had planted on the lawn for Mrs. Denmark had had no chance to sprout.

Mrs. Denmark said it was more important to save the garden than to try to grow grass, so that was how Ben would spend the afternoon. There were sprinklers and hoses in the barn and he would carry them down to the garden to try to keep the ground there moist. Water spilled directly on the plants would boil and scald the leaves, but it would be some help to keep the earth around them from hardening. When he pulled the barn door open it dragged roughly across the small stones fixed in the ground. He needed to raise the hinges.

It was no cooler in the hall of the barn, though the darkness there was a relief to the eyes. Ben's thick shoes sank deeply and coated themselves in the dust of the dirt floor, a much finer powder than the dust outside. He walked up a pair of wooden steps and opened the door to the room where the saddles were kept. The same grit covered the saddles and the shelves that ran along the walls. Ben knelt down and felt in the corners below the lowest shelf for the hose-pipes that had been stored there. He pulled out a length of hose and flexed it in his hands to see if the drought and heat had cracked it. The particles that his motion raised glowed in the flat shafts of sunlight which came through the cracks between the boards of the wall.

He tested all the pieces of pipe he could find and tied them into coils with bits of baling twine. There were two sprinklers under the shelf that he thought were not broken and he took these out also. His tongue felt rough and swollen, too large for his mouth, and he began to think of how thirsty he was. The dim space of the barn smelled of musty straw and dried horse manure. He wished there would be a breeze.

When he came outside again he saw Lisa walking down the steps from the door of her mother's white house. She walked in the dense shade under the big trees of the yard, watching her feet on the brick path and swinging her hands. The dress she wore was pale blue and hung straight to her calves, unbelted. Looking at her across the bare lot, Ben thought that she seemed to be moving in an improbably cool globe, although he knew it was as hot in the yard as anywhere else.

With the coils of hose slung over his shoulder he walked back to the horse trough and sat down on one of the large pocked stones beside the faucet. He reached for the cup that he kept there, filled it from the tap and drank. When he was halfway down the second cupful he looked back toward the house. Lisa had come to the end of the walk and mounted the low brick wall that ran to the gate of the barn lot. She walked along the top of the wall and climbed the square brick post that met the wire fence enclosing the lot. She stood poised on top of the post, her hands out a little from her sides, and stared away over the drying pasture and wooded hill in the direction of Ben's own house. The hem of her dress and the ends of her hair seemed to flutter slightly, though there was no wind to move them. Ben thought that when he had finished his water he would go over and talk to her a little, before he went to the garden.

In the Tyler house it was dark and sweltering; the windows were small and didn't admit much light or air. Amelia had dressed as lightly as possible in a cotton print skirt, but she felt like her huge body was burning from inside. There were four rooms in the house and each was small and low-ceilinged, so that she always felt cramped. The doors between them were almost too narrow for her to pass through.

The front room with the woodstove seemed unnatural in hot weather, for it was meant to hold heat and keep the air out. There were several layers of wallpaper on the walls, too torn and dirty to be decorative. The paper insulation fixed the heat in the room, as did the ragged stuffed furniture. The room was grey with the dirty light that came through the windows. Amelia walked to the door, pushing aside some litter with her feet, newspapers, part of a child's tea set, and a headless doll. She swung the door open, hoping to start some air moving through the house, and stopped to rest a moment, looking down the concrete steps to the gravel road a few yards away.

The toys belonged to Amelia's granddaughter, Jenny's child. Jenny couldn't get along with the man she was married to so she was staying at home for a while. She had never been able to get along well in life and she hadn't married Prester until the baby was almost born. Now she said he was a no-count and she wouldn't stay at his house anymore. She kept the baby, who was four now, but she didn't seem to understand how to take care of her. So Amelia had to watch over the girl whenever she was here, but today she was with Prester's old mother.

From the time she was a baby Jenny never seemed to have good sense, and she didn't have any head for school. She would often stand and stare blankly like she couldn't hear whatever you were saying to her, but it was not until she grew up to the age of sixteen that she began to have the sickness that makes people holler and fall down. When Mrs. Denmark got to know about the falling down she said for Jenny to be taken to the hospital of Central State. There a doctor told Amelia that Jenny would never be smart, which everyone had already known, and it was also discovered that she had become pregnant. They gave names to the things that were wrong with her but Amelia couldn't remember them after they got home, any more than she had remembered the name of the thing that had been growing in her brain that other time. Jenny was given a medicine for the falling sickness, but it often seemed that either she did not take it or it did not work.

When Son, so called because he was named for his daddy, came on leave from the Army, he tried to bring Jenny into the arms of the Lord. For days she had turned her head away when he talked, but when he got her to go to a meeting she became as excited about it as she ever was about anything. Soon she became more devoted than Son had ever been, and she began to go to the meetings where people cry out and speak in unknown tongues, not like the church the Tylers had always belonged to.

It was then, just before Son went back to the Army camp, that Jenny had gone to Prester and got him to marry her. All the family was cheered by this act, and they made the best celebration for her they could. But later it appeared that her life had not really been changed.

Amelia was in the kitchen now, shaking pepper into the pot of pork backbone she was boiling on the electric stove. She felt so hot and bad that it was tiresome to do the smallest things. Some days she couldn't understand what she was working for anymore, when it seemed to take all her efforts just to stay in one place.

Out of all her children only Son had not been a disappointment to everybody. He had gone in that program in the Army where they give you school for nothing. He had a safe job in the Service and now he was an officer. Everyone could tell he had a serious mind.

But the other boy, Henry, had never been able to find a straight path for himself. For short stretches he would work and seem to live right, but it always turned out that he would break loose and spend all his money on wickedness. Because of that he never had any job that amounted to much and in the end no one around wanted to hire him anymore. Finally he got angry with them all and declared he would go to New York or Chicago, where he said there was a better life. No one in the family believed he had the money for such a trip and it was not until he had been gone a few days that they began to notice the small things of value that were missing. They never heard from him and he didn't write to them even for money.

Now she couldn't even talk to Benjamin anymore about all the problems. In her heart she still felt that he was a good man but she could never understand how the bad seed had come into the family. She remembered how he was when they both were young, quick and funny and so strong for his size that everyone was amazed by it. These days his mind was no longer clear and he would always think of drinking whisky and it would be up to her to stop him.

In the bedroom at the front of the house Jenny was still asleep, and she had not undressed yet from coming in the night before. She would often sleep until late in the afternoon, and she never cared to do anything useful. Amelia thought of waking her up, but it seemed there was no reason to. She couldn't think of any direction she herself should move in. She was tired, so tired, and looked forward only to the day when everything would be explained to her. Wiping big drops of sweat from her forehead, she took a step back from the heat of the stove.

Secretly, without at first declaring itself, the malignancy in Amelia's brain had returned and grown to a painful size. As she moved it broke apart and swirled forcefully all through her head. The picture that the room made in her eye diminished to the size of a postage stamp and then disappeared completely, as she fell across the top of the stove. Her elbow struck the boiling pot, which bounced from the wall to the floor, spilling the meat and the water. The crook of her arm rested on the glowing coil of the stove, and after she had lain there for a while the arm began to char.

In the room by the road Jenny turned over on her back and swung her feet to the floor. She put her head into her hands and rubbed at her eyes for a minute or two. Her mouth was sticky and stale, and she rose and moved toward the kitchen to look for something to drink. She walked a little unsteadily, bumping against the door as she left the room.

There was a little sick smell of burning that met her from the kitchen before she entered. When she stepped into the room her eyes grew round and white, and her mouth opened itself and hung waiting. For a moment she stood breathing deeply, and then her hands rose and waved twice in front of her face.

"Oh little Jesus," she said. "Send the demons out of my body." On the last word she threw herself at the floor and rolled there, flailing her arms and legs. Moaning came from her mouth and her spine moved in long violent jerks. A wild sweep of her leg upset a wooden chair, which fell across the door that opened to the back yard. The convulsions of her trunk became stronger and her body thrashed like a snake after it has been hit and before it dies. Her limbs and head were tossed at random by the motion that came from the center of her body, and foam appeared at the edges of her chewing mouth. With each jerk her head slammed soundly against the floor. Gradually the jerks became less frequent, and Jenny lay slackly on her side, knees drawn up toward her chest.

Out in the yard a starling skipped toward the open door in zigzags, picking at the dirt. He hopped onto the edge of the fallen chair and turned his scruffy head sideways to the room. Jenny twitched and raised her head, and the starling flapped sloppily into the air. Jenny clasped the edge of a shelf and raised herself to her feet. She stood and stared at the spilled pot and the massive body humped on the stove. Then she turned and ran out the door, catching her loose shoe on the chair. She rushed into the clumps of buckbushes and cedars at the edge of the yard, following the straightest way to the Denmark house. Her mouth flew open and she began to cry out, not in grunts as she had before, but in high pure screams. As she moved into the thicket her clothes caught on thorned vines, and she began to tear at the front of her garments with her hands, not slowing her pace.

Lisa stayed standing when Benjamin came over to the post; she moved lightly from foot to foot. She would turn her head to look at him and then look away, back to the hill and the trees. Ben's voice rolled out smoothly, explaining how the heat sapped all the life from him, how the weather didn't give a man a chance, how he was feeling his age. All of this Lisa had heard before, too often to be interested, but she loved to hear the sound of his speaking. She shifted her feet and swung her head in rhythm to the talk. An object detached itself from the trees at the edge of the pasture, and Lisa's head stopped moving. Her eyes sharpened and began to track the object on its path down the hill.

Ben was facing away from the hillside, so he couldn't see the running figure. Lisa kept watching and saw that it was a person, that the person was waving its arms and stumbling as it rushed toward the gate between the field and the lot. As it fumbled with the gate latch Lisa recognized it as a woman. The woman thrust the gate open and ran through, leaving the gate swinging. Her feet, sockless in heavy unlaced boots, beat a cloud of dust from the cracked ground. A twig of bramble hung from the skirt of her dark dress, which was torn in front to disclose white underwear and heaving black skin. Her eyes rolled and her mouth flopped exhaustedly, and it was not until Benjamin turned to look at her that she began to scream again.

Ben turned to follow Lisa's glance and saw her coming through the gate. He stood quietly, looking toward Jenny's pumping legs as she came on, crying, "Mama done dead, mama dead," over and over, with other sounds that were not words. Lisa looked down at him from the post and he seemed to bend and shrink smaller in her eyes. Then she felt her mother's hands on her shoulders, turning her back to the house, and heard her voice telling her to go back, to go up to her room and wait, to take a nap. Almost frightened now, Lisa hurried away along the wall, looking back over her shoulder to where Mrs. Denmark was speaking, first to Ben who was shriveling so small, then to shrieking Jenny, trying to extract some form of sense from this mad situation. The scene contracted under the burning sun, as Lisa moved through the green shade into the cool shadows of the house.

III

One hog stood half hidden by a drooping branch of a cedar tree, halfway up the little rising from the shed where they all were fed. He was white with many black blotches, and was covered with wet brown mud, which the rainy winter kept stirred up in the hog lot. The hog and his four brothers of the litter had churned the mud constantly with their small heavy feet, so that around the shed it was worked into a soft gripping paste, several inches deep. But up the rising and back in the lot the ground was firmer, though slick, and there were rocks and roots to stiffen it. The mud on the prickly back of the hog beneath the tree was streaked by the cold morning drizzle.

Inside the feed room Benjamin was sitting on a sack of shelled corn, stopping to breathe a while, for he often felt bad in the mornings now. He took a little drink from the secret bottle that he had left under the empty sacks. The room had a small window and with the door shut it was so dark he could see nothing but shadows. The bottle glinted a little in the dim light and clanked when he set it down. After he had replaced it in the hiding place he could hear disturbed mice moving, under the sacks. He kept several bottles now, hidden in the outbuildings, and believed that no one knew about them. He had told Lisa to wait for him outside the gate, so she wouldn't see him take his drink.

He heard her voice, clear in the foggy air, saying, "Look, Benjamin, the hogs are out." He got up slowly to peer out of the high window, and there was the hog, wrinkling his long snout. Ben picked up a coffee can from the floor and scooped it half full of corn. He opened the door and went out into the lot, rattling the corn to attract the hogs back to the shed. The hog by the cedar tree stiffened and then bolted, and Ben could see the backs of all five of them through the trees as they ran grunting into the brush. Somehow he must have forgotten to latch the door tight the night before, and Jack Lee and Luther were coming to kill this morning. He knew Mrs. Denmark was going to bite his head off when she found out about this.

Lisa leaned all the way back, supporting herself with a hand on the wire gate, and looked up at the sky. There was nothing to see but the mist drifting and a cover of dull-colored cloud. Light rain fell on her face, and she lowered her head and pulled up the hood of her raincoat. Then she turned around and leaned her back against the gate. She could now see Luther's old battered truck coming unevenly across the rough ground, past the cow barn and toward the hog lot.

The truck pulled up beside the lot fence and Luther got out and let down the tailgate, so that later they could load the hogs and haul them away for cleaning and blocking. Lisa could see that both men had white stubble on their faces, and she smelled liquor when they came near. Each carried a light rifle. Ben had come around to the gate to meet them, bringing his own gun.

Ben scratched the back of his neck while he explained that the hogs had got loose, and Luther answered him, mumbling. Luther and Jack Lee came through the gate and the three of them walked up toward the thicket, with Lisa following at a little distance. The hogs had stopped under some low bushes and they had all turned their heads back to the sheds. They tensed as the men came near them but they kept watching and did not run. When the three men raised their rifles a couple of hogs grunted and the group began to swing away. There was a ragged sound of gunfire and squealing as the hogs scattered through the thorn bushes. One burst out into the clearing and ran to the creek bank behind the shed, where it collapsed, floundering. Ben pursued it, almost falling in the mud which clung to his feet as he tried to run, and as he drew near he pulled the butcher knife from his pocket. When he reached the twitching body he dropped onto his knees, shoved the knife hard into the side of the hog's throat, and made a quick slash all across it. The hog kicked and twisted, and a great rush of fresh blood came out and ran into the creek water. Ben stood up and began to walk back toward the others. Lisa, who had been standing apart, trailed behind him, watching everything sharply.

All of the men were laughing and shouting, excited and out of breath. They came together and leaned on their rifle barrels, trying to get their wind back. Only two hogs had been killed by the shots, and they weren't sure how many might have been hit. They didn't rest long before they spread out into the thicket, holding their guns at their hips. Lisa tried to follow them but she was quickly outdistanced. She slowed to a walk and wandered down near the fence at the far end of the lot.

On a high rocky place there was a hog waiting, partly concealed by grey shoots of thorns. Its nostrils were widened and its long flanks moved heavily with its breath. Lisa was near enough to hear the sound of the breathing from the place where she stood. As she watched the hog there were a couple quick cracks and she saw two round red holes appear in the hog's dirty hide. She heard a man yelling and the hog squealed and ran at her, scattering rocks on its path down the slope. When it came near her it sheered away and plunged into the creek bed, heading toward the fence. Lisa turned to follow the hog with her eyes and saw it wriggle through a broken water-gate and disappear into the woods. She ran along the creek to the fence and scrambled over, then followed the hog among the trees.

The hog had run far ahead of her and she had no idea where it could have gone. She looked on the wet ground for tracks, but there were no clear prints, because of the fallen leaves. With her head lowered she moved on into the woods, looking for tracks or traces of blood. These woods were strange to her and they were not on her mother's land, so she knew she should stay near the sound of the creek to be sure of finding her way back again. The noise of running and shooting died away behind her as she went farther into the forest.

Walking, she began to forget about the killing and the hog she was looking for. Around her, everything was pleasantly calm. Brown sparrows were hopping on the ground and fluttering in the trees. Above the tree tops the sky had cleared of rain clouds, though it was still the color of damp limestone. All along the sky looked flat and even, and Lisa thought she saw a buzzard turning through a gap in the branches. It had not become much lighter.

The creek bent across Lisa's path and as she started to cross it she saw that for several feet the stream was heavily stained with blood. For a moment she thought of the hog she was looking for, but then she remembered the one that had fallen in the water earlier. She was surprised, because she wouldn't have expected all the blood to hang together so far down the creek. She began to follow the red patch as it slipped and wound along the stream.

Lisa was fascinated by the quality of the moving blood, how it seemed to be so much more solid than the water. It floated in many small strands which wove themselves in a complicated matrix, and each strand looked as solid as a piece of fiber. Yet when Lisa put her hand into the water the strands divided around it and became insubstantial. She wondered what blood looked like when it was inside a body, and this thought absorbed her so deeply that she would never have noticed the hog if it had not fallen very near the creek.

It lay dully on its side with its hind feet at the edge of the water. Lisa could see no wounds on it, and she thought they must be on the side against the ground. Its body had not stiffened yet, but the eyes were glazing over. Lisa was glad to have found it, and proud that she knew what needed to be done. Then she realized that she had no knife.

Benjamin climbed over the hog lot fence near the place where Lisa had done so and hurried into the woods. He couldn't clear his mind of the picture of Mrs. Denmark's angry face. It had been bad enough when she saw how the hogs had escaped, but when she learned that Lisa was missing she had become almost too furious to speak.

Luther had told Ben that he thought he had seen the girl going over the fence, and so Ben had a chance to be the first to find her. He felt sure that the child would have the sense to stay near the creek, for she had lived around the woods all her life. He moved as fast as he could along the bank, afraid to call her name because there might be no answer. His fear was about to break out in a shout when he came around a turn in the stream and saw her.

She was sitting on the ribs of the warm dead hog, with her hands holding each other in her lap. She wasn't looking in his direction, but away through the trees. At once he saw that she was unhurt and no terrible harm had been done, and his head throbbed with the relief. The thrill of safety made him feel young again, and he ran up to touch her as she turned to look at him. He lifted her under the shoulders and stared into her face, and her eyes were clear and empty as the sky.

Mary Ward Brown

TONGUES OF FLAME

(from *Prairie Schooner*)

The Rev. Zack Benefield, evangelist, had been called in to Rehoboth Church like a doctor to a patient. Rehoboth was more
than a hundred years old and, some thought, dying. A country
church, surrounded by large farms that had swallowed up the small
ones, many of its members had moved away. A few were attending
churches in town, but the majority had simply lost interest and,
more often than not, stayed home on Sunday morning.

Tonight, the third night of a week-long revival, Rehoboth held
more people than in twenty years.

Benefield's sermon was over. His doubleknit coat hung on the
back of the pulpit chair. In spite of two fans directed on him, his
short-sleeved shirt clung wetly to his skin. His broad face was
flushed and his eyes seemed to send out charged blue rays. He had
left the pulpit to come down near the congregation.

"Before I came out here," he said, "I looked up the word 'revival'
in my son's new college dictionary. Just out of curiosity. What it
said was, 'to return to consciousness, to life.' Now . . ." He lowered
his head, then raised it. "If you really want a new life, for your-
selves and this old church, I want you to stand up and be counted
tonight. I want you to come down here and give me your hand.
Because if you don't want that, I'd just as well pack up my suitcase
and head on back home."

On the third row from the front, Dovey Goodwin sat listening,
her hands in her lap, palms up, one inside the other. A farm wife,

middle-aged and overweight, with a sweet face and brown eyes, she was one of the few who kept Rehoboth going. On her left was her husband, Floyd, and next to Floyd, E. L. Nichols, in church for the third time in anyone's memory.

Floyd sat slumped in the pew, his thin legs crossed at the crotch, watching Benefield as he would watch a bird in a tree.

E. L. had begun to shift his weight from one side to the other, and to change the position of his hands and feet. From time to time he stifled a cough. He was a farm overseer and spent his days in the sun, yet his skin never tanned but stayed tender and red as if inflamed. When drunk, his color sank to a clammy white from which it rose like a thermometer as he sobered up.

Benefield called out the hymn number and raised both arms, on which thick, wheat-colored hair sprang up golden in the light.

"While we sing now, won't you come?"

From behind him, to the left, came a piano introduction full of bold off-notes. Abigail Wright, whose forebears had founded and named Rehoboth, was the white-haired pianist. Bringing an evangelist to Rehoboth had been her idea. He was a guest in her home. Never married, since no suitor had been good enough for her parents, she lived alone in the homeplace, its cedar-lined lane within sight of the church.

Benefield unleashed a powerful baritone to get the song under way, and people began to fill the aisles coming forward.

Dovey squeezed past Floyd and E. L. Yes, she wanted a new life for Rehoboth. What would she do if its doors ever closed? She had come to this church for as long as she remembered, and even before, in the arms of her mother. She had in turn brought babies of her own. Her people were buried in the graveyard behind it. Sunday and Rehoboth were the same to her.

She was also here on Saturdays, dusting and cleaning, usually alone. Depending on the weather, Floyd took a nap in the truck or came back to get her. Now and then other women helped wax floors or wash windows. Miss Abby gave money, fixed flowers, and fed the preacher with the help of a cook, but she did not clean up the church. "Dovey is our housekeeper," she said.

"God bless you, Sister." Benefield clasped her hand, looked her in the eye, and turned to the next in line. "Thank you. God bless you."

Half the congregation was already at the front. Others followed, one at a time. Floyd stayed behind with E. L.

On the last verse Benefield lifted a hand to Miss Abby, who stopped playing. "Anyone else?" He checked the pews like an auctioneer. "Will you come?"

E. L. lowered his head, covered his mouth with his hand, and coughed. When singing resumed, Floyd kept his eyes on the song book and sang in a drone like a far-away tractor.

Afterwards, as they turned to leave, hands reached out in all directions to touch E. L. on the arm, pat him on the shoulder.

"Glad to have you, boy."

"See you tomorrow night."

Miss Abby hurried through the crowd. "I wouldn't take anything for you being here, E. L.," she said.

E. L. had worked for her family most of his life, first for her father, then for her brothers who farmed the family land but made their homes in town. "Drunk or sober, he's the best farmer around," everyone agreed.

Benefield stood at the door shaking hands. The church was small, with a vestibule in front and Sunday School walled off in back. The rest of the building was a rectangle focused on the pulpit. Rows of pews lined the center, with shorter pews down each side. Two aisles divided the sections. There was a smell of old wood and musty song books and, over all, an aura of quiet. When empty of people, the sound of dirtdaubers building nests went on all day.

Above the vestibule rose a modest steeple in which hung an iron bell, the end of its rope just above the heads of the people. The bell, once rung each Sunday morning, had been silent so long it was no longer missed.

There was no light in the churchyard except from windows of the building, and the sudden blinding headlights of departing cars and trucks. Behind it the adjoining cemetery lay in darkness. From time to time a pair of headlights picked out several tombstones, to flash them briefly on the screen of night.

People lingered in shadowy groups near the steps. When Benefield had clasped the last hand and let it go, he took out a handkerchief and mopped off his face, neck, and arms. Then he came down the steps like a winning athlete. Smiling and joking, but still on the job, he made his way to where E. L. stood with Floyd and Dovey. Without looking at E. L., he spoke from the side.

"You're on my heart, Brother. I'm praying for you."

As soon as E. L. drove off, everyone turned to the Goodwins.

"Three nights in a row!" someone said. "How did you do it?"

Floyd looked at Dovey.

"All I did was feed him a time or two," she said modestly.

The patent leather purse on Miss Abby's arm flirted with light from the vestibule. "My hat's off to you, Dove," she said. "He never would let me feed him."

On the way home, Floyd and Dovey met no other cars. Rabbits ran across the road in front of them. The eyes of small animals glowed from the woods and the roadside ditches. The air dried Dovey's hair, damp around the edges.

"I hope they don't scare E. L. off," she said. "Carrying on so much."

"Shoot. He might like it," said Floyd.

It had all begun in the spring. All winter, after work, E. L. had been passing out in his parked truck, sometimes in the middle of the road. On the way home one night Floyd, who worked on a neighboring farm, decided to bring him home and sober him up.

Dovey had helped willingly.

"He hasn't got a soul in the world," she would say, as she made hot coffee and warmed up food night after night.

The Goodwin children, grown, married, all in different places, called home regularly. When they realized how often E. L. was there, being sobered up and looked after by their parents, they did not approve. Gertrude, the oldest, finally spoke for the rest.

"You don't have enough to do since you got rid of us, Mama."

"Now that's not so," Dovey had protested. "But E. L. is just so pathetic."

"Well, don't get the idea you and Daddy can straighten him out, after all this time. He's got psychological problems, with all that drinking and stuttering and being a loner all his life. He needs more help than you can give him."

"What do they expect us to do, let him *die?*" Dovey asked Floyd later, telling him what Trudy had said. "Besides, he hasn't been drunk in a month."

"He ain't quit, though, Dove. By no means. You know that."

"But he's just drinking beer now. You said so yourself."

What Floyd did for E. L. he did without faith, Dovey thought. Floyd was a good man and would help anybody. What she did was different. She could see E. L. sober and happy like other people. He could have a good life if only he stopped drinking.

Once or twice she had seen him dressed up. In a suit, with his pink skin, prematurely white hair, and pale blue eyes, he did not look like other farmers. There was an air of refinement about him, especially his manners. He was careful about ashes, for instance. If she forgot to give him an ashtray, he caught ashes in his cupped hand or, if he thought no one was looking, dropped them into the pocket of his shirt. Though he smoked all the time, one cigarette after another, he had never once dropped ashes on her floor.

She liked to watch him eat. Floyd took her cooking for granted, but E. L. seemed to enjoy every bite. After a meal he folded his napkin exactly as it was before, no matter how long it took. The way his hands shook, it was touching, like the efforts of a child.

"A f-f-fine meal," he would say. "M-m-mighty good. Everything."

The night after Trudy's call, Floyd had to stop and move E. L.'s pickup before he could get by on the road; but he did not bring E. L. home as before. Instead, he took him to the overseer's house and put him to bed.

The first thing Dovey said was, *"Why?"* Then right away, "We'll have to go down there after supper."

E. L.'s home was white with a tin roof, and a yard full of bird dogs barking all together when they drove up. The only company he has, Dovey thought.

On the porch, a single straight chair had been turned over and propped against the wall to protect it from the rain. The front room was furnished in what E. L. called "Mama's things." A picture of his mother in late middle age hung on the wall. There was a painting of a stag at dawn, antlers high, eyes straight ahead, and a bookcase filled with books.

Everything needed dusting. In his own house E. L. paid no attention to ashes, Dovey noticed. There were ashes on the arm of his mother's sofa and on her hand-hooked rug. The kitchen sink was full of dirty dishes. An empty pork and beans can, with a teaspoon still in it, sat on the kitchen table.

E. L. lay in a stupor in the bedroom, where Floyd pulled up a chair to watch TV. Dovey cleaned up the kitchen, then brought scrambled eggs, bacon, and grits to the bed.

"E. L.," she said firmly. "Wake up."

Floyd had turned around to watch. "You better let sleeping dogs lie," he said.

"He's got to have something in his stomach," she said. "He'll go right back to sleep."

On the way home, Floyd kept yawning. He had been up since four-thirty in the morning. "Trudy may be right," he said. "We can't do nothing with E. L."

"Well, if we can't, maybe the Lord can," Dovey said shortly. She'd been up even longer than he had, since she had cooked his breakfast. "Miss Abby says there's to be a big revival at Rehoboth. Maybe we can get him to go."

When the time came, it had been easy.

"Revival starts tomorrow night, E. L.," she said on Saturday. "Come eat supper and go with us."

"O-k-k-kay," he said. "What time?"

But when they had eaten and started to go, he had balked unexpectedly. "I'll c-c-come on behind you," he said. "Y'all might want to s-s-stay a while, and I got to get up in the m-m-m . . ."

"Morning." She had said it for him, and he'd seemed to be relieved.

So now he had been there sober each night. Dovey held the thought with deep satisfaction as they drove into their yard. In the kitchen they stopped to drink water. A geranium, framed by ruffled curtains, bloomed in the window. It was canning season and jars of freshly canned tomatoes were ready to be put away on the pantry shelves.

"You know, E. L. is listening to that preacher," she said, as she poured ice water into glasses.

"Yeah." Floyd smiled. "Old Zack puts on a good show, him and Miss Abby."

"I'm not talking about any show, Floyd." She opened the refrigerator door. "Want a piece of pie?"

"Might as well." He took his place at the kitchen table and waited to be served.

She got out a lemon ice-box pie, two plates, and a knife. Knife in hand, she paused to look at Floyd.

"I believe in miracles, myself," she said.

He took the perfect piece of pie she handed him. "I don't know why," he said. "You sure ain't never saw one."

Since childhood Dovey had knelt by her bed at night, to pray before getting in it. Except in times of trouble, she went quickly over the names of her friends and loved ones, prayed for the sick and needy, asked daily strength and guidance for herself. She prayed for sunshine or rain for the crops. If she stayed on her knees overlong, Floyd knew something was wrong and moved to the far side of the bed. Tonight she prayed somewhat longer than usual, for E. L. and his soul, he suspected. He moved on over, just in case.

During the night Dovey had a dream. E. L. was in bed with them, and she was in the middle. Floyd slept soundly, but she was awake and aware that E. L. was too. She wished E. L. would move closer, and he did. When he put his arm around her and began to fondle her breast, she was flooded with pleasure.

She awoke shocked and ashamed. Why would she dream a thing like that? She hoped to forget it when she went back to sleep, but it popped up in her mind the first thing next morning. She turned off the alarm on the clock and got out of bed. She didn't know where dreams came from, but they came in the darkness of night and should stay there. Now it was almost daylight. In the kitchen, since there was time, she decided to make biscuits.

That night the Rev. Benefield wore a suit he hadn't worn before. The tooth marks of a comb still showed wetly in his hair. As people came in and found seats, he sat in the pulpit chair reading from a small New Testament. From time to time he raised his head and stared at the ceiling, or sat with eyes closed in meditation. He did not look at the audience.

On the pulpit, someone had put a vase of zinnias beside the large gilt-edged Bible given by Miss Abby's family. A pitcher of ice water and a glass were ready on a tray. The collection plate was in place on a small side table. The plate was of dark varnished wood with a wide brim for handling and a removable pad of worn red velvet in the bottom.

In the rapidly filling pews, people sat quietly or spoke in whispers. To make more room, Floyd and E. L. sat like half-folded shirts, arms out of the way and knees close together. Dovey didn't know where all the people came from. Over against one wall, she recognized a girl who rode the school bus with her years ago. She looked old and worn-out already.

As the last arrivals tiptoed in to sit on the front row or in folding chairs in the back (all other places were taken), Benefield glanced at his wrist watch. Without haste, he took his place behind the pulpit. All movement ceased. The faces before him were like sunflowers fixed on the sun. The only sound was that of oscillating fans.

"Shall we come to the Lord in prayer?" he said.

Every head bowed and most eyes closed, but his prayer was short and spare, a quick formality before getting down to business.

"God's Holy Spirit is here tonight, my friends," he said. "I never felt it more strongly in my ministry."

He shut the big Bible and laid his hand on the cover. "So I'm going to forget about the sermon I prepared for you. I'm going to talk about something else entirely. I'm going to go where the Spirit leads me."

He left the pulpit and came around to stand in front of it.

"Just look at this congregation!" he exulted. "Isn't this something? If half you people came to Rehoboth every Sunday, you wouldn't be sending for me." He raised an eyebrow. "I'd be sending for you!"

Laughter sprinkled the pews.

"Do you know *why* you're not here every Sunday?" He waited a moment. "I'll tell you why! Because we all have crutches to keep going, from one day to the next, one week to the next. Your crutch is whatever you use to keep from falling down before the throne of grace and saying, 'Lord, I can't make it on my own. I can't stand up to all the trials, temptations, and disappointments of this life. You've got to help me. *You* take over!'"

As more words poured out his voice began to vibrate, then soar. It rose to the ceiling and resounded, amplified. It plummeted to a whisper and rose again, stronger than ever. He threw back his head and reached for handfuls of heaven, looked down into a flaming abyss. He took off his coat and flung it on the chair.

When a baby began to cry, people glared until the mother got up and took it out. No one noticed when she came back to stand in the vestibule and listen, jiggling the baby to keep it quiet. Spent at last, Benefield filled a glass with water and drank it off. He wiped his face with a handkerchief.

"We will stand and sing 'Revive Us Again,'" he announced. "We all know it. Let's sing it from our hearts—all four verses, please."

Halfway through the song, he got down on one knee by the pulpit. Until the song was over, he prayed alone, eyes tightly shut.

"Now then." He was back on his feet. "I'm going to ask for something I've never asked for before. Not money." He pushed back the idea with his hand.

"I know that some of you good people, like people everywhere else today, lean on drugs to keep going. Tranquilizers, sedatives, pills. You have to have help and you go to the doctor. He writes out a prescription.

"Some of you rely on alcohol." He paused. His eyes moved slowly over the congregation without coming to rest on a face. "Do you know how many alcoholics we've got in America today? So many we have to have not only AA for them, but Al-Anon for the people who live with them.

"I'm sure a few of you fine young people, living in this good, wholesome environment, will try marijuana if you haven't already. We smoke cigarettes. We eat too much, *buy* too much, just to keep ourselves pacified. Temporarily. The Scripture says, 'My God shall supply all your need according to His riches in Christ Jesus.' Philippians: four, nineteen."

"Amen," a man's voice called out from the back row.

"Now, my friends, we're going to sing an old gospel song, 'Leaning On The Everlasting Arms.' That's what we need today, the arms of God Almighty! That's what our fathers and forefathers leaned on. They never heard of a tranquilizer, and they crossed the wilderness in covered wagons.

"As we sing, we'll pass the collection plate. I'm asking you *not* to put money in it. Not this time. But if you've got a crutch with you, and if it will go in that plate, I want you to put it there. I want you to throw away, tonight, everything that keeps you from the saving grace of our Lord and Savior, Jesus Christ!"

Miss Abby found the number, opened her hymn book and

propped it open. Before she began to play, she took a bottle of pills from her purse and carefully set it on top of the piano.

Dovey had no pills and neither did Floyd, but several bottles were in the plate when it reached them. There was also a package of cigarettes, to which E. L. added his own.

As the plate moved back, collections rattled in all the way. Down front again, it was piled so high a package of cigarettes fell off and had to be picked up from the floor. Besides prescription drugs, there were over-the-counter pain relievers, antacids, stimulants, cough suppressants, antihistamines.

Dovey glanced at E. L. Hunched over, he gripped the edge of the pew with both hands. The knuckles of his fingers were white.

"I don't think the law is here tonight," Benefield joked, "in case we got a joint or two!"

Several young people laughed, then glanced around guiltily to see if anyone had noticed. Everyone looked at the plate, then at Benefield.

"I know some of you will regret giving up your crutches," he said. "They cost money for one thing. I also know if you get home and can't sleep without your pills, you might not come back to-morrow night! So I'm asking you, when the service is over, to come down and take back whatever belongs to you. We did this to make you think, my friends. When you get home tonight I want you to think, and to pray for God's help as you've never prayed before."

After the closing prayer, people did not look at each other directly as usual. Everyone was reluctant to go down for his crutch, so someone picked up the plate and began handing it around. Those hunting through it looked sheepish.

When Dovey turned toward E. L., he was gone.

"Brother Benefield went too far this time," she said to Floyd, in the car headed home.

"He's an evangelist, Dove," Floyd said. "They're supposed to stir people up. They're all red hot."

"But did you look at E. L.?"

"Yeah. He was nervous."

"That's what I mean. And he slipped off without a word about tomorrow night, or anything. I didn't even tell him to come on to supper."

"He wouldn't go back for his cigarettes and didn't have no smoke. That's why he took off so quick."

At home they drank water in silence. Having been up four nights in a row, they were tired. Dovey's prayer, instead of being longer, was shorter.

But once in bed, she couldn't sleep. This would be the turning point for E. L., she felt. Brother Benefield had preached straight at him. She kept bringing her thoughts back from pictures of him passed out in his truck or his unmade bed, sick of Rehoboth, and sick of her for ever getting him there. At the same time, she could plainly see him sober, in a clean blue shirt, sitting beside her and Floyd with every pew in the church filled, as tonight.

"Help him, Lord," she prayed. "Now it's up to you."

Asleep at last, she dreamed the church bell was ringing, and when she woke up, it was. She held her breath and waited to be sure, then shook Floyd. A church bell ringing in the night was a call for help in an emergency.

Floyd reached for his pants. While she slipped on her house coat, he unlocked the door.

"Something's on fire!" He was already down the steps, calling back to her. "Get the buckets while I turn the truck around."

"It's Miss Abby's house or the church," he said, starting off before she could shut the door to the cab. They sat up straight, trying to see ahead, as he drove fifty miles an hour down the dirt road.

Tongues of flame, in billowing smoke, leapt into the dark sky before them. The flames were red-gold and glowing, with sparks shooting off in the night like fireworks. All around was a reddish haze and, in the air, a malignant crackle.

"Lord God," Floyd said, when the blaze came in sight. "It's the church!"

Dovey opened her mouth to speak, but no sound came out. She forgot to close it as she looked at Rehoboth, flames coming out of the roof.

Cars, trucks, and people in night clothes were everywhere, but the fire department from town was already there and in charge. Up close, most of the flames were confined to one wall. A fire hose, snaked in through the vestibule, was trained on the bottom of the blaze. There was a loud rushing of water and hissing of steam. People stood watching with small flames in their eyes.

Brother Benefield was the first to see it, someone said. He was also the one who called the fire department and rang the bell.

The wet pulpit, with the Bible still on it, had been brought out into the churchyard. Pews sat haphazardly about. Song books, Sunday School books, and Bible pictures for children were scattered on the grass. Off to one side, someone was lying on the ground beneath a tree. Two men were standing nearby, as if on guard. Floyd looked at the man on the ground.

"How did it start?" he asked suspiciously.

Dovey felt her heart stop, then lurch forward.

"Oh, E. L. Nichols was in there drunk." The voice that answered was filled with disgust. "Smoking, they think. Miss Abby kept hollering, 'Get the Bible, save the Bible.' That's the only way they found him. He could have died from the smoke."

"That bottle was still in his hand, though." There was a short, bitter laugh.

Dovey took hold of Floyd's arm. When he went to look at E. L., she went too, holding on.

In the smoky orange light, E. L. lay on his back, his head turned to one side. He no longer wore a shirt. Over his undershirt, the coat to his suit spread beneath him like failed wings. One pant leg was up above his sock. From time to time a hand twitched, or a foot. Once he halfway opened his eyes, then groaned and shut them.

As the flames were drowned, people began to move around, talking, laughing, asking questions.

"How did they ever stop it?" someone asked. "It was all heart pine."

"Why, the hand of God was in it, that's all."

Another voice spoke up. "They had it insured, didn't they?"

Dovey held to Floyd's arm and said nothing. For a time he seemed not to notice, then turned to look at her. "You ain't about to pass out too, are you?" he asked. "I got to go speak to the preacher."

She let his arm go but walked close behind him.

"I'll take E. L. on home, Reverend," Floyd said.

"Brother, that would help," Benefield said, and added a thought of his own. "If you could bring me back here, I'd follow in his truck and get it out of the way."

Dovey climbed into the cab. She did not watch as they lifted E. L. into the bed of their truck. She paid no attention to the preacher behind them, his headlights politely dimmed.

Floyd drove slowly, easing over bumps and washouts. "Well, I guess that takes care of the revival," he said.

She looked at the road and said nothing.

At E. L.'s house, Floyd and Benefield took E. L. from the truck bed and, draping his arms around their necks, carried him up the steps to his door. Dogs barked at their heels all the way.

"Shut your mouth!" Floyd finally burst out at one beside his leg.

While she waited in the truck, Dovey saw without interest that trees and bushes were all still black, but the sky had turned a gun-metal gray. It was almost morning.

Floyd and Benefield came out and closed the door behind them. They got in the truck, one on each side of Dovey. Doors slammed. The preacher adjusted his bathrobe and the legs of his pajamas. The cab was crowded, so he eased his right shoulder out the open window. No one spoke as they headed back to Rehoboth.

Benefield shook his head. "I've been accused of preaching hell and brimstone all my life," he said. "But that's the first time I ever set a church afire."

When the meaning sank in, Floyd guffawed. He couldn't stop laughing. He set off Benefield, and they laughed together.

"Yes, sir," Floyd said, when he stopped to catch his breath. "You outpreached yourself that time!"

They laughed again. The crisis was over. They had done what they could, and nothing was ruined except the wall of a church.

Dovey did not join in the laughter. She saw nothing funny in anything, anywhere. Staring before her in the gray, breaking dawn, she felt she had never been through such a night in her life. Her mind still blazed out of control, and there was no one to put it out for her. Not Floyd. Not the preacher. No one.

Suzanne Brown

COMMUNION

(from *The Southern Review*)

"Mama." Gladys had stopped shucking. She braced her foot against the bucket of corn beside her.

Mamie continued to brush the silks off the ears. "Go ahead. I'm listening."

"Can't you stop a minute?"

Even when they grew up and had children of their own, your children always wanted your full attention. Mamie set the brush aside. "Here's a corn worm. Shall I call Little Don?"

"Better not, he'll just put it down Stan's back." Gladys gathered her breath, folded her hands in her lap. "Don and me—we're having trouble."

"I wondered why he didn't fly out with you and the children. Never known him not to be able to get a vacation before."

Gladys didn't seem to hear. "Every day when he comes home he just wants to sit. He says he's ready to rest after he's done working under cars all day. I say I been home all day. He says, so go ahead out, I'll look after the kids. But I don't *know* anybody in Lawton. He says—"

"Sounds to me like this is between you and Don."

"He won't listen to me and now you won't listen to me either. I don't see why you're taking his side."

"I'm not taking his side. But some things is private between a husband and wife. Listen to me, I been married twice and I know. Least said, soonest mended."

While her mother was talking, Blackie had jumped into Gladys' lap and she stroked the cat behind the ears. Blackie jerked away.

"He don't like being petted around his head," said Mamie. "Do his stomach. He's a funny cat. I never knew another cat liked tomatoes."

It was just like her mother to refuse to talk about it, to want to cover things up with some old saying. And Gladys had been looking forward to a good talk; there was nobody in Oklahoma to talk to. She remembered the article on expressing emotions she'd read in *Woman's Day.* That was her mother's trouble, always had been. "Mama, it don't help to keep things bottled up. That's why you got a bleeding ulcer. You got to confront things—"

"Well, you—confront things—with Don, then." Mamie stood up, shook out her apron. "I'm going in to blanch this. Wash your hands before you come in to supper; you been playing with the cat."

Gladys smiled as her mother shut the screen door to the beauty shop. She should have been mad that her mother was still saying the same thing she'd said when Gladys was eight. But rocking on the porch at dusk, looking at the old fig bush, somehow Gladys found it comforting. Best to take her mother like she was. It was peaceful here.

They kept the television on during supper. It was Walter Cronkite's last night on the air. "He's been doing the news every night since I can remember," said Gladys. "Not that I hear it with the kids screaming—it's just a habit to turn it on. Stan, be quiet so Grandmama can hear the news."

"Let them play," said Mamie, "I don't listen neither, just used to having it on for company when you're not here." Mamie turned to Miss Ethel with a spoonful of peas. "Mama," she said distinctly, "this is Walter Cronkite's last night." The old lady continued to chew on a mouthful of peas, but she nodded. You couldn't tell if she understood or if she was just being polite. Mamie thought, Mama always had good manners.

After supper, Gladys said, "Why don't you read the kids a story and I'll put Grandmama to bed? Give us both a break."

Mamie hesitated. "I better do Grandmama," she said. "If you

don't bend her left arm right undressing her, it hurts her. Took me a while to learn how to do it."

Gladys shrugged all right. "Kiss Nana goodnight," she told her children. Don Jr. and Stan and Ben lined up to kiss their great-grandmother on the cheek. They had been scared at first, but they were used to Miss Ethel now. Miss Ethel smiled at them like she did at the cat.

Gladys stood up from the table. "My fingers is sore from shucking," she said. "I'm not used to doing it no more." She wouldn't have said "no more" in Lawton, or "is" either. She'd learned which phrases were country. But it came back easy when she came home. Don always laughed at her when she called Mama; he said she talked different just as soon as she got on the phone to North Carolina.

"You going to help me in the shop tomorrow?" asked Mamie.

"I reckon so."

"Good. You was always better at cutting young people's hair. Peggy Davis is coming in at ten. You can do her."

"Peggy Davis isn't so young. Hasn't she got two kids?"

"She's the youngest comes here, 'cept for children."

Last Christmas, Gladys and Mamie had sat together by Miss Ethel's bed. "Shall I read the Bible?" Mamie had asked her mother. Miss Ethel blinked. "Yes, I think she means yes," said Mamie. The King James lay on the night table. Mamie began First Corinthians 13: "Though I speak with the tongues of men and of angels, and have not charity, I am become as sounding brass or a clanging cymbal."

Water came in the corner of the old woman's eye and overflowed. "Are you in pain?" Gladys asked.

"It's the reading," said Mamie.

Gladys looked skeptical. "I don't know if she can follow something like that, Mama," she said. She leaned over the shrunken form, spoke loudly with pauses between the words, "Are—you—hurting—somewheres?"

"It's the First Corinthians, Mama always loved Saint Paul," Mamie insisted.

"I don't think Grandmama can understand."

"She knows it though. She had this whole chapter by heart."

"Mama, she don't even perk up when I tell her about her own great-grandchildren—"

Mamie frowned at Gladys, mouthed the words "She—can—hear—you." Gladys rolled her eyes but followed her mother out of the room anyway. "Gladys, I'm telling you. Grandmama knows a lot more of what's going on than she lets on."

That night after church, Gladys had said to Don, "I'm worried about Mama."

He took off his dark jacket, laid it on the bed in the spare room. "Why? God, I'm glad to get out of this thing."

"You should have heard how she talked to her, Don. She can't accept that Grandmama's mind is gone. I don't think that's healthy. It reminded me of how people talk to their cats, you know"— Gladys raised her voice in imitation of their neighbor in Lawton— "Prince is so smart, just seems to understand everything I say—"

Don had taken off his tie and lain back in his undershorts. Gladys shook her head.

As soon as she entered Miss Ethel's room with the breakfast tray next morning, Mamie knew that her mother was dead. Miss Ethel's eyes were open, and her left arm lay at a funny angle. The muscles around her mouth were loosened as they never were in sleep. She wasn't breathing.

Mamie set the tray with the grits, bacon, biscuits, and coffee down on the night table and sagged into the chair by the bed. She intended to have a quiet moment before she broke the news to Gladys and started calling Hayden and Suzie Grey and all the others. She was shocked. Yet everyone had been waiting for years for Miss Ethel to die. All through the days of the funeral, people would keep saying, "Well, it's not like you weren't expecting it." But she *hadn't* been expecting it, even though her mother was so old. Precisely because her mother's existence was so low-key, so little conscious, it had seemed to Mamie that it might go on forever. She had been less surprised by the sudden deaths of Ben and Aaron, her two husbands. "So young to go," people had said about both men. Ben had been thirty-one; Aaron, forty-six. But Mamie had known life before Ben and before Aaron, and, deep as her grief had been, it had not been difficult to imagine life without them, however bitter it had been to endure. But she had never known life without her mother. Miss Ethel's death seemed impossible, though not especially sad.

After only a few minutes, Gladys opened the bedroom door that Mamie had closed.

"Grandmama has passed away," said Mamie.

Gladys' mouth relaxed, almost like Miss Ethel's, then her face drew together and she walked to the bed and covered the face with a sheet. Of course, thought Mamie, why didn't I think to do that?

Gladys called and canceled all Mamie's appointments. The beauty shop was off the kitchen. Mamie worked there from eight to five, six days a week.

Mamie looked at Miss Ethel's breakfast tray and gave a shaky laugh. "I don't know what to do with this food," she called from the kitchen.

"The kids will eat it," Gladys called back.

"Where are they?"

"Outside painting a gourd to be a birdhouse. I'll tell them later." Mamie could hear her dialing another number. "I can't believe Irma Parker's still coming Mondays at ten. Do you remember when I was a kid and she was giving me piano lessons? I hated how she made me practice while you were doing her hair. I was always glad when she went under the dryer and couldn't hear."

"People don't usually change appointments around too much." Most of Mamie's customers were friends who had standing weekly appointments. "Only time I has to shift folks around is when somebody wants a permanent." Mamie put the grits in the refrigerator and listened while Gladys fielded condolences. The children would eat it if she sliced the cold grits and fried them in butter.

Mamie went next door to call Herman Parker, the undertaker. When he came to the house, he wondered what to say to Mamie. She was the bereaved, but Mamie had worked for him for years and knew the inside of the funeral business. Mamie knew everybody in Stantonsburg, and relatives usually asked her to do the hair before a viewing. "You did Aunt's hair all her life, I'm sure she'd want you to fix it now she's gone. It would mean so much to us," they'd say to Mamie. And she always did, usually at no charge. Over the years Herman had got to depend on her for other things. "You've got that corset on backwards," she'd told him when they'd buried old Miss Lula Martin. He hadn't known—nobody had worn a corset for years.

Now he asked her, "Who will you get to do the hair?"

"I'll do it myself," said Mamie.

"You sure?" he asked her sympathetically. "We can get somebody to come over from Wilson."

"I'm sure," she said.

Herman kept coming in to check on her while she was rinsing Miss Ethel's hair. "You all right in here?" he'd ask.

Finally she said, "Herman, I'm not ever going to get this set if you keep interrupting." He looked hurt, so she said, "Mama looks real good."

"I tried hard to make her look nice," he said. "Folks tell me that when somebody's been sick such a long time like Miss Ethel was, it helps 'em remember the time before they got sick."

"Thank you," said Mamie, and Herman looked gratified as he left. He *had* smoothed the age and sickness from her mother's face, but Mama had never looked like that. The plates and fluid used to mold the cheeks and extend Miss Ethel's drawn face had made it look broader than her face had ever been in life. They'd been right to bury Mama in the blue wool. Gladys had wanted to choose a summer dress since it was late August, but Mamie had insisted on Miss Ethel's favorite dress. Besides nothing thin would have been suitable. Herman put thick rubber diapers on the corpses to prevent accidents, and the bulk could show through. Funny how bodily functions went on after death. Fingernails, and they said the hair still grew. Mama had always had nice hair. Thick. A little coarse, but then that was why it held a permanent. Her hair had never greyed; it had been black until Miss Ethel was almost eighty, then had gone white almost overnight.

Mamie set the hair the way Miss Ethel would have wanted it. After going to hair demonstrations in Raleigh, Mamie had tried to get her mother to wear her hair softer, fluffier, but Miss Ethel had insisted on having it curled tightly, clamped to her head. Miss Ethel wore a hairnet to bed every night—said she couldn't sleep without it. Her mother had judged a hairstyle by how little it moved—the more anchored, the better. A lot of Mamie's customers felt that way—always asked "Will it last?" to find out if they were getting their money's worth. Mamie, who tried to keep up with the new hairstyles, felt frustrated that nobody in Stantonsburg wanted to try the cuts she learned from the young, award-winning stylists, mostly men, that the hairdressers' association brought to the capital for demonstrations. These young men came from establishments—Mamie had learned not to call them beauty shops—with names like Mr. Ralph's or else with some clever pun—Great Lengths or Shear Madness. Mamie had once changed the name of her own shop, the Stantonsburg Beauty Shop, to Hair Today.

"Why'd you do that?" everyone had asked.

"You know," Mamie had said, "Here today, gone tomorrow."

"Yeah?"

"Well, when you get a haircut, it's *hair* today, gone tomorrow."

"Yeah?"

She'd changed the name back after two weeks. And after all, she'd not been sorry. Mamie wondered herself if those young hairstylists didn't go in for those crazy cuts just because they couldn't cut hair even. Anybody could tell when you'd done a bad job on a blunt cut that wasn't layered. All that talk about sculpturing hair and hair as a medium was just to hide that they didn't know what they were doing.

She had to trim some around Miss Ethel's neck. When Mamie had started setting hair on dead people, it had given her the willies, but now she'd got used to it. It bothered Herman that she was tending to her own mother, but this seemed right to Mamie. Used to be done all the time. Hadn't Mama told her that women used to do all the laying out? Not much use for the undertakers then; no wonder Herman was bothered. Deftly Mamie twirled another pincurl. Now she had the moment to be still that she'd wanted this morning. "Almost finished on this side," said Mamie, then stopped as she realized she'd spoken to a dead person. But Mama hadn't said much for ten years, so this didn't seem that different. Mamie was used to commenting on the weather or the crops while she fed her mother, dressed and undressed her, bathed that body where the skin of her mother's arms hung from the bones like a quilt on the line. So Mamie continued to speak. "Getting dark out.

Could use the rain, but I hope it holds off 'til I can get home." She wasn't crazy, it was just comforting to talk out loud, like reminding yourself of what you had to do. "I'm going home for a couple of hours, let you dry natural, then I'll be back to comb you out." Her hands seemed to move more efficiently to the rhythm of her own speech. "There's gonna be a crowd, but there won't be no trouble about food. Irma Parker sent over enough ham biscuits to feed an army already this morning, and Lynette brought over deviled eggs and a bowl of chicken salad. There's a lemon meringue pie in the kitchen too—don't know who brought that. The meringue ain't so high as you used to make, but it'll be good anyway—"

The viewing was two nights later, at seven o'clock in the evening. Herman hadn't wanted to delay things so long, but with Hayden flying in from Washington and Valeria coming from Knoxville, they'd had to wait. And there were the cousins from Raleigh and Greensboro. Don was taking personal leave, so he was coming too. Mamie had told Gladys that tragedy brought people closer together, but Gladys said she wasn't sure she wanted to see him. Gladys had started sobbing when he stepped off the plane.

Mournful organ music was piped into the funeral hall, but it trembled through the room as if there were a real organ somewhere in the basement. The room seemed too empty: the open coffin all alone at one end, the few folding chairs and potted trees scattered about. The viewing felt more like a family reunion. People were there who hadn't seen each other for ten years, not since Aunt Ruth died. A spurt of laughter would rise above the dirge and the chill before the relative remembered he was supposed to be mourning. It wasn't that Miss Ethel hadn't been loved; she'd just been sick so long that to most of them it seemed like she'd died a long time ago. Suzie Grey said to Hayden, "Anybody who's seen her like I have these past years can't help but think of this as a release." The men were the worst offenders. Mamie heard Clyde, Lynette's husband, discussing sports with Hayden in the corner. She caught bits of other conversations as she walked through the parlor:

"That your youngest? I thought he must be David. Don't think I've seen any of you since—were you at Hazel's wedding?"

"No, Doris was having her wisdom teeth out."

"Then it must have been when Aunt Ruth died. You still at the same place? I—"

And over near the coffin:

"So distinguished and wise. I'm really going to miss him." Only with the pronoun did Mamie realize that Doris meant Walter Cronkite. She had to keep reminding herself that Walter Cronkite wasn't dead, even though she hadn't seen him on the news for two nights.

People said the same things to Mamie they'd said when Ben and Aaron had died:

"She looks so peaceful."

"I want you to know we're thinking of you."

The preacher was the only one besides Herman who looked comfortable in the funeral hall. He held Mamie's hand between his and said, "The Lord hasn't promised not to try us, but he has said he'll not ask us to carry any burden that is too heavy for us to bear." He'd said exactly the same thing to her at Aaron's funeral, and Mamie wondered if he remembered this. Now she saw Lynette coming towards her, her navy polyester dress riding a little on her bountiful hips.

Lynette hugged her and said, "You've got to get out more now. It's what Miss Ethel would have wanted."

How did Lynette know what Mama would have wanted? People were always doing that and usually to suit themselves. Like last fall when the preacher had said God wanted the old maple in the churchyard cut down. But hadn't she done the same thing herself? She watched Lynette drift away. All these years when Mama couldn't or wouldn't talk and Mamie had interpreted her struggles. Who was to say if she'd stilled herself enough to feel with Miss Ethel, or if she'd only projected herself onto the silent woman?

The thought was disturbing, so Mamie was glad to see Miss Irma Parker coming toward her. She must be leaving. People spoke to Mamie just before going out the door, like it was a party. At Ben's funeral, Mamie had hated Miss Irma most of all. Irma had hugged her at the graveside and said, "Time heals all things, child." Mamie had thought, you don't know, none of you know, why couldn't anyone say something *real*, really *talk* to her. But she had been young then. Now the familiar words seemed right, a graceful acknowledgment that in the face of some things nothing *could* be said, or at least nothing personal or new. Because Miss Irma had been so strict when she taught both Mamie and Gladys piano, Mamie was startled to see that Miss Irma's dress was dirty. Looked like gravy. Nobody to look after her, and Miss Irma probably couldn't see too well. The women's circle would have to start checking on her.

Over Irma's shoulder Mamie could see Howie Beckton by one of the plastic trees, waiting his chance to speak to Mamie. He'd been the one to bring her the news when Ben had been hit by lightning plowing the lower field. It was a comfort to have them all around her. What was that show, *This Is Your Life*, where they flew in all someone's old friends and neighbors and teachers and relatives? Mamie saw most of these people every day, and every time there was a funeral or wedding even the wandering relations were gathered together in one room.

Gladys and Don looked like they were getting along fine now, his arm around her shoulder. Still not easy raising those three boys away from home. Stan was peeking out from between two of the folding chairs. He was Mamie's favorite. That was the the good thing about grandchildren; you could have favorites without feeling guilty.

"It was a nice funeral, just the way Grandmama would have wanted it."

This time the comment didn't bother Mamie. She was relaxed. Gladys had cushioned her mother's neck with a towel and was running warm water from a hose over her scalp. Mamie gave herself over to those massaging fingertips. No wonder all her customers gave contented grunts while Mamie was scrubbing their scalps.

"That feels so good," she murmured. "It's a real treat for a beauty operator to have her own hair done. Only time I do is when you come home."

Gladys just went on scrubbing, with all four fingers like Mamie had taught her. "I'll do your nails, after," she offered.

"That would be nice." Mamie could hear *As the World Turns* coming from the corner. The young lawyer on the show asked Penny, "Would you like a moment alone with your daughter?"

"Why is she leaving the baby?" Gladys asked.

"She's going to prison. They think she's the one murdered Judge Brenner."

"Oh, that's sad." They were silent a moment. "Things is better with Don and me," said Gladys. "He's been real good since Grandmama died. Really *there* for me, you know, real supportive."

There for me? Mamie felt their communion broken. It always offended her when Gladys used phrases from the magazines Mamie kept around the shop for customers. Only thing worthwhile in them was the recipes, and those used too many shortcuts and canned soups.

"Don, Little Don," Gladys called her son. When he appeared in the doorway of the shop, she said, "Why don't you sweep up these cuttings on the floor?" He dashed about with a broom, gathering piles of severed curls on the linoleum. "He's still young enough to like helping," said Gladys. "Wonder how long that will last."

"Which rollers shall I use," she asked her mother.

"The medium ones. They're purple." Once again Mamie relaxed as Gladys began to roll her hair. "Last night," she said, "I went and sat in that rocking chair in Grandmama's room, where I fed her every night. And I could swear she was right there. I felt that close to her."

Gladys glanced at her son. "Don't talk like that in front of Little Don," she said. "He'll have nightmares." Actually the boy didn't pay much attention to them.

Gladys rifled the tray of nail polish, decided on Zanzibar Sunset. Something bright to cheer Mama up.

Gladys held her mother's hands to remove the old polish while Mamie was under the dryer. They smiled at each other; they couldn't talk above the roar of the dryer. Mamie closed her eyes. She wondered if Gladys would do her hair when she died. Most likely not—Gladys would have to fly in and Herman couldn't wait that long. Poor Gladys. That will be hard on her.

James Lee Burke

THE CONVICT

(from *The Kenyon Review*)

For Lyle Williams

My father was a popular man in New Iberia, even though his ideas were different from most people's and his attitudes were uncompromising. On Friday afternoons he and my mother and I would drive down the long yellow dirt road through the sugarcane fields until it became a blacktop and followed the Bayou Teche into town, where my father would drop my mother off at Musemeche's Produce Market and take me with him to the bar at the Frederic Hotel. The Frederic was a wonderful old place with slot machines and potted palms and marble columns in the lobby and a gleaming mahogany and brass barroom that was cooled by long-bladed wooden fans. I always sat at a table with a bottle of Dr. Nut and a glass of ice and watched with fascination the drinking rituals of my father and his friends: the warm handshakes, the pats on the shoulder, the laughter that was genuine but never uncontrolled. In the summer, which seemed like the only season in south Louisiana, the men wore seersucker suits and straw hats, and the amber light in their glasses of whiskey with ice and their Havana cigars and Picayune cigarettes held between their ringed fingers made them seem everything gentlemen and my father's friends should be.

But sometimes I would suddenly realize that there was not only a fundamental difference between my father and other men but also that his presence would eventually expose that difference, and a flaw, a deep one that existed in him or them, would surface like an aching wisdom tooth.

"Do you fellows really believe we should close the schools because of a few little Negro children?" my father said.

"My Lord, Will. We've lived one way here all our lives," one man said. He owned a restaurant in town and a farm with oil on it near Saint Martinville.

My father took the cigar out of his teeth, smiled, sipped his whiskey, and looked with his bright green eyes at the restaurant owner. My father was a real farmer, not an absentee landlord, and his skin was brown and his body straight and hard. He could pick up a washtub full of bricks and throw it over a fence.

"That's the point," he said. "We've lived among Negroes all our lives. They work in our homes, take care of our children, drive our wives on errands. Where are you going to send our own children if you close the school? Did you think of that?"

The bartender looked at the Negro porter who ran the shoe shine stand in the bar. He was bald and wore an apron and was quietly brushing a pair of shoes left him by a hotel guest.

"Alcide, go down to the corner and pick up the newspapers," the bartender said.

"Yes suh."

"It's not ever going to come to that," another man said. "Our darkies don't want it."

"It's coming, all right," my father said. His face was composed now, his eyes looking through the open wood shutters at the oak tree in the courtyard outside. "Harry Truman is integrating the army, and those Negro soldiers aren't going to come home and walk around to the back door anymore."

"Charlie, give Mr. Broussard another Manhattan," the restaurant owner said. "In fact, give everybody one. This conversation puts me in mind of the town council."

Everyone laughed, including my father, who put his cigar in his teeth and smiled good-naturedly with his hands folded on the bar. But I knew that he wasn't laughing inside, that he would finish his drink quietly, then wink at me, and we'd wave good-bye to everyone and leave their Friday afternoon good humor intact.

On the way home he didn't talk and instead pretended that he was interested in Mother's conversation about the New Iberia ladies' book club. The sun was red on the bayou, and the cypress and oaks along the bank were a dark green in the gathering dusk. Families of Negroes were cane-fishing in the shallows for goggle-eye perch and bullheads.

"Why do you drink with them, Daddy? You all always have an argument," I said.

His eyes flicked sideways at my mother.

"That's not an argument, just a gentlemen's disagreement," he said.

"I agree with him," my mother said, "Why provoke them?"

"They're good fellows. They just don't see things clearly sometimes."

My mother looked at me in the back seat, her eyes smiling so he could see them. She was beautiful when she looked like that.

"You should be aware that your father is the foremost authority in Louisiana on the subject of colored people."

"It isn't a joke, Margaret. We've kept them poor and uneducated, and we're going to have to settle accounts for it one day."

"Well, you haven't underpaid them," she said. "I don't believe there's a darkie in town you haven't lent money to."

I wished I hadn't said anything. I knew he was feeling the same pain now that he had felt in the bar. Nobody understood him— not my mother, not me, none of the men he drank with.

The air suddenly became cool, the twilight turned a yellowish green, and it started to rain. Up the blacktop we saw a blockade and men in raincoats with flashlights in their hands. They wore flat campaign hats, and water was dancing on the brims. My father stopped at the blockade and rolled down the window. A state policeman leaned his head down and moved his eyes around the inside of the car.

"We got a nigger and a white convict out on the ground. Don't pick up no hitchhikers," he said.

"Where were they last seen?" my father asked.

"They got loose from a prison truck just east of the four corners," he said.

We drove on in the rain. My father turned on the headlights, and I saw the anxiety in my mother's face in the glow from the dashboard.

"Will, that's only a mile from us," she said.

"They're probably gone by now or hid out under a bridge somewhere," he said.

"They must be dangerous or they wouldn't have so many police officers out," she said.

"If they were really dangerous they'd be in Angola, not riding around in a truck. Besides, I bet when we get home and turn on the radio we'll find out they're back in jail."

"I don't like it. It's like when all those Germans were here."

During the war there had been a POW camp outside New Iberia. We used to see them chopping in the sugarcane, with a big white P on their backs. Mother kept the doors locked until they were sent back to Germany. My father always said they were harmless and they wouldn't escape from their camp if they were pushed out the front door at gunpoint.

The wind was blowing hard when we got home, and leaves from the pecan orchard were scattered across the lawn. My pirogue, which was tied to a small dock on the bayou behind the house, was knocking loudly against a piling. Mother waited for my father to open the front door, even though she had her own key; then she turned on all the lights in the house and closed the curtains. She began to peel crawfish in the sink for our supper, then turned on the radio in the window as though she were bored for something to listen to. Outside, the door on the tractor shed began to bang violently in the wind. My father went to the closet for his hat and raincoat.

"Let it go, Will. It's raining too hard," she said.

"Turn on the outside light. You'll be able to see me from the window," he said.

He ran through the rain, stopped at the barn for a hammer and a wood stob, then bent over in front of the tractor shed and drove the stob securely against the door.

He walked back into the kitchen, hitting his hat against his pants leg.

"I've got to get a new latch for that door. But at least the wind won't be banging it for a while," he said.

"There was a news story on the radio about the convicts," my mother said. "They had been taken from Angola to Franklin for a trial. One of them is a murderer."

"Angola?" For the first time my father's face showed concern.

"The truck wrecked and they got out the back and later made a man cut their handcuffs."

He picked up a shelled crawfish, bit it in half, and looked out the window at the rain slanting in the light. His face was empty now.

"Well, if I was in Angola I'd try to get out, too," he said, "Do we have some beer? I can't eat crawfish without beer."

"Call the sheriff's department and ask where they think they are."

"I can't do that, Margaret. Now, let's put a stop to all this." He walked out of the kitchen, and I saw my mother's jawbone flex under the skin.

It was about three in the morning when I heard the shed door begin slamming in the wind again. A moment later I saw my father walk past my bedroom door buttoning his denim coat over his undershirt, I followed him halfway down the stairs and watched him take a flashlight from the kitchen drawer and lift the twelve-gauge pump out of the rack on the dining room wall. He saw me, then paused for a moment as though he were caught between two thoughts.

Then, "Come on down a minute, Son. I guess I didn't get that stob hammered in as well as I thought. But bolt the door behind me, will you?"

"Did you see something, Daddy?"

"No, no. I'm just taking this to satisfy your mother. Those men are probably all the way to New Orleans by now."

He turned on the outside light and went out the back door. I watched through the kitchen window as he crossed the lawn. He had the flashlight pointed in front of him, and as he approached the tractor shed he raised the shotgun and held it with one hand against his waist. He pushed the swinging door all the way back against the wall with his foot, shined the light over the tractor and the rolls of chicken wire, then stepped inside the darkness.

I could hear my own breathing as I watched the flashlight beam bounce through the cracks in the shed. Then I saw the light steady in the far corner where we hung the tools and tack. I waited for something awful to happen—the shotgun to streak fire through the boards, a pick in murderous hands to rake downwards in a tangle of harness. Instead, my father appeared in the doorway a moment later, waved the flashlight at me, then replaced the stob and pressed it into the wet earth with his boot. I unbolted the back door and went up to bed, relieved that the convicts were far away and that my father was my father, a truly brave man who kept my mother's and my world a secure place.

But he didn't go back to bed. I heard him first in the upstairs hall cabinet, then in the icebox, and finally on the back porch. I went to my window and looked down into the moonlit yard and saw him walking with the shotgun under one arm and a lunch pail and folded towels in the other.

Just at false dawn, when the mist from the marsh hung thick on the lawn and the gray light began to define the black trees along the bayou, I heard my parents arguing in the next room. Then my father snapped:

"Damn it, Margaret. The man's hurt."

Mother didn't come out of their room that morning. My father banged out the back door, and was gone a half hour, then returned and cooked a breakfast of cush-cush and sausages for us.

"You want to go to a picture show today?" he said.

"I was going fishing with Tee Batist." He was a little Negro boy whose father worked for us sometimes.

"It won't be any good after all that rain. Your mother doesn't want you tracking mud in from the bank, either."

"Is something going on, Daddy?"

"Oh, Mother and I have our little discussions sometimes. It's nothing." He smiled at me over his coffee cup.

I almost always obeyed my father, but that morning I found ways to put myself among the trees on the bank of the bayou. First, I went down on the dock to empty the rainwater out of my pirogue, then I threw dirt clods at the heads of water moccasins on the far side, then I made a game of jumping from cypress root to cypress root along the water's edge without actually touching the bank, and finally I was near what I knew my father wanted me to stay away from that day: the old houseboat that had been washed up and left stranded among the oak trees in the great flood of 1927. Wild morning glories grew over the rotting deck, kids had riddled the cabin walls with .22 holes, and a slender oak had rooted in the collapsed floor and grown up through one window. Two sets of sharply etched footprints, side by side, led down from the levee to a sawed-off cypress stump that someone had used to climb up on the deck.

The air among the trees was still, humid, and dappled with broken shards of sunlight. I wished I had brought my .22, and then I wondered at my own foolishness in involving myself in something my father had been willing to lie about in order to protect me. But I had to know what he was hiding, what or who it was that would make him choose the welfare of another over my mother's anxiety and fear.

I stepped up on the cypress stump and leaned forward until I could see into the doorless cabin. There were an empty dynamite box and a half-dozen beer bottles moted with dust in one corner, and I remembered the seismograph company that had used the houseboat as a storage shack for their explosives two years before. I stepped up on the deck more bravely now, sure that I would find nothing else in the cabin than possibly a possum's nest or a squirrel's cache of acorns. Then I saw the booted pants leg in the gloom just as I smelled his odor. It was like a slap in the face—a mixture of dried sweat and blood and the sour stench of swamp mud. He was sleeping on his side, his knees drawn up before him, his green and white pinstriped uniform streaked black, his bald brown head tucked under one arm. On each wrist was a silver manacle with a short length of broken chain. Someone had slipped a narrow piece of cable through one manacle and had nailed both looped ends to an oak floor beam with a twelve-inch iron spike. In that heart-pounding moment the length of cable and the long spike leaped at my eye even more than the convict did, because both of them had come from the back of my father's pickup truck.

I wanted to run, but I was transfixed. There was a bloody tear across the front of his shirt, as though he had run through barbed wire, and even in sleep his round hard body seemed to radiate a primitive energy and power. He breathed hoarsely through his open mouth, and I could see the stumps of his teeth and the snuff stains on his soft pink gums. A deerfly hummed in the heat and settled on his forehead, and when his face twitched like a snapping rubber band I jumped backwards involuntarily. Then I felt my father's strong hands grab me like vise grips on each arm.

My father was seldom angry with me, but this time his eyes were hot and his mouth was a tight line as we walked back through the trees towards the house. Finally I heard him blow out his breath and slow his step next to me. I looked up at him and his face had gone soft again.

"You ought to listen to me, Son. I had a reason not to want you back there," he said.

"What are you going to do with him?"

"I haven't decided. I need to talk with your mother a little bit."

"What did he do to go to prison?"

"He says he robbed a laundromat. For that they gave him fifty-six years."

A few minutes later he was talking to Mother again in their room. This time the door was open, and neither one of them cared what I heard.

"You should see his back. There are whip scars on it as thick as my finger," my father said.

"You don't have an obligation to every person in the world. He's an escaped convict. He could come in here and cut our throats for all you know."

"He's a human being who happens to be a convict. They do things up in that penitentiary that ought to make every civilized man in this state ashamed."

"I won't have this, Will."

"He's going tonight. I promise. And he's no danger to us."

"You're breaking the law. Don't you know that?"

"You have to make choices in this world, and right now I choose not to be responsible for any more suffering in this man's life."

They avoided speaking to each other the rest of the day. My mother fixed lunch for us, pretended she wasn't hungry, and washed the dishes while my father and I ate at the kitchen table. I saw him looking at her back, his eyelids blinking for a moment, and just when I thought he was going to speak she dropped a pan loudly in the dish rack and walked out of the room. I hated to see them like that. But I particularly hated to see the loneliness that was in his eyes. He tried to hide it but I knew how miserable he was.

"They all respect you. Even though they argue with you, all those men look up to you," I said.

"What's that, Son?" he said, and turned his gaze away from the window. He was smiling, but his mind was still out there on the bayou and the houseboat.

"I heard some men from Lafayette talking about you in the bank. One of them said, 'Will Broussard's word is better than any damned signature on a contract.'"

"Oh, well, that's good of you to say, Son. You're a good boy."

"Daddy, it'll be over soon. He'll be gone and everything will be just the same as before."

"That's right. So how about you and I take our poles and see if we can't catch us a few goggle-eye?"

We fished until almost dinnertime, then cleaned and scraped our stringer of bluegill, goggle-eye perch, and *sacalait* in the sluice of water from the windmill. Mother had left wax-paper-covered plates of cold fried chicken and potato salad for us on the kitchen table. She listened to the radio in the living room while we ate, then picked up our dishes and washed them without ever speaking to my father. The western sky was aflame with the sunset, fireflies spun circles of light in the darkening oaks on the lawn, and at eight o'clock, when I usually listened to "Gangbusters," I heard my father get up out of his straw chair on the porch and walk around the side of the house towards the bayou.

I watched him pick up a gunnysack weighted heavily at the bottom from inside the barn door and walk through the trees and up the levee. I felt guilty when I followed him, but he hadn't taken the shotgun and he would be alone and unarmed when he freed the convict, whose odor still reached up and struck at my face. I was probably only fifty feet behind him, my face prepared to smile instantly if he turned around, but the weighted gunnysack rattled dully against his leg and he never heard me. He stepped up on the cypress stump and stooped inside the door of the houseboat cabin; then I heard the convict's voice: "What game you playing, white man?"

"I'm going to give you a choice. I'll drive you to the sheriff's office in New Iberia, or I'll cut you loose. It's up to you."

"What you doing this for?"

"Make up your mind."

"I done that when I went out the back of that truck. What you doing this for?"

I was standing behind a tree on a small rise, and I saw my father take a flashlight and a hand ax out of the gunnysack. He squatted on one knee, raised the ax over his head, and whipped it down into the floor of the cabin.

"You're on your own now. There's some canned goods and an opener in the sack, and you can have the flashlight. If you follow the levee you'll come out on a dirt road that'll lead you to a railway track. That's the Southern Pacific and it'll take you to Texas."

"Gimme the ax."

"Nope. You already have everything you're going to get."

"You got a reason you don't want the law here, ain't you? Maybe a still in that barn."

"You're a lucky man today. Don't undo it."

"What you does is your business, white man."

The convict wrapped the gunnysack around his wrist and dropped off the deck onto the ground. He looked backwards with his cannonball head, then walked away through the darkening oaks that grew beside the levee. I wondered if he would make that freight train, or if he would be run to ground by dogs and state police and maybe blown apart with shotguns in a cane field before he ever got out of the parish. But mostly I wondered at the incredible behavior of my father, who had turned Mother against him and broken the law himself for a man who didn't even care enough to say thank you.

It was hot and still all day Sunday; then a thundershower blew in from the Gulf and cooled everything off just before suppertime. The sky was violet and pink, and the cranes flying over the cypress in the marsh were touched with fire from the red sun on the horizon. I could smell the sweetness of the fields in the cooling wind and the wild four-o'clocks that grew in a gold and crimson spray by the swamp. My father said it was a perfect evening to drive down to Cypremort Point for boiled crabs. Mother didn't answer, but a moment later she said she had promised her sister to go a motion picture in Lafayette. My father lit a cigar and looked at her directly through the flame.

"It's all right, Margaret. I don't blame you," he said.

Her face colored, and she had trouble finding her hat and her car keys before she left.

The moon was bright over the marsh that night, and I decided to walk down the road to Tee Batist's cabin and go frog-gigging with him. I was on the back porch sharpening the point of my gig with a file when I saw the flashlight wink out of the trees behind the house. I ran into the living room, my heart racing, the file still in my hand, my face evidently so alarmed that my father's mouth opened when he saw me.

"He's back. He's flashing your light in the trees," I said.

"It's probably somebody running a trot line."

"It's him, Daddy."

He pressed his lips together, then folded his newspaper and set it on the table next to him.

"Lock up the house while I'm outside," he said. "If I don't come back in ten minutes, call the sheriff's office."

He walked through the dining room towards the kitchen peeling the wrapper off a fresh cigar.

"I want to go too. I don't want to stay here by myself," I said.

"It's better that you do."

"He won't do anything if two of us are there."

"Maybe you're right," he said. He smiled and winked at me, then took the shotgun out of the wall rack.

We saw the flashlight again as soon as we stepped off the back porch. We walked past the tractor shed and the barn into the trees. The light flashed once more from the top of the levee; then it went off and I saw him outlined against the moon's reflection off the bayou. Then I heard his breathing—heated, constricted, like a cornered animal's.

"There's a roadblock just before that railway track. You didn't tell me about that," he said.

"I didn't know about it. You shouldn't have come back here," my father said.

"They run me four hours through a woods. I could hear them yelling to each other, like they was driving a deer."

His prison uniform was gone. He wore a brown short-sleeved shirt and a pair of slacks that wouldn't button at the top. A butcher knife stuck through one of the belt loops.

"Where did you get that?" my father said.

"I taken it. What do you care? You got a bird gun there, ain't you?"

"Who did you take the clothes from?"

"I didn't bother no white people. Listen, I need to stay here two or three days. I'll work for you. There ain't no kind of work I can't do. I can make whiskey, too."

"Throw the knife in the bayou."

"What'chu talking about?"

"I said to throw it away."

"The old man I taken it from put an inch of it in my side. I don't throw it in no bayou. I ain't no threat to you, no how. I can't go nowheres else. Why I'm going to hurt you or the boy?"

"You're the murderer, aren't you? The other convict is the robber. That's right, isn't it?"

The convict's eyes narrowed. I could see his tongue on his teeth.

"In Angola that means I won't steal from you," he said.

I saw my father's jaw work. His right hand was tight on the stock of the shotgun.

"Did you kill somebody after you left here?" he said.

"I done told you, it was me they was trying to kill. All them people out there, they'd like me drug behind a car. But that don't make no never-mind, do it? You worried about some no-good nigger that put a dirk in my neck and cost me eight years."

"You get out of here," my father said.

"I ain't going nowhere. You done already broke the law. You got to help me."

"Go back to the house, Son,"

I was frightened by the sound in my father's voice.

"What you doing?" the convict said.

"Do what I say. I'll be along in a minute," my father said.

"Listen, I ain't did you no harm," the convict said.

"Avery!" my father said.

I backed away through the trees, my eyes fixed on the shotgun that my father now leveled at the convict's chest. In the moonlight I could see the sweat running down the Negro's face.

"I'm throwing away the knife," he said.

"Avery, you run to the house and stay there. You hear me?"

I turned and ran through the dark, the tree limbs slapping against my face, the morning glory vines on the ground tangling around my ankles like snakes. Then I heard the twelve-gauge explode, and by the time I ran through the back screen into the house I was crying uncontrollably.

A moment later I heard my father's boot on the back step. Then he stopped, pumped the spent casing out of the breech, and walked inside with the shotgun over his shoulder and the red shells visible in the magazine. He was breathing hard, and his face was darker than I had ever seen it. I knew then that neither he, nor my mother, nor I would ever know happiness again.

He took his bottle of Four Roses out of the cabinet and poured a jelly glass half full. He drank from it, then took a cigar stub out of his shirt pocket, put it between his teeth, and leaned on his arms against the drainboard. The muscles in his back stood out as though a nail were driven between his shoulder blades. Then he seemed to realize for the first time that I was in the room.

"Hey there, little fellow. What are you carrying on about?" he said.

"You killed a man, Daddy."

"Oh no, no. I just scared him and made him run back in the marsh. But I have to call the sheriff now, and I'm not happy about what I have to tell him."

I didn't think I had ever heard more joyous words. I felt as though my breast, my head, were filled with light, that a wind had blown through my soul. I could smell the bayou on the night air, the watermelons and strawberries growing beside the barn, the endlessly youthful scent of summer itself.

Two hours later my father and mother stood on the front lawn with the sheriff and watched four mud-streaked deputies lead the convict in manacles to a squad car. The convict's arms were pulled behind him, and he smoked a cigarette with his head tilted to one side. A deputy took it out of his mouth and flipped it away just before they locked him in the back of the car behind the wire screen.

"Now, tell me this again, Will. You say he was here yesterday and you gave him some canned goods?" the sheriff said. He was a thick-bodied man who wore blue suits, a pearl-gray Stetson, and a fat watch in his vest pocket.

"That's right. I cleaned up the cut on his chest, and I gave him a flashlight, too," my father said. Mother put her arm in his.

"What was that fellow wearing when you did all this?"

"A green and white work uniform of some kind."

"Well, it must have been somebody else because I think this man stole that shirt and pants soon as he got out of the prison van. You probably run into one of them niggers that's been setting traps out of season."

"I appreciate what you're trying to do, but I helped the fellow in that car to get away."

"The same man who turned him in also helped him escape? Who's going to believe a story like that, Will?" The sheriff tipped his hat to my mother. "Goodnight, Mrs. Broussard. You drop by and say hello to my wife when you have a chance. Goodnight, Will. And you, too, Avery."

We walked back up on the porch as they drove down the dirt road through the sugarcane fields. Heat lightning flickered across the blue-black sky.

"I'm afraid you're fated to be disbelieved," Mother said, and kissed my father on the cheek.

"It's the battered innocence in us," he said.

I didn't understand what he meant, but I didn't care, either. Mother fixed strawberries and plums and hand-cranked ice cream, and I fell asleep under the big fan in the living room with the spoon still in my hand. I heard the heat thunder roll once more, like a hard apple rattling in the bottom of a barrel, and then die somewhere out over the Gulf. In my dream I prayed for my mother and father, the men in the bar at the Frederic Hotel, the sheriff and his deputies, and finally for myself and the Negro convict. Many years would pass before I would learn that it is our collective helplessness, the frailty and imperfection of our vision that ennobles us and saves us from ourselves; but that night, when I awoke while my father was carrying me up to bed, I knew from the beat of his heart that he and I had taken pause in our contention with the world.

Ron Carlson

AIR

(from *Carolina Quarterly*)

I

Butch is under pressure. He swings his crazy new tennis racket with a malice that has little to do with sport. It has been building in him for eleven days, since his sister, Karen, went to her room after the incident at Lannie's club and didn't come out. She's been in there a week and a half and it's got everybody nervous. Budd, their father, has always been the kind of man who hits those things he can't understand, and so there has been a struggle. Each time Butch smashes the ball, he exhales a sharp, "Hup!" as if tennis is a game full of little tortures.

It's not really tennis; it's a test. He found three new guitar strings in the garbage behind the pharmacy and wired them through an old warped Jack Kramer racket frame. It looks like a kitchen utensil with those silver strings, and it strikes like a cleaver.

I stand on the rough side of the court, the side that has been shifted like the continents by the largest poplar in the park into four uneven quadrants. Some days we lie on it to dry off after running through the sprinklers, and Fenn says he can feel it move. "Yeah," Butch always says, "and one of the roots is going to pop through and grab your neck." I lob the black tennis ball, tapping it with my racket, a Sears Pro Star Model (Blue), and Butch stands like an exterminator, slicing it back at me at rocket speed. As always when he is trying something new, he is having fun. I lob the ball over and he smashes it back. I dodge it and fetch it and then tap it back. Each time he strikes the ball, the racket makes a *bimming* sound, not unlike someone bumping a piano. The ball is shredding, and finally Butch really swings and the ball knifes right onto the face of the strings and stays there like a piece of cheese. Our game is over.

Behind Butch, I can see Fenn and four or five other kids playing fencetag on the tennis court fence. Roto, Keith Gerber, the Starkey twins. They skitter along the ancient wooden four-by-fours crashing through the intertwined vines, fingers in the chain-link like monkeys. Every once in a while, someone will lose hold and fall to the ground and cry for a while and then get up and be *it*. They all scramble from one end of the courts to another, climbing over both sides of the fence, straddling the top, twenty feet off the ground, and occasionally when someone reaches the far end (across the other court where Linda Aikens and Carol Wilkes are playing), and the guy who's *it* will close in, the victim will try the great leap to the restroom roof. It's something to see. The best anyone has done is Roto, Butch's little brother, who leaped one time and grabbed the edge of the roof where he was able to hang for at least twenty minutes until his pursuer grew impatient of spitting at him to make him fall and climbed off after other quarry. Most kids who attempt the leap simply try a little scream, hit the wall with their feet, and fall to the ground to be *it*.

Butch and I sit on the lawn while he picks pieces of the ball out of his weapon. "It's going to change the game," he says. "Metal strings. In six months nylon and catgut are over, you'll see." I already know that Butch doesn't think much of tennis. "The tennis *ball* is a great thing," he always says, "But the game is for girls. Any game where you don't get your last ups is not even worth watching."

He hits the racket against his palm a few times to spring loose the last bits of black rubber: bong, bong, bong. But there is something in his face that isn't satisfaction; he shakes his head and simply says, "Karen."

Eleven days ago, Tiny ran away. Now, Tiny, because of the B-U-T-C-H printed in his hide, is an easy dog to find, and Karen, his best friend, found him loitering under Lannie's clubhouse, leaning against one of the crooked stilts that holds the whole terrible shack eight feet off the ground. Tiny has a way of standing against things because of his hip problem that makes him look like some greaser waiting for a bus. All he needs is a cigarette. As it is, he always stands with his mouth open in the off chance for some flying insect nourishment. When Karen approached Tiny that day, he was listening to the rancid commotions from upstairs.

The clubhouse itself has no first floor. Four warped two-by-fours hold the cabin aloft just the way Butch designed it. It was going to be a simple eight-foot cube, because Lannie and Cling were too lazy to saw any lumber. But when Butch constructed the frame, he made a critical mistake: he nailed the flat roof on first, and the two bullies had so much fun sitting up there spitting on anything that came down the alley, that they told Butch to build the clubhouse *up there*. The wood was all discard from the lumberyard, dragged down the middle of Concord Street by Cling, six boards under each arm. When a car would pull up behind him and honk for him to move, he wouldn't even pause to give them the finger. He just stayed where he was, in the center of the roadway, and pulled the monstrous load forward. He had taken six eight-foot boards under each arm because Cling is not the kind of soul who would make anything into two trips.

Every single two-by-four and plank in the bunch was twisted, warped, knotted or rotten, which Butch took as a challenge, and he put the structure together like a puzzle. Where one board bowed out, he would counter it with one that twisted the other way. And when he was finished with the second roof, the little window and the half door, he even constructed a five-rung ladder that could be raised and lowered. The clubhouse looked a lot like a treehouse without the tree.

When I asked Butch why he was doing it, he told me so those guys would leave us alone for a few weeks. "If those guys are in here," he told me one day as we sat up in the little room, "they can't be down in my yard pulling my hair out and stealing our tennis balls."

I told him it was a mistake. But it was no use; Butch loved building things, even if they were for the enemy. I looked around the dark little clubhouse and felt the old dread. It had to be a mistake to enable guys like Lannie and Cling to get eight feet off the ground, ever. I also felt the shiver each time Butch's hammer struck a nail. The entire construction had a trembling fragility which made me glad to go down the ladder and head for home.

Before I left that day, I said, "Butch, I'm not too sure. They're just going to use it as a place to plan their murders."

He had put his head out the window and said down to me: "It doesn't matter. It's like the atom bomb. We had to create it; it was possible, for chrissakes. How they use it is up to them."

And they did use it. They spent so much time up there that for a week I kind of missed them. I went through entire days with nothing to avoid, nobody to go the long way around the block for. They had gotten, Butch told me, "into sex."

And when Karen came upon Tiny that day, she had no idea that Lannie and Cling were up there in a frenzy over the new copy of *Tits Ahoy* that Cling had stolen from some vagrant. It was common knowledge that Lannie's club was organized around the principle of looking at dirty magazines. I think they acquired their first batch from us, the magazines we'd found one day in the vacant lot. We had gone over to play army and found six or seven cover-less pulp magazines full of large naked ladies in our foxhole. Most of the ladies wore little aprons. One woman lay naked on a rug squashing her large white breasts. It looked like she was trying to smother a puppy. And it was common knowledge that Lannie and those guys went up the little ladder into the clubhouse to look at the magazines and to do things to themselves. After all, it was a club wasn't it?

At first, Karen thought that Tiny's scratching himself had set the clubhouse into motion, but then even he became alarmed enough to stand up straight, close his mouth and look up. It was too late.

The little plank compartment assumed a rhythmic and overwhelming wobble. It took one weird circular tour around the air on those four twisted stilts, looking like a drunk daddy-longlegs, and then it poised against the very limit of falling as the nails in one entire side fired out three at a time like bullets, and the house exploded, or so it seemed, and began an everlasting arc out, out, out on two legs and then down, down, down toward the ground.

The far wall had been ripped away and the planks hurled into the alley, revealing to Karen the startled occupants of this sad spaceship. She was, as far as I can tell, able to get her two eyes full of Lannie, his pants knotted around his knees, his hands clutching his privates in the full blasting bloom of sexual excitement. It was said later that the jet of his emission traveled nineteen feet, if you can count where he ended up after hitting the ground and rolling three times. Oh, it was a mess. Cling, who had not begun his club activities in earnest yet that day (he still had his pants on) was able to stand, just as the house rocked to forty-five degrees, and cry, "Timber!" as he hurled the copy of *Tits Ahoy* into the bright air. By the time that publication hit the ground, Karen had forgotten Tiny, and she had fled down the alley in a beeline toward her room, where she has been for eleven days.

Though one of the shattered uprights did strike the dog sharply across the nose, he didn't yelp, but simply loped down the alley in his usual sideways canter toward home, where he crawled up into Karen's room through the place where Budd smashed the corner off their house that night in his pink Ford.

So, the upshot is simple: Karen and Tiny disappear, and Lannie and Cling, their magazine repository smashed, are loosed once again on the streets. Cling carries the rolled tube of *Tits Ahoy* in his back pocket, and Lannie has a scab clear over one elbow. They slink around the neighborhood, hanging out in Butch's alley quite a bit. Rumor is they want to kill him and nail him to some of the crooked plank remnants of the clubhouse. Lannie walks bent over slightly, the way you limp to first after taking an inside pitch in the nuts.

I've seen them a few times and they've asked about Butch, but Butch, himself, has avoided them easily. He doesn't go home that often and now—with his new tennis invention—we've been spending a lot of time in the park.

Across from where Butch and I sit today, Linda and Carol tap the ball softly to each other. They're getting better; they can hit it three and sometimes four times in a row before it sails over one of their heads or crashes into the net. The nets here are chain-link also, with a canvas liner at the top. Last summer a crew came and replaced the old warped chain-link nets with brown cloth ones. They were beautiful nets, each square woven in with perfect little knots. We marveled at them; they were something to touch. The second day they were up, Cling set them both on fire, burning them into short little fringes which didn't really serve the purpose.

The chain-links were brought back; the very same nets. They make a small crash when hit with a tennis ball that I will always associate with a short serve.

I lie back in the grass and cock my head so I can watch Fenn moving in the fence. Fenn is highly skilled in fencetag. It's all touch and besides he practices a lot at home. He's admitted to me that he plays furniture tag a lot even when he's alone. His father caught him in the living room once, leaping from the coffee table to the sofa, and even though Fenn was just wearing socks, he was banned from coming upstairs for a week and had to eat his dinner sitting in the hall off the kitchen. Actually, I admired Fenn for it. He was ardent. He told me once, "There is no thrill like coming off the couch without looking and taking a toe-hold on the bookcase and feeling it start to fall. It's the point of the whole game."

"Why do you think they do that?" Butch says to me, indicating Carol and Linda, but he doesn't stay around for my "I don't know." He's up and into the fence. When he reaches the midpoint four-by-four, he calls, "Two new players! Larry's it."

So I rise and pull myself up the huge fence and start moving along the board, like a man on a ledge, herding the six or seven kids down toward the restrooms. I grab a vine instead of fence and nearly fall to my death once, but other than that, I'm cornering everybody. When one of Roto's friends tries to slip back by edging along the bottom of the fence, I nearly miss him. Roto yells "Go Ekins!" and I look and there is this kid trying to midget his way underneath my feet. When he looks up into my face, he says, "No spitting." Carefully I kneel on the timber and drop into a free hang, swinging my legs a bit too briskly because I kick the kid, Ekins, in the ear and he drops to the ground and starts crying. As apology I can only offer: "You're it, kid." And I hustle along the ledge toward the others.

At the end of the fence, we're stacked five deep, and here comes Ekins. Fenn has gone up, over the top of the fence, hoping to skitter back when Ekins makes his move. The rest of us await our doom. Our options are to follow Fenn (a risky venture); to go low along the bottom of the fence (hoping, as Ekins had, to sneak by when the bad guy is busy); wait in the crowd (hoping someone else will get tagged and have to count to forty while we scramble for the open fence); or, to leap for the restroom roof.

Ekins is inching toward us deliberately; no one will escape. Then Butch grabs my shoulder and whispers his plan. It is a bizarre plan. I crouch, fingers in the wire, arms straight, so that I lean away from the fence. Butch climbs up above me on the fence and then steps out onto my shoulders. I know what he is thinking. He is not thinking about the game or being *it* or not being *it* or falling the ten feet to the ground; he is thinking "This is something new; this is a move they'll be imitating two summers from now!"

Ekins has stopped to witness our acrobatics. In fact, everybody has moved away so as not to be dragged to their deaths with us, and they are watching. Fenn says: "What are those two doing?" I wonder what Carol and Linda think of our stunts but I don't have time to develop an embarrassment. Butch, one hand in the fence, is stomping around my shoulders reaching for balance. Each shift wants to tear my fingers from the fence. Finally, he settles, almost sitting on my head. "Hold on," he says. "Just hold on." I feel a new pressure and realize he is standing up. The roof is only one giant step away from him now. "Okay," he says, "Now, one, two, and theereee!"

Remarkably, I am not hurled to the ground by his springing leap. I simply recoil and change positions in the fence to massage my fingers. Butch made it easily. He made it standing up. In fact, he nearly ran off the other side of the restroom. Now, as I rub the deep red creases inside all my knuckles, Butch walks in circles on the restroom roof, gloating.

"How'd he get on the roof?" Fenn asks from where he sits cocked on the top of the fence.

"Now, jump!" Butch says to me. "I'll grab you."

I look over at him. "It only works in movies, Butch."

"Jump!"

I don't want to jump. I don't want to hit the wall, feel my palms torn off as they scrape across the asphalt shingles, and fall on my skull. But I ready myself, as if I could do it. Ekins is coming. He's moving along the fence a little higher than I am to cut off Fenn's escape.

"One, two . . ."

"Butch," I say.

"I'll catch you."

The Starkey twins, who have both tried this maneuver and battered themselves doing it, are rapt. They cling to the fence just below me for a good view of the suicide.

"Wait a minute," Butch says. "Try this." He retrieves a five-foot two-by-four that for some reason lies on the far side of the roof near two old bicycle tires. He jams the plank against the fence crossbar under my feet and the other edge sits nicely on the roof with four inches to spare. "I'll hold it. Come across." He puts his foot against his end.

I lean back against the chain-link and then push and propel myself in two steps right across the narrow bridge onto the roof. I've made it! As soon as I set foot onto the shingles, the two-by-four slips and clatters to the ground nearly knocking the Starkeys' heads off.

"Hey!" Ekins calls. "No fair! You can't do that!"

Butch answers: "Did we touch the ground? What rule did we break? The roof is in bounds."

"You can't use a board."

"Yes we can. Shut up. Catch somebody or we'll toss a few shingles in your face." Butch tears a wicked triangle out of the roof and holds it up for everyone to see. Then he turns and wings it powerfully out into the sky where it rises suddenly like a flying saucer and then spins and slices into the grass above the tennis courts. "Go on," Butch says. "Catch somebody. Get Fenn. He deserves it."

We sit on the roof in the sweet fumes of the two Russian olive trees and the tar shingles and watch the mayhem. Ekins is now way up, one leg over the very top of the fence and he is sideshifting straight toward Fenn. Fenn himself is all fake; he moves left, moves right, but ends up exactly where he was. Keith Gerber, Roto, and the Starkeys are hunkered against the bottom rung of the fence, as low as they can be without touching the ground. They know they are safe now, so they just hang and watch.

"I want you to talk to Karen," Butch says.

"Karen? Karen who?"

Ekins is closing in on Fenn. And since Fenn is an ace in this game, everyone is pretty interested in whatever move he's planning.

"Will you talk to her?"

"Me?"

"Yeah. It's got to be you. She knows you; she doesn't trust Fenn; and I can't touch it. She thinks I'm going to pound her, which I would really like to do. She's got the whole house crazy. Budd's on the warpath like nothing and my mother is crying all the time. We can't have any fun down there until she comes out of her room. *You* can talk to her. If I get started explaining any sex stuff, it's over." Butch tears another little piece out of the roof and loops it out over Fenn's head. It lands on the tennis court right in front of Carol Wilkes.

"Please, boys," she says without turning.

"Fenn, grow up," Butch says.

Fenn doesn't even defend himself; he's lost in concentrating on Ekins. He's perched on the top fence rail like a cowboy, balancing, pretending he isn't twenty feet off the ground.

"Butch, I can't talk to her. I don't know what to say."

"It doesn't matter what you say. Just go in her room and talk to her. Tell her it's okay if she comes out. Tell her summer is not over. Tell her Lannie and Cling and those guys were just kidding."

"She's really going to believe that."

"She might. You're believable." He looks at Fenn on the fence. "You're the only believable kid in the neighborhood. Just tell her it was some game. Yeah, some game, and those guys were practicing."

I don't want to talk to Karen. I'm more confused than she is. I'm sorry I walked the plank over to this roof. Talk to Karen. I can't explain what Lannie and Cling were doing; it mystifies me too. What older kids do is two things: 1—their business, or 2—beyond me.

Something new has developed in the game of fencetag. Just as Ekins was about to tag Fenn, he stopped and looked down. Then here comes the Starkeys, Keith Gerber, and Roto climbing up the fence like prison escapees, scrambling for their lives. All five boys sit astride the top rail of the tall tennis court fence and look down. I can't see what mad dog has scared them all, but then I hear it: the saliva-filled chortle of Cling's laughter.

"Hey suckers!" Cling says.

I whisper to Butch to lie flat and I crawl over to the edge of the restroom roof to see what is going on. Lannie and Cling stand against the fence, smoking, blowing the smoke up at the boys. They can't see us, but Butch and I are trapped.

"Where's that dipshit Butch?" Lannie says, rattling the chain-link.

"We don't know," Fenn says. He can be a hero sometimes. There is a chance, though, that he just can't see us over here anymore.

"That little sucker move away or just crawl in a hole?" Lannie says and Cling chokes out his laugh again. They are good friends because they each laugh at what the other says.

"Why do you want him?" Fenn says.

"Oh, we want to talk to the runt bastard about why he can't build a clubhouse worth a shit."

Just as I move back from the edge, a silver gob of spit sails over my head and on down toward Lannie and Cling. Butch has spit at them! Butch is smiling, but his mouth is cocked open as if to eject another missile. I wave my hands frantically in front of him, shaking my head with a rapidity that is utter fear.

"I've always wanted to do that," he whispers to me. "It was worth it. I'll fight them."

But he is not going to have to fight them, yet. From the gutteral hubbub coming from below, my guess is that—sight unseen—he was able to strike Cling about the head and shoulders.

"You pissants!" Cling screams, and I see the fence shake a little. "You chickenshit pissants!" The five boys on top of the fence haven't moved. They look across at us, their faces wide open in fear and surprise. Then they begin to move. Involuntarily. Lannie and Cling are pushing the fence back and forth in a little rhythm.

"It was an accident!" Max Starkey tries, but it is no use. The fence continues rocking, back and forth, back and forth. The waves are slower, but wider; the boys have to lean to keep from falling. They must be swaying six feet, back and forth.

"Yee-hah!" Cling calls, enjoying the exercise. This fence must be one of the biggest things he's wrecked this week. "Yee-hah!"

The old fence is going to break. Now with each swing, it groans. The boys are flying through the air like apples on a branch. Each time they swing our way, we can see their faces clearly. If I stood up, I could touch them. Roto's face is the only one which shows pleasure; he considers this, like every accident in his life, to be a free ride, and his mouth is open to taste the wind. Ekins looks flat scared; he's never experienced anything like the wrath of Cling before. Keith Gerber has been pantsed twice already this summer by Lannie and Cling, and so his face is more resolved, the fear tempered by the fact that he understands these things to be inevitable. Fenn's face is determined. He is holding on skillfully, practicing a few new positions. But it is the Starkey twins whose faces bother me the most. They look at us helplessly, a cross between a curse and a plea, as if to say, "Thanks very much for having us killed in this way."

Now there is a little sharp snapping at the end of each deep sway, and that is coupled with a small moaning Ekins has begun. Butch watches the murder calmly, curiously, the way he watches every little violent spectacle in this neighborhood, but he is still lying low. I am too. On the last swing our way before the fence goes down, Max Starkey nearly falls off onto the restroom roof, but he is able to crane his neck up at us and say quietly, "You shits!" And then, instead of crashing in an explosion of timber and wire, the old fence leans way out over the tennis courts and lets go. It slumps down, down, down, snaps six or seven times, moans once and stops, three feet from the ground.

Carol Wilkes and Linda Aikens have played tennis through all of this. It is like there is a time zone between all of us and the two girls. I've learned that is the way the world works: boys are being killed and twenty feet away girls are playing tennis. Carol is now running back to swat a high one, and she runs over Keith Gerber who has just dismounted the hairiest ride of his life. They both go down in a pile. Keith gets up and runs away. Carol gets up and says to all of us, our five friends fleeing to the far corners of the park, Lannie and Cling who stand triumphantly on the fallen fence as if it is an elephant they have slain, and to Butch and me where we cower on the roof, "Grow up! Why don't you all just grow up!"

Cling flips his cigarette at her, steps off the fence, and he and Lannie swagger off, through the swings, past the bandstand, and out of the park.

Linda and Carol take their sweaters and move to the lower court. It is amazing to watch. They just move to the lower court and commence playing their version of tennis. Girls. What planet are they from? What magical thing surrounds them and enables them to advise Cling to *grow up*? If I suggested that to him, he would strike me in the face with his left fist. What is this? And now, Karen. I'm supposed to "talk" to Karen, a person who, even though she is a year younger than I am, is still a girl, and therefore, lost in the time warp. I feel the hot grainy surface of the asphalt shingles on the restroom roof and I watch the two girls bat the tennis ball back and forth.

Finally, Butch sits up, and instead of commenting on the assault, the destruction of the fence, Carol's collision with Keith, the uselessness of everyone running away since Cling can't run twenty feet, he says, "Did she say *grow up? Grow up?* What for? So we can play tennis?"

I watch how gracefully Wilkes moves around that broken tennis court. She backs across the jagged cracks as if the court were smooth; she glides left, glides right, runs to the net. She is not going to fall.

II

I'm feeling the pressure. I am riding down Concord Street toward Butch's house, but it never seemed uphill before. There is a stiff wind in my face and I have to stand up to pedal from time to time, but it's more than that: I don't want to talk to Karen. The big trees are riding in the wind and several pink Quall's Market fliers skitter past me along the street and sidewalk. Keith Gerber has the job of distributing 500 pink sheets every Thursday about Quall's butcher specials, but he's too timid to put them on the porches. He leaves them in the yards, so that Thursdays every standing fence in the neighborhood has a little pink cache along the bottom. They get distributed all right; I'm surprised Keith doesn't get a raise. But today, as the pink sheets flee by me, I realize too well that they are going the right way. For the first time this summer, I don't want to go to Butch's. I don't want to talk to Karen. All around me on Concord, things are trying for summer: weeds have grown up through the wreck in front of Oshiro's; every tree waves a load of leaves in my face; Mr. Haslam is mowing his yard, spraying the fresh clippings and a few shredded pink advertisements into the air. The whole neighborhood smells of late lilacs, weed musk, and cut grass. Everything is right except the dusty sky, the wind, and this terrible errand I'm on.

Butch is waiting for me in his backlot. I can tell this whole interview means a lot to him, because the first thing he says to me is, "She's in her room." Then as a gesture of goodwill, a gesture meant to say, "Hey, it's still summer; everything is going to be all right," he says, "Come here. Look at this." He leads me back through the forest of weeds on a toad path to the old round-topped Amana refrigerator sitting near the fence. It still has two old notes taped to the door along with a photo of Butch as a baby. Butch taps on the door twice, and two muffled knocks come back. Checking his watch, Butch says to the fridge door, "Four minutes. You all right?"

"No problem." It's Roto's voice.

"He can breathe in there," Butch says.

"That's good to know."

"Yeah, but the experiment is costing me a penny a minute, and I'm not real sure how normal Roto is. It'd be nice to have somebody else. But who else is going to get in the fridge to find out? It's tough to get people into a fridge."

I look at Butch. I want to say, "Not for you, Butch. It's not hard for you." But I turn and walk back toward the house. "You say she's in her room?"

"Yeah," Butch says. "Let me know how it goes."

As I round the corner toward Karen's room, I hear the refrigerator say, "What? What'd you say?"

It feels real funny standing at the corner of the house, saying into the jagged hole: "Karen? Karen, you in there?" The wind hustles litter across the front yard. "Karen?" A passerby would think I was having a short conversation with the house. As I'm about to ask for the third time if Karen is there, a hideous, drooling spectre focuses in the dark hole. I jump back, thinking this is it: I am finally encountering a witch. Then Tiny pokes his head clear out and licks my face. Regrouping, I push his dangling head aside and look right into the room. "Karen?"

"What?"

Okay. She's there. I want to move fast, get this over with. Tiny retreats into the cave, and I move right up to the house, duck in the hole, my feet still on the ground, and lean in, my elbows on the floor. The room is a suffocation chamber of dog breath and darkness. At first, I can't see anything in the rank humidity, and then my eyes adjust slightly and I can make out a hump on the bed.

"Karen?"

"What do you want?" The bundle of blankets speaks. I've seen it before: in "Curse of the Mummy's Tomb."

"Now, listen. This is Larry. Those guys . . ."

"I know what those guys were doing."

"Karen. Summer's not over. There is no reason not to come out of your room." She doesn't move. "Your friends are asking where you've been."

"Who?"

I don't even know who her friends are; I made that up. But I'm in it now: "That blond girl who isn't as good as you are on the tricky bars."

"Shawnee?"

"Yeah, I think so. Shawnee."

"What'd she say?"

This is tough. I wonder what anybody outside who can see my legs is thinking. I wonder if anybody knows I'm in here lying my head off. "She said she wondered where you've been. She said she hoped you'd come out and play, teach her some tricks on the bars."

I can see the Mummy shift, and Karen sits up on her bed. Her voice is husky and she says, "You know why I'm staying in here?"

"Because Lannie and those guys scared you? I'm here to tell you they were only . . ."

"I'm staying in here because of the flying sperm."

"What?" I don't want to hear any more, but I can't stop myself: "What? What are you talking about?"

"I saw it. It's everywhere. It's in the air all around here. It's filthy. It gets you. I hate every boy in the whole world."

"You don't hate me."

The Mummy whispers, "I hate your guts!" I can tell that she means it. The interview is over. But instead of pulling back into the windy daylight, I stay in the dank space a moment longer. I want to say one final thing, but I don't know what it is. I slump on my elbows on the torn floor and say, "Karen. It's okay. There is no flying sperm. It's okay to come outside. Summer's not over." And then I duck back out into the fresh air. The warm wind hits my moist face and cools it. I feel better. I did what I could. Everything is better outside. I grab one of the passing pink sheets for the butcher specials and crumple it in my hand and throw it onto the roof. When it floats down, I make the catch. Oh, it feels good to be outside.

However, in the backlot, things look bad. Lannie and Cling have finally, after all these days, caught up with Butch. Actually, all I can see are their heads above the blowing weeds. They are looking down. I imagine they have clobbered Butch fully and now are taking turns kicking him.

If they are going to batter him senseless, I can't stop it, but perhaps I can interrupt it for a while. "Hey!" I call. "Hey, you guys. What's going on?" But when I arrive through the jungle trail at the old Amana refrigerator, it is all different than I supposed.

"Butch killed his little brother," Lannie explains.

The fridge door is open, releasing a stale odor too concentrated to be dispersed by this wind, and Roto is limp on the ground with Butch kneeling above him. Roto is a light green, the color of celery. In fact, he smells like rotten celery.

"Seventeen minutes," Butch says to me.

"Yeah, well, you're a weird kid, Butch," Cling says, "to kill your little brother."

"We were pissed at you because of the shitty job you did on the clubhouse, but, hell, we're not going to beat you up in front of your dead little brother."

The two guys move back through the weeds and into the alley. "We'll see you around," Lannie calls. "Sorry about your brother."

"Yeah," Cling adds from the distance. "I did a lot of shit, but I never killed my brother!"

Butch stands up and closes the fridge door. Then he opens it again. Then he closes it. Then he opens it and runs his fingers along the rubber door liner. "That's quite a seal they put in these things."

Roto is still sprawled green beneath us.

"Seventeen minutes," Butch says. "Have you got a quarter? Lend me a quarter. Don't worry, I'll write it in the book."

I hand Butch my quarter. He kneels again and deposits it in Roto's open palm. I am amazed to see the fingers close around it.

Butch sees my surprise and says, "Yeah, it was only seventeen minutes, but, what the heck, I'll give him a bonus this time." I see Roto's open mouth close and then open again. He moves his head to the side. He's either less green now or a different shade of green. Maybe it's yellow. "Let's go before he throws up," Butch says, pushing me back toward the house.

I want away from here. I want to mount my bike and fly with the wind down to the park where kids will be just playing games. I throw my leg over the bike. Butch comes up and puts his hand on the handlebars. "Is she coming out?"

"You didn't tell me that she thinks there is flying sperm."

"Oh yeah, the flying sperm. Is she coming out?"

"You should have told me, Butch. I didn't know what to say to her. Is there flying sperm, Butch? Is it in the air?"

Butch lets go of my bike. "I don't know, Larry. Why not? I only know that if Karen doesn't come out of the house, Budd is going to keep on killing everybody."

I leave him there, where he sits in the wheelbarrow without a wheel, and I rise on one pedal and drift around the house. I rush the street and rise into the sweet wind, turning with it in a fast sweep down Concord. I race a dust devil which is spinning old spelling tests and dirt across the school yard, when I hear my name in the wind. Coasting, I turn in time to see Karen wave at me from the front yard. I can see the wind pulling at one end of her blanket and Tiny at the other.

The wind pushes my shirt for a moment, but then I'm flying faster than the air; I outrace fleets of pink paper and cut through the narrow gate at the park without slowing down. Down on the little league diamond, I can see Fenn's team being driven from the field in a dust storm. A few kids chase their caps in the brown air. Ekins and the Starkey twins are horsing around on the restroom roof, throwing torn shingles high into the crazy wind and watching them rise and dive.

But what stops me in this joyous maelstrom, what makes me slow and stop and lean a handlebar against the side of the old bandstand and balance there on my bike, is not all of these activities, nor the blasting summer whirlwind, the grit hitting my face, not the dusky haze hovering over the park, but the two girls playing tennis. I see Linda and Carol, their hair winging away from their heads, playing tennis in this warm wind, and I stop to watch them.

It stuns me. My eyes almost water against the air as I watch Carol and Linda struggle against the elements. I will never understand girls, but I see now that they are braver than I thought. They run and bat the ball into the unreliable sky, even though they must know, as I do now, that the air is full of things and anything could happen.

Doug Crowell

SAYS VELMA

(from *Mississippi Review*)

When I was in the sixth grade, I'm pretty sure it was the sixth grade, there was a group of kids. Well, you know, it didn't all start in the sixth grade. Where I went to school, we all went to school together, from the first. But probably in about the third grade is when we all sort of started to become separate. You know? Groups and things. Though there were overlaps of course. Yeah, I think the third grade is about right. All these groups started to come about. So I was in the smart kids' group, mainly in the smart group, you know, but I was also in the rich kids' group, and so on. You know what I mean. Not rich, really, but well-off, or something like that. In the minds of third graders, you see. Well-off. Right. I still remember the poor girl in the class that we used to make fun of. And I mean real fun of. Kids are so mean. But to this day I remember her, how we made fun of her. I was as bad as anyone. Isn't that funny? So I was smart and rich, but I was never in, say, the fast girls' group, see, though we never used that word then. I forget what word we did use. But those girls were in a group of their own, and all that. But like I say, there were overlaps. So I knew some of those girls. You know, from being in other groups with them. But not the fast girls' group. Me, I never caused any trouble in school or disobeyed, though some of the other smart kids did. But then in the sixth grade, that spring of the end of that year, I began to get to know again, to get to know again a girl I had been friends with, on up to the third grade about. Maybe the fourth grade. But we had sort of drifted apart back then. But then in the sixth grade we were starting to become friends again. For some reason. I don't remember why. Our parents weren't friends, I know that, and they hadn't ever been. Her name, I think, I'm pretty sure, was Evelyn, but I don't remember the last name at all. But Evelyn was fast, one of the fast girls. It's really funny now, of course—fast, how ridiculous. But we thought of her that way. Her and a few of the others. Never many fast girls at any one time you know. But Evelyn was a smart one too, and that was my connection, she was one of the smart ones, a member of the smart group. Smart and fast. Lord. She smoked too, and in the fifth grade had been caught at that, a big scandal. But she kept on smoking in the sixth. So she was definitely one of the fast ones. And tits. She had tits too. Of course. Between fifth and sixth grade, she just grew these tits, big ones for that time, and so she was definitely fast. Cigarettes and tits. All during the sixth grade the rest of us talked about her. We were very curious. What would it be like to have tits? To smoke? Evelyn smiled a lot, she seemed to know things. Another thing I just remembered—both her parents worked, which was odd for our school, odd for that time. So every day after school she had time alone, at her house. I know some of the kids, even boys sometimes, used to go over there now and then. We talked about that too, the rest of us. Actually it was only a couple, three or four of the kids, went over there ever, so a lot of us wondered about it. What went on. I'm just trying to set this up is all, to give you the background. It's not much of a story really, just one of the ones I've remembered, one I've never forgotten. So spring of the sixth grade, I remember two things—Evelyn and I were getting to be friends again, first, and second, rumors began to circulate that spring among us. Rumors about things that happened in Evelyn's house, after school. Before her parents came home. They were sex things of course, which we were all intrigued with anyway, since none of us knew anything, not back then. But I would get the rumors from a guy named Dan, who liked me, and who was friends with, I think his name was Ricky, who was Evelyn's boyfriend, or so we thought. Nothing was ever revealed to us from Evelyn's side, see. But I remember Dan would tell me things, not really tell, more like hint. Because of course he didn't know anything, he just wanted to impress me, because he liked me. I remember that. He didn't go over to Evelyn's house very often, but he liked to pretend he did. I realize now that no one went over to her house very often, but at the time it seemed to all of us who didn't go at all that hot stuff was going on. It had to be, you know. So we wondered about it, soaked up the rumors, and we were excited. Anyway, this was the situation, what was going on, when Evelyn and I, for some reason, started becoming friends again. And then one day, she invited me over to her house after school. All day long I sat in class and just tingled, and that visit started a month or so of an extreme state of titillation for me. To this day I remember how intensely I walked around feeling, for a while there. Sexual, you know. Of course I didn't know what it was, really, I just felt it, and it was great. To this day, the events of that time are blurred, but the way I felt then is still very, very vivid to me. I wish I could ever feel that way these days, that titillated. I'm just joking. But look, just a few days before all this, a dance had been announced, for the sixth graders. A formal sort of dance. Now it was going to be sponsored by a local dance studio, which hoped to drum up lesson business, but the school had endorsed it, and all of us had gotten fancy invitations in the mail and all that. Basically, we were all very excited by the idea of a dance, we were going to be grownups for a night. You know. So when Evelyn asked me over that day, she asked me if I liked Dan. I told her Dan liked me, that it wasn't me who liked him necessarily. And why, I asked. Well, I sort of want to go to the dance with Dan, she said. But what about Ricky, I asked. Well, Ricky likes you, she said. Well, I was surprised at that, to say the least. And I didn't like Ricky anyway. He was way too fast, or so the stories went. He was loud and talked a lot. And just the day before, Dan had told me that Ricky had kissed Evelyn, tongue-kissed her, while she was wearing nothing but a bra and panties. So I didn't know what to think. A couple of days later, I was back at Evelyn's, with some other girls, and we all talked about boys, and the dance that was coming up. The others were all talking about kissing boys, and whether they were planning to at the dance, and so on. I didn't say much. Evelyn didn't either, really. All this while, Dan kept telling me rumors that he was getting from Ricky. One day he told me that Ricky had touched Evelyn's breast. Through her bra, but he had put his hand right on it. He said that, put his hand right on it, and his eyes grew wide. I thought about having a hand on my own tit, what there was of it. But I had been hanging out with Evelyn for a while by then, and being around her, she didn't seem to be so fast as we all thought of her as being. But I didn't know anything, so I didn't quite know what to think. I guess I thought maybe Evelyn's not talking about it all was a sign of her knowing things. And that that was why boys were so silly, because all they did was talk about it. But I didn't know anything for sure. I never asked Evelyn about what I heard from Dan. I just thought Evelyn was very, very smart, and knew a lot. And what did I know. Now, when I said that Evelyn wanted to go to the dance with Dan, I didn't really mean go with, since no one was actually going to go with anyone of the opposite sex, but it just meant that she wanted to hang out with him at the dance, while we were all there. I guess that doesn't matter anyway. But all the while, Evelyn had been trying to get me to like Ricky more, and all that. To clear the way for her with Dan, I suppose. And then one day I just asked her, about the rumors I mean. Not telling her Dan had told me. I just asked her right out, about the kissing, the bra and panties, the breast. She turned real red. Well, she admitted the kissing, but denied the rest, and went on being red. Now, of course, I believe that she was telling the truth then, but at the time I didn't believe her, for whatever reason. I misread her red, you see. I believed that her red face hid even more things than those I had heard about through Dan. And the thing is, she turned into a sort of hero for me, right then. A heroine. I found myself standing there in awe of her, for some reason. What *had* she done really? I asked myself. The funny thing is, she felt then—I realized this all later—but Evelyn felt then, at that moment, that she had lost some edge, some mystery. I'm sure of it. Because as time went on, after that day, she began more and more to look to me. And by high school, say, I had far eclipsed her, in all sorts of ways. But that's another story altogether, a whole other story, right. At that moment, I looked at her red face, and thought it indicated that she knew everything, absolutely everything, that I didn't know. And didn't even really want to know, not then anyway. But I felt that I should know, you know? The point that I'm making, or trying to make, is that I was highly agitated as I stood there looking at her red face. Even stimulated, I suppose, wouldn't be too far off. But my blood was definitely racing, I remember that very well. Now this is going to sound completely ridiculous, but it's true. But right at that very moment, the doorbell rang. We both just jumped, we were very startled, but Evelyn finally went to answer it. Who else could it be? It was Dan and Ricky, dropping by, before Evelyn's folks got home. They seemed real nervous too, the boys did. And again I misread that. I thought all three of them were in on some big secret that I was outside of. And in the physical sort of mood I was in, I didn't want to be outside of anything. I wanted to be in on it, I wanted to be right in the middle of things. So I was really swirling, swirling all over, my brain and my body too. What is really going on here? I kept asking myself. What is really going on here? And I thought something really was going on, among the three of them. And I was absolutely excited, just absolutely. Am I making myself clear? At all clear? About the excitement I mean. Because, look, before I go on, I'm going to tell you what the real situation was, or what I much later on came to decide that it was. And I'm sure that I'm not far wrong. I mean, it's fairly obvious, right. And I'm sure that you can surmise the case even though it's my story. So I've already told you about Evelyn and me, what that situation was. And I'm sure Dan and Ricky were something like this. The thing is, as the dance had been approaching, we had all been changing. We didn't realize it, but we had all been changing. Just in simple ways, goofy ways even. But that's what growing up is. And here's what I think. Ricky had obviously been lying to Dan about what had gone on with Evelyn, about the rumors. And in some way or other, explicit or not, Dan had finally called him on it, that very day, the same day I had asked Evelyn. For what that's worth. So anyway, Ricky had brought Dan over that day to prove something or other to him. Evelyn sure wasn't expecting them, though at the time I thought she was. I thought they all were in on whatever it was they were in on. See? And that's why I ended up doing what I ended up doing. But I'm not there yet, so just hold on. So there Dan and Ricky were, standing at the door, right. With these sixth grade sort of shit-eating grins, right. And Evelyn asked them in. She's still red-faced, I'm thinking they're all playing a joke on me. Ricky makes some sort of crack about Evelyn and me, whether we were doing something we shouldn't have been. Because of her red face, see. And then it got even redder. Only this time, even then I knew why she was red—because she was really mad. Look Ricky, I want to talk to you, she said, and then she and Ricky went off down the hall to some back room. Now the thing is, Evelyn's folks were pretty well-off, had a big house, and it had this intercom system. So as soon as they left, Dan went over to the buttons in the living room and pushed it on. And we just waited there. I didn't know what was going on. And I just thought it was all another part of whatever it was they were all three in on. So after what seemed a long time, we heard a click through the intercom, Dan and I did, and then comes Ricky's voice. Hey, Evelyn, what if this was on in the living room, and they could hear what we were doing? Evelyn's voice was indistinct in the background. It wasn't a sophisticated intercom, right, and you had to be pretty close to it for anyone in another room to hear you. But Ricky was obviously right there beside it, and we could hear him all right. Wow, you look really good, Evelyn. Another mumble from the background. Dan and Velma would sure be surprised to see you now, wouldn't they? Another mumble. Dan sort of murmured, or moaned. That bra and panties looks real good on you, came Ricky's voice. This time Evelyn's voice was a bit stronger, but it came through with a sort of puzzled Huh? that my fevered state of mind was hearing as a low moan. Jesus, said Dan beside me, it's all true, it really is true. What's true? I asked him. That feels great, came Ricky's voice. A sort of high-pitched scream came from Evelyn then. Dan, came the voice then, Dan, hissed Ricky, come on back right now, Evelyn's in her bra and panties back here, she just kissed me and touched me, down there. Oh wow! shouted Dan, jumping up, completely awestruck. He was looking off into space. Then came Evelyn's voice, loud and clear. I am not! I did not! Then she screamed again, sort of. Ricky, what are you doing? we heard her say. Then came Ricky's voice again. Dan, come on back and see for yourself. So we just ran, Dan and I did, back to the back of the house, back to Evelyn's bedroom. Ricky was standing there with his shirt off, and his pants sort of half-unzipped, standing right next to the intercom. He was grinning. Evelyn was all the way across the room, her eyes wide, her clothes on. You missed it all, Dan, said Ricky, she had her clothes off, she was just bra and panties. I was not! screamed Evelyn, turning a bright red. She even tried to grab me here, said Ricky, indicating his half-zipped pants. I did not! shouted Evelyn, real loud. Oh wow, oh wow, Dan was saying over and over, it's all true, it's true, it's all true, oh wow, oh wow. What's true? yelled Evelyn, true? nothing's true! She was bra and panties, yelled Ricky back, she was bra and panties, I'm telling you. Dan moaned. I looked over at Ricky, and his half-zipped pants had started to slip down a little, and when I looked down at him, down there, you know, I could just see the hairless top of his "thing," as we called it, and that's when what's the point of my story took place. Not the point exactly, I guess I have no point really, but what I started out to tell you. Why I'm telling you this story. Even though it's not worth telling. But even back there in Evelyn's room, as I was watching all this, was hearing Evelyn's denials, and Ricky's hyena-like barks, and Dan's mesmerized fascination, even as I watched and heard what later would become much, much clearer, even then I had the definite sense that they were all performing all of this for me, that there was some sort of joke being played on me, that they all knew something I didn't, but that they were willing to let me in on it all, on the whole thing, if only I responded rightly. And you know what I did? How I responded? Can you guess? Because even today I'm still astonished, a little, when I think back on what I did. I was eleven, in the sixth grade, knew nothing, hadn't even kissed a boy, was nowhere near fast, in fact was slow, very slow. But you know what I did? It shows you what excitement can do, even to a child. Sexual excitement. And I had been excited, for a month at least. That day was just the culmination of the process. Do you see? The dance, getting to know Evelyn again, the rumors about her, how fast she was, the things Dan had told me. Oh, I was excited all right, and had been, like I say. And at that moment at least, there in the bedroom, the thing I wanted most in the world was to know whatever it was I thought Evelyn knew, must know. Ricky and Dan too, I suppose, what they knew too, but mostly Evelyn. And I wanted her to let me know that I knew. Whatever it was. She had to give me the signal, that was part of it. And what that meant was that I had to respond rightly, I had to do the right thing, react rightly to this joke they were all performing for me. So you know what I did? You probably won't believe this, but it's true, it's all true, every last penny of it. So you know what I did? Can you guess? Well, here's what I did, here's it exactly. And I'll tell it quickly from now on, because I can see you're tired of listening to me. But here's what I did. I ran over to Ricky and finished unzipping his zipper and pulled his pants down to his knees. He had no underwear on, and he was about half hard. I'd never even seen a boy's thing before, not really, just crude pictures. What did I know? But you know what I did? I grabbed his thing and started, well, basically just jerking him off. Though that wasn't a phrase I knew at the time. I didn't know what I was doing, I just started pulling on it. I was just standing there, pulling it, back and forth, back and forth. Just standing there facing him, and pulling on his cock, his pants down around his knees. I have no idea what I was even thinking at that time, I just remember what I did. And what I'm telling you now is what I came later to see was the case. Because one thing I do know I was thinking at the time, was that they were in control, not me. But later on in my life I saw that that wasn't the case. They were all just eleven-year-old kids in the sixth grade, who were curious and had played at kissing, and now here I was, coming into Evelyn's house, and pulling on Ricky's cock. They were astonished, just blown away. Evelyn stopped her denying, Dan stopped his exclaiming, and Ricky was simply frozen, with a look of fear on his face. He had no idea what was going on. All he knew was that here was this girl, pulling *on his cock*. It did get harder though, fear or no. And there I was, pulling on it, back and forth, back and forth, and he was terrified, looking from Dan to Evelyn and back again, and Dan and Evelyn behind me were completely silent, not at all believing what they were seeing. And I don't know how long all this went on, but there I was, in the middle of this great, huge silence, jerking Ricky off. And I'd never even kissed a boy before! Can you imagine all this? I had no idea what I was doing. So finally, get this, I'm standing there, pulling away, facing Ricky, reaching out like this, back and forth, back and forth, and finally Ricky starts trembling in the legs. He's standing there with his pants down around his knees, and his legs just start shaking like crazy. Just like crazy! And he's got the most peculiar look on his face that I have ever seen in my life. I had no idea! And then he *comes!* His eyes open wide, with just this horrible look in them, this look of absolute terror. I realized that later, you understand. I mean, he'd never come before, and he didn't

know what was happening. And I sure didn't. And later I realized—that is, he didn't *come* exactly, I mean he didn't ejaculate, he
just had this orgasm, he wasn't ready for coming yet. And later on,
I realized it must have been his first time, you know. Which is why
he was so scared. He had no idea what was happening. But he gets
this incredible look on his face, then he comes, and then he sort of
lets out this really strange scream. And his legs are shaking like
crazy, I mean he's almost hopping, you know, hopping up and
down in front of me, his legs are so trembly. But he had come, and
he had let out this horrible scream, and then he just passed flat
out, right flat out. By that time I was holding his cock so tightly
that I had to remember to let go. When he passed out, it was
tugging on my hand. So I let go of it, and Ricky just collapsed in
a heap on the floor. He was passed out cold. It was the most incredible thing. I mean, I had no idea, and I guess I just assumed
that that was what boys did. So—and this is the end, nearly the
end—I turned around and said to Dan and Evelyn, who were
standing there with their eyes open like this and their mouths
hanging down. They were both just standing there amazed. And
so I turned around and said, just as pretty as you please, just as
calm as a rock. I said something like, well, I need to go home now,
I guess I'll see y'all in school tomorrow. And then I just walked
out of the room and down the hall and out the front door and
went home and ate supper and went to bed. And I'll tell you one
thing for sure, neither Dan nor Ricky showed up at that dance
after all. And so Evelyn and I just sat around with the other girls.
Actually, not too many of the boys showed up anyway, though
most of the girls in the class did. Sometimes I wonder what exactly
went on in that room after I so calmly walked out. Actually, I think
none of them ever mentioned it. They probably didn't believe it
had happened really, in some way. You know? I know that no one
ever mentioned it to me, not even Evelyn, not even later on in
high school, when I began to be the one that she looked up to. Or
if not up to, at least to. Like I said, Evelyn later on came to be in
awe of me. And I certainly didn't become one of the fast girls.
That was because, I came to see, none of them ever mentioned it
to anyone. But even if they had, people wouldn't have called me
fast, you see. Because I had gone way beyond fast. I had, for that
one moment at least, been in some place beyond speech. And I

just mean for us in that time, in that place. You see. Because I, absolutely without knowing it, had done something that was completely unimaginable, to us then, even to Evelyn. But I didn't know that, of course, not then. That would come later. Do you see? I just didn't have any idea, I just had no idea at all. I thought the whole thing had just been set up by them, was some sort of special test just for me. So I did what I thought I should. And I just thought that that was what boys did, dropping out cold like that. It's pretty funny, isn't it, the things people do sometimes?

Leon V. Driskell

MARTHA JEAN

(from *Prairie Schooner*)

A good many years back, when I was a kid trying to grow up down South, all of the soft drink companies took to giving prizes for numbers they put inside the bottlecaps. That was before you could buy just about anything you wanted to drink in an aluminum can with a snap top and throw away the can when you were done. That goes to show you about how many years ago what I am going to tell happened.

If you wanted to try and win a prize, you had to gouge out the number that was between the metal top of the cap and a thin pad of rubbery, or cork stuff. Sometimes you had to have a special card to paste all your numbers on, kind of like bingo. One company had what they called Magic Numbers, and if you got one of the good numbers you got a prize just for sending it off to that company's district office. Some of the prizes were things like an electric can opener, which nobody would want unless they had a heap of cans to open. Other prizes were worth a considerable amount of money.

Some of them were worth cash, and those were the ones Martha Jean was after.

Not that she wouldn't have taken a can opener or anything else she happened to win, but she was out for big prizes and for a special reason. Cash would have suited her best, but she would find a way to use anything she got. Every little bit helps, she said. That was her way, and still is.

Martha Jean is a girl I grew up with but never thought much about until our last year in school. If you lived where I did, in the town of Whitehall, Georgia, as I did then and still do, you didn't have much choice but to grow up with just about everybody in the county who happened to be born about the time you were.

There wasn't much to Whitehall except the people, and not many of them. Whitehall has grown a lot since then, but we still do not have what you would call a population explosion: town is maybe five stores, a restaurant, and a movie theater. In addition to which we have three churches, not counting the Jehovah's Witness Church, which was then in a lady's basement and is now in that same lady's attic. All the churches are Protestant except for the one they call backdoor-Catholic and that nobody much goes to.

Back then, we had just two kinds of schools to go to, white and colored, separate like they said but equal. So Martha Jean and I grew up together and went to the same schools but not to the same church.

Martha Jean wasn't what anybody would call ugly. They just didn't think much about how she looked. I know I didn't. She was not the kind of girl you would think about kissing or holding hands with. She had what all the girls called "a good personality"; other girls, the ones who secretly disliked her, called her "sweet." They said it the way they would say that a little bitty diamond in a so-called friend's engagement ring was "sweet."

For a long time none of us boys noticed her personality any more than we noticed that she had violet-colored eyes and curly brown hair which she kept pinned down and half the time under a kerchief. If anybody had asked me about Martha Jean I would probably have said that she was good and would be a missionary or something when she got older. If I had known about nuns, I would have guessed that she might become one of them.

Knowing how good Martha Jean was didn't make us like her. Mostly we boys didn't dislike her, but we regarded her as a nuisance. Sometimes one of us would go by to see some girl we thought we liked and there would be Martha Jean spending the night. Had it been almost any other girl any of us knew, we could say, "Hey, I know this boy I'll call, and we'll all go to ride and maybe stop at Uppy's and get some onion rings and a Nu-Grape."

But any friend you had wouldn't be caught dead riding around with Martha Jean, and if he would, he wouldn't be your friend.

Those nights, Martha Jean would have this awful glitter about her. You could tell she knew she was in the way and did not know what to do about it. It never occurred to us boys that we were maybe in the way. Martha Jean would talk a mile a minute, and you'd sit there in the girl's living room, or maybe on her porch depending on the season, and you'd wish Martha Jean would say excuse me and get herself lost. You'd look hard at the other girl, who would frown and shake her head and try to carry on nonsense with Martha Jean, but you could tell she would like to be rid of Martha Jean as much as you would. Martha Jean never let on, but she knew too.

What was wrong with Martha Jean was not how she looked or even that we boys knew better than to try and touch her or fool around any. Everybody could tell that Martha Jean had a purpose in everything she did, even when she was cutting up and trying to make everybody laugh. She was always proving something, being fun so that everybody could see how much fun it was to be a Christian. Everybody I knew could tell the difference between really having fun and having fun to show that they could do it.

Martha Jean probably never had any fun in her whole life, though she talked lots about Joy, which I take to be different from fun.

Parents liked for their daughters to be around Martha Jean, for she was both serious and, from the parents' point of view, fun; she was a kind of model. She did not wear makeup, and she taught Sunday School at the Church of Christ and went away summers to work at some church camp or another. She was probably a great swimmer, but I bet she did that for Jesus too. She went to a different camp every summer, for, though she could sell almost any camp director the first time, they thought hard about having her back two summers in a row.

Martha Jean knew every game and joke in the book, but when she got done with them, they might as well have stayed in the book. You know the kind of books I mean. She was always reading things like "Object Lessons for Intermediates," and "True Fellowship," and "Stories of Faith." Later, she took to reading books like "The Christian Home."

I have watched Martha Jean read books like that, and I know she was not doing it for fun. She was dead serious, and when she tried out the games and jokes she had studied up on, she just naturally made people feel like they were in church or something. The more she glittered at you and tried to make you have fun, the more you felt solemn and serious. That was just how Martha Jean was.

Everybody knew she planned to go away to Columbia Bible College after high school and get a degree, maybe two or three, in what she called Christian Education. You could not ask Martha Jean how she was doing without getting a full report on what she had lately learned about Christian Education.

The way Martha Jean talked about Christian Education made me shiver. She meant it when she said she was *thrilled* or *excited* about it. You could tell she was going to be hell on wheels once she got ready to start teaching in earnest. She was just trying out on those kids down at the Church of Christ and on us at the Whitehall High School.

Well, Martha Jean was one of the commencement speakers at our high school graduation, and everybody wondered which of the girls' spend-the-night parties she was going to afterwards. All the boys wanted the girls they were with to go to another party, for we did not think Martha Jean was likely to approve of what all went on. It was the custom for the boys to drive back and forth from one girl's house to another's. The girls would slip out to see certain boys, even after all the girls were supposed to be in bed. Sometimes a whole gang of girls and boys would pile into the cars and go away and do crazy things like singing and dancing in front of a teacher's house, or eating pickles in the cemetery.

Nobody could imagine Martha Jean slipping out to go riding or anything else, and nobody wanted to spend more time on graduation night with her than they had to. You can just bet that if Martha Jean could, she would have everybody, boys *and* girls, sitting around playing the games she had worked up special for the occasion. It was hard to tell which would be worse, doing what Martha Jean would regard as fun or hurting her feelings by refusing.

It may not be the same everywhere, but in Whitehall, where we grew up, all the boys in the graduating class would ask some girl to walk down the aisle at commencement exercises with them. There was always a girl or two left over, sometimes more, and they always paired off and walked down the aisle together. The boys naturally liked this practice; we never thought that we could be the ones left out, and neither had the girls. At about Christmas, the girls in the senior class began to realize that they might be the ones left out. If they did not have steady boyfriends, they would start being extra nice to anybody they thought might ask them to walk down the aisle.

There was a saying that you always walked down the aisle twice with the same person, which made girls think it was romantic for a boy to ask them to walk down the aisle. The saying really meant that you would go down the aisle twice, once at rehearsal and again at the exercises. Still, even if a girl didn't like a particular boy very much, she would start to think about him different if he asked her to walk with him at graduation. Graduation and marriage seemed almost equally significant then, and it would occur to boys as well as girls that they just might marry the person they walked down the aisle with on graduation night. The odds were for it.

About a dozen of us planned to go to college, and we knew that three of us would most likely be picked as graduation speakers. Our pictures would be in the county newspaper, and we would get to sit on the front row, no matter what our names began with. Mostly, the same ones of us who were officers of practically everything and honor graduates would be the ones nominated as speakers. The way the speakers were selected was that the school principal and the teachers all had a meeting and made their pick first. Then the senior class got to vote on the five they had picked.

I was going to the State University, and, though I didn't count Columbia Bible College as being the same, I knew that Martha Jean might be one of the speakers along with me and Henry Elder. As it turned out, my name did show up on the list the teachers picked, and I got busy right away planning my speech. Once I made it by the teachers (especially Mrs. Schneider, the librarian), I thought I had it made. Anyhow, I did not think I had to worry about Martha Jean beating me out, so I voted for her—though in second place. It was the first time I ever voted for myself, and I lost.

The way Henry Elder and I figured it is that everybody thought we were sure to be speakers, so they voted for Martha Jean either first or second. The balance of us got the scattered votes. Nobody had expected Martha Jean to be elected, but we knew she would make exactly the kind of speech everybody expected to hear, and she did.

After the election, which took place late in April, everybody began to worry about who would walk down the aisle with Martha Jean. Naturally, she did not have a boyfriend. Everybody agreed that it would look funny for a speaker to walk down the aisle with another girl. Generally, the girls walking together were put back on the back row so they wouldn't show up much, but you couldn't put a speaker on the back row.

I had spent most of my senior year being in love with a sophomore drum majorette named Juanita Langley, but I obviously could not walk down the aisle with somebody who was not even graduating. Besides, Juanita had suddenly taken an interest in a truck driver she met at a Coca Cola stand during half time at the State Football Tournament. Though the driver had a wife and what Juanita called three and a half children, she later quit school to ride with him back and forth to Birmingham.

Commencement was on a Friday, the eighth of June, and by the time I got over not being elected a speaker and got around to asking first one girl and then another to walk down the aisle with me, they had all said yes to somebody else. I had thought all along I could walk down the aisle with just about anybody I asked, but all the girls knew I would probably go off after the graduation exercises to be with Juanita. My stock had slipped some too because I had not been elected a speaker. I made a list of everybody graduating and who I knew, or thought, everybody had paired off with. Nobody much was left, and I began to think of ways I could miss graduation completely.

There was this one goon in our class that nobody had anything to do with unless they couldn't help it. He was a real oddball, whose father was a one-legged carpenter, which of course he couldn't help. A week or two before time for graduation rehearsal, I had this awful thought. What if I ended up at graduation without anybody to walk with, and all the girls, even the ones I didn't want to walk with anyhow, were all paired off, and I ended up walking down the aisle with old Lowell?

It would be the first time in the history of Whitehall High School that two boys had to walk down the aisle together. That would be what everybody would remember me by.

I didn't even bother to check with the one or two girls whose names I had written down as "possibilities." I knew one certain bet, and I lit out for Martha Jean's house. I half expected to get there and find Lowell had beaten me to it.

For a minute, I thought Martha Jean would not do it.

As soon as her mother had left us alone, I asked her. She stared at me hard and then looked away.

"Well," she said. That word sounded like the *amen* to a prayer the way Martha Jean said it. "Well, Katie and I—." Katie was this girl almost as bad as Lowell. Her only supposed friend in the world was Martha Jean, and everybody said that even Martha Jean had a hard time being nice to her. I about died to think that it might get out that I had gone so far as to ask Martha Jean to walk with me and she had turned me down for Katie. I'd end up with Lowell anyhow, or, if I was lucky, with some girl about twice as awful as Katie, though that would take some doing.

"Martha Jean," I began, and then I couldn't say any more. I kept wishing I knew her better and had been nicer, so I could go ahead and beg. She fiddled with her new class ring, and I could tell she was thinking hard about me and what I had asked her.

"I'll do anything," I said finally, not quite knowing what I meant I would do. She looked at me in a way that made me sorry I had said it; she looked like she really pitied me, and I realized she knew without my telling her why I had come roaring into her house. I started to tell her to forget it, that I would try to break my leg or preferably my neck, or catch Something Awful so I could spend June 8 in the hospital. I didn't do it though; I sat there waiting for her to decide.

"Well, Jim," she said. She begins nearly every sentence with *well*, which seems a small thing but gets irritating after awhile. "Well," she says, "if it means so much to you, I will."

I knew I had won, but I wasn't certain what.

Graduation night was terrible, and I don't even want to talk about it. Juanita, as I was soon to learn, was stringing me along so she could make her family think she was with me when, in fact, she was with her truck driver at a motor court called The Blue

Pines. So, Juanita got mad that I was walking down the aisle with Martha Jean and made me promise I would take Martha Jean home, or somewhere, by eleven so I could come to her house. I said I would do it, for I did not know that Juanita meant to have me drive her to the Blue Pines Cafe where her boyfriend would be waiting. I didn't mind getting rid of Martha Jean early, and I had an idea that our disappearing early was not going to break anybody else's heart.

Half the people in my class thought I had been noble to ask Martha Jean to walk down the aisle with me, thus preventing her having to walk with another girl. They kept giving me these pitying looks and trying to be jolly. The other half thought I had asked Martha Jean so I could sit on the front row though I had not been elected to speak. No matter which side they took, nobody wanted to be around me long at a time on graduation night. To make it worse, Martha Jean had got Katie and Lowell together, and we double dated.

To top it all off, Juanita's truck driver, whose name turned out to be Ed Greenway, kept buying me beers at the Blue Pines Cafe, and I was dumb enough and gloomy enough to drink them. Wouldn't you know I would get sick, and Ed had to lug me to the toilet to throw up. The odor made me twice as sick, and so Ed had to help me back past Juanita and out to my car. Juanita was simpering and shaking her head the way older women do when children get into trouble. For the next hour or two, Ed kept coming out to rouse me where I was half sitting, half lying on the front seat. He brought me coffee, and once Juanita came and peeped in and sniffed. I mumbled something to her and she went back in the cafe.

I had meant to hate Ed, and there I was depending on him and saying "Thanks, Ed, thanks" every other minute. I even said thank you when he came out a few minutes later and offered to take Juanita home for me. I didn't even say good night to Juanita, for I did not intend to call her again and I doubted she would call me.

Two or three nights later, the telephone rings and my mother answers it and calls me to the phone in her supersweet voice and gives me this knowing look. I had hoped it might be Juanita so I could tell her she had the wrong number and hang up, but my mother's look let me know it was probably somebody I did not want to talk to. It was Martha Jean so naturally my mother, who normally does not approve of girls calling up boys, thought it was just great.

Martha Jean said she had a proposal for me, and I nearly choked. She wanted to see me the next day, or, if possible, that night. I chose the next day, thinking that nobody seeing me going into her house in broad daylight could possibly think I was having a second date with her. I had been thinking lots about that saying that you will walk down the aisle with the same person twice, for Martha Jean had been sick and could not go to the rehearsal.

I didn't think I ever wanted to see Martha Jean again, but I could not think of any good reason not to go to her house the next day. She had said she would like for me to "drop by," and I started to tell her that she knew as well as I did that you could not live much further from one another than we did and still be in the same small town. Anyhow, I went.

When I got to the door, I could see Martha Jean sitting at her desk, which took up half of one wall and which I could see through the window at the top of the front door was mostly dedicated to Christian Education. I rang the bell and Mrs. Foley let me in, though she had to come all the way from the back of the house and Martha Jean was sitting just ten steps from the door.

When I saw Mrs. Foley tiptoeing down the hall to let me in, I thought "By God, she has even got her own mother thinking it's church time—on a Tuesday afternoon in her own house." Mrs. Foley did not exactly whisper, but I had to strain to hear what she was telling me. She said Martha Jean was studying so she would be ahead in her courses at the junior college at Carrolton that summer, which she was taking so she would be ahead when she went to Columbia Bible College.

Martha Jean had not looked around when I rang or when I came in, but now she closed her book and looked back at me almost as if she was surprised to see I was on time. She looked at her watch, as if to calculate how much time she could take off and not miss too much.

I began to smart a little at that, for it was not what I had expected. I thought she would be waiting at the door for me. Her mother tiptoed out. She hunched her shoulders up and poked her neck forward every step she took, and I could tell tiptoeing had got to be a habit with her.

I sat down where Martha Jean told me to, and she began the conversation right to the point.

"You acted as if it was important for me to walk down the aisle with you," she said. "And I did it."

She said that last as if it was to her credit, almost as if she had made some sacrifice for me, which was not the way I saw it at all. I started to tell her, but thought better of it.

"You said you'd do anything," Martha Jean said.

I nodded, and she went on.

"Katie had meant to help me," she said, "but now she's mad at me, I guess you'll have to do."

I knew she thought it was my fault Katie was mad, though I wondered why Katie had not let on she was mad on graduation night, if my walking down the aisle with Martha Jean was the trouble. Martha Jean frowned a little, and I knew she was thinking some of what I was thinking and I wondered if she knew some of the reasons people said I had asked her to walk with me. Then she seemed to soften up some. She almost smiled.

"If Katie gets over it—me walking down the aisle with you, I mean—we can get twice as many."

"Twice as many what?" I asked.

"Bottlecaps," she snapped as if I hadn't been keeping up.

She told me her plans. She intended to win all the prizes she could in the bottlecap contests, and use the cash proceeds to fully equip a recreation center in the Church of Christ basement. If there was anything left over, she might use some of it to help defray her expenses in learning Christian Education. (I swear that's the word she used—*defray*.)

"After all," Martha Jean says, beginning to glitter a little, "it's all for the same goal." I knew better than to ask her what goal she meant.

I stood up and rattled my car keys in my pocket.

"What exactly do you want *me* to do?" I asked, trying to stop feeling sorry for Martha Jean as I had begun to do. It seemed to me like Martha Jean talked about going to Columbia Bible College but did not really expect ever to get there. I decided that probably her daddy did not have the money to pay, and she had not got a scholarship as I had done. I had made a promise, though I did not know she would hold me to it, and I meant to keep it.

What Martha Jean wanted me to do was to use my car and go twice a week to a bunch of cafes and restaurants she had already contacted and get the bottlecaps out of the little boxes under the openers. The way Martha Jean had led up to it, I expected it to be harder.

"I added a few places to the list when Katie backed out," she confessed. "There are some places you wouldn't ask a girl to go." She waited a minute and then added, "Even for the Lord." I shivered and nodded. I thought I would rather go to all that trouble for Martha Jean than for the Lord, though the truth was I would just as soon not do it at all.

"After you make all your stops," she instructed, all business now, "you bring the bottlecaps here and we'll gouge out the numbers and put all the prize winners in a special pile, and I'll write off for them to send me the prizes. What we don't need, we'll sell and use the money to buy what we do need."

Martha Jean was so thrilled about what we were going to do for the Lord that what she was saying almost made sense. I did not think she'd need many stamps to write off for prizes and I hated to see her building up for a big disappointment. I guess she could tell I was cool to her idea, so she says, "If there's something you especially want, Jim, you can have it." That was like Martha Jean, and I said thank you, though I doubted she would win anything I wanted.

A minute later she cut her eyes toward her desk and I took the hint and tiptoed out. She was reading again before I got off the porch.

I began that same week. Martha Jean gave me two gunnysacks to put all the bottlecaps in and I went everywhere she told me, though I did feel a perfect idiot carrying a gunnysack into the Elks Club and the American Legion and places like that. I drove past the Blue Pines Cafe twice before I got up nerve to go in, but, fortunately, neither Ed nor Juanita was there. I had one of the bags nearly full when I got to Martha Jean's house.

"Where's the other one?" she says as soon as she sees me.

"This is all," I tell her. She frowned and led me back to the porch where we were going to gouge out the numbers. I knew she thought I had somehow failed.

She began gouging right off and I watched how quick and easy she did it. I could tell she'd had considerable experience. All the time she was gouging, she was thinking.

"Wednesday is a bad day," she said. "We'll have to change the collection day, but do you know where some of these places put their garbage?"

"In the garbage can," I say sarcastically, for I know already what she's about to ask me to do.

"Fine," she smiles. "While I work on these, you go back and see if you can't find the ones they threw away. There's no telling what wonderful prizes are sitting in garbage cans going to waste." I told her there was no telling what kind of nasty stuff I would have to root through to get all those lovely prizes, but she hardly listened to me.

"You won't have to do that again," she said, "for you're going to go on Friday and Monday from now on, especially to those places Katie couldn't go."

I started to tell her that the places Katie couldn't go to mostly made their money selling beer and illegal whiskey and that the beer companies and the bootleggers do not need to give people prizes for what they sell. I didn't have the heart to say any of that, for I had this funny feeling I would end up scrounging around in garbage cans no matter what I said.

When I got back to Martha Jean's house the second time, I had maybe four or five hundred more bottlecaps. She was still gouging and from the look on her face I could tell she had not come up with any winners.

She brushed her hair back from her face and said, "You sure this is all you got?" It sounded like she thought maybe I had held out all the winners, but I knew she was tired and sad she hadn't already got a ping-pong table or something for the church basement.

I dumped the new bottlecaps out on the table for her to see and sat down and started gouging.

This went on for over a month. Twice a week I'd go around with my gunnysacks and deliver them to Martha Jean's. I became real well acquainted with the help at some of the most regularly raided joints in the county. At first I did not want to tell these characters that I was collecting bottlecaps to try and outfit a recreation center in a church basement. When I did, they began to take an interest and sometimes gouged out the numbers for me when they didn't have anything else to do. I was sure they gouged them out without even checking to see if the numbers were good ones, but Martha Jean was not so sure. Sometimes, if the bartenders and dishwashers had not had any time to gouge out bottlecaps, one of them would come to where I was emptying the bottlecap containers and stand around, looking mad for a minute or two. Then they would stick a crumpled-up dollar bill, or sometimes a five, at me, and mumble something about maybe this would help.

When I took the bottlecaps to Martha Jean, I would always give her the money first, all smoothed out and neat. She would mist up and say "Even if we do not win anything, Jim, we are doing some good." It turned out she thought we were *helping* the people who gave me those dollars. I didn't quite understand, for it seemed to me *they* were the ones doing good. I did not try to explain that to Martha Jean.

I would nearly always try to help Martha Jean gouge out the numbers to see if we had won anything, but this made her nervous. She thought I might throw away a winning number, or gouge into one so hard she would not be able to read it. Sometimes she looked as if she might start to cry. Still, she never suggested we should give up, and neither did I.

In the middle of gouging out a thousand or more bottlecaps and checking to see that she still had not won anything worth mentioning, she would say, "Jim, how do you feel about a pool table in a church? Don't you think we should have one?"

I told her a recreation center would be nothing at all without at least one pool table, and we should most definitely have one if we could get it. I felt funny about saying "we," for I was not a member of her church and hadn't any intention of ever going down to its basement if I could help it. After a conversation like that, she would gouge away faster than ever, and if pure spunk could have come up with a pool table she would have had a dozen of them.

Toward the end of summer, I was dragging. It seemed summer hadn't been summer at all, and I wondered where those long, carefree days I used to know had gone. Martha Jean would not admit she was tired too. She had finished her courses at the junior college, and from what I could see she was not doing anything now but gouging bottlecaps. Once or twice, I started to ask her to ride along with me when I did the collecting, but I decided Martha Jean would not like sitting out front at places like the Blue Pines Cafe.

Katie was helping some now, and I learned that she and old Lowell were going out together regularly. Lowell was helping his father build houses, and I thought that maybe between them they might make a passable carpenter. A bunch of Martha Jean's Sunday School students were going all over town asking the women who answered the door to save their bottlecaps for Martha Jean. When Martha Jean won an electric mixer, the newspaper carried an article about her and what she was hoping to do. People began to drive up and ring the doorbell and hand Martha Jean a sack full of bottlecaps. Martha Jean always asked them to come in, but they would edge away and she would call out "God bless you" when she saw they were really leaving.

Martha Jean said that our testimony was having a good effect, and I told her I would appreciate it more if the folks who dumped their bottlecaps on her front porch would gouge out the numbers and leave her the winners. That way, I said, they would know what they were giving away.

Martha Jean took it as a personal victory when we won a prize from some of those bottlecaps left on her front porch. The prize—a year's supply of one of the drinks—wasn't much, but Martha Jean got excited about it. She even wrote to the company and suggested that they should supply the church with drinks for all its social functions.

"That's two prizes, Jim," she said. "The third will be the big one." She was almost hysterical and kept saying the same thing over and over: "The third will be the big one."

To make her stop, I grabbed her and whirled her around. I hadn't meant to pick her up, but she was light as anything and I spun around and around with her held up against me.

"Sure it does," I yelled. "This changes our luck for sure."

When I put her down, she looked at me funny but she did not seem mad or anything.

It was almost time for me to leave to go to college, and I knew

Martha Jean would be looking for a job and that Columbia Bible College was going to have to wait for awhile. To make myself feel better about how unfair it was that I could go off to college and Martha Jean couldn't, I told her I thought she ought to use all the prizes she had won, or might win, to help her pay for studying Christian Education. As I expected, she said no to that. She had set out to equip a recreation center and that would have to come first.

She wrote me at the University that fall, and more than halfway suggested I should go around and collect bottlecaps to bring home with me at Thanksgiving and Christmas. I could tell that she had not even thought of giving up yet, and I wrote her back that I was staying at school for Thanksgiving because of the big football game. I didn't mention Christmas, for I hoped that by then she would have given up.

When I came home for Christmas, Martha Jean's daddy was sick and I only saw her once. She didn't mention the bottlecaps until I asked about them. She said she was way behind with gouging them out, for people still brought her bags full of them and, now it was cold weather, she had no place to work without disturbing her daddy. She had been doing some typing at home, but that bothered her daddy too, so she was about to get busy and find herself a job.

About February, I got this letter at school that was so damn cheerful I couldn't stand it. Martha Jean wrote that her daddy was in the hospital and that he was much more comfortable there, and she was getting caught up with the bottlecaps. It was like she didn't even care about winning any longer; she just wanted to keep up.

She said she had got a good job as secretary at a lumber company. "I am plane board," she wrote. "Get it?"

She went on to say that she collected the bottlecaps out of the cold-drink machine in her office and that the men who drove the lumber trucks picked up bottlecaps at all the places they stopped. "Everybody has been so sweet," she wrote.

She said she had won an electric hairdryer since she last saw me, and I wondered if she had kept it or sold it. I wouldn't put it past her to give the hairdryer to the church as she had done with the electric mixer. (I could not think of anyone needing to dry their hair at church, unless, of course, they had just been baptized, but that wouldn't make any difference to Martha Jean. She would put it there even if nobody ever used it.)

After I read that letter, I got to thinking how rich Martha Jean would be if she had been paid even fifty cents an hour, which was the rate of pay back then for babysitters, for all the time she had put in gouging bottlecaps. She would be about ready to retire if she had been doing anything worthwhile. I began to hate the sight of a drink machine, for I felt guilty if I did not stop and get the bottlecaps for Martha Jean and I felt silly if I did.

I could not answer Martha Jean's letter. I had nothing to tell her but the one thing I knew she would not listen to. Which was to give up. While I was still trying to answer that letter, I got a second one, and then my mother wrote me to say that Martha Jean's daddy had died and it looked as if she would be working at the lumber yard the rest of her days to pay off the hospital and funeral bills.

I knew I had to write Martha Jean, but I did not know what to say to her. I worried about not writing, and every time I thought about her I got this heavy guilty feeling. Nothing was any fun anymore. I could not go to a party and see a girl drinking a Coca Cola without thinking of Martha Jean on that dingy back porch of hers gouging out bottlecaps and working the rest of her life to pay off doctors and undertakers. Once or twice, I got to feeling so bad I would go out late at night and fill up my briefcase with bottlecaps. I would come back to my dormitory room and gouge out all the caps to see if I could win a prize for Martha Jean.

When I went home for spring holiday, I called the lumber company and Martha Jean answered the phone. From the sound of her, you would have thought she was on top of the world. That made me feel so bad I asked if I could come by and pick her up after work and drive her home. She sounded glad about that and said she had something to show me at her house. I thought it would be something she had won, and I hated the prospect of pretending to think it was great.

I got to the lumber company just before five o'clock and went in for Martha Jean. We shook hands very solemnly, though I do not think I had ever shook hands with a girl my age before. I could tell everybody in the office thought the world and all of Martha

Jean and that they were hanging around to see if they thought I was good enough for her.

Old Mr. Rossiter came out from behind the glass cage that was his private office. He said he was coming out to inspect Martha Jean's young man. He talked like he thought I was taking Martha Jean out on a date, and I wanted to explain to him about Martha Jean and me, but then I couldn't decide what to say.

I held Martha Jean's coat for her, and somebody said it looked like a shower. I looked outside real quick, for I had left the top down on my car. Martha Jean blushed and said April showers would bring May flowers, and everybody laughed. You could trust Martha Jean to think of something like that and never think about the rain ruining my car seats. Mr. Rossiter said that April showers also bring June weddings, and everybody but me laughed again.

"You behave yourself," Martha Jean said. She tossed her head as if maybe there was some truth in what he said, and I wished I had never called her up at all.

Because I could not think of much else to say when we got in the car, I asked if she wanted to stop anywhere before I took her home. She shook her head, and I asked if she would maybe like to stop and get something to eat.

"I'd love to," she said real quick, "but if we do that it will be too late for me to show you what it is I said I wanted to show you. It's out back."

Without much thinking, I said, "Okay, we'll go out to eat after we've been by your house."

"If you want to, James," she said. I looked at her quick, for she had never called me James before, always Jim. She was sitting straight up and staring out the windshield ahead.

In a minute she said that she wouldn't want to be too late getting home without letting her mother know where she was. I asked if she could not call her mother, and she said no. They had probably taken out the telephone to save the money. I was feeling about as bad by then as when I got her first letter.

Martha Jean began talking a blue streak when we hit her front porch. I guess it was to let her mother know she was home and had company, or maybe it was to let her mother know she was having a good time. We went into the living room, where Martha

Jean's desk was still loaded down with books, and I had hardly sat down (in the same chair I sat in the first time there) before I had to get up again because Martha Jean's mother came in to say hello.

As soon as I saw Mrs. Foley, I knew why Martha Jean had to be so cheerful all the time. Her mother looked like she had cried until she had no more tears, but none of the tears had helped her any. I would not have known her had she not been tiptoeing.

I guess she knew how bad she looked, for she had tried to fix up a little when she realized Martha Jean had company. She had a big blot of rouge on each cheek, and she had turned up the edges of her mouth with a little bit of lipstick. She made me think of that clown in a movie I had seen with Juanita; he was always singing "I'm laughing on the outside, crying on the inside."

"Jim," she says, turning her mouth upward in an even bigger smile, "I haven't seen you in ages. Not since—."

She trailed off, and it was not hard for me to guess that she was thinking she hadn't seen me since her husband died. Martha Jean was smiling and trying to encourage me to say something, but I didn't know anything to say.

Martha Jean pipes up, "Not since James went off to college, Mama."

"That's right," Mrs. Foley agreed. "And do you like your teachers, Jim?" She was clouding up again, possibly thinking about how Martha Jean had counted on going off to Columbia Bible College but hadn't been able to go.

I talked awhile about my teachers and even made up one or two. Finally, Mrs. Foley said she would go and finish up supper and I should stay and eat with them. I knew I had to say something quick so I could get out of there. I was about to die I was feeling so sorry for Martha Jean and her mama. I don't know which made me feel worse, the old lady breaking down every other minute or Martha Jean chirping away like she was Queen for a Day.

I said it would be too much trouble for Mrs. Foley to cook for me without any notice, and I thought maybe Martha Jean and I had better hurry so we could get something to eat in town before time for the early movie. I had not mentioned a movie before, but neither Martha Jean nor her mama looked surprised.

I remembered all of a sudden that Mr. and Mrs. Foley and Martha Jean did not use to think very highly of people going to the

movies, and I wondered if I had said the wrong thing. I said quick,
"Or, if you don't want to go to the movie, Martha Jean, we can do
something else." Which was silly of me, for everybody knows there
is nothing else to do in Whitehall on a date but go to a movie.

I had not meant to do it, but there I was going out on a date
with Martha Jean Foley.

Martha Jean said she would love to go to the movie, but then
she settled right down to entertain me and her mama as if she had
all night. She talked about everybody she had seen, or spoken to
on the telephone, at the lumber company that day. She made
everything that had happened sound so funny that Mrs. Foley and
I sat there in that dusky room staring at Martha Jean as if she was
one of the Wonders of the World.

Once or twice, Martha Jean made her mama laugh, and I could
tell that that tickled her, but then Mrs. Foley would get sad again.
She would laugh and then she'd look like laughing had made her
think of when she used to be happy and she'd cloud up again. Still,
Martha Jean had said no more about what it was she had wanted
to show me.

I stood up and told them that we could still make the late movie,
if Martha Jean didn't mind staying out later, but that unless we
got started we would miss supper or the movie, or maybe both.

"Goodness," says Martha Jean, "Time flies when you're having
fun." And she began to glitter a little.

"It's about dark already," I hinted, and Martha Jean shot a look
at her mother.

"Mama," she says softlike, "we're going out the back door. I
want to show James what we've made." Her mother nodded, almost as solemn and serious as Martha Jean had sounded.

After a minute, Martha Jean added, "James helped. Without
James, we might not have done it." I could not imagine what she
was talking about.

I saw it as soon as we got to the back door. Martha Jean had
gone ahead of me, and Mrs. Foley followed me. I stopped short
at what I saw, and Mrs. Foley nearly ran me down.

Toward the back of the yard were eight or ten big trees with the
last light of day showing through them. Just in front of the trees,
and sticking up almost even with the lowest branches of the trees
was what Martha Jean wanted to show me. It was glittering in

what light was left, and its shadow fell on Martha Jean when she turned and smiled back at me as if to say, "Look what I have done."

It was a twenty-foot cross made out of strips of lumber and covered all over with bottlecaps of all kinds. That is what made it glitter, thousands and thousands of bottlecaps. I did not know what to say. I felt as I had the one time I went inside a Catholic church and saw all those candles glittering up front and reflecting in the silver candlesticks and other things.

"It's not a recreation center," Martha Jean says in a funny, high voice. "But I decided to use all those bottlecaps and all our work. I wanted them to go to a good use, not go back to the garbage heap." She was smiling and looking desperately sad all at the same time, and I wanted to run to her and touch her or say something to tell her what she had done was good.

That backyard felt like a church, and Mrs. Foley and I were the congregation. Martha Jean looked small and almost helpless, but she also looked as if she wanted to understand why she had done what she had done. I was so overwhelmed that if I had known then how to genuflect, I would have done it although Martha Jean would have disapproved.

"Mr. Rossiter let me have the lumber free," Martha Jean said in a quiet voice. It was almost as if she was a wife trying to explain some extravagance to her husband. "I drew up the plans," she went on, "and some of the drivers put the pieces together and brought them out here. I decided to do it when I first knew things weren't going to happen the way I had planned them."

She turned back toward the cross and seemed almost to be talking to it. "I didn't know how I was going to do it," she said, "but I had the idea ages and ages ago. Getting a job at a lumber company wasn't my idea either, but there it is."

She turned back to me. Her mother had gone quietly back to the house. "I knew," she said, "ages and ages ago." I nodded as if Martha Jean was revealing some mystery to me. I went to the cross and touched the bottlecaps.

"I see," I said. "I see."

"It's sunk in concrete," Martha Jean said, giving it a good hard tug to show me how steady it was. "It's there for keeps. I nailed the bottlecaps at the highest parts before we set it up, but Mama and I got impatient so we sunk it in concrete and every day I nail a few more on."

"Yes," I said, and Martha Jean smiled as if I had said the perfect thing.

"The back's not finished yet," she told me. "Only the front."

I walked behind the cross and into the dark shade of the trees. I smelled the spring growth and became conscious of the sounds of crickets and birds in the trees. Nobody could see the back of the cross unless they came through the woods, and Martha Jean had nailed bottlecaps only at the very top of the cross. Down low, you could still see the rough grain of the wood.

"With the stepladder, I can reach the top," Martha Jean told me, "and now the days are getting longer, I'll nail more on than I have this winter."

Martha Jean showed up gray in the dark against the light her mother had turned on. I stood in the dark watching her and knowing she could not see me except as a shadow behind the cross. Listening to her that way was like hearing somebody's confession, as I had seen priests do in the movies. But I didn't know why Martha Jean Foley should confess to me.

She went on: "I still gouge out the tops of most of them before I nail them up," she said, "but some of the companies have stopped their contests by now. Those things come and go, you know."

"Most things do," I said. "Most things come and go." I felt paralyzed, and Martha Jean's face when she turned it a certain way shimmered. I seemed to have lost control of myself, but I did not regret losing what I had never understood anyhow.

"I told Mama," Martha Jean confided, "that it would be good if I could go ahead and nail up all the rest of the bottlecaps on the cross without wondering what I would find inside if I gouged them, but she said I had worked too hard for a recreation center to give up." She was smiling. "It wouldn't be giving up at all," she said.

"Sometimes, I nail up one without looking to see if it is worth a prize. It's kind of like an offering—you don't know what it's worth, but it's all you have."

I stepped out, and without meaning to do it, I took Martha Jean's hand in mine. "You mustn't do that," I said. "He doesn't want that. He wants you to give yourself a chance." I am not, and was not, sure who He was, or is, or how I knew what I said was true, but I believed it. And still do.

Martha Jean looked at me as if she believed what I had said too. I took her other hand and we stood there in front of that giant cross, not looking at each other but looking at It.

I felt as if I had stood up at church and testified. I also felt the need to say something practical.

"While I'm home, we'll finish the cross," I promised. "We'll gouge out the rest of the bottlecaps before I nail them on, and if that's not enough I'll get some more." I laughed and said that while I was nailing up the bottlecaps, Martha Jean could write off for all the prizes we would win.

Martha Jean said nothing, and I said, "Okay, Martha Jean? Okay?" It sounded as if I was begging her.

"If you want to, James," she said, "we'll do it."

That night after the movie, we gouged out bottlecaps. The next night we stayed home and ate sandwiches and did the same. None of the numbers were worth prizes, but we kept at it as if the next one would make up for all the rest. It seemed like old times, and that I had spent my life gouging out bottlecaps. I did not think I could tell my parents what Martha Jean and I were doing.

The next day, which was Saturday, I finished nailing on the bottlecaps, and I took some pictures of Martha Jean and her mother in front of the cross. Since the next day was my last day at home, I said I would drive Martha Jean and her mother to church. Afterwards, Martha Jean took me down and showed me the basement where she wanted to put the recreation center. I went home to have Easter lunch with my own family, and the excuse I gave was that I had lots to do to get ready to drive back to the University. I didn't have all that much to do, though, and the last thing I did before I drove out of town was to take my gunnysacks (which I found in the garage) and fill one of them up with bottlecaps and leave it on Martha Jean's porch.

The next night, somebody yelled up to me in my dormitory room that I had a long distance call in the lobby and to come quick.

I thought, "My God, first Martha Jean's daddy and now mine." I was sure I would find out my daddy was sick or dead.

I ran down the steps and grabbed the phone, and the operator asked me my name and said, "Sixty cents for the first three minutes, please." My throat unstopped then, so I could breathe and talk, for I knew it was not my mother calling from a pay phone.

It was Martha Jean and she was laughing and crying and jabbering all at once, and I couldn't tell what she was talking about. At first, I thought something awful had happened, and then she settled down enough I could understand some of what she was saying.

" I ran straight out of the house to call and tell you, James," she said. "Mama doesn't even know yet. All I said was 'I'll be right back.'"

Before I knew it, I was laughing too and saying, "Come on, Martha Jean, come on and tell me."

I knew we had won something, and from how happy she sounded, it had to be something big—like a pool table, maybe. The more I laughed, the more settled and serious she got.

She cleared her throat and said, "Your faith did it, James, your faith did it."

I began to tighten up inside and didn't want to laugh anymore, for I didn't think faith had anything to do with it, and, besides, it was just exactly like Martha Jean to try and give all the credit for something she had done to somebody else. I did not want her to give the credit to me, for I did not think I could live up to it, or escape from it either.

The telephone connection wasn't too good, and everything I said rang back in my ears. I felt as I had felt in Martha Jean's backyard, when I saw the Cross. I felt like I was listening in on somebody else's conversation.

"What is it, Martha Jean? What did we win? What?"

"Nothing for the recreation center, but it's one of the biggest prizes." She laughed again, and I thought maybe Martha Jean was beginning to have fun. I hoped so, for I wanted to stop having to worry about her all the time.

"Great," I said. I listened to that word echo in the telephone and went on. "We'll sell it and buy what you need for the recreation center—or maybe we'll just haul off and send you to Columbia Bible College."

I hoped we could get it over with quick. I was losing interest now Martha Jean had finally won something big. Maybe she could be happy now and stop pretending everything was great when it wasn't. She would have her recreation center and her cross, and maybe I could have some peace of mind. I had blisters on my hands from all that gouging and hammering I had done, and I wondered what on earth had made me do it. When my friends at school asked me what I had done during the spring holiday, I didn't know what to tell them.

From then on, I had to strain to hear Martha Jean. My hands were sweating and cramped from holding the phone so close and hard. Martha Jean sounded different now, and I could not tell if she was still happy or about to cry. What she said was this:

"If you want to, we'll get the money for it, Jim, but what we have won—is a trip for two to Bermuda."

"For two?" I asked, and then softer: "For two?"

Martha Jean whispered, "Yes, for two." The operator came in and was saying our time was up, and I said I'd better come home that weekend so we could talk. Martha Jean asked me if I was thinking about coming Friday or Saturday. I said Friday, for we had a lot to decide. And then we hung up.

On the way back to my room, I stopped at the Coke machine and felt in the box under the opener. I guess I did that from force of habit. It was almost empty, and I went on upstairs to my room wondering how on earth I had gone and fallen in love with Martha Jean Foley.

Elizabeth Harris

THE WORLD RECORD HOLDER

(from *Southwest Review*)

Balancing on One Foot. The longest recorded duration for continuously balancing on one foot without any rests is 35 hours by Mary Eileen Maloney, Wichita Falls, Texas, on March 3, 198–. The disengaged foot may not be rested on the standing foot nor may any sticks be used for support or balance.

198– World Book of Records

I

We've both changed—even from the beginning of our acquaintance, in the two sides of a new duplex full of cold construction errors in blatant Fort Worth, we were moving in opposite directions. I was married, wanting to be single, and she was single, wanting to be married—a thin rapid intelligent woman, christened Mary Eileen, called Emmy. She was sharing the other side of the duplex with another schoolteacher and a nurse, a tall clear-eyed blond named Marilyn, and Marilyn was getting married, and this had set Emmy's mind like a bright weathervane, gargoyle and arrow, at the same angle for days on end.

"I hate her," Emmy would say. "She's so happy. And she gets into his car with him"—it was an unshiny old red Ford convertible, Marilyn's, not his, but this was no help to Emmy—"and they drive off together, and I can't *stand* it, I'm so jealous, I want somebody to *love* me." And we would laugh, at the absurd persistence of ambition, or longing, or something.

It seems like a long time ago, now that I wake up alone so many different places later, with the light diffused softly through the curtains, the pyracantha outside, lacy or brilliant with the season. I'm simpler, easier now, like the birds—a cardinal flew into the room one time and miraculously made it out unbroken; another time a mockingbird flew against the window outside, cracking the pane, and was killed.

But when I met Emmy, who was a stranger in town, accidental, like my then-husband and me, she offered the kindness of distraction, a life even more difficult-seeming than my own. At home all day alone—the other schoolteacher did something else, and Marilyn worked a day shift—Emmy would wait for me to drive up and would rush out and leap on me conversationally. She would invite me in, make me iced tea for the shimmering Texas summer, and tell me all about herself and everything she was thinking.

"I'm thirty-one!" she said. "Can you believe it? I hate my job, my car is broken, my family is crazy, and I want a man!"

Crazy was one of her words, not as casual comment but as serious assessment ("Of course, I'm crazy, *you're* crazy—you must be or you wouldn't've married him—but he's *really* crazy"). Also necessary credential ("I mean," she said, "if they weren't crazy, why would we care about them?"), ambiguous good ("But what I really want to know," she said, "is just how crazy a person can *be* and still walk around in the world?"), and generally significant topic of inquiry—what it all meant that you had to be crazy but not too crazy.

She was preoccupied, as well, with larger and larger questions ("I mean, what's it all *good* for?" she would say. "What's it all *about*? I mean, okay, great, if you can be James Joyce, or Picasso, or Duke Ellington, but what if you can't?"), so that conversations with her were likely to end in a companionship of exhaustion and irresolution on the outer margins of human circumstance. "I used to think about committing suicide," she said, "after I read Camus—silly, isn't it, kill yourself because of a book?—but really, what's the good of even that? I mean, we're just *here*."

And I could agree with her, for all the else I knew about it at the time, or know now, only for me, it's more like a song we used to sing in the Scouts—Here we stand like birds in the wilderness . . . waiting to be fed. I never really shared her noble desperation.

I'm a gardener now—I seed and feed and cherish new roots and shoots, and when I die, I'm going to be composted, and it's enough for me—or I make do.

But if I was not to have a future like her, I didn't have such a past, either. She had an unusual family history—she was the daughter of a jockey named Eddie Maloney, who had been famous once, when he rode a horse named War Department to win the Belmont Stake in 1930-something. He had been an Irish kid from Canada, an orphan, or maybe a runaway—he had grown up around racing and started riding races in New York in the early thirties.

And one time in New Orleans for the winter racing, her father had met her mother—he was in traction in the hospital, and she was a nurse. They had sold their story to MGM—I saw it when I was a kid, years before I knew Emmy: at first he's the rough-tongued young jock, desperate over this setback to his career; then sweet-faced Jane Wyman, playing the good Catholic girl, nurses him back to health; and in the end War Department wins and it's all going to be so perfect.

I wonder, did they ever see the movie. He would've—a devotee of his own myth; she probably wouldn't've—she would be working the evening shift at some hospital so she could get the kids off to school in the morning. He had made money, and spent it like all the jocks—on custom-made suits and a silver fox topcoat and a 1936 Cord 810 and a claque of friends. Because, of course, he thought it would go on and on, that he had well and truly made it—and he almost became what they call a legendary figure in racing. Was it drinking?—they all drank. Maybe it wasn't anything he did or didn't do. Somehow, in the gradual algebra of opinion that meant you got the winning mounts, he didn't anymore, though he had continued to ride; it was what he knew how to do.

"The last year my father raced," Emmy said—I think it was 1950—"he rode eighty races and made altogether less than two thousand dollars."

So he had retired from racing and moved the family to New Orleans, which had been the mother's home.

"I'm from nowhere," Emmy said. "One time we lived in a trailer. When I was sixteen, I became the Yankee kid. I think that's what I like about the South."

"In the house we lived in," she said, "you could see the fair-grounds race track from one upstairs window and the St. Louis Number Three Cemetery from the other one. Now they live on Mystery Street."

He still did things around the track—"Oh, he drinks," Emmy said. "He hangs out with his racing buddies and they talk"—and her mother was still a nurse. She worked at the Emergency Room of a hospital in New Orleans called the Hotel Dieux.

A little poorer year by year as the children were growing up, they had sent Emmy's younger brother to college, but not Emmy—she had had to work her way through.

"So here I am with a lousy degree from a lousy university," she said, "so I can't get into a really good graduate school, like Harvard or Yale, or Berkeley or Columbia—though those places are sort of crazy right now—I mean, the list of places I can't get into is posi-tively depressing. So what can I do? Teach high school in Grape-vine, Texas, and waste away to nothing." She had taken the job in Texas sight unseen, for the strangeness of it ("I mean, Grapevine!" she said), as if her personal supply of improbability wouldn't've been enough.

She had freckles on her arms that ran together in places and a head of spiky blond hair that she bleached some and cut herself, short, like on Giulietta Masina playing the idiot girl in *La Strada*. At one time in life, she had wanted to travel, and she had been to Europe and the Middle East and had once taught at a private girl's school in Iran for a year and caught typhoid and lost all her hair, but it had grown back.

"I was kind of sorry," she said. "Think if I was bald. At least that would be *something*."

It wasn't enough, I suppose, that she looked like her father—or maybe it was too much. I met him once—he looked like an Irish-faced mummy, about four feet eleven, with skin like wood, and a narrow, angular little body—like a Chinese woman's foot, when they used to do that, or a crippled child.

They had driven up from New Orleans for a visit, and I had been invited over to meet them, to water down this family com-bination the exact asperity of which I could never truly share, and we were standing in Emmy's avocado kitchen, where there were gaps around the all-electric appliances.

"Say," Eddie said to me, "I bet you didn't get up as early this morning as I did." He was drinking Canadian Club poured out of a bottle he had brought with him into a cloudy Flintstones glass his daughter had undoubtedly had to wash for him.

"You have to get up early to be a jockey," he said, and looked up from under white eyebrows with the calculated timing of a man who makes jokes for a living or as a regular mode of conversation. "It's a profession, you might say, singularly unforgiving of lateness."

Only I laughed, and he went on smoothly, "There was once a jock at our track"—as if he had already linked all his stock of remarks and stories in all possible combinations, so that none of them could be difficult or unfamiliar—"name of George Woolf, a diabetic, by the way, who fell asleep one morning in a Turkish bath trying to sweat off a couple of pounds for the weigh-in and missed the mount of the summer meet."

He had on a suit in the cut of the forties, neither new nor worn-looking, clean and pressed, with an air of the closet about it, and expensive-looking wingtips laced tight on insignificant bunioned feet. He saw me looking at them.

"I had the right feet for a jock. That was how they knew I wouldn't grow."

Emmy had taken a Librium for the visit and smoked Salems one after another and seemed divided: should she show him off, the once-famous jockey father who told stories—he was, after all, what she had—or was he really, as he had seemed to her in the family for years, a terrible bore?

"Oh, Poppy," she said. Her mother was a tall cool brunette, still a beauty in her fifties, with a perfect mask, the discipline, maybe, of thirty years' listening.

"Get up early and stay late," he said. "There was another rider—steeplechase rider—name of Hayes, who rode a horse name of Sweet Kiss home first in Belmont Park and fell out of the saddle dead.

"Now that's dedication for you."

Eventually we changed the subject, while Eddie's memories ran on silently under him, like the horses of the past. Finishing his drink, reaching to pour another, he shook his head and smiled out of one corner of his stiff mouth.

"Like asking a Cadillac for mercy," he said, as if to himself, without rancor.

II

We moved away after the summer—we didn't live in that house but a few months—and spent the last thin year of the marriage in Atlanta, Georgia, where getting divorced turned out to be vastly and surprisingly simple. Emmy and I wrote letters about how strangely simple it was, and about other things—she, long, inchoate letters that seemed to have gone on like her conversations, until she was exhausted. Our friendship settled into a long-distance pattern not so different from the way it had been when we lived next door to each other, except there was no iced tea. The next year she did go to graduate school, though not to any of the places on the list of places she couldn't get into. Then she wrote me about "how *crazy* this place is" and how much she was in love with one of the professors, who was married, and what a shit he was, but she got over him.

Then she wrote, as a postscript to some other circling self-examination, "There's this man—this man—I don't know."

Months later, he was still there, having moved in, or rather, she wrote, come over one night and never left, introducing his things, a clean shirt, a pair of forgotten underdrawers, one at a time.

"We share our disillusion," she wrote. "We laugh a lot, and he's a great big warm bear. He's younger than me—eleven years, can you believe it?"

But it was a surprise when they decided one weekend and got married the next, in New Orleans at the registry office.

"Unbelievable," she wrote, "that I can be this happy—though, of course, the wedding itself was ridiculous."

She sent me a Polaroid taken indoors, the color too yellow, of herself, with her tiny waist in a blue and white polka-dotted wrap dress, holding a plastic champagne glass and laughing, next to a large, reassuring-looking young man with brown eyes and a large brown beard.

"Of course, my father was drunk, and the rest of the family—my brother, my mother's cousins, who don't like him—were just standing around. And none of Doyle's family came down from

Texas, though we invited them, not even his mother—they're like that."

After this, unsurprisingly, she wrote less often and less when she wrote, as if her conversational energy were being spent elsewhere. And when she did write, of course, it was not about what it was like to have gotten what she wanted, but about the medium-sized details of their life. Graduate school, which neither of them liked much. "If you could just read great literature," she wrote, but there was so much other bullshit, but on the other hand, it *was* an education. ("Why do we think that's good?" she wrote. "Maybe it's just another shibboleth. Or are doubts about the value of education becoming themselves a new shibboleth? What a word.") Then before they had been married a year, Doyle was about to be drafted. "He tried to flunk the physical," she wrote, "—his blood pressure is naturally high—staying up all night the night before, taking dexies and drinking Coca-Cola and telling me to *shout* at him, so I screamed and screamed, but when he went in, it was just under."

It all worked out, though, since they could be saved by moving to Doyle's hometown, so he could take a public service job there. "They don't really *need* any more bodies from Wichita Falls," she wrote. "Volunteering is popular there." So they quit graduate school, gratefully, it seemed, and moved to Wichita Falls, where Doyle got a job with Child and Family Services ("I never knew they *had* that here," she wrote), and they bought a house and were having a baby.

Only then was she disposed to reflect on what she had achieved. "I never thought I'd do this," she wrote, "—sit home all day in my own little house in my own little town (actually, it's Doyle's little town). I even cook, sort of—remember Fort Worth, with the books on the oven shelf? And it's fine, it's perfectly all right."

And I thought perhaps it was true, perhaps I was only unconvinced because my own experience had been different—though she did still seem afflicted with a certain nervous, half-resentful distance from her life. But that might just have been the burden of a naturally ironic outlook.

After the baby was born, she wrote, "I look at her, and I'm supposed to feel something—what is this word *motherhood* that I'm supposed to feel?"

And when Melissa was a couple of years old, Emmy wrote, "I look at her when she's decided she *won't* do something and I think, who are you? You're not my child. You're not *mine*. Of course, she looks *exactly* like me."

It was around this time that—back in Fort Worth—I went up to see them, to flat Wichita Falls, and we sat around in their little white frame house in their grownup living room, which had carpeting and drapes and a green plaid Early American sofa and some maple tables covered with glass, and it all seemed to have been bought secondhand at the same time and put there and not thought about since. But they were happy—they said so, and they looked happy. They were standing together at one point in front of the cold fireplace, Emmy with her head tucked under Doyle's chin, facing me.

I said, "You're the only people I know for whom marriage has actually seemed to make life better."

"Oh, it has," she said.

"We are too," he said, "the only people we know," and I thought, yes, it must happen sometimes. I liked Doyle—he was easygoing, noncommittal, humorous; she seemed to have made a stabilizing choice.

On another visit, though, months later, I was less convinced—things seemed less blissful, more familiar, somehow, as if an early reality of Emmy's life had reasserted itself. "I just vegetate," she said. "I don't have any friends. I've turned into a *lump*. I try to write and can't. Then I sit down and drink gin every day. Or I go out to the thrift shop and buy—ugly things to cheer myself up, just because they're two-fifty—and I come home and look at them and wonder what I bought *that* for, and Doyle makes fun of me."

They'd been married about four years, then. She laughed about their sex life. "He used to wake me *up* at 6 o'clock in the morning. I couldn't believe it. I'm a *rag* at 6 A.M., a *rag*."

But none of this seemed serious, or any worse than the known blunt ordinary of marriage, so I didn't doubt that they would make out—laugh at her discontent together, do something sensible about it.

Instead, they decided to have another baby. Emmy wrote, "I'm a nervous wreck. Doyle made me give up smoking this time. I can't even drink, because it nauseates me. All I do is sleep—I fall asleep in the middle of meals, like the dormouse, or I'll just be sitting there."

But when the baby was born, she wrote, "This is my child. I look at Adam and I just love him. Melissa is so jealous—no wonder, I never felt this way about her."

And then, passing through Dallas–Fort Worth on another one of those crossings of the South that seem to have been part of my own affliction at the time, I ran up on short notice for a weekend visit and got sucked into their misery without knowing.

In the back yard, the grass was brown and dry and the ground as hard as fired clay, and Emmy and Doyle, standing apart from me, went on with some discussion they had apparently started before I got there. I was pushing Melissa on the swing and didn't hear, but Emmy was earnest, gesturing with her arms, saying most of the words; Doyle was looking, as if absentmindedly, away.

Privately (with Adam asleep in the basinette in the dining room) Emmy worried to me. "I'm going to waste," she said. "I try to write, but I can't. We have crazy friends. We see this couple—Doyle's social work professor at Midwestern." Doyle was having to get credits toward an M.S.W. to get promoted in his job. "I think both of us are in love with him. Last time they came over, all four of us ended up shouting at each other. I can't stand this guy. He intimidates me so—you should see the way Doyle and him exclude me."

And hearing it all again, I didn't feel as sympathetic as I had—I thought maybe her capacity for dissatisfaction was constant, and only its objects would change.

She did have a friend of her own, which I thought might help her, a well-known landscape painter—we went to see her vapory watercolors in the lobby of a famous old hotel—but the woman herself I didn't like much.

"Sylvia's crazy, too," Emmy said. "She threw her husband out, but they're still married. He comes around in his pickup truck begging her to let him move back into the house. It's embarrassing." He was a toolpusher in the oilfield. Sylvia hadn't known how to tell him she wanted a divorce, so she had the papers served on him as a way of bringing up the subject. One Sunday morning they were in the bathtub fooling around, and he got out of the tub to answer the door, and there it was: his wife wanted a divorce.

I had arrived complaining about money, worrying whether I had enough for the cross-country move I was in the middle of, doubting even whether I should've spent the money to come to Wichita Falls. Seeing me off on Sunday night, cordial as always, or so it seemed, Doyle stuffed a twenty-dollar bill into my hand. "Anyway, it'll cover your bus ticket," he said, and though I tried to give it back, he wouldn't take it, saying, "Keep it, keep it. I can afford it more than you."

I tried to give it to Emmy, who I thought would've taken it, but instead she just laughed. "Oh, you have to indulge him. He gives people canned goods when they come over. They say something like, 'We have to go shopping, there's absolutely nothing to eat in the house,' and he gives them a can of tunafish to take with them."

Years later, Emmy confessed to me in a letter that after I had left, there had been a terrible fight about that money. "When was the last time you gave me twenty dollars?" she screamed at him. "When did you just *give* me twenty dollars because you had it and I didn't?" But for months after that visit, we hardly wrote—maybe not even friends anymore.

Then, in a couple of years, it was all over—they were breaking up, and who could really say why?

"It's horrible," she wrote after a long time, as if diverted by desperation into letters again. "Doyle is being horrible. He's a stone. He disappears behind the newspaper. He sleeps on the sofa. I say, 'Do you love me?' and he says nothing. I drink and take pills. My shrink says I have low self-esteem and I demand too much of myself, but, I ask you, what do I do that I should hold in esteem? I hate my daughter, love my son madly, no longer even try to write, and drink gin in the afternoons. Then my husband comes home and won't talk to me. Once he didn't say a single word, I swear, not one single word, for two solid weeks. I would sit on the arm of the chair where he was reading the paper and *scream* at him, 'I'm here. Talk to me,' and he'd never move a muscle."

I wrote back—advice she couldn't follow, probably—and we were friends again, in disaster: another marriage in trouble. I felt sorry for Doyle and thought she might have been kinder to him, but it was clear that she couldn't be, and though I liked him and didn't blame him the way she did, *she* was my friend, not he. I remember the very moment when, reading some letters of hers, I knew and regretted I'd never see him again. The marriage lasted altogether about eight years.

She wrote, "It's over. It's completely and forever over, though we're still living in the house together until he can afford to move out. One night in December after he came home, I don't know why I did this, I went into the bedroom and looked in his coat pocket and found this expensive turquoise necklace—much nicer than anything he ever bought me. So I went downstairs and said, 'Do you love me?' and he said, 'No,' and that was that. I never told him I found the necklace.

"And I know—I'm so crazy—I know they're going to take my kids away from me, and I can't stand the thought, can't stand the *idea* of Doyle trying to raise them. Doyle the stone. As crazy as I am, I *know* I'm a better parent than he is. But I can't *stand* either, the idea of having to go in and try to convince somebody I'm sane."

She did it, though, surprising herself but not me. "After *seventeen*—would you believe it?—*seventeen* sessions of psychiatric evaluation," she wrote, "I've got the kids. Doyle brought out all the *horrible* stuff in court—my *diary*, for God's sake, that I've been keeping off and on since I was twenty. I mean, what do you *do* when you're home all day with nobody to talk to? Only, it's all, you know, not what's really happening. I mean, in my life I'm getting the kids up and fixing breakfast for everybody and getting Melissa off to school and doing the laundry and cleaning up where the cat was sick and going out to the Safeway for two cans of tomato sauce and a package of Rice-a-Roni, but, of course, none of that's in the *diary*. What's in the *diary* is how crazy and miserable I am, how I'm losing my mind, and how much Valium I'm taking. That was the other big exhibit: my Valium prescriptions."

"So now it's over, and I have the children, and Doyle the stone is living in an apartment and seeing some woman—not the same one, I think—and I have collapsed in total relief."

And that was the apparent end of the ambition I'd first known her with.

She wrote, "I feel totally empty, exhausted." Her friend Sylvia had painted a picture called something like, *Out of Luck in the*

Oilfield, that I remembered, a man in an aluminum hardhat, a human line of despair against the angle of the derrick, with the impervious expanse of prairie behind.

III

Afterward, she was just holding on, just maintaining—herself and the children. She got a job at the last minute, right before school started in September.

"They want me to teach something called Multi-media Communication, about which I know nothing. What it is, really, is non-college-prep required English. Can you imagine that? Teaching semiliterate high school students about television and popular music, when what's *wrong* with them is all they've done all their lives is watch television and listen to popular music?" (By spring she was writing, "I dread going to work. I hate my students, and they hate me. It's so absurd. Every day we all—most of us, anyway—force ourselves to go to this place where we don't want to be, and we hate every minute that we're there—and in this atmosphere somebody is supposed to *learn* something? What a joke.")

She struggled to take care of the children. "And then, every afternoon, I drag myself home, pick up the kids from *two separate* daycare centers (in one of which they are turning my son into a Baptist!) and then I try to make dinner. Tonight we had peanut butter and jelly, because I was too tired even to make Kraft Dinner. And now I'm supposed to grade papers!"

Doyle did pay child support—"Big deal!" she wrote. "If anybody had ever told me I would be supporting two children on the amount of money I am, and that it would buy this little, I wouldn't've believed them."

By the end of the school year she wrote, "I am never going to enter a classroom again. I will do *anything* else."

And she must've looked for jobs, and it must've been that, with everything else, that overwhelmed her, but she didn't write me about it—she waited till I was there, the next summer, a year later. In Dallas for something, I had taken the bus up to spend an evening with her, and we were sitting out in the back yard on aluminum lawnchairs on the unwatered grass, watching five-year-old Adam play soberly by himself.

"It's been hard for me to accept that he's a very ordinary child," she said. "In fact, he's slow-average. When he was born, I thought . . . oh, everything." She laughed.

Melissa was nine, freckled, strawberry blond, somehow appearing only around the edges of any scene. She did look like Emmy, and like Eddie Maloney, but with a baleful aplomb in place of Emmy's manic activity, so she seemed more like Doyle; I hoped it would help her.

Emmy said, "I, ha-ha, did a very foolish thing. I had quit teaching forever, after that awful year, and I couldn't find a job, and I decided that I just couldn't struggle any more. I mean, I was so tired, and I had hardly any money left, and there was going to be a nuclear war, anyway, and Wichita Falls will get it because of the Air Force base, so I decided to kill the children and myself. I went out to buy a gun. I had this whole elaborate story cooked up to tell them about why I wanted it, in case they were suspicious. And you know what? The cheapest one you could get—I think it was $89.95—was more money than I had in the world. I couldn't afford to kill myself."

Instead she had found a job, "working for a bunch of psychologists," she had written at the time. "It might be a sort of secretary-editorial job." But by the time I saw her, months later, she knew, "All I'll ever be there is a secretary. What I do all day is fill out forms on the typewriter just as fast as I can, with these guys standing over me telling me to hurry up. I walk out of there at night *shaking*, I'm not kidding."

It was better than teaching, though, "If I *do* have to go to work in July," she said. "At least when I get off, I'm *off*—no essays to read. And these guys (these guys are so weird), at least they're grownups and they don't tell you to get fucked."

There were men in her life again, but they were indistinct, rising to the surface of her conversation only to be glimpsed now and then ("Oh, *Mike*," she said. "Mike always wanted to go to *bed*. I wanted to go to the *movies* or something"). She didn't seem positively to care about anything except performing the motions of household and family life, and I wondered if she would always be this way now, like a stuffed hawk in the children's museum, legs outthrust insincerely by something that had gotten away some time before.

Six months or so later—the Christmas letter, probably—she wrote that her father had died of a heart attack and her mother had intestinal cancer—a diagnosis which, oddly for a nurse, she rejected until the end, which came quickly. And partly, it seemed, under the influence of grief, Emmy left the psychologists' job ("I couldn't stand it after awhile—all that fake *understanding* going around, when none of those people really gives a shit about me," she wrote), and in a curious generational pattern, worked briefly as a clerk in the emergency ward of a hospital. She also went back into psychotherapy, where she was prescribed lithium, which she thought changed things for her ("I'm so *calm*," she wrote, "What have I become? Hopelessly and unutterably boring, and you know what? I don't *care*. My kids even like me better—I don't *yell* at them like I used to").

In the fall, she took her new calmness back to teaching. "It's the only halfway interesting job I have any qualifications for. Plus the bottom tracks seem a little more cowed here. I can make them sit there and shut up and *read*—even if the only thing some of them can read is comic books. And I am *calm*—whatever they do, it doesn't get my goat. I'm not even sure I still have a goat.

"I don't do much else. I come home from teaching and I'm *tired*. Still, I tell myself, I'm doing something. I'm supporting myself and my children, and it's *hard*.

"When I have the strength, though, I sometimes wonder, is this all there is?"

Around this time—encouragingly, I thought—she began looking for whatever else there might be. Possibly under advice from her psychiatrist ("None of my gym teachers would believe this," she wrote), she took up running ("I go out after work and pound around the track like one of my father's two-year-olds, in a little red shiny outfit that I got from the secondhand shop, shorts and a tank top, with a white stripe, and wonder if my children are anything like psychologically normal"). It did not satisfy her, and she wrote, "You should see me. I have to stop this before I disappear. I weigh ninety-one pounds. And it's so *boring*, so *boring*, it has no *soul*, no *meaning*. Is that what makes it good? That it's like life? I don't need this for recreation."

But she needed something, for something, and at this time in her life the physical seemed to compel her, so she switched to

Jazzercise. She wrote, "I go to Adult Ed twice a week. It's silly, of course, paying somebody twenty dollars to stand up there and show you how to 'work your body.' When I first heard that, I thought it was 'walk your body,' like a dog. Christ, listening to that mindless music, sometimes I think I'll—but then the endorphines or whatever they are hit and I don't care. I feel good. (Is that what life is all about? Just feeling good?)

"Of course, a lot of these people have religion. It's popular again everywhere right now, isn't it? and especially down here. But I went to Catholic schools and I got out of that once and for all. I mean, where do they get off? Telling people that God hasn't ac- tually *spoken* to anybody but a few cracked saints for centuries and centuries, but *we* know he's still up there, and moreover *we* know what he wants *you* to do!"

In the end, though—or I wouldn't be writing this—she did find what she was looking for or something that would do. Like the whooping cranes that winter down on the coast here and fly up the Great Plains to Canada every spring—they prefer a certain kind of wild tubers, I understand, but in a sparse year, they make do with water rats, insects, aquatic life. After all, they're almost ex- tinct.

It had been months since I heard from her, and she wrote, "You won't believe this, but I am, as they say, 'into' standing around on one foot. And I thought awhile, after I wrote that. What kind of a thing is that to write a friend after six months? (Is this my semi- annual letter to you?) It's true, though. It started when my friend Marty—did I tell you about Marty?—was over and we were drunk and reading *The Guinness Book of Records,* and I read there that somebody in Sri Lanka had set the world record for standing on one foot, and it's thirty-three hours. And I thought, 'I can do that. I mean, I've been doing it all my life, in one way or another. It fits my temperament: it's difficult, demanding in a sort of simple way, but not too demanding, and it's a chance to set a world record, right down there in black and white!'

"Is it worth doing? Of course not—not compared to being Shakespeare (but Shakespeare didn't really *know* he was Shake- speare, did he? I mean, that four hundred years later to people in the English-speaking world, he'd still be *Shakespeare!* So what good was it to him?). Anyhow, I'm not Shakespeare, I'm forty-six years old (can you believe it? I'm old! and I haven't even grown up yet) and the world will probably be blown up in my lifetime, and being in the book of world records for standing on one foot is *something*.

"The first time I tried it, I fainted and fell over after six hours. Everything went black. I was standing in the middle of the living room carpet. I was lucky I didn't hit my head on the hearth or something, I could've been killed. Instead, I fell on a table and broke my arm. Fortunately, I could train with a broken arm—in fact, I couldn't do much else. I think if I'd quit right then, I never would've tried it again. Maybe I kept on *because* I broke my arm. Now I'm up to thirteen hours and there's *no* doubt in my mind that I can do it eventually—unless I get varicose veins or cancer or something."

And that was how she came to it, by what might be called chance. Any doubts I might've raised, she had raised herself and disposed of already, so (myself raking and piling up in one season, strewing and scattering in another) I wrote to her soothing, favorable things, a selection of the best you *can* write to an old friend newly standing competitively on one foot.

She kept me up on her progress: "I'm up to nineteen hours. I work out while I read high school students' essays. I used to hold them in my hands, but that was messing up my stance, so now I leave them on the mantelpiece and just turn the pages. And I make jokes about it—that at least I have a leg to stand on, or that I have a leg up, or that I'm going to lift a leg (you're allowed hourly pee breaks)."

Toward the end, she wrote, "It's hard to find time to test endurance and still get everything done. I've given up sleeping on Saturday nights. I'm up to twenty-six hours, free stand on one foot. My friend Lola comes in and helps out. (Did you know people will just help you sometimes, because you ask for it? I never knew that.)

"I drink green Kool Aid and nibble on something. The children feed themselves, and they know they can come and talk to me, but I cannot come and take care of anything unless they need to go to the hospital. (Did I write you about the time I did have to take Adam? He fell down the back steps and broke his ankle. Do you think that was so he could only stand on one foot too? He was calling me from out there, saying 'Mommy, I can't stand up,' and I was saying, 'Adam, you better be really hurt, or I am going to be very angry with you.' He was in a cast for a month. Eight-year-olds heal fast.)

"I'm not going to overtrain. When I can almost do it, I'm going to set up the verification procedures and go for it. Listen to me, 'go for it.' Have I simply found a way to be the same kind of idiot everybody else is?"

The rest appears in the public annals of unusual achievement. "On March 2–3," she wrote, "a day of local historical interest, for whatever it's worth. And I wasn't, I honestly wasn't sure I was going to make it from hour thirty to hour thirty-three. But then, I thought, why not go on and on? and I believed I could. Marty says I was hallucinating mildly by then. So I did it, and it's been accepted by the *Book* and will come out, I don't know when.

"It's absurd, isn't it? But what isn't, anymore? There's a certain letdown afterward. So I did it, so what? What now? I suppose there's always terminal boredom; I've had a lot of experience with that. It's not easy coming to terms with your own mediocrity."

No. At first I'd planned to be composted and fed to roses—I've always loved roses—it was in my will that way, but now I've decided to change it to a simpler flower, a native flower. Bitterweed? Bull nettle?—a surprisingly beautiful blossom. Dayflower? that was in another codicil, but now I'm thinking fire-wheel: I'll be composted and fed to fire-wheels, along the never-plowed right-of-way, maybe, where the native grasses still seed.

Now Emmy writes, "I'm keeping in training. Every day I come home from work and stand on one foot for several hours. I mean, sometime the record is bound to be challenged—maybe even by the man in Sri Lanka next year."

I have plans to go up for a visit soon—I feel concerned about her daughter, somehow, who's eleven—almost a young woman herself, with who knows what ambitions? Emmy writes, "Melissa has gotten to be a very good cook. She makes things out of *The Joy of Cooking* and other books that people gave me—you know, the ones I always used to look at and think I *could* make something out of there, but instead would make something out of a package? She even seems to enjoy it, though it's hard to tell with Melissa."

Mary Hood

SOMETHING GOOD
FOR GINNIE

(from *The Georgia Review*)

The summer Ginger Daniels was twelve years old she no longer needed her mother's feet on the gas or brake pedal to help her drive. She could do it all, big enough and willing. Her mother never knew how to stop her except by going along. Ginnie pushed it to the limit and past, on the straight stretches through the pinelands between black-water ditches, cutting a swath through the swarming lovebugs, her mother riding beside her, not thinking, just answering, "Sure, Baby," if Ginnie asked was she happy "*now, this exact very minute I mean now?*"

Neither of them knew if Harve Powell ever got elected, but they laughed about his sturdy ads rusting away several to a mile: YOU CAN TRUST HARVE POWELL IN CONGRESS. "I don't know about Congress, but he sure was thorough with his *signs,*" her mother said. Several times they started to count them, but lost track—something else always caught their attention. What difference did it make anyway? They didn't come from around there.

"That was before my time," Ginnie said.

"Don't wish your life away," her mother warned.

On their getaway sprees they sang to the radio and laughed and yelled at cattle in the fields—miles before their courage drooped and they had to turn back. Sometimes they picked berries or wildflowers. Ginnie teased the pitcher plants and sundews with the tip of a reed. She knew just how little or how much it took to cause the involuntary carnivorous snap of the fly traps. She ran through the congregations of sulfur butterflies and they settled on her like petals shattered by wind.

Her mother always told her she was going to be beautiful, a heartbreaker. "If you could *see* yourself," she'd say.

Long before she qualified for her learner's permit, Ginnie was driving solo.

"Why do you *let* her?" someone asked Mrs. Daniels, before her fall.

"She's going to anyway," Ginnie's mother said. "I want her to know how."

When Ginnie was thirteen, her mother fell out of a live oak on a camping trip, way out on a limb after a bird's nest for Ginnie. She broke her back on a POSTED sign, but they couldn't operate immediately; she had to be detoxed first. This was down in Jacksonville, and when the hospital released her, she went to a halfway house. She didn't come back to Georgia right away. Ginnie's father, Doc Daniels, told people it was snakebite. He knew better, and so did the ones around Dover Bluff who always kept up with things like that.

Word got back across the state line that Doc's wife had been feeding her habit straight from his shelves. As long as something's possible, rumor doesn't stop to ask, *Is it true?* His pharmacy—never number one in town before that—endured harder times afterward. He couldn't afford to reopen the snack bar, closed since integration, or to stock more than a few of any of the items that lay dusting and yellowing toward their expiration dates on the sparse shelves. Most of his regular customers kept charge accounts, usually delinquent, with hard cash trickling in a few dollars at a time from oldtimers who didn't feel like driving out to the new mall or from tourists who sometimes stopped to ask directions back to the Interstate.

He had a Coke machine out on the sidewalk which brought in a little income, not much, not reliably. More often, vandals picked the coin box and made off with the profits—and small change made a big difference some weeks. That made Doc shrewd, restless. He got a gun and kept it in his cash drawer. There was room.

He had returned to Dover Bluff several years earlier—had packed up his life entire and moved back home to become his father's partner—even though his father and the store were both failing, and they had never been able to work together before. There was still friction, but not like the kind after his mother died that had driven Doc all the way to North Georgia to establish himself there. Doc had come back thinking that he could turn around the losses, and things had looked pretty good—until the new Interstate opened and business moved east. His father died the second year of their partnership, but Doc left the sign up: *Daniels & Son, Drugs.* Ginnie was Doc's only child.

Now, with both his parents gone, Doc got restless again. Dover Bluff was a dead end for him, and his wife had never given up hoping they'd move back to the mountains. Doc decided she was right; he was finally free to please himself, and a fresh start for him meant a fresh start for all of them. They stuck it out in South Georgia for another year, making their plans, then moved back to Deerfield, north of Atlanta, where Ginnie had been born.

Doc leased a brand-new building at the plaza south of town and built them a house out in the country—no neighbors—on land they had bought years before, thinking of retirement someday. They returned to Deerfield the year Ginnie was supposed to start her junior year. The high school was six miles away. Everything was six miles away, "or more," Ginnie's mother fretted.

"A girl needs friends," Mrs. Daniels said, standing at the window, watching the woods. She no longer used her walker, just a cane.

Ginnie said she didn't care, so long as they didn't make her ride the bus. She wouldn't go to school if she had to ride the bus.

Her mother said, "Be happy, Baby, be happy," and Doc said he'd see.

Her first car was a fifteen-year-old Falcon. "I won't," she said. "I'd rather be dead in a ditch."

"You're the type," he agreed.

Ginnie's mother had a more practical approach. "What'll it take?"

Ginnie knew, exactly. "Red," she said. "I want it painted red. New seatcovers. And shag. And a tape deck."

"Jesus Holy Christ," Doc said. "You want me to rob a bank?"

Ginnie didn't back down: "You want me to, *I* will."

"She doesn't mean that," Ginnie's mother told Doc.

Ginnie said, tightening her barrette, "I didn't want to go to school anyway. Boring."

"They're going to like you, Sugar," her mother said. "You make friends easy, and you already know these kids, went to grade school with them. Remember sixth-grade Talent Night at PTA? They liked you best."

"Well, that's what counts," Doc said.

Mrs. Daniels picked up the keys to the Falcon and offered them to Doc. "It won't always be like this," she said. "This is just the beginning. Look ahead, that's where to look."

When Doc didn't take the keys, and Ginnie stood with her arms crossed, head tilted, not looking, her mother said, "Your daddy finished fifth in his class. He's going to make it right for us, he just hasn't found his niche yet."

"Well, here we all are," Ginnie said,"Hillbilly Heaven."

"When you get back into things—" her mother began.

"Just shut up, both of you," Doc said. "Will you?" He grabbed the keys and went out, cutting along fast down the hill and through the woods.

"He's probably going to throw them into Noonday Creek," Ginnie said, just as he turned back. They could see the white of his tunic flashing far off, a flag of surrender.

"You mustn't hurt people's feelings," her mother told Ginnie. "You won't be able to keep friends if you play like that."

Ginnie watched her father walking slowly back. He didn't come in. He got in the Falcon and drove, hard, toward town. She turned from the window and said, "He's going to do it! Every last bit!"

Her mother hugged her, held and held her. "We love you, Baby."

Ginnie was sixteen when Gid Massey fell in love with her. Gid was a man already. Around school they called him "Drool Lips," but he didn't drool. It was just their way of singling him out. He was a strong, tough, slow man who guarded the parking lot, served in the lunchroom, and swept the halls. He was out in the parking lot the first morning of Ginnie's junior year. She wheeled in late, and backed between two school buses, into the one re-maining space, skilled and cool, indifferent to him standing there, watching. After that, he waited to see her arrive, even though she was usually late, past the first bell. He never waved or spoke. When her arms were full of books, she kicked the car door shut. When she had gone, he'd go over and wipe off the scuff on the paint her shoe had left. Her name was on the door, in pink: *Ginnie*. The *i*'s were dotted with hearts.

Gid stopped by the office one day to see if anyone had claimed a ballpoint pen he'd turned in; he always turned in whatever he found, even money. They teased him. Was he going to write a book?

"Letter," he told them, earnest. He talked slowly, thickly. It sounded as if he said *Let ha*.

Behind his back, they smiled. "He's all right," they said, meaning "not dangerous," meaning "good-natured," meaning "too bad the speech therapist hadn't helped him and a hearing aid couldn't."

Gid watched Ginnie a long time before he wrote that first letter. For practice he ruled the page off, the whole brown grocery sack page, using a two-by-four scrap for a straightedge. He practiced on the scratch sheet till he got it right. He kept the note in his pocket, folded no bigger than a coin. Every day at lunch when he saw Ginnie coming by for her milk, he reached deep and touched that folded paper, but he didn't give it to her. He'd hand her a carton of milk instead, just as always, saying, "Here for you," with an intense look that made Ginnie and her friends exchange sly grins. Once Ginnie said, "You'd think it was heart's blood," and everyone laughed. Gid laughed too, the watchful, mirroring, uncertain, count-me-in laugh of the deaf.

After lunch Ginnie always worked for an hour in the school library, shelving books. He knew that. He had seen her. He had found her with his fugitive glance as he pushed his wide broom by the open door, a glimpse only with each pass he made up and down the oiled planks of the dim hall. He looked from dark into light to find her—the afternoon sun silvering the hair on her arms as she stood watering the philodendron, straightening the magazines on the table, giving the globe a spin as she dusted the quiet world. Ginnie worked in the library every day that semester, penance for misbehavior in study hall. They kept their eye on her, kept her busy. They caught her once in the stacks, kissing Jack Taylor's

pale wrist—he'd just had the cast removed. After that, they kept
her in plain sight, up front.

Gid Massey swept past now, and she turned, about to notice
him in his plaid jacket, pants tucked inside his laced-up boots like
a Marine, his head with its lamb's curls ducked over his work, over
his secrets.

"Hunnay," Ginnie drawled, loud enough for the other worker
to hear and laugh. Ginnie patted her heart, mimicking agitation.
She fanned herself with a limp *Geographic*. Anything for a laugh.

She wasn't the one who found the note. The other girl did, and
brought it to Ginnie the moment Mrs. Grant's back was turned.
It was folded and smudged and tied with blue sewing thread—
and it was for "GINNIE," the *N*'s backward. Ginnie wouldn't read
it right then. Let them wonder. She knew how to play things for
all they were worth.

All it said, and it made her smile in contempt when she at last
unfolded and read it, was PLEASE. The *S* was backward too. The
next day, she stood at the door of the library as he swept. He tossed
a little note ahead of his broom; she might pick it up or not. If
not, he'd sweep it away. She let him wonder. She let it go almost
past, then she plucked it up and pocketed it, her eyes drugged and
shining with her secrets. It never mattered much what the fun was,
to Ginnie, so long as she had a part in it. This note was longer:

> LIKE YOU GINNIE YOU GOOD THANK YOU
> YOU FREND GIDEON

Ginnie wasn't afraid of him. She'd never been afraid of anything
but missing out. She banked each little thread-wrapped message
from Gid in her majorette boots, along with her birth-control pills
and her stash of marijuana. She couldn't wear the boots any
more—they were from long ago. She kept them stuffed with newspapers, the perfect hiding place. Before her parents gave up on
stopping her, she used to hide her cigarettes in the boots, too. She
smoked in public now, anywhere or any time she wanted. Even at
school. That's how she got thrown out of study hall. Three days
suspension for not using the smoking area, and a semester in the
library—in the peace and quiet and order of Mrs. Grant's cedar-

oiled rooms, among timeless and treasured-up thoughts—because
of how she had sassed Mrs. Pilcher, the study-hall keeper, who
wouldn't have her back. The library was a compromise. It had
taken a little for Ginnie to get used to Mrs. Grant and the silence.
She had to learn how to look busy, to keep the librarian off her
back.

"I thought things were going better with me and you," Mrs.
Grant said, the day she found the fifth note. Gid had left it in plain
sight on the poetry shelf.

"Between you and *I*," Ginnie said. "Isn't that correct?"

"No, it isn't, but how would you know?" Mrs. Grant said, walking her to the principal's office. Ginnie had the note, but Mrs.
Grant wanted it back.

"It's a federal offense to tamper with the mails," Ginnie said.

"No way, Sister," Mrs. Grant said. "No stamp, no postmark. You
lose that round too."

Ginnie opened the note and wound the thread tightly around
her finger, round and round.

"Untie it," Mrs. Grant said. "It'll cut off the circulation and your
finger will turn black and fall off and you won't be able to wear a
wedding ring."

Ginnie laughed. "What do you care?"

"Hush now," said Mrs. Grant, as they entered the office.

Ginnie said, "You're not my mamma."

The principal brought it all to a head by saying, "Last chance,"
and reaching for the note.

In the hall, Gid Massey swept by, not looking in, but knowing.
He couldn't hear much of what was going on, but he knew Ginnie
was in trouble, and he hated them for making her unhappy. He
leaned against the wall, trying to hear what the secretary was telling Doc on the phone. He caught Ginnie's voice, too, but no
words. The principal said, "If you *don't*—"

There was a struggle and a chair overturned. Gid heard the principal cry, "Stop her!" and "Don't let her swallow!" and then things
speeded up. The school nurse came running and, as the door
swung shut behind her, he saw Ginnie's foot rising through the
air to kick. The nurse came back out into the hall, calling "Mr.
Massey! Come help us."

He went in and helped hold Ginnie.

"She's having a fit," the nurse said.

When Doc got there, he took one look at her and said, "She's just kidding. Let her go."

Gid had been holding her up in the air, her feet just off the floor, strong but not hurting her. He wouldn't hurt her. If they had laid a hand on her, he'd have struck them down. Mrs. Grant glanced at Gid's eyes, then looked again, wiser. Gid set Ginnie gently down. Her legs didn't buckle and she didn't run.

She turned to Gid and said, "I ate it. The whole thing."

Then they knew who had been writing to her, and they also knew that she hadn't been trying to protect him at all, simply defying them.

"If *we* had said *eat it,* she'd have found a way to publish it on the front page of the *Enterprise,*" Mrs. Grant said.

Ginnie said, "This isn't Russia. I don't have to stay here."

The three o'clock bell rang. "I'm walking," she told them. "I'm sixteen."

"Are you dropping out?" Doc asked, grabbing her arm.

"Some of it's up to us, not Ginnie," the principal reminded him.

"We must get to the bottom of this," Mrs. Grant said.

Gid stood there, watching them talk fast.

"That man is dangerous," Mrs. Grant said, pointing. Gid stepped back, but he didn't relax till Doc released Ginnie; his fingers left marks on her arm.

"We'll just talk it through," the principal said, bringing in another chair. To Gid he said, "You may go." Behind Gid's back, he mouthed to Mrs. Grant, "Fired."

Ginnie saw. She took the principal's desk chair, tipping it back as she unraveled the thread from her finger. The bloodless white skin pinked and plumped with each heartbeat.

"Why do you like trouble?" Mrs. Grant wondered.

Gid didn't shut the door as he went out. In the halls, there was the afternoon chaos of lockers slamming and bus lines and laughter and scraps of song, the roar of normalcy.

"First of all . . . ," the principal said, closing the door on all that.

It was a lengthy conference.

Ginnie rode out a three-day suspension and then was back in class. She didn't see Gid for a long time afterward, but he was watching her. After he lost his job at school, he found work at a sawmill. He stayed gone from Deerfield during the weeks, but he was back in town on Saturdays. That's whose boots left the tracks in the driveway by their mailbox, that's who left kindling on their porch. It was Gid who waited in the woods behind the Baptist Church and watched Ginnie smoking a last cigarette before services, her Sunday shoes flashing like glass, her legs still summer-tan under her choir robe, her hair caught tidy in enameled combs. He saved her cigarette butts, her lips printed on the filter in Frosted Plum.

When she started going with Dean Teague, Gid watched more closely. Some weeks she left church with other boys from school; it wasn't always Dean. They went to dinner at Pizza Hut and sometimes Gid followed them, on his bicycle. He never came close.

Ginnie was popular.

Her mother said, "Baby, now don't give these little old boys heart failure. Don't play them off one against the other."

Meaning what? Fickle? Ginnie just laughed: "Mama, you know anybody but a baby can eat two french fries at once."

At Christmas Ginnie got a card from Gid, a big satiny one proclaiming HAPPY CHRISTMAS BIRTHDAY TO A WONDERFUL DAUGHTER. He had bought it—the most expensive card in the store—from Ginnie's father himself. Gid counted the sawmill dollars into Doc's clean palm, laid the exact change for tax on top, and didn't understand why Doc asked him, twice, "You know what this says?" and read it to him, like Gid couldn't read.

Gid didn't get mad. He thought Doc meant, "Are your intentions serious?"

He liked the card. He knew it was Jesus' birthday, so that was the birthday part of it. And he liked the red satin, like a valentine, and the gold shining on it—that was the Christmas part of it. And he knew Ginnie was a wonderful daughter, and Doc must be so proud to be her father. "Good," he told Doc. "Happy."

Doc rang up the sale. He was uneasy with Gid so near the cash drawer stuffed with holiday money. Doc got the pistol and laid it on the counter in plain sight. "Anything else?" he asked, business-like. "Card like that takes extra stamps."

Gid shook his head, no, no. "Take," he said, taking. He smiled.

Ginnie saw his boot tracks and knew, even before she opened the mailbox and found the card. She was furious as she read what he had written inside:

ALAWAYS LOVE YOU HAPPY DAY YOU LOVE GID.

It wasn't funny any more. When it was happening at school, there had been an audience. Now it was boring. It was nothing. What was she getting out of it? And yet sometimes she thought of how he had lifted her in his arms in the principal's office. That had been interesting. And how he had taken her side, had stood for her and by her. Strong as that, he could be trained, broken. He could serve. "There's something good worth getting at in any soul," her mother always said. Ginnie wanted to get at it if she could; maybe he would be harder to solve than most, but that made it more of a challenge. Once she had seen a man on TV take down a whole round factory chimney by chipping the mortar from the bricks, one course at a time, row on row. When the chimney fell, it swooned in slow motion, ending in rubble. The man was famous for it. He had stood there, just beyond reach of the topmost fallen bricks and rising dust, smiling.

So she went from wishing Gid would get lost forever to watching for him on the road or in town. She went from wanting everyone to see them together—so that they could laugh behind his trusting back—to not wanting to see him at all again, and then, finally, to wanting to see him alone. He wasn't hard to find, once she made up her mind. Everyone knew Gid.

After New Year's, she drove to where they said he lived. She had never been by there before and was just going to look, not stop. But she decided to stop—why not?—and parked behind an old barn, a field over, prying off a hubcap and tossing it into the briars at the turn, in case she needed an alibi. She was always losing hubcaps.

Gid was living as a squatter in an abandoned houseboat, atilt in a cornfield gone to sedge and scrub oak. She had to be careful where she stepped; there were tires and junk everywhere. She could see where his garden had been, outlined in stones, his scarecrow slumped in a broken lawn chair. He'd staked his beans on a bedspring. Everywhere were aluminum cans he'd salvaged from the ditches for scrap. The doghouse was made of sawmill slabs, and the ax he cut kindling with was deep in a stump. His small dog didn't scare her.

The snow had about melted; only the roots of the trees wore little rinds of it. She made a snowball around a rock and threw it at his window. It missed, thudding softly against the houseboat's siding. Gid couldn't hear well, she knew, but she wouldn't shout. She was sure he was in there, so she kicked on the crumpled pontoon, kicked and kicked, till he finally felt it and opened the door. He looked down, not knowing what to do, not even saying hello.

"Come out or ask me in," she told him. He read her lips, puzzled, then jumped to the ground—there were no steps—and they stood in the sunlight while the dog barked and leaped.

"I don't know what you want with me," she said, suddenly wanting to kick Gid instead of the boat. She talked too fast for him to catch it all. She beat at him with her fists and he let her.

She had all his notes in her coat pockets. She took them out and flung them. Then she tore his big red Christmas card into pieces and scattered it on the wind. When a car drove by on the high road, she turned her back and raised her hood over her hair. She wasn't afraid, and she wasn't being discreet; she just didn't want to be stopped.

"Invite me in, dammit!" She didn't wait for him to help her; she planted her boot on the sill and drew herself up by the door frame, strong.

"Oh, God," she said, when she saw how he had painted everything red, barn red. "Massacre," she said.

He had nailed the ceiling over with raw boards. The quilts were folded across the foot of his neat bed. Things looked clean. He even had a few books, missing their covers, that looked as if he had found them in the ditches as he hunted cans. An oil lamp stood on his table, nothing special. He had framed a picture of her, from the newspaper. She shook her head.

He chunked more wood into the fire and latched the stove door, taking his time adjusting the draft. Then he looked at her with those trusting-dog eyes. "Trouble?" he guessed. *Tubba* was how it sounded.

Ginnie laughed. "No trouble at all," she told him. He was slow-blooded, like a lizard in winter. She knew it would be up to her to warm him to living speed. Funny how he acted, standing there looking proud.

"You love this dump, don't you?" she said, checking the old Coleman icebox for beer. No beer. She'd bring some next time.

As she drew him down, down with her cool hands, she warned, "No future, and my terms."

"Friend," he said. It sounded like *fend*.

"All human beings are is animals who can talk," she told him, peeling the watchcap from his big furry skull. "And you can't even talk."

She teased him till he was crazy, till he barked, till he sweated, crawling after her on all fours. She rode him bareback. "Lady Godiva," she called herself. He was "Tennessee Stud." She sang it to him, till he knew the tune. He couldn't sing, but he could keep time. She tied him to the table. She learned him by heart. They played like that for hours, till the sun headed down. She wasn't afraid of a knock on the door. She wasn't afraid of anything. If anyone had come to that grounded boat then, she'd have answered the door herself, wild as God made her.

"As God made me," she asked Gid, "how'd he do?"

"Howdy do," Gid said.

They ate canned soup afterward—she had interrupted his lunch—and she drove home by dark. She warned him again, as she left: "No future, my terms."

Gid couldn't hear her.

Ginnie wasn't crazy about Dean Teague. She could make him do some things, but sometimes he wouldn't. It took her a little time to figure out whether he meant no for now or no forever. Not about sex, but about dope. And not because his father was the police chief, but because he ran on the track team. It would have been something to get him to smoke, or some other thing, to have him beg her for a light or a line. She couldn't make him, though. She liked him better when she couldn't make him, till she figured out she never would be able to. Then he wasn't much fun any more, and she told him so.

She told Jeff Davis about him too. "He's just no fun," she said.

"Why is that?" Jeff asked. He was like a little pony you train on a course to take each jump with a mere flick of the whip. He wanted to know why so he wouldn't make the same mistake. But Ginnie wouldn't say. That was better for business.

She ran Jeff ragged. She called him "Reb," and made him feel special, and called him "Manny," and let her hands rove as they were driving up to Hammermill to the basketball tournament. She rode so close to him she could feel him heating up. It was going to be almost too easy.

Excited, Jeff drove wild. He wasn't used to dope, and he ran them into the ditch, lightheaded. He was almost crying to get out of there, before his father found out. He went all around the car checking on the paint. All he needed was a wrecker, but he beat his hands on the roof of the car, and cursed his luck, and cried.

He even made her put the Miller in the woods, out of sight in case the Law should happen by. "I'm not drunk," he said, over and over. She would have had time to finish the grass, but he knocked the roach out of her hand into the mud and stomped it out of sight. He wasn't thinking party any more.

The first one to stop by was Buck Gilbert. Ginnie told Jeff farewell, and she and Buck drove off for help.

At the first house Buck slowed. "What're you doing?" she said.

"Telephone," Buck said.

"Let the little jerk sweat," Ginnie said. "He's already wasted enough of my precious time."

Buck put the bigfooted four-wheeler in gear and gunned the truck on by. Ginnie liked the way it wallowed on the curves as though it might roll over, but Buck knew how to drive it. He laid it around in the gravel, full circle, twice—no accident the first time, more fun the second. She wanted to try it. He let her. She sat in his lap, the way she had learned to drive in her mother's own lap. She had the hang of it soon.

She wasn't drunk and she wasn't high. She was willing. "Let's go back," she said. "See if he's still sitting in the mud."

They wheeled around and headed back. The ditch was empty, though, and the mud tracks headed south. "Home to his daddy," Ginnie said. She got out and ran into the woods and found the beer she'd stashed.

Buck had the 4×4 turned around, nosing back toward the north.

"Well all right," she yelled. "Party time!"

"Satisfactory," he said, finishing off one of the ponies and tossing the bottle. It shattered into smoke on the road behind them.

Buck knew where to find others in a party mood, so they never
made it to the tournament. They hung out at the video arcade for
an hour or two—nobody was watching the clock. Then, in a convoy, they headed down to the thousand acres where the off-road
vehicles churned up the mud on weekends.

They had picked up Johnny Bates and Chris Olds. "Love makes
room," Ginnie said. She sat across their laps, her back against the
door, washing down Chris's pills with Johnny's vodka. Buck was
tailgating the Trans-Am ahead of them. "Kiss it! Kiss it!" Ginnie
urged, bracing herself for the collision, but the 4 × 4 was too tall;
Buck ran right over the car's trunk, and they had to stop—the
whole convoy—and discuss it. The other driver was so stoned he
couldn't even walk straight; when Buck pushed him down, he
crawled on the road, trying to get up. "Like a spider," Ginnie said.
"Step on him." She stomped, just at his fingertips. He rolled away
and staggered to his feet, as she climbed into the 4 × 4 and revved
the engine. "Where's your balls?" she called, backing the truck off
the Trans-Am. Buck and Johnny and Chris jumped on board,
laughing. The boy in the road didn't step out of the way. The 4 × 4
grazed him, and he grabbed onto the hood, trying to haul himself
up. "Bullfighting!" Ginnie said, jerking the wheel sharply left, then
right. He slid away into the dark. Everybody was laughing. Ginnie
drove on, leading the pack now.

They prowled on down to the landing, where there was moon
enough to party. Ginnie felt the light hit her arms like blows as the
shadows of the pines laddered over her flesh. "I *feel* it!" she said,
jumping from the truck, spinning, savoring. She fell in the sand
and sat, looking around. She didn't even get up when the headlights of another truck swung across the sky and headed toward
her. The other truck's radio was on the same station as theirs. Full
blast.

They danced, then, Ginnie and the others. She didn't know
quite who they were, but she liked them. She wanted to take off
her clothes and dance on the dock in the moonlight. She wanted
to swim all the way to Thompson Beach. She was the only one. It
was still winter.

When the fight started, Ginnie pitched right in. She didn't like the other girl and began tearing at her face and clothes and calling her "slut" and "whore" and kicking sand and cursing. She found a pine limb and wielded it like a bat, trying for serious damage. The girl was screaming and crying loud enough to turn the lights on in the windows across the cove. They could hear sirens far off, nearing.

Buck and Chris got Ginnie into the truck and got out of there— not waiting for Johnny, who had disappeared as soon as the fight started. They pulled into a side road, lights off, till the deputies had passed.

Ginnie didn't want to go home. She thought of Gid's houseboat. It wasn't far.

"Let's stop here," she dared.

She knew Gid wasn't there except on weekends. He boarded up at Dixon now, since it was too far to commute weekdays on his bicycle. Too cold.

"It's abandoned," Ginnie said, crawling up inside. She lit the lamp and turned to give a hand to Chris.

He climbed up, looked around, and whistled. "I know this guy," Chris said. "He—"

"He's dandruff on the shoulders of life," Ginnie said.

Buck was wild enough for anything, and Ginnie was ready, but Chris edged toward the door, saying, "I need air."

"Did you say prayer?" Ginnie asked, her scorn so sudden and hot it made her want to kill him. He was the one she wanted right then, Chris. She'd make him.

She stood blocking the open door, all the night behind her, dark, nothing to break her fall. "Say the word," she teased. She didn't lay a hand on him, just waited for him to try to get past. She could change anybody's mind.

"What're you doing these days, Ginnie?" Chris asked, as if they were meeting on the street at noon. "Found one that fits yet?"

She looked at their faces as they laughed at her, Buck laughing louder.

"Y'all just get out!" she screamed, kicking at them wildly. "Out!" She was still raging and cursing as the 4 × 4 roared away.

After they had gone, she trashed Gid's houseboat, broke and tore and spattered and fouled it from bow to stern. Then she made a fire in the stove, stoking it till the flue glowed red, and left the place to find its own fate. It would look like an accident. She knew Chris and Buck wouldn't tell. If they did, what could they prove?

She cut across the sedgefields toward home. It was miles, and she had blisters the size of silver dollars on both heels by the time she got there, sober and vomit-hollowed, her hair tangled with burrs. She chewed some Dentyne and thought fast. There was a light on. She began crying.

Her mother met her at the door and cried too.

Ginnie told her, "I've walked miles. I made them let me out. They weren't Christians, Mama. They weren't good boys at all."

"Did they hurt you, Baby?"

"I'd die first," she said.

Doc didn't do anything except turn out the yard light, lock the door, and listen. He knew Ginnie well enough not to swear out warrants. He knew where the birth-control pills missing from his inventory were going. He never challenged her, just went on pretending she was who she thought they thought she was. "We all ought to be in bed," he said.

"Let her talk it out," Ginnie's mother said. "Talk it out, Honey." She drew Ginnie to her, shoulder to shoulder, so alike that time was the only thing that made the difference: Before and After, Doc thought, clicking the three-way bulb to low.

Ginnie said, "I just want to put it behind me, you know? Like, it's over." She bent to pry off her boots and look at her heels.

"Vitamin E," Mrs. Daniels said, going to the cabinet to get a capsule. She believed in *Prevention;* she kept a stack of the magazines by her bed, and could rattle off the names of vitamins and minerals and their uses the way some people name saints and their miracles. She might question Doc about some vitamin controversy, but she believed in miller's bran, aloe vera, and D-alpha tocopherol with the same blind faith she put in Ginnie: a wholesomeness never to be doubted, and possibilities worth any expense. If Doc was a realist, and hated talking things out, just getting on with it instead, his wife had a softer eye and heart. Maybe she didn't really know her daughter. She didn't worry; she trusted. Not to trust seemed dishonorable; when doubt shaded in, and chilled her, she turned her mind's channel to another station, just like she did the TV. She kept herself busy, living in a world of her own making, putting her own crazy captions to the pictures in the

news, watching TV for hours with the sound off. When they were
driving along and passed a road-killed animal, she said, "Probably
just playing possum," even if you could *smell* it. Doc always said,
"Goddam!" and laughed. "What'll it take to convince you?" he
wondered.

Mrs. Daniels came back with the vitamin E. "There won't be
any scars, if you'll just start this early." She knelt and helped smear
the oil on Ginnie's wounded heels.

Ginnie laid her hand on her mother's head. "Mama," she said,
"Did you save the receipt for these boots? They're going back."

"Tomorrow," her mother said. "First thing."

"It's already tomorrow," Doc said.

Mrs. Daniels stood and wiped her hands. "It may already be
tomorrow, but it's never too late." She headed for the kitchen to
cook them something special for breakfast.

"I bet you didn't sleep a wink all night," Ginnie said to Doc. She
tossed her ruined boots over by the hearth and sat down in Doc's
recliner, shoving it all the way back. She looked up at him. "Your
bags have bags." Doc had been about to yawn, but he forced it
into a smile.

"Slept great. Your mother got me up when you came home."

Doc never slept great. Sometimes he woke in the night and felt
like breaking things, or shooting up the whole world, every lying
thieving cheat in it. He'd been burglarized again, and often, and
not always petty thefts: they knew what they wanted, what was
worth anything. He had changed his whole anti-theft system after
the Bland boy broke in and stole the drugs that killed him. He'd
installed alarm systems connected to the police direct by radio
signal, and new deadbolts and wires on the windows. From time
to time he bought another gun and registered it. What more could
a man do? All that trouble and expense at work, and at home,
Ginnie and her mother would be unruffled, calmly paging through
their catalogs for custom curtains, brass bedsteads, Fair Isle sweaters, Hummel figurines . . .

"What do you say, Daddy?" Ginnie sounded serious. Doc hadn't
been listening. He tried to catch up, then decided against asking
her flat out. She had something to say? He waited to hear more.

"I'm going to graduate next year," she vowed. "I'm going to
settle down and study and make me some *A*'s. What do you say?"

Her mother, in the kitchen making banana waffles from scratch, always a big deal out of something, deliverance this time, hummed "Come Thou Fount of Many Blessings," beating eggs in time.

"This is the turning point of my *life*," Ginnie told him. "You hear me?"

"I'm listening," Doc said. The anniversary clock chimed six-thirty.

"What do you say to Beta Club and some *A*'s and all that Glee Club stuff and a diploma and graduation with my class and all that?"

Doc bent and picked a section of briar from the toe of Ginnie's boot.

"How much will it cost me?"

Ginnie didn't even open her eyes.

"Have you seen the new T-roof-Z's?"

He flung the bit of briar in the fireplace. "No way," he said. He laughed. "Not for straight *A*'s and perfect attendance." He took off his glasses and polished them, settling them back on his face again, giving the room a clear hard look. "You should have started sooner."

"I'm starting now," she said.

"No sale," he told her. "Besides, I thought you were dropping out. Going to cosmetology school or something."

"You say that like it was worm-farming, Daddy," Ginnie said. "People change."

In the first light, she looked like herself at ten, scolded too hard, afraid to raise her face to their anger and disappointment. He didn't really believe in evil, born in, unchangeable. People could change. We all start off even, her mother was always saying. Some of us learn a little slower and whose fault is that?

The recliner snapped upright and Ginnie sat staring at her hands.

"Shit!" She held her hand out for him to see. "I broke my fingernail getting off those damn boots."

Doc didn't move and Ginnie glanced up. Then he reached over to the cat's scratching post and handed it to her. "Here," he said.

She couldn't believe her eyes and ears. She looked at him as at a stranger. He *was!*

"Daddy?"

She was gifted, he knew, by all her test scores. Genius. *Under-challenged,* they had told him and his wife. "Keep her busy," they had said. "Keep her motivated." He resumed himself. "T-roof-Z?" he said, thinking it over.

To help him calculate, she asked, "Can you stroke it? Are you good for it?"

"I'll tell you the truth," he said. "I don't think *you* are."

Ginnie reclined her chair again, smiling. "I guess it's up to me."

She was asleep at breakfast time. Her mother called, then came to see. She laid an afghan over Ginnie and tiptoed back to the kitchen to serve Doc. "Sleeping like a baby, like an angel." She moved around to Doc's chair and poured his coffee. She set the pot down and hugged him, rocked him to her, and let him go.

"She's going to straighten up," she told Doc. "This time she's on her way. I pray it for her all the time: something good for Ginnie."

Doc said, "It's her deal, and she knows it."

"I'm happy, *happy!* Thank you, Doc. Thank you, God," she said, and then sat down and cried. She was still crying, and Ginnie was still asleep, when Doc left for work.

Ginnie didn't see Gid much any more. After his boat burned—it went down as accidental—he took a permanent place at Dixon and didn't even come back on weekends. He was saving his money, had an account in the bank—one of the mill workers helped him open it—and he was careful of his pay. He planned to marry Ginnie. She had plans of her own.

She quit dating. Quit partying. Dropped out of sight except for school and church. In the afternoons, twice a week, Jordan Kilgore came to the house to tutor her in geometry. This was Doc's idea. Jordan was fifteen, sprouting his first manly bristles and nervous around Ginnie, who was a little older and beyond wild hope. Jordan lived with his grandfather, who owned the yacht club across the lake, but he didn't go to school at Deerfield. He went to Atlanta to special classes for the gifted. He was already taking college courses twice a week. Those were the afternoons he had free to help Ginnie. He was a virgin, Ginnie could tell—as much fun as a newborn kitten. She played little games all through the lessons; he never even suspected. She'd let the top button on her blouse gape, and then button it quick, shy. She wore scent on her hands so when he went home, her flavor was on his books. She didn't have anything in mind, just to drive him crazy a little and pass off time. On lesson days she wore her daintiest clothes, no leather, no makeup, no angora, no jeans. She wore dresses or full skirts and eyelet and never said *damn*. When his cat died, she cried and came down to the lesson with her eyes red and swollen.

On her birthday in March he gave her a silver cross set with aquamarines, for studying so hard.

She kissed it and said, "I'll wear it always, when I marry, forever, I'll never take it off!" She let him clasp it, his hands clumsy and slow, tangling in the stray curls she had left out as she pinned her hair up. When it was fastened, she had him kiss it too, and she dropped it down her blouse, out of sight, but known.

"You look like a valentine," he said.

She looked down at the tucks and laces and white white shirtfront and bit her lip. "Thank you," she said.

"Ginnie," he said, hurting. They were alone.

She shook her head. "Let's pray," she said. But it was too much, too strong. They embraced, and she let him—soft lips! untrained shy questing shy lips—kiss her. He quivered like a horse wearing its first saddle. She was almost bored, but not quite. She drew away, and stood, tucking her blouse in and smoothing her hair. "We mustn't."

"I have wicked thoughts," she said, as he looked away. "But we have just an hour, and it's for geometry."

"You—you're making progress," he agreed. He turned to the lesson.

"I think about you all the time!" she said, just as his mind had gotten fixed on the matter at hand. Ginnie was having trouble proving triangles. "I dream about you," she said. She checked the clock. Her mother was at a luncheon.

He drew a triangle. "I dream about you too," he said.

He could smell her shampoo. He leaned into the fragrance, inhaling, all the time drawing another triangle inside the first triangle, and numbering from one to ten.

"Tell me," she whispered, stopping his pencil with her fingertip.

He leaned away.

"What do you dream?" She got up and went to the window and looked out. "What did you do with those magazines?"

"They—I burned them."

"Daddy has more. New ones. He keeps them under the counter. You have to ask, people always ask."

"They're trash," he said.

"Slime," Ginnie agreed. "Filth. Don't think about them!" She watched as his color burned higher. "Do you dream about them? Things like that?"

Her mother's car was turning in the driveway. Ginnie slapped her book closed. "We ought to burn them all! It could be—" she drew a breath, "—*noble*, like Jesus running the moneylenders out of the temple." He gathered his papers and books. They hadn't done a thing for the hour except those two triangles, one inside the other.

"Don't tell!" she cautioned him, and ran outside to meet her mother. He passed them in the drive as they were picking daffodils. He was on his ten-speed, bent forward, his bookbag strapped across his back, his legs strong on the hill.

Ginnie's mother worried what he'd do when it rained. Ginnie said, "With an uncle who's a bishop and a granddaddy who's got a wad on his hip the size of Stone Mountain, he could have a Porsche if he wanted it, if he knew how to ask."

Doc was paying Jordan five dollars an hour for the tutoring. Sometimes Ginnie borrowed a little of it, just a few dollars now and then. "I'll pay you back," she always promised. "Somehow."

"He's a darling boy," Ginnie's mother agreed.

All through Lent she tormented him like that, till she left the note in his book. Unsigned. Who could prove a thing if it went wrong? "Tonight, back door at Doc's, midnight, god's sake don't leave your bike in plain view." She typed it at school, in a spare moment.

He'll never show, Ginnie thought. And if he did, she'd think of something.

She left her car at the roller rink, and walked back to town. Two, three blocks, no street lights till the post office, where the sidewalk began.

Anne Summerday, charge nurse for the 11 to 7 shift at Tri-County Hospital, saw Ginnie walking along the road toward town, all in white. Anne pulled alongside the girl, thinking she might be a nurse in some kind of trouble. When she saw it was Ginnie, dressed like a bride in a dream, vacant-eyed, ghostly, she knew better. "Anything the matter?"

Ginnie said, "One of your headlights is out."

"I meant with you—need any help? Anything?"

"Nothing radical," Ginnie said. "Just airing it out, y'know?" She played with the ribbons at her waist. "Massive weather, hunh?" She blew a gum bubble, perfected it, inhaled it whole, and popped it with a blink of her eyes. Then started over.

"Take care of yourself," Anne told her.

"Not going far," Ginnie assured her.

"It's dark as an egg's inside," Ginnie complained as Jordan came in. She had opened the door at his third tap. She groped over to the partition between the storeroom and the pharmacy, pulling open the golden plastic curtains that served for a door. An eerie light, green as the aurora, streamed through the gap she made.

"I can't stay," Jordan said.

Her eyes glinted alien in the strange light that pulsed from a cosmetic display in the front of the store.

"Why did you come?"

"I shouldn't be here."

She shoved him away toward the door. "That one-eyed grand-daddy of yours, I bet, calling frog and you hop." She covered her eye with her hand and tilted her head at him, saying in a mocking mannish voice, "Jordan, boy, you better love Jesus, my Jesus yes!" She had smoked a roach on the way. He couldn't ever catch up with her.

"I do!"

"I *do!*" she mocked. "Is this a wedding?"

She slipped into the store and brought back a hairbrush and handed it to him. "Do me," she said.

He began stroking her hair, too lightly, tangling as he went, then smoother, firmer, from her crown to her waist.

"How I like it," she said, leaning into the stroke.

"You smell like clover," he noticed.

She spit out her bubblegum and stuck it under a shelf. "Sweet Honesty," she said. "Avon. I don't sell it any more. Daddy says it's competition for the store." She took the hairbrush from him and threw it over a pile of cartons in the corner. It scuttered out of sight.

"Everything in this store is *mine*," she told Jordan. "I can help myself. What would you like to have?"

"I have to go now," he said.

"You ought to teach your folks a lesson," she told him.

"How?" Like a man in a dream, he kept on walking toward the cavemouth, his heart pounding.

"Make them afraid. Afraid you'll die. Afraid you'll run away." She turned to face him and got close. "You scared of me?"

"No."

She laughed. "Miles to go to mean it," she said. She drew the cross he had given her up from her blouse, saying, "Feel, it's as warm as I am."

He touched it but didn't touch her.

"I could wash your feet and dry them with my hair," she suggested. "I think as highly of you as I do of Jesus." She said, "Take off your shoes."

She didn't figure he would. There was a slight film of sweat on his face.

"Do you really believe God made me out of your ribs?" She put her hand out and touched his chest. "I just want to see the scar," she said.

He thought he heard something.

"What could you hear?" she said. "Your heart?" She leaned her ear and listened.

Ginnie heard something else.

"Did you lock the door?" she wondered.

"I—"

"*Did* you?"

"I—"

A flashlight beam prowled across the ceiling over their heads. They ducked to the floor. "Night watchman!" he whispered.

"No," Ginnie said. "There isn't one. It's somebody breaking in!" She almost laughed aloud. Luck! She couldn't think fast enough. She was excited and almost danced. Which way? Which way? "In here," she decided, and they crept around behind the curtains into the store and waited. Ginnie leaned around to look.

"Get behind me," Jordan said.

"You! In there! I hear you!"

"Daddy!" Ginnie breathed. "Oh shit!"

Doc kicked the door open and yelled, "Freeze!" just as Jordan stepped forward, his hands out in the dark. "It's all right, sir," he began to say.

Doc fired, both barrels.

The impact knocked Jordan backward, the ribs Ginnie had touched a moment ago gone like the plastic curtain in their faces, and then Jordan fell. There was nothing between Ginnie and Doc but that spilled blood.

Ginnie didn't scream but once, then she bent there, trying to pull her skirt out of Jordan's grip. Doc stood looking down.

"*Goddam mess,*" he said.

Jordan tried to say something, but he couldn't remember what. He rested. When the sirens neared, he asked, "Who's hurt?"

When Ginnie said, "This didn't happen," he asked, "Who is it?" already forgetting, with each emptying pulse, time running backward as it ran down.

"You're hurt," Doc told him, facing facts. The emergency unit arrived.

"I'm not afraid," Jordan said. The technician stripped back Jordan's sleeve to start plasma.

"Take it easy, son," the attendant said. "Stay with us." They lifted him up and even then Jordan was awake, gripping Ginnie's skirt. She rode beside him in the ambulance.

"Notify trauma," they radioed ahead.

Ginnie said, "I need to wash my hands," and someone gave her a towlette. There were bits of the curtain in her hair. They kept drifting randomly down.

Doc said, mile after mile after mile, "It was self-defense."

In emergency, they all waited together. Jordan's grandfather was there, his sports coat pulled on over his pajamas, no socks on his pale feet, the elastic to his eye patch lost in a rumple of white hair under the yachting cap. Doc sat in the corner on a straight chair. Ginnie stood at the window, looking down at traffic. She had washed her face and arms. All of the blood was Jordan's. She hadn't even got one pellet, she was that lucky.

Jordan's grandfather said, "Seven units of blood already."

A policeman was standing in the doorway, filling out reports. Doc answered most of the questions. Ginnie moved back and forth in front of the windows, like a fox in a cage. Finally she sat. She drew another chair over and propped her feet on it.

From the hall, footsteps brought them all to attention. A woman looked in at them, waiting. Her left hand was cupped to catch her cigarette ash, her eyes witness to some unspeakable anxiety. She looked at them all, one by one, then studied the policeman's insignia, the flag on his sleeve, his badge. She shook her head, lost in her own anguish, tears brimming. "Mine's not a police matter," she said, going on by, down the hall, out of sight.

Jordan's grandfather said, "Sonofabitch!" and pounded his fist into his thigh. He passed his hands over his face, and blinked at Doc.

"I thought he was reaching for a gun," Doc said.

At the door, the policeman cleared his throat.

They looked at him, for news. He said, "I was just clearing my throat."

"They ought to have a TV in here," Ginnie said.

"I could see them moving around—the silhouettes, you know?" Doc spoke to the Deputy. "I did what I thought right at the time."

Jordan's grandfather said, "He was born right here in this hospital."

Doc said, "She was too."

Jordan's grandfather said, "The night you made her, you should have shot it in the sink instead."

Ginnie laughed.

Doc didn't. He jumped up so fast his chair turned over. The two men kept hitting each other, and sobbing, till the orderlies and the officer pulled them apart. The old man sat down, still crisp with anger, and pressed his handkerchief to his lip. A nurse brought Doc a plastic glove filled with ice for his eye.

Doc blew his nose.

Ginnie shook out her dress and sat again. "This was a Laura Ashley," she explained. She looked down inside the blouse, then stood and shook her skirt. The cross didn't fall out. It was gone.

"And I lost my necklace too," she said. She started looking for it on the floor.

"Sit down and shut up," Doc told her.

It was another hour before the surgeon came in. He was as bloody as Ginnie. He paused a moment, then said, "Kilgore?" and the old man stood, slowly but tall.

"Alive," the doctor said. "I came to let you know we've had a look around. It's bad, couldn't have been much worse. Spine's not hurt, but the bleeding has to be stopped. We do that, he's got a chance. I don't kid you, abdominal's second only to head for tricky. We're layered, not toys. And he's a mess. We have to stop the leaks first. Then we might have a chance," he said. "A chance."

"I'll be here," his grandfather said, in a different voice, and not as tall.

"It'll be hours. There's a snack bar down the hall; we'll keep you posted." At the door he turned back and said, "Good luck."

"And to you the same," the old man said.

When the surgeon had gone, he told Doc, "I don't want you here, none of y'all. I don't want to see you." He looked at Ginnie, "I don't want to *smell* you."

Doc said to Ginnie, low as prayer, "Not a word."

They walked with the lawman to their car. Doc wasn't under arrest; charges pending. "But you'll both have to answer some more questions," the officer told them.

"I'm not going anywhere," Doc said.

Afterward, as they drove home, Ginnie said, "I guess this cooks it about the Datsun for graduation, doesn't it."

"Could you cry for that?" Doc wondered. "Could you?"

The bright moon stared down at itself in the river as they crossed. It was almost dawn.

"This'll put your mother back at Brawner's," Doc said. "If they sue, we're looking at Chapter 7 bankruptcy."

Ginnie clicked on the radio. Doc cut it off instantly. "For God's sake!"

Not that she was listening for news. There wouldn't be any, not for three days. Jordan lived three days. No lawsuits.

Gid didn't die until the next summer, and Ginnie didn't know anything about it at the time. Doc had double-mortgaged to send her away to finish high school at Tallulah, and then she spent the summer at a mountain camp, lifeguarding.

She heard about Gid casually, soon after returning home, and she didn't ask any questions. She went to the library and read about it on microfilm. He had been riding a lumber truck, atop the piled wood. He was leaning against the cab, not watching where he was going, just looking back at the road he had already traveled; they went under a low railroad bridge and he was killed instantly. It made her feel funny, reading about it like that. She hadn't thought of him in a long time.

Home again, she went to her room and got her majorette boots out of their box, dumping the newspaper stuffing on the bed. There wasn't much to sort through. She didn't even have to hide her pills anymore.

She found the matchbox crammed in the left toe, filled to roundness with cotton. In the center of that cotton was the ring. It wasn't worth anything. All its pawnable worth had fallen from it the day it arrived in the mail. She had carried the little package upstairs to open it and had dropped it on the bathroom floor. The laid-on stone, turquoise paste, had crumbled off. The silver was so thin the brass showed through. It had a coppery smell, like blood. Its flashiness was plated on, and inside, engraved within its tarnished perfect greening circle was "REMEBER GIDEON." He'd paid for that. It still made her laugh. She said it: "Remeber." Had the engraver made the mistake, or Gid? When she stepped on the broken blue stone from the ring, it had powdered to dust. She had cleaned it off the floor with a tissue and flushed it away.

She had never worn the ring and had never seen Gid again. A week later she had gone away to school. Now she tried it on, and it fit so tight it frightened her. She had to work it off with soapy water.

She put it back in the box and headed downstairs, with the box in her pocket. As she went by her mother's door, her mother called, over the top of her latest Harlequin, "Seat belt!"

The Datsun was backed into the garage. She opened the door and drove out, leaving rubber on the cement. That was for her mother, listening upstairs. She tapped the horn at the end of the drive. That was for the dogs. They jumped in and rode with her, nosing out the T-roof, taking the air.

It was a fine day, a late autumn day. The lake wasn't busy—a few sails on the far channel, a bassboat on the west cove, and no skiers. She let the dogs out to run; they drank from the lake and chased each other clumsily along the muddy shore, turning over rocks, sniffing at debris. Ginnie stood at the car a moment watching them. She left the door open, sliding the keys on their jailer's bracelet onto her wrist, walking easily down to the water and along the littered and slippery beach. She stepped over the cable anchoring someone's dock to the shore. The "Private" sign nailed to the dock stuck up just enough so she could clean the mud off her boots on its sharp edge. The wood was so sun-warm she could feel it through her soles. A kingfisher buzzed her, and flew past, settling on the reef-warning, looking this way, then that, at the green reflection of the pines in the water. Out in the channel the lake was blue as the sky. The dock dipped under Ginnie's feet, slow, drowsy, on the lapping rim of the lake.

She shaded her eyes and looked as far as she could, claiming it all. She felt as free and right as she did in her own home. The untrammeling world was widening in ripples around her, and she was the stone at the center that set things moving. She took out the box from her pocket and shook the ring out of its cotton, like a seed. The cotton blew away, and the lake took it, dragged it down slowly. She held the ring on her palm in the sun till it burned hot, hotter than her blood. Then she tossed it as far as she could, out past the low-water reef. It skipped once—plook!—and vanished. The dogs chewed up the matchbox, playing on past her, barking off on trails into the woods. Ginnie stood there a moment in that impersonal vantage and solitude, breathing deep.

She reached high over her head and clawed the sky, then folded up, right at the edge of the dock which tipped a little with her hundred pounds. Her hands smelled brassy. She dipped them in the lake, troubling the clear water, then drew them up, splashing her cheeks with the cool. Refreshed, she looked up, as though something on the horizon had caught her attention. She stood, flinging the last drops from her hands, drying them on her skirt. She walked back to the car, whistling the dogs in, and churned the car slowly uphill through that sand onto the lane between the windbreak pines, heading toward the main road in no particular hurry. It wasn't life or death.

David Huddle

SUMMER OF THE
MAGIC SHOW

(from *Grand Street*)

One October night in his second year at the University of Virginia, my brother persuaded a young woman to drive him to a scenic overlook at the top of Afton Mountain. They sat in the dark car a few moments, but they didn't talk. The young woman lit a cigarette just before they both climbed out. There were no stars, no moon, no street or house or car lights.

And they stayed quiet. The woman leaned against her car's front fender, crossed one arm in front of her, held the cigarette near her face, and kept her eyes on Duncan.

It was so dark, Duncan says, he could step away from her only a pace and a half and still see her face and her blond hair. He took a white handkerchief from his jacket pocket—U. Va. students wore coats and ties then—shook the folds out, and held it at arm's length.

A rifle shot went off not ten yards from them, so loud that Duncan, who knew it was coming, says he couldn't help flinching. The young woman yelped, crouched, dropped her cigarette, crossed her arms in front of her face to protect herself. Duncan had been too startled to notice if the handkerchief had flapped or not, but it had the bullet hole through it, and he carried it over to show to the young woman. He made the desired impression on her: the night so frightened her that she moved away from Charlottesville, where she'd lived most of her life.

Duncan says he regrets what he did. He had arranged for his friend Bobby Langston to wait with his squirrel rifle up there on the Skyline Drive, and he's lucky Bobby had his night vision and was such an accurate shot as to be able to hit that handkerchief, dark as it was. With the shot, Duncan stopped wanting to harm the woman, but by then, of course, he had already done it. I regret knowing the story and what it tells about him.

Back when he was fourteen, Duncan was taller than anybody in our town, six-five, and thin, but very strong. No matter how much needling he took from the coaches over at Madison High School, he wouldn't play basketball or football for them. Duncan was an intellectual, and he was an innocent boy. He was pale and hairy, wore glasses, was not what anybody'd call handsome. He never really had a date until his senior year of high school.

He was the smartest one ever to come out of our town. No one begrudged him his brains, though my father often shook his head over what he called "the ways Duncan chooses to put his intelligence to use." Duncan's passion was magic. He found an old *Tarbell Correspondence Course for the Apprentice Magician* in my grandparents' attic, and he read through the year's worth of lessons in about a week.

When he was thirteen he put on his first magic show, in our living room, for Uncle Jack and Aunt Mary Alice. I remember that he messed up the Mystical Multiplying Balls, dropped one of the hollow shells right in the middle of his audience and had to stop, humiliatingly, and pick it up. But he went on, and when he finished the show, my parents and aunt and uncle applauded. What else could they do? They didn't know it was going to have a permanent effect on him.

Duncan went on doing tricks for the kids on the bus, who thought he was a freak, and for the kids in his homeroom, who were happy to have him pass the time for them, and so on, until finally Mrs. Pug Jones promised him five dollars if he'd come to Buntsy's birthday party and keep the kids from tearing her house apart. When he came back from Buntsy's party, Duncan showed me the five-dollar bill and said that now he was a professional.

The time I was closest to Duncan was the summer between his first and second years in engineering school at the University of Virginia. He was a National Merit Scholar, the only one we'd had from our whole county. He'd gotten a summer job running the scales for Pendleton over at the rock quarry, and he'd decided to put on a magic show for the town of Rosemary. He told us his plans and started working on us at the supper Mother fixed to celebrate his homecoming from Charlottesville. He wanted my mother to get the Ladies' Aid to sponsor him and my father to talk to the Superintendent of Schools to get him the use of the auditorium. My mother was still a little intoxicated from seeing the Lawn and the Rotunda at the University of Virginia when she drove up there to get him. My father gave Duncan his old slow shake of the head, but he didn't say no. It was a supper where Duncan did all the talking anyway, which was his right, having managed not to flunk out of school like everybody else from Rosemary who went away to college. The plans he told us about for the show were modest ones, a lot of card tricks and sleight-of-hand stuff he'd been practicing for his roommate, Will Green-wood. My father and I packed in the steak and mashed potatoes and peas that were Duncan's celebration supper, and my mother listened to his newly sophisticated talk, hardly touching what was on her plate.

Duncan just assumed I'd help him with the magic show, but that didn't bother me. I had nothing else to do that summer except mow yards for the three or four people in town who wanted them mowed. Rosemary probably had more houses in it that were surrounded by packed-down dirt, with chickens pecking in the dust and dogs under the porch, than it had houses with grass around them. Even the people who were willing to pay me to cut their grass were doing me a favor. So was Duncan, who pronounced me his "stage manager and first assistant."

The more Duncan thought about it—mostly while he was wearing a hardhat and making checkmarks on a clipboard over at the rock quarry—the more he realized card tricks and sleight-of-hand wouldn't be good enough for his show. We had to have more illusions, a Chinese Disappearing Cabinet, a Flaming Omelet Bowl that changed the fire into dozens of silk scarves and then changed them into two white doves, a Guillotined Girl, and a

Floating Lady. He talked my grandfather into helping him weld together an elaborate device of heavy pipes that he needed for The Floating Lady. He set me to work building, according to diagrams he drew, the Chinese Cabinet. He saw Toots Polk down at the post office one morning, and he persuaded her to be his Guillotined Girl. While he was at it, he asked her if she wouldn't mind doing a few of her dance numbers.

He decided I'd do a couple of trumpet solos, too, just to balance out Toots's tap dancing. I'd gotten to be pretty good at "Cherry Pink and Apple Blossom White." Duncan said I could do that one and one more. I chose "Tammy," which in my opinion I played with a great deal of feeling.

On weekends when Duncan didn't have to work for Pendleton, he and I spent most of the days in the empty schoolhouse, building and painting flats for the set, working on the lighting, blocking out the show. There was a battered upright school piano in there, below and to the right of the stage. I plunked around on that when things got slow. Duncan always asked me to play one of the two songs he liked to sing, "Old Man River" and "Unchained Melody." He stood at center stage and bellowed out the words at the top of his voice, but he held himself formally, as if he had on white tie and tails. At least once every time he and I were in there alone, he had a go at "Unchained Melody."

Duncan had been getting letters from Charlottesville, and he'd mentioned a woman's name in connection with the theater group for which he had done some lighting work. So it wasn't quite a surprise when he announced that Susan O'Meara would be visiting us for a week at the beginning of July.

Susan was twenty-three. Duncan was nineteen. She smoked, wore jeans and men's shirts untucked, and no makeup; what her blond hair looked like didn't seem to matter to her. She drove up to our house one afternoon in a beat-up white Ford. She got there before Duncan had come home from the rock quarry, and right off she told Mother that it was so damn hot in that car, could she please take a bath? I couldn't remember when a woman had ever said damn in front of my mother; it startled me to have a strange woman come into our house and go straight upstairs to take a bath. I waited for a sign from Mother, but she remained calm. I was dumbfounded at supper that evening, halfway through my first piece of fried chicken, when I looked and saw, first, that Susan O'Meara was cutting hers with a knife and fork, and then that Mother and Duncan were doing the same with theirs. My father and I stuck to our usual method, but neither of us went beyond our second piece.

Susan talked about the heat in Charlottesville, about her father, who was a doctor, about her mother, who taught biology at St. Ann's. Susan said damn again during the meal; then during dessert, she laughed and said she had recently told David Weiss of the Virginia Players to go to hell.

I figured my mother was bound to correct that kind of talk at her supper table, but they all went on eating their berry pie, and I was the only one who'd drowned his in sugar and milk because my mother had given my father a look when he reached for the cream pitcher.

Duncan, for once, wasn't saying much, but he sure was listening to every word Susan spoke. Finally the two of them excused themselves and left the house to go to the drive-in. When I stepped to the window to see which one of them was going to drive, Mother snapped at me to stop spying on them.

I saw Duncan open the door of her Ford and Susan climb in on the driver's side.

I waited around the table hoping to hear some interesting opinions of Susan from one or the other of my parents, but they offered nothing. My father did have seconds on the berry pie, and this time he treated himself to plenty of sugar and milk. I asked them straight out, "What do you think of her?"

It was one of the most reasonable questions I'd ever asked them, but I didn't get an answer. What I did get was a look from each of them, neither of which I understood. Then they gave each other another look, and I didn't understand that either.

On the weekend Susan, in her jeans and a sweat shirt, worked over at the schoolhouse with Duncan and me. Mostly she sat in the second row, dangling her feet over the wooden back of the seat in front of her, smoking, and offering suggestions to Duncan. Anything I had to say he always had only half listened to, but he took notes when Susan told him something. Once she climbed up on a ladder to examine some of the lights above the stage. For a long while she shouted down remarks for Duncan who stood holding the ladder and gazing up at her.

She wasn't rude to me or to my father, but she dealt with us as if we were photographs of Duncan's cute little brother and his old codger of a father. She never asked us questions the way she sometimes did Mother.

On the last evening she spent with us, Susan wore this little diamond ring Duncan had bought her with his Pendleton money. It couldn't have been anything but the smallest stone they had at Smith's Jewelry, but it probably cost Duncan every cent he had in his savings account at the time. I wouldn't have noticed it if I hadn't caught Mother with her eye on it during the meal.

Obviously Duncan and Susan meant the rest of us to understand that they were engaged, but for some reason neither of them said anything aloud about it. My father and I weren't about to say anything on our own, and so it was up to my mother to mention it if anybody was going to, and she chose not to. It was as if since nobody gave voice to it, the engagement hadn't really come about. There was the ring on Susan's finger—she chewed her nails, by the way—but without any words being spoken there was no engagement. That last night I did notice a way Susan had of widening her eyes when she talked that made me understand just for an instant what Duncan saw in her, "one of the most brilliant minds in Albemarle County," as he put it.

Next morning, to see her leave, I snuck out of bed and knelt by the window. It was early because Duncan had to go to work at the quarry. My mother and Duncan and Susan all came out to the car together. Mother gave Susan a sort of official kiss on the cheek, so measured that I imagined she must have thought about it all through their breakfast, and Susan had to hold her cigarette away from Mother with her free hand. Then Mother went back inside, Susan stamped out her cigarette in our driveway, and she and Duncan went into this farewell embrace and kiss. I was surprised at how embarrassed I felt to be seeing it, though I confess it was exactly what I had come to the window to see. Maybe I thought it was going to be funny or sexy, but it was neither of those, and I can't really say what it was. When Susan climbed in behind the steering wheel, Duncan leaned in to kiss her goodbye again. And when she was gone, with the dust from her car still hanging above the driveway, Duncan stood out there alone with his hands in his pockets, toeing at something on the ground. I noticed then how skinny he was, how the sun had burned his neck and arms.

This was the same morning my mother decided, as she put it, "to inaugurate a custom for the good of our family." She meant to correct the social behavior of my father and me who had not gracefully carried off Susan O'Meara's visit. Mother didn't ask us what we thought about it, and we knew from her tone of voice not to argue. She commissioned me to ask a girl to our house for my birthday supper. Every birthday, she added, a girl should be invited.

To put it in straightforward terms, girls made my father uncomfortable. Susan O'Meara had come close to paralyzing him. He was a courtly man. When we sat in the dining room, which was when we had company, he stood and held my mother's chair for her until she came in to sit down. He spoke with elaborate courtesy to all the women on my mother's side of the family and said yes ma'am and no ma'am to most of them. In fact, I felt that in the presence of women, my mother excepted, my father was never himself. He limited his conversation to expressing agreement with the people around him or to asking questions of them. If questioned himself, he phrased his replies in such a way as to generalize or abstract whatever he was telling, so that his opinions in his voice were dull, his experiences hardly worth mentioning. My father was a man who had faced an old toolshed full of rattlesnakes, had been shot at by union strikers, had taken a knife away from Bernard Seeger at a high school dance, but around women who came to our house as company, and especially around Susan O'Meara that past week, my father took on the personality of somebody who'd stayed indoors all his life and eaten nothing but cheese sandwiches.

I didn't resent my mother's decision, as perhaps I might have any other summer. I had noticed that my parents treated Duncan like a grown-up while Susan was in the house; I knew a girl who was almost as formidable as Susan: Jean Sharp. She was from Palm Beach, Florida. Even though she was only thirteen, I'd heard her say things that showed she thought Rosemary, Virginia, was far back in the wilderness.

I was Jean's grandmother's yard boy. When I finished mowing

her yard, old Mrs. Sharp had me come inside for lemonade before she paid me. While I stood there, sweating in her kitchen, she coaxed some conversation out of me, then some out of Jean standing in the kitchen doorway. Jean had very fine dark hair, a small nose and mouth, a lanky frame. When Jean and I gave the appearance of being able to talk with each other, Mrs. Sharp handed me the money and suggested that we go into the living room and play cards. Jean taught me cribbage while sitting forward on the sofa with her back very straight, her knees bent and together, her ankles crossed. All that summer Jean had worn sundresses; they emphasized her flatchestedness, but there was something about her in those dresses, her thin shoulders maybe, that was sexy. Her fingers playing the cards or moving the pegs on the cribbage board held my attention. Her soft voice, her precise diction, made me feel I was learning something every time she spoke to me.

My father had seen Jean only a few times in all her summers of visiting her grandmother in Rosemary, but he knew about her. When my mother and I talked it through to the conclusion that Jean was the one I would ask to my fourteenth birthday supper, my father's face showed that he dreaded it. I dreaded it, too, a little bit.

Duncan, of course, when he heard about it, got a bright idea. His turn of mind that summer was one where everything that came to his attention had to be connected in some way to his magic show. He would ask Jean to be his Floating Lady. He was so excited about the notion that he drove me up to old Mrs. Sharp's house that Saturday so that I could ask Jean to the supper and so that he could get a fresh look at her to see how she'd work on stage. He didn't get out of the car, but while I was talking to Jean on her grandmother's front porch, I could feel Duncan staring at us from the car window. Then driving up to the schoolhouse, Duncan chattered away about Jean, how it was great she was so thin and wouldn't be likely to break down the Floating Lady apparatus, as we'd both joked that Toots might have done, and how Jean's "ethereal face," as he put it, would appeal to the audience. He'd stopped thinking about a Rosemary audience, which would be made up mostly of a bunch of antsy, loud-mouthed, bad-smelling, runny-nosed kids, Jeep Alley, Big-Face Limeberry, Thelma Darby and all her freckle-faced family, Mr. and Mrs. Pug

Jones and Buntsy, people like that. Duncan was thinking about *audience* in the way they probably thought about it in Charlottesville.

He had this hyperbolic way of talking about everybody: Will Greenwood was the greatest drum major in the history of his high school, Bobby Langston was a fearless and diabolical genius, and so on. About Jean Sharp, I heard him telling our mother in the kitchen, "She's truly beautiful, don't you think?" This was just before Jean's grandmother drove her up to our house, and my father and I, in the living room, exchanged glances when we heard Duncan talking like that. We knew Jean wasn't "truly beautiful." She was just a girl who was visiting in our town. Duncan didn't have to exaggerate what she was just because he wanted her to be in his show. But my father and I were used to his ways that summer. We were grateful to him for doing most of the talking when Jean first walked into our house.

She had on another sundress, this one white with a sort of primly high front to it. It set off her tanned shoulders and face, her dark hair. Something about the way that dress fit her at the arms bothered me, though. It made a loose place where, I knew, if I looked at the right angle, I'd see her breast, or what should have been her breast.

There were girls in my classes at school whose breasts or bras I'd strained my neck trying to get a peek at, but they weren't like Jean. I didn't want to see into her dress, but sitting beside her at the table, I could hardly help noticing that opening every time I cast my eyes in her direction. To make things worse, I became aware of the sounds my father made as he ate.

Courtly man that he was, his table manners, or rather the things that went on between him and the food on his plate, were pretty crude. He took large bites of things, and there was a kind of liquid inhaling noise that went with each bite. Often he chewed with his mouth open, so that you could hear it, and he liked to roll the food around in his mouth so that he made sloshing noises. It bothered me even though I knew why he did it. It was the result of his courtliness: his way of signaling to my mother that he liked the food was to make eating noises that expressed his pleasure, his gratitude to her for cooking the food for him. The noises had to be loud enough for her to hear him at the opposite end of the table, and I expect they were that evening even though I knew he was holding back on Jean's account.

I thought about asking to be excused when suddenly Duncan asked Jean if she would be his Floating Lady, and she got choked on a sip of iced tea.

She was all right, of course. Nobody ever died of iced tea going down the wrong way, at least not that I know of, and you would think the incident—Jean gasping and coughing into her napkin, my father and brother and I rising and coming around behind her chair, ready to pound on her back (though not one of us was going to touch those elegant shoulders unless she got really serious about her choking), my mother coming around the table, too, carrying her napkin for some reason and saying, "Oh, you poor dear, you poor thing"—you'd think the incident would have humanized us all. It didn't. There was a short moment after Jean recovered and we'd all gone back to our places where nobody made a sound, one of those embarrassing lulls in the conversation that are usually broken by somebody's polite giggle. In this case my mother managed a feeble, "Well . . . ," and then we had more silence before we fell back to eating, and my father's mouth noises recommenced.

After a while Jean managed to squeak out to Duncan that, yes, she would be happy to be his Floating Lady, and he was released from responsibility for her condition. He went on with his inflated jabbering about the show. But because she had made such a red-faced, watery-eyed, spluttering spectacle of herself, she who was as serene as a piece of sculpture in every other circumstance of my seeing her, Jean now was repulsive to me. Sitting beside her I lost my appetite.

My mother must also have experienced some kind of pivotal moment that summer evening when Jean Sharp choked in our dining room. That was the last angel food cake with pink icing that she ever made for my birthday, though I have never stopped thinking of it as the only legitimate kind of birthday cake.

Next morning as usual, Duncan and I walked down to the post office where I waited with him while he waited for his ride to Pendleton's quarry. It was an occasion for talking about the magic show. He'd glance at his letter from Susan, if he got one. Then when he left, I'd take my parents' mail back up the hill to our house.

That morning, though, Duncan had to sign for a little package from Susan. He opened it while he and I were discussing what we were going to do about the kids who'd go around behind the schoolhouse to try to peek in the windows and cracks in the doors to see how the tricks worked. All of a sudden he was holding the diamond ring in his fingers, and I was looking at it, and it was registering on both of us what that meant.

"Aw God, Duncan," I said, "that's a shame." I didn't know what else to say. I wanted to put my arm around his shoulder, but we weren't that kind of a family, and this was in the post office anyway. So I just got out of there as quick as I could and left him standing there staring at the ring with no expression on his face.

I guess he went to work, though I don't know how he got through the day. He came home at the regular time, and he sat with us at the table in the kitchen where we ate supper. But he just dangled his fork over his food and wouldn't eat, wouldn't talk. We'd gotten used to all his jabber-jabber, as my father called it, and the three of us had a hard time filling up the silence. We'd have understood if he'd called off the show. We'd have even understood if he'd taken the car out, gotten drunk, and run that thing up the side of a tree—there was a tradition of that kind of behavior in our county.

But Duncan was his own man. He worked harder than ever on the magic show, and he said what was necessary to make me work harder on it, too. We'd begun rehearsing in earnest. It wasn't fun for us any more, what with him losing his temper and going off to sulk when one of us made a mistake. "There is no margin for error in magic," he spat at me once when I lost my balance on the tiny little platform of the Chinese Disappearing Cabinet and put a foot down where the whole audience would have seen it.

Toots asked him to leave the auditorium while she ran through her tap numbers. She said they weren't magic, and she didn't want to know what he thought if she made a mistake. I was surprised when he agreed to leave, and I found that my pleasure in watching the little shimmering of her thighs had increased with Duncan out of the room. When I went outside to tell him Toots was finished,

I saw him walking over at the far end of the red-dirt elementary school playground. He had his head down, and I first thought maybe he was crying and then that maybe he was thinking real hard about something. But then I could see little puffs of red dust coming up from his footsteps, and I knew he was stomping the ground, was raging to himself. I went back inside and waited for him to come back in on his own.

I had become a good deal more objective about Jean Sharp by that time. I didn't like to be around her, but I continued to think that I ought to be attracted to her. She was prettier in the face than Toots Polk, and I knew I ought to like looking at her just as much as I liked looking at Toots. But I didn't. The *didn't* and the *ought to* canceled each other out, and I felt nothing.

One night Herky Thompson and Toots took Jean and me out with them on a double date to the drive-in. (Toots's mother made them do it, I expect, because she didn't trust Herky, who was from Piney.) After dark, Jean and I sat in the back seat doing our best to concentrate on *Miss Tatlock's Millions* while Herky and Toots coiled around each other in Toots's corner of the front seat.

I snuck an arm around Jean—she was wearing a sweater—and though I knew she was aware of my arm, I felt no loosening of her good posture, no impulse on her part to lean my way. At the time I resented her for that coldness, but later I decided that she was in the right: she felt no real affection or desire in that arm behind her, those fingers lightly touching her shoulder. She didn't respond because I didn't offer her any part of myself to which she could respond.

All through the final rehearsals Duncan growled at us and cursed under his breath and once put his fist through one of the flats so that we had to repair it. Jean and Toots and I had grown frightened of him. Jean, who rarely said much, told Toots and me she thought he was going to scare the audience right out of their seats. Toots nodded. I thought about telling them how it had been, earlier in the summer, when Duncan and I had performed "Unchained Melody" to the empty auditorium, but I didn't.

I opened the show out in front of the curtain, ignoring the giggles that Thelma Darby started in the audience when I stepped into the spotlight. I couldn't see past the first row anyway, though my father had passed back the word that we had a full house. I lifted my trumpet and silenced everybody with "It's Cherry Pink and Apple Blossom White."

I finished, the curtain opened, and there was "Duncan the Great" standing in his tuxedo at center stage with Toots a step or two to the side holding the top hat out of which shortly Duncan would yank the three-pound white rabbit I'd bought from Gilmer Hyatt two weeks ago. But he had time for small talk, or "patter," as magicians call it, before the trick. In the most lighthearted tone I'd ever heard him use, he paid me a compliment: "That's Reed Bryant, my brother, ladies and gentlemen, and isn't he some musician?" I got another feeble little round of applause, along with a couple of jeers which I ignored.

Jean really didn't have many duties for the show. She assisted Duncan for a couple of little tricks, but she didn't have any talents that we really needed; so she spent a lot of time standing around near me when I was offstage. Sometimes it was pitch dark back there when Duncan was doing one of the tricks with flames or working with a deck of cards in the spotlight out front. I could feel Jean standing there with me and reminding me of how much I dreaded the Floating Lady trick.

Toots and I were both assistants for that one. We were to pull the chairs out from each end of the Floating Lady's little platform. Toots was at Jean's head, and I was at her feet. I'd bargained with Toots to trade sides, but Duncan hadn't allowed it. I had to get back to the lighting board immediately after the trick to douse the lights, and so it had to be the feet side for me. I had been anxious all through the rehearsals when Jean had worn shorts or slacks, because I knew that in the performance she was to wear a dress. There was a good chance I'd have to see all the way to the north pole, whether I wanted to or not, and in front of half the town of Rosemary. In any circumstance Jean was a girl up whose dress I did not want to see.

The apparatus for the Floating Lady was heavy and elaborate, because of course it had to hold the lady up, but it had to be so cleverly arranged and concealed that the audience couldn't see it or imagine how it might be set up. Duncan had to brace himself against part of it and stand so that he hid one huge black pipe from the audience. Even then there had to be a four-by-four post holding that thing down behind the rear curtain and braced against the top of a window well. In rehearsal, Toots and I had laughed because all those pipes looked so crude to us that we couldn't believe anybody would ever be fooled. Duncan assured us that the trick would work.

In the performance Duncan and Toots and I were sweating out there under the lights. When Jean in her yellow sundress walked out on stage, she was loudly and somewhat lewdly cheered, but then something about her appearance quieted the audience right down. She really did appear to fall under Duncan's hypnotic spell when he had her sit and then lie down on the platform. Toots fixed Jean's dark hair to lie prettily at the side of her head, and Jean's face and body became waxen, spiritless.

A hush came down over the audience when Toots removed the first chair. Duncan, standing directly behind her, kept his hands held high over Jean while she lay there, and he looked like a crazy preacher held in a spell himself. I looked up at his face then, just before my chair was to be pulled. Duncan was charged with some kind of emotion I'd never seen in anybody. I knew that some part of it must have had to do with Susan O'Meara, but another part of it was willing that illusion into being: Jean Sharp was by God going to float in the air on the stage of Rosemary Elementary School!

With exaggerated wariness, I removed my chair. Jean wobbled a little bit. Then she held steady. A noise came from the audience as if everyone had inhaled at once. Clarence Shinault, who'd gone through seventh grade with Duncan, said clearly from way in the back, "Gah-odd damn, Duncan."

Gravely Duncan passed the hoop, with agonizing slowness, from Jean's feet to her head and then back again from her head to her feet. Then he held the hoop up for everyone to see. The applause came just when it should have, Toots and I put our chairs back under the platform, Jean waked from her spell, smiled, and began climbing down while I skipped back to the lighting board. The trick was over, and I couldn't remember whether or not I'd seen up Jean's dress.

In the week or two before he went back to Charlottesville, thanks to his success with the show, Duncan recovered some of his good spirits. Once he asked me why I wasn't trying to see more of "The Exquisite Miss Sharp," as he had taken to calling her. I wouldn't have been inclined to explain it to him even if I had understood my feelings about her and even if he had been free enough of his own troubles to be more than halfway interested.

It was my father who gave me the most comfort in that time. Even earlier in the summer he'd started helping me, at the end of the terrible birthday supper when my mother had herded us all into the living room to chat with Jean before she went home. We sat there for an excruciating length of time. I found myself copying my father's manner. I agreed with things Duncan said, things my mother said, and especially with any slight remark of Jean's. Once the rhythm of conversation demanded that I say something, and so I asked Jean a question about Palm Beach, then pretended to listen while she, with much graceful gesturing of her slender arms and hands, tried to make us understand where in the city she lived and how far that was from the actual beach.

When my father stood up to signal that he wished the occasion to be over, I was the first one to rise and second his motion. Duncan wanted to ride with us on the way over to Jean's grandmother's house so that he could tell her more about the magic show. I'd have been glad to have him along, but my mother put a hand on his sleeve, and he said that well, now he remembered that he had a letter he had to write before he went to sleep.

Outside, standing by the car, my father instructed Jean and me to ride in the back seat. By that time the fireflies were out, the bats were swooping over our heads, it was warm, and there was the scent of honeysuckle over the whole yard, but Jean seemed glad to be climbing into the car. When my father saw that she and I weren't going to have much to say to each other on the drive across the ridge and around the town, he turned on the radio. I've always been grateful to him for that, because I know for a fact that he hated the car radio, especially the hillbilly and the rhythm and blues stations that were all we could get at night in our part of the country.

In the cool air I walked Jean up onto her grandmother's front porch, said a quickly retreating good night, and scuttled back to sit in the front seat with my father. In his kindness he neither asked me anything nor said a word to me. He'd turned off the radio, and he took his time driving back home. The two of us were quiet, except once when we came to a place where we could see a light way up on the hill at our house.

I said, "I'll bet that's the light in Duncan's room," and my father chuckled and said yes, he guessed Duncan was writing that letter to Charlottesville. That was the night before Duncan got the ring back in the mail from Susan O'Meara, and it was several months before the night he sent Bobby Langston with his squirrel rifle up on Afton Mountain to wait for him and Susan. It was almost a full year before Duncan flunked out of the University of Virginia. That night, sitting at his bedside table to write that letter to Susan, all Duncan knew that was coming to him was his magic show. My father and I kept driving slowly around the ridge, both he and I watching the road in the headlights and occasionally glancing out our side windows at the dark. Then, at almost exactly the same moment, though our tunes were different, we each began whistling through our teeth.

Gloria Norris

HOLDING ON

(from *The Sewanee Review*)

The woman who started it all was a Mrs. Filburton. Mrs. Arkin met this remarkable person while visiting her sister Beulah in the Delta. Mrs. Arkin had packed her battered old suitcase and left Pinola on the Greyhound bus as her first act of defiance against Mr. Arkin. He didn't see why he should be expected to cook for himself for a week. He never had in thirty-eight years of marriage.

But Mrs. Arkin found the courage to oppose him because she knew she was, after all the years of thinking so, truly at the end of her rope. And the only thing in the world that would relieve her would be not to see Mr. Arkin for a week, not to see his bachelor brother L.B., and, most of all, not to see L.B.'s dogs lying around her front yard. The dogs were one of the heaviest crosses she had had to bear in life.

The truth was—it hit her one morning while she stood cleaning her rimless glasses, her shoulders sagging—that she had never had one single thing she wanted in all her fifty-four years. Not one single thing that she had wanted and set out to get and gotten. All her life she had tried her best to be good and, when things didn't work out as she wanted, she held on and prayed they would, some-how, someday. But it struck her that morning, looking at one of L.B.'s hounds stretched on her front steps, that all she was doing was holding on, not ever going one step forward.

So to have a perfect stranger like Mrs. Filburton change her life was the last thing she expected. Later she came to believe that God arranged it all from the moment she stepped off the bus in Belzoni. Because that very afternoon Beulah, who was the most dependable nurse in town, left her to answer an emergency call from the hospital. Mrs. Arkin was all alone when the two visitors arrived out of the blue—the old lady who lived next door and her visiting daughter.

The visit started off by giving her the shock of her life. As she opened Beulah's front door, a woman's voice brayed, "Now don't hide that whiskey bottle we caught you with, just pass it around!" Raucous laughter followed as the younger woman steered her mother through the door.

The old lady was dressed in a neat black dress. She trembled on her cane from St. Vitus' dance, and, despite coils of hearing aid, couldn't hear thunder. Mrs. Arkin was sure she was a sweet old lady—providing you were used to invalid old folks as she was, having cared for twelve years for Mr. Arkin's ancient father, who spit tobacco juice on her clean floors, and for a penniless Arkin aunt who never showed a speck of gratitude. But Mrs. Arkin quickly saw that the daughter was common as dirt. She was dressed in red shorts that exposed white middle-aged legs crisscrossed by lumpy varicose veins. She had hennaed hair and pencilled-on eyebrows black as the ace of spades. And to Mrs. Arkin's horror the woman pushed right by her and plunked herself down on Beulah's couch while puffing a Pall Mall, letting the ash fall on the carpet.

As the visit wore on, Mrs. Filburton's hoarse voice strained at the ceiling while she talked without pause about problems with her colon and about her daughter's three beautiful and unbelievably smart children and the big two-story Jackson house this daughter lived in, with the latest and best of everything.

She moved on finally to tell about a father of ten children in her hometown who just last week fell into a vat of boiling peanut oil at the peanut mill. "Burned to a crisp, like a potato chip," Mrs. Filburton pronounced grimly. She *was* lively company, Mrs. Arkin had to admit.

The next day Beulah went off to the hospital, again neglecting her own sister. Being alone in the strange house on the flat Delta made Mrs. Arkin so blue she was actually relieved to look through the side window and see Mrs. Filburton's red shorts zigzagging toward her through Beulah's rose beds. She was by herself this time.

For the first two hours Mrs. Filburton told about all the troubles that had been caused by her three separate husbands, none of whom had enough get-up-and-go and one of whom had an artificial stomach. Warmed by this talk, Mrs. Arkin blurted out her own troubles. "Now that my children are grown and gone, and Mr. Arkin is always worrying about his job managing the cotton gin . . . Well, I'd just like to have work of my own, but what can a lady do?"

What she couldn't put into words was that in her whole life no one had thought she deserved one moment of happiness. L.B.'s dogs had been given the run of her yard and dug up every one of the rosebushes she lovingly set out. L.B. and the old father and aunt had eaten Mrs. Arkin's meals day in and day out without a single thank-you. And during all their years together Mr. Arkin had regarded her as a fencepost: deaf, dumb, and there to serve.

Mrs. Filburton lit a fresh Pall Mall from her butt. "Why I can see that you're just like any woman without a independent income. Under *his* thumb. Why don't you open your own cafe? Now, don't laugh. I sold mine last year, and if I had it to do over, I'd hold onto that cafe."

Puffing out blue smoke, Mrs. Filburton rasped on: "Let me tell you this, cafes all over Missippi are gonna *get rich*. Because we're gonna have tourists crawling out of the woodwork. I know that for a fact—one of my high-up friends that's a governor's colonel told me that the governor himself is determined to make north-erners aware of all the lovely things we got for them to come see. Why he's already got a public relations firm in New York City talking up the Natchez pilgrimage and the Gulf coast and Vicks-burg. Vicksburg's lucky—they got all those Yankee graves. And they're going to make Miss Hospitality a girl that will *work* to attract tourists," Mrs. Filburton continued, suddenly angry, "since you know Miss Hospitality has never been anything more than a *title* for a society girl to put in her engagement write-up. Oh, I nearly died of the unfairness when my beautiful Lula lost in '52 to a *bowlegged* banker's daughter!"

Mrs. Arkin wished she would get back to the cafe business, but she murmured, "What a shame."

"Now they're going to make it a fair contest, where the prettiest girl will win it, although my Lula didn't and is still perfectly happy, thank you, married to a Jitney Jungle manager with three of the most beautiful children you ever saw."

Mrs. Filburton launched back into cafes. "They're getting ready for the tourists by building roads all over. And you know what highway building means to cafes?"

"Why no."

"It means they'll be swamped with bidness. The crews will come, and they eat like horses—and I mean they eat three times a day, plus a afternoon break for coffee and pie. Oh, I promise you, cafe owners are gonna be rich!"

With a habitual gesture, crossing an arm across her chest and apologetically fingering her collarbone, Mrs. Arkin said that she could cook well enough, but she knew nothing about running a business.

Mrs. Filburton snorted with laughter. "There's nothing so complicated about running a bidness. That's just another idea men have to make theirselves important!" They both laughed, Mrs. Arkin harder than she had in years. She had listened to Mr. Arkin's business problems over the years, and, though she never dared say so, she had often thought a little common sense could have prevented him from having them in the first place.

As the week wore on, Mrs. Arkin's hopes rose as they hadn't in years. And one afternoon, sitting on Beulah's guest bed, lacing up her stout Natural Bridge shoes, Mrs. Arkin was as stricken as if an angel had landed on her bedpost. She suddenly realized the sheer coincidence of her and Mrs. Filburton being at the same spot at the same time. Mrs. Arkin's heart fluttered like a bird's wing. She realized that God was answering her prayers of a lifetime by sending Mrs. Filburton with the cafe idea. Although no one ever even asked her to make change at church suppers, she knew now that God was working to turn her into a financially independent woman, with her own bank account.

By the time her week was up, Mrs. Arkin had made her plans with Mrs. Filburton. She would convert a small vacant house in her own side yard into a cafe, where she could serve dinner at noon to the construction crews, and Coca-Cola and pie in the afternoon to ladies. She would hire a good colored woman she knew to help her, and Ruby Ella's son, Rufus, would be engaged to do the dishes.

Mrs. Filburton thought much bigger, roaring off in her cigarette voice about which wholesale grocers would let you run a bill, how to price items for a profit and fire waitresses, how to avoid Social Security benefits for employees. And, really, this breathtaking talk was what gave Mrs. Arkin confidence for the first time in her life. She tried to store the feeling within herself, bracing herself to face the blistering opposition she would find when she returned to Pinola and told Mr. Arkin of her great plan.

For a week he refused to speak of the matter at all, resting on his first reaction of satiric laughter. But Mrs. Arkin had become crafty as a new religious convert pledged to win over a sinner. She continued to pass along tidbits of Filburton bait, and after two weeks she could tell his resistance was actually breaking down. It was Duncan Hines that broke him.

As Mr. Arkin blundered noisily through the house checking the locks for the night, Mrs. Arkin suddenly remembered what Mrs. Filburton described as "a cafe's sure-fire ticket to success." But she waited until breakfast to bring it up. Mr. Arkin, a fat man with a steady appetite, was at his most congenial at meals.

"There's a man named Duncan Hines," she began, as Mr. Arkin bent over his plate of ham and eggs, "who comes around to cafes and eats, and if he likes it, you get a sign that says he recommends your cafe."

Mr. Arkin said nothing, but she could tell he was listening because he was only chewing, not putting anything more in his mouth. "And when you have that sign up that says Duncan Hines recommends your place, anybody going by will know you have a good cafe and they'll stop and give you business."

Slowly Mr. Arkin buttered three fresh biscuits and thickly spread them with fig preserves. "Not only people coming by," she added, "Duncan Hines puts out a book with the names of cafes he recommends and people traveling make it a point to go by those cafes and eat."

"Just on his say-so?" Mr. Arkin demanded.

"Just on his say-so," Mrs. Arkin answered confidently.

* * *

Unbelievably the day came when the cafe was opened. As soon as Mr. Arkin had given in, won by the notion of free Hines advertising, Mrs. Arkin made arrangements with such frenzy that Mr. Arkin said if she didn't stop running around like a chicken with its head cut off she was likely to drop dead with a heart attack. But though she worked from the moment she got up until far past her bedtime, supervising the renovation of the old house in her side yard and making lists of recipes, she was too excited to notice if she was tired.

The cafe was the first thing she had had just like she wanted it. It was a square room fronted by a door and a large glass window on which she carefully painted MRS. ARKIN'S CAFE. There were four oilclothed tables alongside the counter, which had a hinged flap that opened up for her to go through. Behind the counter were her stove and icebox on either side of the side door. L.B.'s dogs parked themselves outside her side door, as though studying how to ruin it. But even they couldn't dim her satisfaction.

A few weeks after the opening, Mrs. Arkin wrote Mrs. Filburton a postcard: "Thanks to your kind help, I am operating my cafe in Pinola. Business is fine." This last statement was untrue, but Mrs. Arkin thought anything else might sound like a reproach. Her only regular diner was a toothless old bachelor who came by for dinner on alternate Mondays when his welfare check arrived at the post office. A lady or two might drop by in the afternoon for a Coke. But most days the only diners were she and Mr. Arkin, Ruby Ella, and Rufus.

Mrs. Arkin remained excited and happy as a bride-to-be. Very soon the road work would progress within driving distance of Pinola, and she expected to be swamped with business. And by the time the crews worked past Pinola, the road would be nearly complete and the tourists would be coming through. She thought about these future customers so many times that she could hardly believe it when the first stage—the patronage of the construction crews—fell through.

This happened, as she explained to Mr. Arkin, who was sitting at the empty counter finishing his dinner, through no fault in her reasoning. There was no way in the world she could have foreseen that Pinola's bootlegger, P.T. Whitney, would see the potential in her business and set up his own cafe across the railroad tracks, with his brassy daughter as the cook-waitress. "Besides," Mrs. Arkin said with unaccustomed spirit, "if the construction men would just as soon eat some slop cooked by P.T.'s daughter as long as she serves it switching her behind, I don't want them for customers."

Mr. Arkin pushed away his second helping of rice pudding and said tauntingly, sucking a tooth, "If you're so ticky about who your customers are, you should be satisfied—here you are feeding the same fine old customer you've been cooking for for thirty-eight years."

Mr. Arkin also deviled her by reporting daily the crowd of hungry construction workers crowding down at P.T.'s cafe on the wrong side of the tracks. And in the still afternoons she was forced to see P.T. slowly cruise in his pickup past her deserted cafe to check out her lack of customers. A man who inspired respect, if not admiration, he had shot six men dead, several of them in the back, bitten off the thumbs of three men in fistfights, and, in a recent to-do over a stolen hog, knuckled out the eye of a strong boy half his age. A short bald man who wore khakis and eye-magnifying glasses greasy with thumbprints, he had a big belly that hung over his pants like a melon under his shirt. The pants hung precariously below on his skinny hip bones, his armpits were perpetualy darkened, and he smelled yards away of sweat.

But Mrs. Arkin's faith in God rescued her. For three more months she kept up her faith that when the construction men were gone forever from Pinola and the tourists—families that would want good food—made up the town's cafe trade, she would show the bootlegger he couldn't steal her idea and get away with it forever. She expected to watch him go out of business.

Meanwhile she let Ruby Ella go and she cashed the last one of her government postal bonds left by her great-aunt Emma. When the highway was completed and the construction men gone, she threw herself with fresh energy into making each day's meal a feast, expecting every morning a carload of tourists that would be the first trickle of the avalanche. But four months passed and the only stopovers from the new road were occasional salesmen she never saw again.

More and more Mrs. Arkin got the feeling that somewhere

along the line a mistake had been made. She became so angry, thinking of the time after time the reward of her efforts had been delayed, that she considered closing the cafe. Whenever a carefully prepared dish went uneaten, she might have done this if it had not been for Mr. Arkin. He daily reminded her that he had been against the cafe from the first minute. So she held on, still hoping for the best.

One quiet afternoon, with the sun over the railroad tracks reflecting only the tangled shadows of chair legs on the cafe's shiny clean linoleum, she looked up at the sound of a car. The car, strange to her, had a New York license plate on the front of its silver grillwork, and her heart began to pound.

Two young men and a girl got out, squinting in the direction of the cafe. As they came inside the front screened door, Mrs. Arkin gasped.

All three of the Yankee tourists were dressed in blue jeans, shirts with the tails hanging out, and thong sandals with dirty toes sticking out. The girl had little slitty brown eyes and greasy dark braids over each shoulder, and for a horrified second Mrs. Arkin thought she was an Indian until she saw the paleness of the girl's face, colorless without rouge or lipstick. The young men were thin and they slouched down, kept from collapsing entirely only by some invisible support in their lower chests.

Both men had beards and long hair, and they looked over the cafe motionlessly, barely moving their eyes—like goats about to butt, Mrs. Arkin thought—then drifted until they sank into the cane chairs at the table farthest from the front door.

She avanced toward them, beaming as if they were her own long-lost children restored to life.

"Je-suz," said the dark-bearded man looking around, "when's the next lynching?"

He talked in such a hard Yankee accent that Mrs. Arkin could hardly make out what he was saying. They were all three wearing denim work clothes like tenant farmers—the most faded worn-thin jeans imaginable. But their jeans had extra decorations, like silver studs running down the sides of the legs, and the girl's blue shirt, unbuttoned shamefully low to expose the rims of her breasts, was sewn with red flowers. In an instant Mrs. Arkin saw through their obvious disguise. They must not be ordinary tourists but Duncan Hines representatives, sent to test the Arkin cafe. Praise God! Her very first real customers and they would be in a position to bring more to her. Now was the big moment of her life, if only she could do everything right!

Mrs. Arkin snatched off her hairnet and put menus before them and rushed to bring icewater and silverware. In between, she hollered out the side door where Rufus was sleeping stretched out on newspapers in the shade to get himself inside, ready to wash dishes. Since there was nothing to wash, the truth was she wanted an audience for her triumph.

"Well, well, well," she said brightly as she laid menus around, "I guess you boys must be growing beards for your town centennial someplace. Whereabouts are you from?"

The three looked blankly up at her, and, seeing their unfriendly Yankee faces, Mrs. Arkin shivered. The dark-bearded man who had spoken had thick kinky hair of a kind she had never seen on a white man. It stood out around his head in a halo of black snakes and swept like volcano lava down the sides of his face, down the back of his neck, and parted in the front of his neck only briefly before rushing on over his chest. He had big arm muscles and wore leather wristlets buckled tight around each hairy wrist.

The girl suddenly giggled.

"Linda," said the redheaded boy, "are you laughing about such a serious matter? Didn't you know Lennie was celebrating the hundredth birthday of his hometown, the picturesque old town of Queens, home of one million bourgeois, including his parents, the dry-cleaners Silverstein?"

Linda dropped her face into her hands in glee. The redhead laughed with her until they both choked. Lennie glared at them.

"All right, you jackoffs, you want to eat or you wanna make me mad? You wanna tell Grandma here what you want to eat, or you wanna go without eating? I'm telling ya, I'm getting to New Orleans before midnight." He sounded as though it was his burden in life to give orders because he was so much smarter.

"I urge you to try our fried chicken, sir, it'll be fresh-fried."

Linda turned her slitty eyes at Mrs. Arkin and said in a nasal voice, "Oh, no, Grandma, I'd rather have some, like, corned beef. You got that?"

Mrs. Arkin felt her heart contract apprehensively. She'd never heard of that.

"Why . . . ah . . . no."

"How about some pastrami on rye?"

"Well, we . . . uh . . . don't have that, whatever it is."

"Bagel and lox?"

"I'm sorry, no."

All three now fell over their china plates laughing. The redheaded one straightened at last, spread some tobaccolike substance on a cigarette tissue, rolled it, and looked around for a match. Mrs. Arkin called back to the kitchen, "Rufus . . . get a match in here for our customers." Flustered, she spoke in a commanding shout. Rufus came through the open flap carrying the big box of kitchen matches. Mrs. Arkin hissed, "No . . . no . . . the little crystal glass of matches, Rufus."

"Aha . . ." said Lennie. "What do we have here? Is Grandma an oppressor? Is this a racist cafe we've stopped at, Markie and Linda?"

They giggled, but Lennie cut them off. "Awright, jackoffs, shut your face. And hold that stuff until we get to New Orleans. You want to run into some state trooper schmuck with that stuff?"

Rufus, dumbstruck as Lot's wife turned to a pillar of salt, held the kitchen box of matches before this trio apparition, unable to move forward or backward. Markie reached out and plucked a match from the box, struck it on the side, held rigidly by Rufus, and lighted up. A sweet odor permeated the Arkin cafe.

"May I suggest the fried chicken, sir?" Mrs. Arkin said.

"Awright, awright, bring us three fried chickens," said Lennie.

Mrs. Arkin rushed to her stove, whisked the floured chicken from the icebox, and began to cook as though her life depended on it.

Rufus had skittered back behind the counter, but Lennie called him back. "Hey, come over here."

Rufus ambled over, walking bent forward so it would look like he was moving fast but in fact shuffling as slow as possible. He was short, and skinny as a beanpole in his bright chartreuse pants and red shirt, his brown forearms sticking out below the short shirtsleeves like brown twigs. Mrs. Arkin had known him from the age of two weeks when Ruby Ella brought him to the house nearly dead with colic. Mrs. Arkin took one look at the tiny twisted face, like a dying brown leaf, and called Dr. Hill. Mrs. Arkin and Ruby Ella spent the next week taking turns giving Dr. Hill's paregoric and carrying the baby in their arms, pressed to the warmth of their bodies, until the dried leaf slowly uncurled, started to suck its bottle, and stopped crying.

Since then Rufus had grown up to be like any other nigra, but Mrs. Arkin could not forget the curled little leaf he had been. He looked frightened at the visitors, his eyes rolling.

"How much money you make here?" demanded the black-bearded man.

Rufus jumped. "Don't make no money, just eats." Mrs. Arkin could have speared him with her red-handled turning fork at this revelation. She had paid him as long as she could afford to.

The young red-bearded one spoke up now. "Eats is all you get, huh?" He had an undemanding redhead's face that did not ask to be remembered. Small light-blue eyes fringed with blond lashes and pink lips too big for the eyes. He was younger than the other two, and his red beard looked like a toy doctor's beard stuck on a child's face. He grinned through it in a silly way, puffing on the sweet-smelling cigarette.

"You know what Markie here gets just for an allowance?" demanded Lennie. "A hundred fifty dollars a week. But then his old man pulls down four hundred thousand a year from his box factory on Long Island, and he feels guilty because he wouldn't let little Markie study the cello like he wanted to."

Markie squirmed and looked—properly, thought Mrs. Arkin—embarrassed at this bragging on his fortune.

"Now, Linda, her daddy is a divorce lawyer, a bomber, and he pulls down two hundred thousand a year from all that marital discord. And he gives little Linda three hundred a week because she's daddy's little girl."

Linda blew out the smoke from the cigarette, narrowing her slitty little eyes and tossing her braids forward over her unbuttoned shirt. Mrs. Arkin looked up from her frying chicken and decided that, whatever her daddy made, Linda acted like a sharecropper.

"And you live off us both," snapped Linda, and Lennie glared at her.

"Whatcha doing with that ax back there against the wall?" asked the redheaded one.

Nervously Mrs. Arkin considered calling Rufus away. He was certainly not a feature of the Arkin cafe, and she did not want him creeping into *her* review. And of course now after getting over his fright at the visitors he was in his element. In another minute he'd be showing off.

"That *aks!*" Rufus crowed. "That aks for Mr. Blue!"

"Is he the law around here?" Lennie demanded.

"Mr. Blue, he sure the law around here!" Rufus brayed a huge laugh, and the visitors looked in awe at Rufus's strong yellow teeth opened before them, serried and perfect as a lion's.

"There he sit!" Rufus pointed dramatically, sure of his audience now, to the side door where L.B.'s pack of hungry hounds sat pressing their wet black noses and scrabbling at the cross-hatching of the screen. In the center, regally unmoving amidst the hounds, sat the scourge of Mrs. Arkin's rose beds, a bluetick hound with infinitely wise amber eyes, waiting confidently for the day's pleasures. The other common brown- and black-spotted dogs struggled to get to the screen door through the pack, each dog working his way to the front but holding his place only for seconds until others scrabbled over his shoulders. None of them disturbed Mr. Blue in the center.

"You use that ax on the dog?" asked Lennie, for the first time not speaking as though he were giving them all orders.

"Yessah. Mr. Blue like his Co-Cola, he do, so once a day Miz Arkin, she pour Co-Cola in a Dixie cup, and I push em out of the way with that aks and give it to Mr. Blue, and I use that aks to keep the others off while he drink it."

Lennie turned to his friends. "Jesuz, no wonder the NAACP got rid of whites. Here you got a black kid can hardly spell his name and he's sporting around with the whites' dogs giving them Cokes. Who can even understand what he's saying? But I think I got it—you leave out the main verbs."

Lennie turned back to Rufus. "You-out-of-here-someday?"

But before Rufus could embarrass Mrs. Arkin any further, another unexpected visitor pulled his muddy pickup in front of the cafe. The sun was clouding up as it sank behind the railroad track, which stretched straight as a board along the main street of Pinola.

The sun silhouetted in the pickup's back window two rifles, a Franchi rimfire auto-loader for squirrels and a Mannlicher Safari, designed for shooting elephants in Africa.

P.T. Whitney came in bold as brass, his pistol popped into his belt. "How-do, Miz Arkin," he said politely. "How-do, Rufus," he added, looking the visitors over slowly like a herd of elephants that had miraculously appeared in Pinola. "Well, well, I see you got customers from out of town," he said, obviously bursting with curiosity. He must have seen their license plate.

Taking the table between the visitors and the front door, P.T. turned a cane chair backwards and lazily straddled it, as though he were settling down on his own front porch. The sun at this moment disappeared behind a moving wall of ugly thunderclouds. The threat of rain made the air heavy. Mrs. Arkin had to breathe harder, as though she had sunk suddenly into an ocean.

"Yew boys from New York City?" P.T. drawled. His eyes set on Linda's open shirtfront like a cat sighting a fat bird.

"What's it to you?" Lennie tossed over his shoulder like he was spitting. Mrs. Arkin wanted to rush over and shake him. *Watch out! It's P.T. you're spitting at!* The roll of thunder overhead echoed Mrs. Arkin's own thundering heartbeats.

"Sir, how far to New Orleans?" the redheaded one cut in, polite as could be, and Mrs. Arkin allowed herself to breathe out. Here was a placator like herself, the type that always saved the day.

"Rufus, how far to New Awlins?" growled P.T., arresting Rufus who had been sidestepping to the flap at the first sign of white folks' trouble.

"I be guessing 400 miles, Mr. P.T.," Rufus quavered. P.T. shot a quick, satisfied look at Linda. She could see from the way this nigger jumped to his word that P.T. was a big man hereabouts.

"Guess you all got some driving to do," P.T. said, not able to take his stare from the girl's nipples. "But I guess you got something to smoke to keep you going."

"You the sheriff around here or something?" demanded Lennie, turning slowly to P.T. for the first time with a withering stare, as though it was his habit to order sheriffs around too.

The first green flash of lightning forked over the darkening sky outside the cafe. Placating in the only way she could think of, Mrs. Arkin yanked up the hot chicken from her skillet, dumped it onto a plate, and rushed to P.T., carrying a long-stemmed goblet of ice tea. In the cheerful voice of a church hostess she cried, "Here, P.T., try my fresh-fried chicken."

At this point the two placators, Markie and Mrs. Arkin, might still have stopped the trouble. The thunderclouds that wrapped Pinola in their darkness might have spewed down their rain and passed on in ten minutes as Mississippi thunderstorms do, leaving the cafe occupants just as they were. But Lennie didn't allow that.

"Hey," he snarled at Mrs. Arkin, "how come he got served before us? We were here first!"

Rufus's mouth fell open, his teeth bared in fear. Mrs. Arkin held her turning fork in midair and couldn't help squeezing her eyes shut in prayer.

But P.T. didn't jump up and seize Lennie by the throat. Grinning, he only cocked his head at Linda and piped in a fake girl's voice, "Well, sugar, maybe you better line up with me to get good service." His voice dropped back to its usual commanding growl. "All kind of service you ain't been gitting. You come over here and sit by me."

Linda stuck her small pink chin in the air and tossed her braids over her shoulders. "You stupid old hillbilly, I wouldn't sit by you if you were the last man on earth."

P.T.'s face twisted like a man who's accidentally swallowed a whole chili pepper. He turned redder than a ham. His mouth untwisting and suddenly opening, he flung the silverware to the floor and howled like Mr. Blue, a howl that shook the glasses on the tables.

Lennie jumped up, his hair vibrating like live snakes. He grabbed Linda up and slung her toward P.T. "You little asshole, get over there and sit down like he says and shut up!"

With his muddy high-topped work shoe P.T. shoved out a cane chair, and when Linda sank wide-eyed into it, his big red hand snaked out and locked around her tiny forearm.

Markie half-rose. "N-n-nooo, Linda, come back."

Lennie seized him by the collar and dragged him back. "Shut up, I got a plan. Let me talk, I'll get us out of here. You don't and I won't answer for you."

He waited till Markie sat down, then he marched back toward P.T., twisting the armband on his left wrist. "Listen, P.T.," he said in a voice so compelling and deep that Mrs. Arkin and Rufus leaned toward it as though to the Sunday preacher on the radio. "I'm going to let you in on a secret."

Lennie waited for P.T. to look up, but P.T. was grinning again, his nose inching closer to Linda's low shirtfront. She looked back at him like a five-year-old who has been told her mother has died. Such things, her frightened brown eyes said, could not happen to her.

Lennie blared on in his loud voice. "We are from New York and we are on our way to New Orleans. But we're not ordinary tourists. We're working for an organization, a *powerful* organization."

P.T. dipped his nose right into Linda's shirtfront, holding her tight in his big red hand.

"You want to know the name of our organization?" Lennie shot out. "The FBI!"

"Not from Duncan Hines?" Mrs. Arkin whispered, gripping a dishtowel.

"Oh, the FBI." P.T. shifted in disgust, leaning back to look at Lennie with his big red face and greasy glasses shining. "I've seed that teevee program. *The FBI in peace and war.* They drove those little Pintos. I wouldn't give a nigger a Pinto."

"The fucking FBI you're fooling with!" Lennie screamed in a terrible threatening voice. "You lay a hand on her or him or me, and you'll have the whole FBI down on you!"

"Who's talking about her or him, we'll just go one on one," P.T. shouted back. He smashed his ice-tea goblet into a jagged spear on the table and threw the table down before him, smashing dishes on the floor. "I'm going to cut you good, boy." He crouched over his glass spear and stalked Lennie.

"The ax, get the ax!" Markie shouted, running to the back wall where Rufus was plastered, frozen in fear.

Lennie ran back and yanked the heavy ax down from its hooks, then suddenly grabbed Rufus by the neck. Pushing Rufus ahead of him and hiding behind him as though he was a shield, he swung the big ax in his left hand and advanced on P.T.

Quick as an attack dog, P.T. lunged left, right, nicking Lennie on each arm with his glass spear, drawing blood and cackling at it.

Lennie raised the ax high and swung it down toward the middle of P.T.'s skull. P.T. sidestepped and the ax sank into the floor with a thud. But before Lennie could raise it, P.T. seized the handle.

They struggled silently for the ax, the muscles in their arms bulging. Lennie threw Rufus aside on the floor to use his right hand, but P.T. held onto his spear and used only one powerful arm. Veins swelling, they battled for thirty seconds; then P.T. yanked the ax from Lennie and threw it easily back over his head. The ax sailed through Mrs. Arkin's front window, shattering the glass and letting in a gale of rain.

Grinning again, P.T. raised his glass spear high over Lennie's chest. Lennie stumbled back a step. "No," he gasped, his face chalky white. Then he seized Rufus from the floor and held the boy before him.

"You want this nigger to die with you?" P.T. screamed.

"I ain't no FBI, Mr. P.T.," Rufus pleaded.

"Please God, take the cafe," Mrs. Arkin prayed. "Just don't let P.T. kill Rufus. Save Rufus first and them second if You will."

Thunder suddenly rent the air as though the sky was a giant bedsheet and someone had ripped it apart. Everyone froze except Mrs. Arkin, who marched from behind the counter, her mild gray eyes burning behind her glasses. What was happening was worse even than Mr. Arkin's slow destruction of her love, worse than L.B.'s dogs digging up her rose beds, worse than the ingratitude of the invalids. In the thunder's crack she saw things she had never seen in her whole life, and she knew what she must do.

"You let Rufus go, you P.T." She shook the fork at him. "You let him and them go or you'll never live another happy day."

P.T. reached out and pulled Rufus from Lennie. Rufus ran out the side door, leaving it blowing open in the rain.

The dogs spotted the chance of a lifetime. Dripping wet, they plunged into the warm cafe and dived between people's legs, rattling their long chains like Attila the Hun's hordes. Hemmed in by the dogs, P.T. pulled his pistol from his belt and aimed at Lennie's heart. But Mr. Blue, his chain swinging aloft like a runaway chain-gang prisoner's, broke across P.T. and dashed toward the front door. The flying chain hit P.T.'s shins like a crowbar, and he fell, his shot singing out and shattering a glass jar of sugar.

Stunned, Lennie gazed down at his fallen opponent among the

milling dogs. Markie grabbed Linda's arm and dragged her through the front door, Mr. Blue at their heels. They plunged into the car. As the motor roared, P.T., shouting curses, grabbed through the dogs for his pistol, and Lennie sprang back to life. He sprinted through the door, caught the car racing backwards, flung open a door. The car tires squealed as the car raced forwards and Lennie jumped inside. The Yankees disappeared in the wall of rain.

Alone, Mrs. Arkin looked around her wrecked cafe. She shook her head in pure fury at P.T., who was hobbling out to his pickup. Maybe if P.T. hadn't barged in, her cafe might have made a go of it. But she shook her head, remembering what she had realized during that rip of thunder. She went to the front door and locked it. Then she took the broom out from behind the icebox and began sweeping up the broken glass and blood. She would not let herself cry.

The last rays of sunlight had broken through after the thunderstorm. The old bachelor shuffled up and shook the door, but Mrs. Arkin waved her hand at him to go away, and went on sweeping. What she realized was that people like P.T. and Lennie didn't give a hoot about being good themselves, but they knew what went on in other people's heads and how to use that to their own advantage. But people like herself, they knew so little about P.T.'s kind of people, not pee-doodle, and when they ran up against that kind they ran smack into trouble.

That was what was heartbreaking. She had tried just this once to break out and do something in her life, and she had held on and held on through the long months. But all the time it was too late. P.T. can have the cafe trade, she muttered to herself. The old man kept rattling the door, but she went on sweeping without looking up. Holding on would be a kind of losing. The Arkin cafe was closed.

Kurt Rheinheimer

UMPIRE

(from *Quarterly West*)

The town of Blueston sits on a little flat piece of flood plain
confined by the river at one edge and by the abrupt start of Cullhat
Mountain at the other. It is a foundry town that had its best days
in the forties and fifties, when the hot waste water ran freely down
into the river, and gawky steel forms rolled away on big flatcars
headed north. The weeds around the foundry offices are as tall as
the men who once worked in the thick wooden chairs inside, and
reach up as if to look into the high, wavy-glassed windows, each
of which has a trim arc of on-end brick above it. On a summer day
in Blueston the heat builds along the river in the midday hours
and then rises to collect—late in the afternoon—in a little low spot
between the flat and the first quick rise of the mountain. It is on
this little scoop of land, amid a few small and poorly kept houses
and a thin line of rock road that runs up the mountain, that Callis
Field is located. It sits with its back to the town, and in 1937, when
the diamond was laid out, either nobody had the power to hit the
ball more than 284 feet into the thick air to right, or someone just
stuck the plate down somewhere and forgot to think about the
fact that the start of the mountain was going to dictate that the
right field line would be unnaturally short.

Reid hates the field because of the heat. The whole league is
hot, but this field seems to draw it and hold it, so densely that the
dust doesn't rise right on a slide. The outfield—in deep left-
center—is damp even in dry spells, and downright mushy in the

spring. As Reid brushes the plate in preparation for the start of the game he watches the red-orange dust as it hangs low to the ground, clinging to his shoes more thoroughly than dry dust would. He comes up from the plate, kicking the heels of his shoes against his shin guards, and allows himself a furtive glance up into the stands, just behind the plate. There is no sign of Ellen, as he knew there wouldn't be—it is too early—and there are no more than twenty-five people on the long rows of two-plank, deep blue benches that make up the "box seats" behind the plate. Above those seats, in a home-made-looking booth, are the two guys from WBLS, already barking out information to their vast audience. Reid likes to see them up there because they are a consolation to him. They broadcast rookie league baseball—Class D, it used to be called—to a town of 16,000 people over an FM station way down at one end of the dial. And all this while anyone who is really interested in the game can come out to Callis Field, pay a dollar, and see the game in person. The WBLS guys are seven million miles from the big league broadcast booth they dream about at night, especially with all the ex-players bouncing in front of men like these, who probably decided at age ten they were going to be broadcasters. The two men up behind Reid are farther from their hope than Reid is from a big league plate with an inside chest protector and real meal money.

Kammler, a big square man of German descent who is thirty-three years old, will work the bases. He comes slowly in toward Reid as they wait for the Blueston Braves to hit the field. "Anything in those shadows out there deep, cover me," he says to Reid, as if Reid doesn't know to do it. "Right," Reid says. "Foul pops by the screen, you watch the runners," he tells Kammler. "Right," Kammler barks back. "No lip and keep it quick." He turns his big body then, claps his hands together twice, and jogs out toward first. Reid doesn't like Kammler because he is too old to be working for $57 a game—$3700 for the whole summer, for Christ's sake—in a hot-town rookie league. Reid has already told himself that this is it for him. This is his third year in the Southern Mountains League—made up of a bunch of little towns you never heard of in Tennessee, Virginia, North Carolina and West Virginia—and he will turn twenty-five in the winter. A year of umpire school and three years at the bottom is more than enough. Either he gets an offer to move up after this season, or he goes back to Fremont, Nebraska, to play softball and drive into Omaha every day to work full time for his brother, who is a lawyer. Reid is a qualified paralegal, and could go farther.

Kammler is clapping his hands again, trying to get the Braves onto the field. He has told Reid that in his eleven years of umpiring the teams have gotten slower and slower to come out, as if they want to make you stand there so everybody gets a good look at you—to let the crowd warm up its collective hatred of umpires. At last the Blueston first baseman breaks out of the dugout. "Number fourteen," the radio/PA team barks into Reid's neck, "the first baseman, Cary Banders." And he stretches out the end of the name. "Banderrrzzz," it comes out, as if to cover for the small applause generated by the crowd. The other players follow by position, each with an elephantine syllable at the end of his name.

The Blueston catcher is a short, squat kid named Lucas. They signed him out of a junior college after they'd already run through three other catchers with broken fingers and pulled hamstrings. You can take one look at Pat Lucas and know he is going no place whatsoever. He reminds Reid of catchers in Little League. The fat kid, basically, who is dumb enough to sit back there and scream and holler and sweat his brains out. Lucas is that red-faced kid grown up a little, and he is so surprised, so damned amazed to be in professional baseball that he has lost all perspective on the fact that he really is still that red-faced fat kid. As Reid settles in behind the plate, Lucas is already shouting out orders to his infielders, who are casually picking up grounders and ignoring the catcher completely.

"Gonna call them strikes when they're strikes, balls when they're balls," Reid tells the pudgy red neck beneath him. "Anything you don't like has already been called and won't be called again. Stay down there to give me a good look and everything will be fine." Reid used to give this little soft-voiced talk to all the catchers, but has let it go as the summers have worn on and his reputation has begun to precede him. But Pat Lucas needs it. And as Reid speaks, the neck gets redder. Reid sighs deeply, motioning the leadoff man for Prestonburg into the box. Another night of listening to gripes on everything up to a half foot off the plate.

Ellen Childress is Reid's entire version of the collective girl-in-every-town dream of the Southern Mountains League. There are two or three players in the league—tall, statuesque young men out of colleges—who will have you believe they've long since accomplished the feat. Reid weighs the factors of girls' love for baseball players against the size and conservatism of the towns, and he doubts it. If anybody has done it, he suspects it might be some runty little infielder with a whole lot to prove. It is Reid's opinion that the farther up into these hills you get, the ropier the women are. Or else fat. No middle ground between the lean, hard-armed girls with freckles and straight, no-color hair, and the ones who grew up round. Ellen, he tells himself, is almost an exception. Her hair is dark brown, and she fills out the back of a pair of Levis the way a girl is supposed to. Smooth and full, but not too full. Ellen has a daughter who is ten and a son who is nine, and they come to the games on some nights, and stay at their grandmother's on others, when Ellen comes by herself. Henry Childress, Reid learned one soft summer night, left the county when the children were six and five, with a woman who has since made the local paper on two separate occasions for flimflam schemes on the Amtrak train that comes through Blueston at three in the morning without stopping. So Ellen has raised the kids by herself and taught fourth grade at Blueston Elementary and, as she tells it, had no inclination at all to have anything to do with another man from her home town. Reid tells himself that before he came along she was well on her way into the process of shriveling up into a dried vine and turning in her femininity in return for martyrized motherhood. If she brings the kids she's there by eight, and if not a little later, staying to talk with her mother before heading to the park.

"Like hell," the beef-necked catcher squawks. "It wasn't even on the black."

Reid easily resists the temptation to agree—the pitch was indeed four inches *off* the black—as the Prestonburg leadoff man trots down to first with a walk. Reid feels heat at his own neck. Already there are voices behind him. "Yeah, get them off to a good start, ump," says one. "Just keep it on your shoulder," comes another, ostensibly talking to the second hitter. "He'll send you on down to first too." Reid thinks often about levels of intimidation in different leagues. He has decided that it is worst in these little one-show towns where people have nothing to do with their anger except spit it out at an umpire on a baseball field. So they sit, just ten or twelve feet away, and rip him to pieces. In the major league cities, Reid's logic goes on, there are a few major league hecklers, to be sure, but at least they are farther away, and held there by something more substantial than the thin, undulating chicken wire that separates Reid from the locals in this town. They will gain strength as their numbers increase through the innings. And as their volume increases so too does their daring, as they prod each other on to greater insults, in the manner of children trying to get each other into trouble in a classroom.

The second Prestonburg hitter, mercifully, pops out on a 3-1 pitch that was a ball, and Reid is spared the crowd's momentum being built more rapidly than it needs to be. But as the Blueston team comes to bat in their half of the first, he is aware that the town's biggest voice—a man Reid has shouted at through the chicken wire—has arrived. He is a middle-aged, roly-poly man with hair worn in a flat-top. There is no drinking in Callis Field, and so the flat-top and his buddies have to step outside the park every inning or so for a nip—a situation which gives Reid a small break, but which also tends to build the level of comment and to destroy their notion of the flow of the game just enough to allow them to make mistakes of judgment—condensing batting orders, confusing hitters and situations just enough to be able to berate Reid for something that is not quite related to the actual progress of the game.

The level of pitching in the Southern Mountains League has gone up a notch or two this season. The consensus among the umpires is that these things go in cycles, while the hitters of course attribute it to a core of umpires which favors pitching over hitting. On this night Reid is particularly impressed. The Prestonburg team is using a small left-hander of the Whitey Ford–Dave Mc-Nally mold, who nibbles at the corners and fields like a cat when they try to bunt on him. He is a college graduate, and about twelve steps ahead of the league in guile and craft. Reid is sure he will move up fast—perhaps before the season is over. And Blueston is using a tall right-hander who is just out of high school—of the type who will walk the bases full and strike out the side in the same inning. By the end of the fourth inning each team has no runs and one hit, and Reid feels the game settling into a pitcher's duel—so long as neither team has a fielding lapse and the tall right-hander doesn't lose the plate.

After the fifth Reid brushes off the plate even though it is clean, and stares openly up into the stands to look for Ellen, having conquered the temptation at the end of each of the last two innings. "Don't look up here for help," the flat-top screams immediately. "There ain't no eye doctor up here." Reid feels his face warm. He has left his mask on to cover his eyes, but a good umpire baiter does not let any opportunity slip by. Reid waits, expecting— dreading—the first comment on why he is really looking up there. Somehow, through dumb luck or perhaps respect for a school teacher in a small town, or maybe just plain stupidity, his big talkers have never mentioned her. And again, as he settles in to start the sixth, they have let him look and made no mention. They are staying with the eyesight theme, their favorite. "You realize he does see well enough to find the plate to dust it off, anyway," someone yells, to general laughter. Reid misses Ellen behind him. In her silence through the jeers she helps him absorb, allows him to remain stoic when he would rather not. Her absence annoys him to a degree that he knows it should not. He has no claim on her. One of her kids could be sick. Or her mother maybe. Or maybe a PTA meeting. No, not in summer. Reid has traveled through six ratty little mountain towns to have Ellen sit behind him for these three games, and now he is finally here and she is not.

In the top of the sixth the big right-hander walks the first two batters. The pitches are all high, and there is not much static from behind. The Blueston manager, a no-hit shortstop who made it to the big leagues for a cup of coffee in the early seventies, trots to the mound and tilts his head back to talk to his pitcher. The kid nods, hands on hips, and the manager trots back. No delay. No casual shot at Reid. No nothing. Reid goes back to his crouch and calls a ball high. "Wait till it gets there," comes a voice from behind. The next two pitches are also high, and down along the right field line people are moving around in the Blueston bullpen. As Reid calls a strike on the next pitch, with some protest from the Prestonburg bench, he feels a strap snap at his left shin guard. It is one of the criss-crossing straps which hold the shin guard in place, and the feeling of looseness annoys Reid immediately and deeply. He has always associated umpiring with tight control. And especially when you are as little as he is, you need a feeling of total firmness and containedness—a secure possession of the game. And the sloppiness at the inside of his left knee—the shin guard will not fall, but will slip slightly until the arch of his foot stops it—is just enough to compromise Reid's feel of control. If things do not feel right you can't do the job right—you don't have the same confidence, and if you don't have the confidence you don't have conviction, and if you don't have conviction people are all over you. Especially if you are small. Reid begins immediately to try to discount the annoyance, to equate it with a lingering drizzle. It is there, and must be dealt with, but it cannot become your whole focus. He cannot stop and fix the strap because it has torn away on the sewn side, and even if he could repair it he would have to endure the complete attention of the crowd while he stopped to work on it. So he has no choice but to deal with the irritation. He reminds himself of other umpiring problems. Guys working with diarrhea. Broken toes. Alone, for God's sake, with a hostile crowd. He glances out at Kammler who is bent, hands on knees, just behind the mound, and is glad he is there.

The hitter walks, loading the bases and putting the potential go-ahead run at third. The Prestonburg catcher—David Harkness—is the batter. He is a tall, strong kid built like Carlton Fisk, and who almost never complains about a call. He is perhaps Reid's favorite player in the league, with a good chance to move up, though Reid has never seen anyone run more slowly on a baseball field. His stride to the plate brings increased chatter from the Prestonburg bench. The first pitch to him is on the corner and Reid shoots up his right arm. "Christ, I didn't know there was called strikes on visiting teams in this town, did you?" comes a voice from behind Reid. "That's the first one tonight, isn't it?" David Harkness steps out briefly—as strong a registering of disagreement as he is likely to make. The next two pitches are high. There are a few shouts from the crowd to take the pitcher out. Reid expects the manager to do just that. But he does not, and the kid comes in with a good pitch that Harkness taps weakly toward short. The drawn-in shortstop, in his eagerness to come home and cut off the run with a force, bobbles the ball momentarily. Pat Lucas is screaming "Home! Home! Home!" as loudly as he can. The shortstop guns the ball in, and Pat Lucas, in his eagerness to get the ball to first for the double play, pulls his foot off the plate far too soon. He has taken a full step before he catches the ball, and Reid has no choice but to call the runner safe at the plate. As Kammler calls Harkness out at first Pat Lucas is throwing his mask at Reid's shins and jumping up and down. The little manager comes out in a hurry, and the chicken wire behind Reid is suddenly a maze of voices and faces. "We had him by a goddamn week," Pat Lucas is screaming again and again as he shoves at his manager's chest to try to get through him to Reid. "You're so goddamn short you can't see to make the call." The manager is pushing at Pat Lucas, trying to keep him from getting kicked out of the game. He doesn't have another catcher. In the infield all is quiet. No one has come in to join the protest because they all know Reid made the call. But at the fence there is pandemonium. "It's a force out, you blind asshole." "You never read the rule book? You don't need a tag on that play. Can you believe this? Guy throws just the pitch he wants, and then a bush ump goes and blows it for him. Could be the difference for that kid on the mound out there." The voices are blended and irrational—too close to Reid. The manager still has not said a word to him, to Reid's relief. The call was so clear as to be indisputable, and the silence confirms that the manager knows it too. But the crowd and Pat Lucas are of one blind mentality. By now they are talking about where Reid stays in Blueston—a line of taunt that frightens him slightly. He hopes against knowledge that Ellen is back there, hearing all of this—but he knows she is not. She would be able to tell him if the threats are real or just the idle blather of half-drunk, small town ball fans.

At last Pat Lucas is calmed and the game resumes. Reid expects an under-the-breath barrage as the catcher settles in, but instead there is total silence. No infield directions, no hum-babe-shoot-it to the pitcher, and not a word to Reid. Maybe the boy has realized that he was wrong. Or, more likely, he has decided to pout because no one took up for him except the crazy fans. Reid hitches the shin guard and settles back to the game. Behind him now the taunts are no longer as consistent. He has come to realize, in his three years, that there is an optimum pace to umpire baiting, and it takes the right kind of game, the right levels of alcohol, and the right kind of weather to have it go just right. There is a certain pace and momentum to be built. When there is one huge explosion, it often kills the momentum for the rest of the game. Reid hopes it will go that way, instead of this being just a lull before another roar.

"He could've went to a Japanese ump school," comes the first distinct voice when things are calm, and after Reid has called strike two on the next Prestonburg hitter. "I'm not too sure they have force outs over in Yagashaki." There is general laughter, and the hitter pops meekly to second.

The Prestonburg right fielder steps in, twitching his neck and back muscles in imitation of Roberto Clemente. "Nah, I doubt it was Japan where he learned," comes another voice. "He didn't meet the height requirements over there." Louder laughter. The batter fouls the next pitch high and toward the screen. Reid jumps out of the way of the catcher and comes back to watch the attempt. The ball falls just on the crowd side of the chicken wire screen, scattering his baiters momentarily. Reid steals a futile glance for Ellen.

"Get up there where you belong," comes a voice.

And when Reid is back in position behind the catcher, "I think he started out in the Three-I League." A pause, while the first pitch comes in. Then the same voice, with the punch line. "You think he would have made it out of there with at least one eye left." Explosive laughter. They use that one game after game. The hitter swings at the next pitch and lines the ball hard toward left field. The Blueston left fielder gets a good jump on the ball and dives for the short hop. But Kammler, running out from behind the pitcher's mound, throws up his thumb immediately and forcefully. Reid looks down, and adjusts the shin guard. The Prestonburg manager, once a pitcher for the old Washington Senators, takes off for Kammler from his third base coaching box. The two Prestonburg baserunners are right behind him, swarming all over the square umpire. Reid could have predicted it. One big rhubarb generally means one more big rhubarb. Kammler walks away from his accusers—out toward center field as the Blueston Braves trot in, some with open grins on their faces. "You just plain totally blew it," Reid can hear the Prestonburg manager shouting. "He trapped it and you took it away from us. Get help. Go ask. You blew it—maybe he saw it." Kammler walks away as Reid thinks of a time in Clairsburg when a rookie ump named Pelouge, of all things, reversed a call of tagging up too soon, that Reid had made. Reid was so mad he couldn't see, and Pelouge made enough similar calls to be out of baseball within two months after that one.

The manager and the runners have moved Kammler out into the short right field corner now, and he has turned to head in toward the plate—along the first base line. He is leading them to me, Reid cannot help but think, but halfway down the line Kammler turns back across the infield. Reid is grateful, and knows that he should start out to break it up, even though Kammler did not help him with the call at the plate. But before Reid starts out, the manager gives up on Kammler and comes in toward Reid, his arms in the air even as he takes his first step. "You gonna let that crap stand?" he said to Reid when he is still forty feet away. "Are you the home plate umpire? Are you?" He is building momentum as he comes in. Reid spreads his legs slightly and folds his arms across his chest, feeling the pounding of his heart. He is, of course, trapped. He can go talk to Kammler, tell him he saw the play differently, back the older man down, and then face the Blueston team and fans, as well as having to establish where the baserunners should be. And risk the wrath of Kammler. Or, he can stonewall for Kammler, and face the loss of some respect from the old pitcher, who knows full well that Reid is a good umpire, and that he cannot desert another ump. Reid has always known that umpiring is the ultimate no-win situation—you call them right and nobody notices—or some drunken fool convinces the crowd that you haven't called them right—and you make one mistake and it hangs there forever. No praise for doing it right and all kinds of hell for one mistake. But this situation is even worse. Reid not only cannot win, he cannot escape with full self-respect intact. If you second-guess another ump you quickly become an outcast among your peers, who are as patient as the devil himself in waiting for their opportunity to hang you out to dry. And if you allow one bad call to stand, a manager will never let you live it down, even if he knows you had no choice but to do what you did.

"Leaving shit like that lay around on the field doesn't get you any closer to the majors, son," the old pitcher is saying to Reid now, calm and almost polite as he stands in front of Reid and goes for the jugular. Reid tells him the call has been made and the inning is over. "There's no real purpose served," the manager goes on, as if Reid had not spoken. "It leaves a big brown ugly spot on the outfield and in your record. You don't think somebody from the League's not up there? You have a chance, son, and the guys that make the majors don't pass those chances up."

Reid turns away, hating the line the manager is taking with him because it is the perfect blend of fatherliness and con. He starts up the first base line, seeing his own instant replay of the short-hop catch in left. Kammler, still out behind second, does not move. He is smoothing the infield dirt with the toe of his shoe. "One call like that sticks with the guy," the manager is saying now. "You eat one here and you'll be eating them the rest of your short umpiring life." Reid knows he is right. And that Kammler is not worth protecting. It is only Kammler's connection with the other umpires in the league that holds Reid back. "Nestor Chylak had a call almost exactly like that one time," the manager all but coos into Reid's ear. "It's tough, I know." Reid realizes that he has changed his own course, and is headed out toward Kammler. He tells himself that it is only a coincidence, but the drumming of his heart at his neck tells him otherwise. He thinks of the fact that he is doing this godforsaken, impossible job for $3700 a summer—that he is out here in the sticky dust and tobacco juice night after night for practically nothing. There is no justice in having to handle two full teams of highly unreasonable men for $57 a night. He wonders what federal mediators make, sitting in air-conditioned offices with people who do not curse them. He straightens, looks at Kammler, pushing the murmuring of the manager's voice out of his head.

"You okay?" he says to Kammler.

Kammler looks up, feigning surprise. "I hit that little dip there, behind short, as he went for it. Could've bounced my head a little." He looks down again, at his infield dirt.

Jesus Christ, Reid thinks above the renewed protests of the Prestonburg manager, he's caving in like a mud dam. Why the hell didn't he do something himself? Why stand out there like some kind of Kraut statue and hope it will all go away, or that the other guy will handle it? Reid fights the intense heat in his face—made of both pity and anger for Kammler—and asks him if he saw the play as a trap.

"Could've been," Kammler says, this time not even raising his head. And all at once Reid is ready. His hatred for Kammler becomes complete, as does his realization that the game is totally his to handle. All of this mingles with his need to see justice prevail. There is simply no call to be an umpire if you aren't after justice, in every sense of the word. Reid remembers that from umpiring school. And he hears his own words to others as he explains why he is a bush league umpire—the courts may get prostituted by plea-bargaining and the inequalities of social station, but on a baseball field, and maybe nowhere else in the world except on a baseball field, there is only one answer. You are either safe or out. There is no second degree safe or involuntary out or any of that crap. Reid starts to go to Kammler, to at least put on the appearance of having conferred and reached a mutual decision. But in his distaste for the older man he turns away and starts toward the plate. He motions for the Blueston manager, who is already running toward him, having read Reid's body as it moves resolutely toward change. "Oh no," he is screaming. "Oh no you don't. Oh no, oh no, oh no. This isn't the Pony League, you little runt, where the daddies talk you into the calls. This is goddamn professional baseball. There is money on the line here, you little runt. This isn't fucking Sunday afternoon slow pitch." Reid tells him to shut up, which has no effect whatsoever, and so Reid begins his explanation in a soft voice, into the rantings.

"The infield umpire and I have conferred," he begins, "and have agreed that the ball was trapped, as we all saw. Therefore, the batter will be at first, the runner at third will come home, and the runner at second will advance to third. There are two outs. Blueston will take the field." He turns to walk away, hoisting his chest protector into place and pulling his mask down over his face.

"Like hell we will," the Blueston manager is screaming. "Like hell. I won't play another goddamn second with you out there making it up as you go along. What's the goddamn sense?"

Reid sets himself behind the plate, as if it might be a haven from the chaos around him. Behind him, at last, the baiters have caught on to what is happening, and are warming to the task. "Look at God out there in the ump uniform," somebody—a female—is screaming. "He runs the world. Reverses history. Walks on water." And then, with the license and encouragement provided by the

female voice, the men begin to curse Reid unmercifully. He is a
runty motherfucker and they'll run him out of the league and the
state. He couldn't umpire with binoculars strapped to his face.
Where did he leave his guts? There is a place in Russia for him and
other traitors and yellow bellies. Why didn't his mother ever teach
him not to make up stories? How much is Prestonburg paying
him to screw over the home team? How long have he and the
Prestonburg manager been queering around together? His ass is
grass. They could find better umpires at the state hospital. And on
and on.

   Reid stands unmoving, suddenly lifted above it all with a vision
of a headline in a newspaper about an umpire being beaten to
death in some obscure southern town on a hot summer night.
With a "Sixty Minutes" crew doing a follow-up investigation.
Reid can see Mike Wallace standing in left field, pointing down to
the spot where the short-hop catch was made. Reid turns toward
the Blueston dugout. "If Blueston is not on the field in thirty
seconds," he says just loudly enough to be heard, "then we will
have a forfeit. It makes no difference to me. This is my game to
call and I will call it correctly." He aims his comments toward the
old shortstop, who is the only person on the field who is his own
height. "You saw him short-hop it, same as I did."

   "Go to hell," the manager says. "Don't tell me what I saw. You
don't go around undoing a baseball game. You want to go back to
the second when you blew that 2-2 pitch to my cleanup hitter?
Maybe we should go back to the first when you called two strikes
in a row on pitches that were down at the shoe tops. Huh, what
do you think?"

   Reid says nothing, refusing to give the manager anything to use
for fuel. Reid can see that he is calming slightly, can see that the
manager knows the umpire is right, and is now doing no more
than going through the obligatory motions of winding down, so
that his team does not lose respect. "Look, if you're going to
change one, you have to do it right away," he is saying now, almost
as if giving Reid advice. "You don't walk around the field for
twenty damn minutes getting your nerve up." He is shooting both
arms up in the air as he talks, in a good imitation of Earl Weaver
in front of a national TV audience. But his words are now much
softer than his gestures. "These are kids out here. They have to

know what to expect. You can't be surprising them all goddamn night." He is heading for the dugout. "Baseball isn't supposed to have trick endings," he says over his shoulder, and then looks ahead to the dugout. "Get the hell out there," he screams at his bench, and the softened din behind Reid erupts again. Someone is hitting one of the support poles with something—a bat perhaps—and the noise is deep, hollow and awful. Reid can feel it go through his head. For the first time he wonders if there is a cop in the place. Or anyone who has some sense, some perspective. "Give them twelve outs this inning, ump. What the hell's the difference?" the tirade begins, and deteriorates from there.

At last, when some order is restored and the baserunners are in position, and Pat Lucas has greeted Reid by going through an extended imitation of someone throwing up, the PA man behind Reid asks the crowd for its attention. "The Blueston Braves are playing this game under protest." Reid starts to spin around, knowing that the announcer has made it up. But he checks himself, repeats his order to play ball, and hitches the shin guard, all at once aware that through the whole hellish sequence he forgot it, and survived with the looseness. He allows the pitcher six warm-ups and they are ready to go. The Prestonburg hitter settles in and Reid tells himself to block out the crowd and get back to the game. The big Blueston pitcher goes into his windup and throws. And just as Reid starts to move his right arm up to call the pitch a strike, he suddenly realizes that Pat Lucas is not going to catch the ball. The fat red neck is falling off to one side of the plate, as if in collapse. Reid realizes that the ball will hit him at the precise moment that it does indeed hit him—high on his upper left thigh. He buckles as the pain registers, immediately grateful for the cup and the fact that the slight break of the ball at the end and his own beginnings of an attempt to jump have spared his genitals. He is aware of cheers from behind the plate as his face hits the soft red dirt of Callis Field. He raises himself back to one knee almost immediately, to watch the field. He is trying to decide if the ball is dead or in play. It has rolled up the first base line, as though he has bunted it with his thigh. Of course it is a live ball. And the runner from third has broken for the plate. The Blueston first baseman scoops the ball with his glove and in the same motion flips it to Pat Lucas, who has raised himself to one knee also, bumping Reid as he does. Lucas takes the throw, whirls and waits for the runner, who realizes he will be out, and therefore barrels into Pat Lucas as hard as he can. Pat Lucas tumbles back through the batter's box but holds onto the ball, and while Reid gives the out call from his kneeling position, Lucas goes after the runner with his mask. Both benches empty immediately, and for one brief moment, when he realizes he cannot yet stand, Reid imagines himself being crushed to death by two groups of sweaty young men fighting over a chunk of rubber set down into the ground at the far edge of some little no-name, no-count town. He has had dreams like that—when there are nine pitchers instead of one, and he has to call all the pitches at one time. As he tries to stand Reid sees Kammler arriving at the plate. He does not come to Reid, but goes to the fight, which is already being broken up by both managers and some of the players. The crowd is at the screen, and as the fight subsides Reid wonders what has kept them from breaking onto the field. Finally, as players begin to straggle back to dugouts, the Blueston manager comes to check on Reid. "Leave him down there," comes from the crowd, several times. Reid accepts the manager's hand and pulls himself to a tentative standing position. As he tries to put weight on the leg Reid hears the manager saying that the fat catcher will never play again for the Blueston Braves. Reid has to fight off the urge to tell the manager that it is Reid's decision on who gets kicked out of a game, and then nods and moves to dust off the plate. "Aw, the little blind guy hurt hisself," comes from behind him. Reid straightens, turns—now not caring what they say—and searches openly for Ellen.

As if to frame the events of the inning—as if to put them into glaring focus—the rest of the game ebbs away peacefully. In their half of the eighth the home team goes in order. In the top of the ninth Prestonburg gets a runner to second with one out but strands him. In the bottom of the ninth, with the crowd thinning and the throbbing in Reid's leg building, the Blueston leadoff man hits a long drive to left that just clears the fence, making the score 2-1, Prestonburg. "Hey ump," comes from a remaining baiter, "you realize the score is now one-nothing us? Do you, you blind cripple?" Another Blueston runner reaches with one out, but the last two hitters strike out against the little left-hander, and the game ends.

As the teams and the umpires head across the field to the club-house beyond the outfield fence, Reid walks alone, trying to minimize the limp, while Kammler talks to the Prestonburg pitching coach, and others walk in little clumps of three or four—motioning, pointing, gesturing—recapping the game. For all but Reid, perhaps, it is no more than one game in the Southern Mountains League schedule, now ready to be tucked away into the records. Another little pile of statistics that will find their way into *The Sporting News* and little newspapers here and there around the country. Reid watches Pat Lucas, perhaps the only other person walking alone on the field, and allows himself one brief moment of feeling sorry for the red-necked fat kid, whose baseball career will consist of three or four games in a rookie league. Back in his hometown—Reid pictures him being from a dying coal town in Pennsylvania—he will brag about the time he took an umpire out with a fastball and got the runner at the plate on the same play. Reid has been a part of the forming of one boy's legend and claim to fame. Reid envisions Pat Lucas as a drunk, semi-toothless man of forty, going to the same bar every day to see if there might be someone who has not heard the story of the catcher and the ump and the play at the plate.

Reid decides that Ellen has met someone new since the last time he was in town, and she has decided that the easiest way to let him down is to just not come back. Reid views this speculation with a calculated calm, as if the events of the evening need a cap—to be sure that he can maintain in the face of total adversity. Near the gate in the deepest part of center field he catches sight of someone running along the fence. He glances up and sees the flat-top baiter moving at bouncing-gut top speed toward the opened gate. He is carrying a bat, and Reid understands immediately what is happening. Ahead of him, the players have not seen the man, and Reid does not call out to them. He brings his chest protector up into his left hand, and prepares to protect himself once again.

"You lousy motherfucking asshole," the man screams as he comes through the gate, and the screams alert those in front of Reid. "You got no reason to pick on Blueston. This is a championship town and you are screwing it all up. And you aren't going to do it anymore."

As the man nears Reid three or four players move in and tackle him easily, and as he lies on the ground Reid sees tears in his eyes. Reid sees the face as if it is being presented to him in a slowed-down pace—almost as if he can see what will happen a fraction of a second before it does. In the eyes Reid sees a boy who grew up in the town and who has perhaps never been out of it, a man who has perhaps held one of the jobs that aren't there any more. As the players rise and move the man back outside of the field a policeman arrives from out of nowhere, so far as Reid can tell, and the drunken fan, now crying freely, is led passively away. Reid waves toward the players as they look back at him just before re-forming their clusters.

In the umpire's showers—they have separate stalls in only two of the Southern Mountains League towns—Kammler is off-hand, nearly jovial. "Good goddamn thing we don't get one of those every night," he says over the opaque divider. Reid is not sure whether he means the blown call or the game as a whole. He does not ask. "How's the leg?" Kammler goes on.

"It's all right," Reid says. Actually, it is a deep, red-purple color, and is raised in the shape of a large male breast. He has tried to touch it to gauge the depth of the injury, but has not been able to. Toward the bottom half of the circle are stitch imprints, almost as perfectly distinct as on a baseball. Reid moves the leg constantly in the shower, trying to keep the swelling and tightening from becoming too severe.

"At least I get the plate tomorrow night," Kammler is saying. "Save you some bending."

"Right," Reid says. He is not sure he will be able to walk, much less run into the outfield to cover fly balls. For one brief moment he considers walking out. He could get in his car and start for Fremont, as soon as he is dry and dressed. He could be there in twenty hours, and walk into Dr. Branch's office and have him look at the leg. He wonders what keeps him here—what real reason there is to stay. With sabotaging catchers and no-show women, he can think of none. But he pushes the thought aside as quickly as it occurred to him, amid new visions of a league commendation as a result of his handling of the game. But of course there was no one from the league in the stands, and so his only hope is that something will come from one of the managers, who don't tend to think past the next day's pitcher, a cold beer, and payday, so far as Reid can tell.

He touches his upper thigh as lightly as he can with a towel, while Kammler is still in the shower, singing Kenny Rogers songs in a voice that is as bad as his umpiring. Kammler, who teaches junior high school history in the off-season, once told Reid over four or five beers that he still thought he could be a pretty fair MOR country singer if he put his mind to it. Reid almost laughs aloud as he remembers this through the pain in his leg. He pulls a yellow pullover down onto his chest, and then steps to the mirror to look at the bruise again. It is bright and large and alive, more riveting than the clump of his sex next to it. He knows he should go to the hospital. The only real benefit that the league offers is that if you are injured in a game they take care of it. Reid doubts he will go, and decides to admire his thinness in the mirror, the hang of the yellow shirt at his waist, the sturdy look of his legs. He grimaces as he bends his left leg to pull up his underwear, and then repeats the pain with dark blue slacks. He slips his sockless feet into cordovan penny loafers, throws his baseball clothing into the laundry cart, and puts his soap and shampoo into his bag. He combs his hair back so that it will dry light and full as it falls back forward, and tells Kammler he'll see him back at the hotel or something.

"You want to wait?" Kammler says, sounding almost offended. Reid is not sure why Kammler wants him to wait. They have not spent an evening together since their first three or four games together. Reid wonders if the older man is offering protection from the bat wielder. Or is just lonely himself, or if he perhaps is looking for a way to apologize for the blown play.

"I think I'll go ahead," Reid says. Outside he decides to be wary, but sees nothing. There are only four or five cars on the forlorn rock lot just outside of Callis Field, and the moon-tinted expanse of space away from the cars appears to be empty, without threat. Reid walks even more slowly now, allowing himself the knowledge that the leg may really need attention. He doesn't know a doctor in Blueston, but is sure that there is one associated with the Braves. He pictures the doctor refusing to treat him, berating him for bad calls, and telling him to see an eye specialist. He is all the way to his car before he realizes that the front tires are flat. He throws his bag against the hood of the car—a six-year-old Toyota Corona he inherited from his father—and then winces as he tries to stoop to see if the tires have been cut or just deflated. He holds his bad leg out straight behind him as he bends to look. Halfway down he comes up again and spins around, fists formed.

"No," she cries, as if already hit. "It's me."

"Jesus," he says, "don't sneak up . . ."

"I'm sorry." She is moon-lit, damp-looking. A plain, thin white blouse allows her tan to show through, even at night. The blouse is tucked into newish blue jeans. Several fingers of each hand are stuck down to the second knuckle in tight front pockets as she narrows her shoulders as a part of an apology. "I guess I really did want to surprise you though. I saw you and Fred Southmire . . ."

"Who?"

"The guy with the bat. I'm sorry I'm so late, Lenny, but Michael has a fever and kept crying, and I really get worried over a fever in summer. I kept trying to leave and Mom kept telling me to. What happened to your leg?"

"I got hit," Reid says, "with a fastball. And now my goddamn tires are flat. How come I didn't see you when you saw this Fred guy?"

"I was on my way in from out here, and then I stopped and decided to let you go ahead and shower. I thought it might embarrass you to have the girl show up right after this guy tries to club you. I have my car, Len." She motions toward her car, an old red Impala that Reid, in his pain and anger, failed to recognize. "I'll get Triple A to come out for you." She touches his arm lightly now, as if sensing that he needs to be approached tentatively.

"Just let me look at the tires," he says.

She pulls more strongly at his arm. "It's okay, Lenny, it's okay. They'll fix it. And we'll get Southmire to pay for it. He's always sorry the next day, and he's one of the few still on at the foundry, so he can handle it. And he will." She guides him away from the Toyota, taking his bag. She moves her arm around his waist, as if to help support the bad leg. Reid conquers a momentary urge to limp more severely, to lean into her. As they move toward her car the first breeze of the night hits the back of his neck.

His body moves in sympathetic motions with hers as she moves him toward the driver's side of her car. He has always driven when they are in a car, and the injured leg will not keep him from doing it now, especially since the car is an automatic. At the wheel, as he turns and looks back over his right shoulder to back the car out, she slides herself in beneath his arm, and brings her own arm across his stomach as she pushes her head to his chest in a soft, quick hug of sympathy and apology.

On the empty little road toward town Reid glances back at Callis Field. The mountain behind it is silhouetted by the moonlight, and the angles of the gates and walls around the field are softened by the light and the huge dark mountain behind them. On down the road the town is still distant enough to be unspecific—to be made of a spread of lights which are yet so small as to be mistaken for reflections of the stars. The tall foundry buildings at the western end of town reach up into the night as if in competition with the mountains for the light of the moon. As Reid drives with Ellen next to him, the town is somehow transformed. Covered with night, it takes on the little-town virtues she talks about so often, and which excited Reid when he first got out a map to see where his new Southern Mountains League job would take him. With her narrow shoulders beneath his arm, he is able to allow her to embody the feel and spirit of the sweet southern town he had expected to find. It is the feel of the shoulders that overtakes him as he aims the car along the last ridge before the road turns to pass the flat-roofed restaurants and bars that signal the beginning of downtown. The dull throb of his leg is all at once no more than evidence that he has done his work for the day and done it well, and has earned this drive into the night. He is poised just then— still high above the harshness of the town, and at the first soft edge of love for the woman.

W. A. Smith

DELIVERY

(from *FM FIVE*)

Emerson Johnson joined up soon after FDR finished his Day of Infamy declaration to Congress. Emerson was twenty-five, putting the final touches on his internship. He and Grace had not yet celebrated their first anniversary when he left. But Grace said later that they both knew he would be coming back.

"So much we hadn't done," she explained.

When the Japanese surprised most of the hemisphere that Sunday in December, Grace was watching a football game with friends. Emerson was an avid fan, but he couldn't be there. He was assisting his father in a delivery which, as it turned out, was not one of the uncomplicated ones we're used to hearing about. Emerson's father, Charley, received a phone call from a man who said he was not the husband, "just a good friend." The man was nervous. He spoke in a whisper that sounded like cold wind blowing through pine, telling Emerson's father that the woman was in awful pain, the baby was coming any minute. "She could die," the man said. Emerson and his father grabbed their black bags and drove to a tenement house on Spring Street.

The woman was lying on a pale cloth mat in the front room. The man was bent over her. There was a sofa, a little wooden table, and two straight-backed chairs. The man's huge hands clenched and opened in dull, broken movements; his eyes stared down at her as if she were at the bottom of a canyon. Emerson's father whispered, "If he's not the husband, there isn't one."

The man told them she had slipped down a flight of stairs two days before. "Should've been there to catch her," he mumbled. The elder doctor looked at his son and said they must get her to the hospital quickly. This was not going to be so easy. Emerson bent down to her, running his fingers through her damp hair, telling her to relax as much as she could. "Have you chosen a name?" he asked.

Each breath was a moan, but she never cried out. Her eyes were open, tracing the comfortable, imperfect line which joined the wall and ceiling. In a clear disciplined voice she said, "Been tryin' to have a baby, seems all my life. Figures I'd stop thinking 'bout it so much and then it'd happen."

She closed her eyes. "Some doctor told me I couldn't have one," turning her face toward the three men. "Said I weren't fertile." She looked at Emerson who still had his fingers moving through her hair. "What you say now?" she asked.

Emerson's father shook his head, pressing his hand against the woman's bloated abdomen. The baby wanted to come in an unorthodox position, its head was wrong.

"I didn't know she was like this," said the man, hands still working the dark air near his pockets. "Not 'til a couple weeks ago. Been outa town." He lifted his eyes from the woman and glanced confidentially at the two doctors. He carried his own hoarse whisper like a cross, sounding as if he wanted to offer his life story right then. "Complete surprise," he said and fell silent.

At Roper Hospital they did a caesarean, attempting to free the child, but he was stillborn. The woman was too weak to withstand the sight of her lost son; she was fifty-two and undernourished. She died on the table with Emerson's left hand on her porcelain forehead. The man who was not her husband had already left the hospital when the two doctors emerged from the delivery room. Their hands dangled uselessly at their sides.

Shortly afterward Emerson left for basic training. In two months he was overseas. There was never any question about going. He promised Grace that he would be back. "Honor and luck will triumph," he said, smiling, then grave: "You and I have so much more to do." He told her he loved her as life's twin. Emerson expected to be a poet in those days.

He was a doctor in his twenties with the marksman's dream painted on his thin helmet. Three and a half years, cutting and tying off, speaking calmly as he'd been taught. "I'm learning this new surgery on my knees," he wrote . . ."bending over the faces' face, needing more hands and tools, more light."

In Belgium, quite by accident, he ran into an old friend from Charleston. He and Cambridge Walker had known each other since before they were born, and Emerson thought the chance reunion was some sort of miracle. They spent an afternoon together. "We were meant to see each other over here," he wrote to Grace. "Each of us was to know the other was surviving."

Emerson and Cambridge had their picture taken standing in a field under the only tree in sight. The light behind them clings like ice to the branches. The expression on their faces makes it seem for the moment there is no war near that place; they might be on a weekend camping trip. Their friendship retouches the photograph. They have their arms around each other's shoulders, relaxed, and Emerson is wearing the vest that Grace sent to keep him warm. Bridge looks as though he has a good joke to tell, soon as the shutter clicks.

Twenty-two years later, Emerson's father, Big Charley, bought a mahogany box with brass handles on the sides and a drawer beneath. He said it looked to him like a music box that could play a symphony. He polished it. Emerson's mother lined it with material from a pair of Army cavalry pants that Big Charley had worn in 1917, during The Great War. In the box they arranged the medals awarded to their son for his part in World War II, "The second one to end 'em all," as Emerson's mother put it.

When the lid of the box was raised, three black cases with gold lettering announced the Silver Star and the two Bronze Stars. Inside the bottom drawer two Purple Hearts and a rainbow of campaign ribbons lay pinned to the olive lining, glistening as if sunlit.

Emerson's parents presented the gift to him on his forty-fifth birthday. When he unwrapped the box and glimpsed its contents he was overcome for a moment, as if he were standing again in some flame-hardened field on the other side of the world. This was the first time Emerson's son, Charley, understood that if he watched closely enough he could see his father's memory working, flashing recorded light there in his dark brown eyes.

Charley once happened upon his mother as she stood in the den, her back to the door, looking down at the mahogany box. Grace ran her hand lightly across the top of it. Charley could tell his mother thought she was alone in the room. She whispered to herself with sad affection. "Above and beyond the call of duty," she said.

The boy looked in the box and smelled the ancient green of his grandfather's cavalry pants. He saw the Purple Hearts, George Washington's cameo face, and he thought of the horseshoe-shaped scar on his father's skull.

When Emerson was still bald from the operation, he traced that scar with an index finger and told his son that a good friend, and great surgeon, had sewn the horseshoe for luck.

"Frank went in there to take a look," he said. "Nothin' but some scar tissue." Emerson patted his shiny head and pulled on the purple fright wig which friends had given him as a joke. He screwed up his face and rolled his eyes at Charley, making the boy laugh. "Now," he said in a clown's bitten voice, "we wait and see. Any way you look at it, Son, I'm better off than I was."

In Czechoslovakia, 1944, a sniper's bullet had found the right side of Emerson's head as he was searching for a pulse along the neck of a young corporal. The blast threw both men into a foxhole. The corporal survived, and Emerson went on to write a handful of poems during his convalescence. One or two years later a certain numbness began to come and go on his left side, in the leg and hand. It drifted in and out. Emerson conjectured that there might be a slight circulatory deficiency, but he kept it to himself. He was young and alive. He was home.

One humid Sunday in 1964, while he was mowing the largest field near the house, his left leg went to sleep on the job. It was not just dozing. It didn't report the time off and apparently gave no consideration to the consequences of its inaction. Emerson had bought one of those large rideable lawnmowers equipped with a seat that unhooked from the machine if the human would rather walk. The doctor elected to ride because the fields were expansive and the numbness sometimes made it unpredictable to walk over uneven ground. He cherished working the land when he had the time off.

He directed the lawnmower in wide, surgical rectangles, thinking about the elegance of an open field. Executing a turn at one end, he hit a hole and the jolt knocked his left foot off the safety bar, but he didn't feel it dislodged. His sleeping limb, numb from the thigh to the toes, trailed in a dream. Before Emerson could do anything the foot was wrenched back and the wheel of the buggy contraption ran over it, jerking him clean out of his seat. Falling, he felt tissue separating from bone, heard ligaments snapping. He called out in pain, but Charley, who happened to be playing with his pellet rifle behind the house, figured the noise came from near the pond; most likely one of those bitchy geese, he thought—then recognizing his father's voice hidden in the stretched, anxious sound and running toward it.

Charley saw Emerson on the ground with his head on one edge of deep grass and the rest of him curled into a tight fetal position on the freshly mown strip of field. The scent of cut grass thickened the air around him. The lawnmower had stopped a few feet ahead, idling, waiting for Emerson to get back on. He clutched his left leg at the knee, and was very quiet, as if any sound greater than a whisper might further injure him. Charley was frightened seeing him like that, so unlike a father.

Emerson's jaw looked as though it had been wired shut. He squeezed the words out: "The safety bar works only while you're on it," he said.

All the cartilage in his knee was severed. He was in the Veterans' Hospital off and on for a year. Once on a weekend home he got up to change the channel on the TV, lost his balance and fell. A week later the doctors discovered a hair-line fracture of the left hip. Emerson said, "Been tellin' you guys for a week something was broken." He looked at the white coats around his bed, gazed at the grey ceiling. . . . From that time on Emerson's left foot was three sizes larger than its mate, forever swollen, and his cane accompanied him everywhere.

The first seizure had come earlier, sneaking up one afternoon in October, 1950. It only hinted at the possible voltages. Emerson was thirty-five years old, a practicing neurologist with a four-year-old daughter. Grace was six months pregnant. If she had a son, they'd decided to name him after Emerson's father.

Emerson was offered a shoe shine as he walked past Frampton's barber shop on Broad Street. He accepted and took a seat. Pigeons and a few stray sea gulls laced the clear sky. The doctor whistled an old Army tune. His right shoe, dappled with spit, was being buffed to a blaze by a small, quick black boy who was eight years old. Right off the boy told Emerson he was eight.

"Maybe I young, but I can shine dem shoe."

"Hey," said Emerson, "don't be hurryin' to get older." He reached over with his right hand and felt along his numb left leg. "You'll be there before you know it," he told the boy.

His left leg shivered, independent of his upper body. His eyes blinked and something dark, blue, squeezed his left eye shut. His right eye closed then too, completing the darkness, and his head laid itself back so that he faced the sky. There was a voice before the face floated up below him.

"What you say now?" she asked him.

A voice the color of birch trees, her face the same. Watching the woman's averted blue eyes, Emerson could tell that she saw her son, suspended above her in Big Charley's hands, dead before he'd tasted a minute of light. The cord stretched between them, and the young doctor felt that he might reach out and grasp it.

A short bolt of electricity knocked his left foot off the brown shine box the boy had set it on. "What you say now?" Emerson repeated with his eyes still closed.

"I say keep dat foot up here an' it'll get what the other got," the boy said. He was a little irritated. "White folks!" he muttered, knowing this dreaming old man wouldn't hear him. He lifted Emerson's foot back on to the box.

Doctor Johnson sat quietly. Finally he opened his tired eyes and saw that several jagged clouds had crept into the sky. He wondered what had just happened to him, and he knew.

Wallace Whatley

SOMETHING TO LOSE

(from *The Southern Review*)

One time I loved an old lady. And I gave her a hard time. She lived next door, and I think she loved me back. Because she gave me a hard time too. I know she enjoyed giving me a hard time. I could see it in her eyes. And they say I was the only one who could make her laugh anymore.

She would shake with laughter and lose her breath, then catch it again and shake some more until water came out of the corners of her eyes. She never cried dramatically. It just leaked out all the corners of her eyes and seeped down to the first wrinkles and filled them and overflowed and then dropped down another level, all of these tears out of control slowly filling the little cradles under her eyes. Then her face would gleam with this crying laughter and she would pick up her old husband's newspaper still rolled with the rubber band holding it around the middle and throw it at me. Not too hard and seldom hitting me. So I knew she didn't mean it. It was just her way of getting shed of me as she put it. I wouldn't go without a show of force of some kind. And she never minded showing some.

You should have seen us run off the Fire Chief when we set her back lot on fire.

"Damn you, Squirrel, you can get your ass off my property!"

The Chief had this unfortunate nickname from his childhood. It was Squirrel. I think he had been a loner, a real squirrel hunter as a young man growing up in the country, quiet, sober, and respectful, the classic loner. As Chief of the Opelika Fire Department he was still a loner, if that is possible in a chief. But he was a good chief and never seen out of uniform: the laced and polished black work boots, matching suspenders and snappy white hat with the brass badge on the front. But he hated his nickname, and no one ever called him that to his face except my old friend.

Finally, she was the only friend I had. The dusty room of her older son—John's room—was full of balsa models of painted biplanes hanging on the walls and from the ceiling, and aeronautical magazines and manuals and engineering and navigational texts shelved neatly in every cabinet and bookcase and stowed away under his bed, which was made as tight as a barrack's cot. And she made all of these things available to me, the planes and the books and magazines, the wrinkled leather aviator's helmet, the souvenir hulls of old cannon shells. In these magazines were the photographs of small and curiously shaped stunt craft and racing planes, of seaplanes and of lumbering bombers with as many bubble turrets as an insect has eyes. And there were air buses and midget planes and the newest lethal, sleek pursuit planes. And around these planes always stood young men in baggy coveralls and the same leather helmets with the goggles pushed up on their heads studying plans or charts spread out on a wing.

The house was huge with only my friend and her husband in it those times he was home, and then he was somewhere silently reading an evening paper. So we had it to ourselves. Or I had it to myself, since she seldom came out of the breakfast room. I had it to myself sharing it with a rusty old black man named Mose who never spoke but pumped his broom and mop and dusted with a turkey-feather whisk and kept it clean. Mose kept it very clean, every long hardwood floor resplendent as a surface of black water flashing with sun where it streamed in through clouds of linen along the windows. There never was any company, so Mose's job was easier for that—a high-ceilinged old house of such space and silence that pigeons were enticed from the sills of the second floor windows to fly through the long bedrooms and out at the other end those times Mose raised windows there in the spring.

But John's room, as high-ceilinged and still as any of the rest, on the first floor across the hall from the kitchen and so the nearest room to it on the morning-sun side of the house, seemed to me the only one of them all somehow lived in. And it was my favorite, smaller than the rest and more narrow and still and quiet and untouched, with its wallpaper of a color and grain like a photograph kept a long time in the bottom of a family trunk. In that room there was a scent, and a light and a quality amber and astringent as sherry, a sense of dust and purpose together. Only Mose and I ever went in. And I spent hours on the floor with the books and pictures in my lap, and the old lacquered airplanes fragile and exact to every detail on the walls, the expended brass of old shells green with corrosion standing as dividers and bookends on the shelves. And on a shelf of its own there was a heavy sextant which I did not bother, probably for its weight as much as mysteriousness, a beautiful instrument like the intricate skeleton of a little tent lifted over a sundial of heavy brass, graduated around the circumference with little serried indentures and numbers, green and black with age. Then there was the shoe box of old fireworks which we exploded that afternoon setting the back lot on fire.

She found an old Zippo lighter somewhere and we set them off one at a time, the dusty cherry bombs and silver salutes, whistling fountains, Black Cats and Roman candles and rockets, so many rockets, and they were every size. Balls of fire spewed away over our heads over the rooftops and trees into the sky visible over all of Opelika before they silently scattered into separate balls of pastel burning a moment before each thundered out with a bang. But the fireworks were old and some only fizzled in the grass, a tail of sparks wagging one way and another until they were exhausted, leaving their crooked path charred on the ground.

"Don't get too close, baby. You might burn yourself. And your mama wouldn't let me have no rest then. Get back now. Let's see what this one will do."

So there sat my old friend on the cement steps off her back porch, with the composure of a summer cloud, lighting firecrackers and tossing them out in the grass and laughing and exclaiming like the Fourth of July. When all of them were gone we simply sat behind the cloud of smoke we had made in a long, immensely satisfied quiet. There was smoke enough to obscure the whole backyard and the garage and the back lot too. Then through this thunderhead we had created appeared our neighbor, the Fire Chief, awakened I think from his after-dinner nap. Because suddenly there he was as if invited, looking into our smoke and stroking his chin.

"I assume you and the boy know the source of this," he suggested in that respectful manner like a man who had slept through a war.

"Get off my property, Squirrel, and mind your own damn business."

And he did, obeying in a second.

She cussed when it was necessary, and she drank a little Budweiser. One time I traded a watergun for a cob pipe and she let me smoke my first rabbit tobacco, showing me how you pick it out from the mullen and ragweed and goldenrod. And we put out the fire begun by a rocket falling on the back lot.

She was my only friend because I was too young for school. My father was out in Texas or Mississippi in the Air Force, and my older brother was in Korea with the activated Alabama National Guard. Mother sent him a birthday cake on his eighteenth birthday through the Fleet Post Office, and by the time that cake got to Korea he couldn't cut it with a bayonet. He cried. He told me later. He never told her. Mother was probably crying at the same time with our neighbor on the other side. Her husband didn't make it to Korea. He wasn't called. He flew in World War II and looked over his shoulder a lot when he was sober. So he and his wife and my mother sat in their kitchen and read my brother's letters together and cried. It was a wet year. Yet with its compensations.

In the thin airmail envelopes with his letters there would be yen notes from the Bank of Seoul with pictures and the sketchy maps of battles he had drawn for me on the back, drawings of stick men on opposite sides connected by dots coming out of their rifles. Once it was a tripod gun in a tree, and the story condensed to a sentence was this: "Wrenn Jr., I got the one in the tree." I was the only kid I knew with Korean money.

Mother put her head on the ironing board and cried. And the old lady and I played.

"Get a pasteboard box, Wrenn Jr., and let's pick up these sot robins."

They got drunk in her cherry tree every spring and fell off onto the ground like pine cones. And we took them up in a box and put them in a place safe from the cats.

"One day you gonna fall off my garage roof just like these damn robins." I guess this was our favorite battle.

Her backyard, taking up approximately a third of the residential city block with the new apartments on one side where my mother and I lived while my father and brother were away, and other, similar, old frame houses with scrolled porches and balconies on the other side, sloped down through the empty lot our fireworks set on fire to the shambling, paintless district where Mose lived. among his people. And lining the slope out on the lot's borders were all varieties of old fruit and ornamental trees brought from the country where she was from, somewhere way below Montgomery. There were turkey-fig and apple and pear and quince and peach trees, with a scuppernong arbor at the bottom, shady and cool to play in in the summer. But the garage roof was grand the year round. I got on this roof by a tree growing at the garage corner nearest our apartment. And there I would sit in the split leather helmet with the goggles pushed up on my head waiting for the nerve to jump or just watching the comings and goings over where Mose lived, until she appeared. Because of all I could do or get into, this upset her the most.

Her hair had already been white a long time, fine and short and shining like silk, and her face could shine like a sack of apples, for this made her mad.

And it went like this:

"Wrenn Jr., you get off that roof!"

"I'll jump down in a minute."

"You get down like you got up there if you don't want to break your neck."

Maybe the distance made me bold, the fact of the real leather hat and goggles, for I always demurred.

"You get down like I say!" she insisted.

"I'll get down when I get ready."

"If you don't get off that roof this minute, I'll call your nurse on you!"

"She can't do nothing, can't catch me."

"Then I'll call your mama!"

"She's gone visiting."

"Wrenn Jr., you get off that roof! I'm old enough to be your mama's mama, and I say come down! Now you do like I say!"

"I like it up here."

"You as stubborn as a mule. Now you gonna break your neck. Go on, break it then."

"Go back in the house and you won't see me."

"It's my roof and I'll look at it long as I please."

"That's the way I feel."

Then one day my brother came home and I let Mrs. Rencher alone for awhile. My brother let me follow him around, and one of the first things we did was to go and see his old girl friend. He wanted to see her so bad he got up early the first morning he was home and went to her house in his khaki with the trousers tucked in the top of his boots. It was so early the cold milk bottles were still on the front steps. We saw her lift a curtain corner in her room and look out right after we rang, then she dropped it back when she saw us looking, too quick even for us to wave. Her father came to the door and acted pleased as everything to see my brother but told him he was sorry but Cordelia had spent the night with a girl friend. And besides, the old guy said next, wasn't it a little early? We stood awhile after he shut the door, neither of us particularly knowing what to do. Then my brother reached down and took up the four white bottles of milk in the long fingers of one hand. Then he turned and leaned back and sailed those full bottles deep into the kudzu of a vacant lot across the street. His hands had grown long and strong in that year. But they were nervous hands, and his fingers shook so that he could not glue together a model plane.

Mrs. Rencher said, "Leave him alone, honey. He's got gettin'-use-to to do."

When I went in the back door off her kitchen porch she would often be in a small chair in the long, dim hall, seated by the little recess in the wall where the telephone was, a little recess about the size of an icon niche and an old phone, the base and stem and cradle kind with a separate receiver you hold to your ear. And she'd be on the phone with my mother, cackling a little in her pleased way as she learned of my brother's returning antics. She always preferred to phone rather than walk next door. It was why her husband had had it put in she said.

Then my father returned. And a few years later when I walked into the house with enlistment papers in a brown folder my father tried to break my arm. But he was old by then and my mother kept him from it. And now all of this is behind us as much as that can be.

The other day Mrs. Rencher died. Everyone close in any way and everyone else who remembered or had ever known her was prepared enough for this. She was old, and for months the realtor's sign had stood in front of the scrolled old house with the stained glass at the stair landing and on the second floor. Because I was expected in a meeting out of town I did not make her funeral.

"It was beautiful," my mother said. "They had her hair fixed, and her skin was as clear and beautiful as when we lived next door to her."

"Well, I wish I had been there," I said.

"They buried her beside John. You know, the words on his stone were the first words I ever heard you read," my mother said.

I wondered how we were on this topic now and asked what she had said.

"You remember John. He's on the terrace above your father as you go back toward the older part of the cemetery, back toward town."

"John, who died." I did remember.

"You remember, Wrenn. You played in his room. And she took you to the cemetery to put flowers on his grave every week. Mrs. Rencher drove, and Mose held the flowers. And that's the first thing I ever heard you read."

They are together a few rows above my father. I don't know what her stone will say, but his is there right next to it, an issued stone leached of color and inscribed

Lt. John L. Rencher

U.S.A. AIR CORPS

died in the service of his country

1920   1942

The mind of a child sifts. I'm sorry I missed your funeral. The meeting was not important, and I'll never forget. Here's to you, love.

Luke Whisnant

WALLWORK

(from *New Mexico Humanities Review*)

SWEAT

This is what you hear Bernard say as he hangs up the phone:
She got me booked two weeks in a row.

It's Regina and the sister in the kitchen with him, and Regina
says, Bernard, all right!

She's gonna get me a raise. She says if it all goes good I'll be at
four-twenty-five after Thanksgiving. Lookit, she got me booked
in Eastland Mall the 26th, 27th, 28th and in Plaza North the 30th
and the first. Then maybe next month I'll be going across the river.

You're lying prone on Regina's bedroom floor, pushing putty
into baseboard corners. Where the two boards, mitered at a 45°
angle, don't quite touch.

I knew you could do it, Bernard, Regina says. 'Cause I *know*
how you do.

That's right. If I got something I really want, I'll work hard and
get it. It's work that gets it. I'm a worker, boy. That's right.

You some hot shit, Bernard, the sister says.

I know it, too.

Bernard.

But see, what I'm worried bout's sweatin. See when I have to
talk in front of people I go and break out in sweat. The doctor says
it's when I start to talk in front—

You know he been like that all his life.

But she put me on the intercom. See, so I won't have to talk to people, just talk into this mike.

Well how we gonna get to see Bernard? We got to come see you, Bernard. How we gonna get way out there to East Land?

They don't have a car. They take the bus everywhere. The putty's cold and grey in your hand like thick toothpaste. Theirs is the last apartment in the building. You've been putting in new walls for days.

Bernard says it's not bad work. See, I'll carry this brochure 'cause there's just too much to remember. Lookit, see, there's four different models and they all got different features. You know, to keep 'em straight I got to pay attention—

Bernard be talking shit to all these old white women. Hoooeee. Old white women toting shopping sacks. With their diamond *jewels* on. Ah ha ha ha, Bernard.

That's right. Listen. That's right.

Bernard—

Now listen, lemme try it out on you. See. There's lotsa features. You can look down this column, see here, right here, it'll tell you— see this, *powerful two-way action,* you know, that means it sucks *and* it sweeps, too.

How much do this cost?

No, see, I don't do that; I'm not a salesman. No. See, I'm a *demonstrator.* I don't make commission. I get a flat rate per hour. You know. See few wanna buy one, I say, "Very good, that gentleman over there, Mr. Larry Brown, will be happy to take your order for the machine I've just described." See and then Larry Brown takes over and I go demonstrate the next one.

Huh.

Yeah, I don't sell. 'Cause see, you a salesman your whole livin depends on what people's buying. Like it snows one day. Nobody's gonna want to buy no vacuum cleaner. And then you don't make no money that day. It's seasonal, sales is seasonal. People don't buy no AC in January. Don't buy down jackets in June. But see, I'm on straight salary. So I'll always make *some* money, the same money every day so long as she can book me.

Bernard finally got him a job, the sister says.

Girl, don't you be making fun of Bernard, Regina says. He's gonna be bringing money into this house and that's more than you do.

They've forgotten you're there. You wipe your putty knife back-handed on your overalls and cock your ear.

SHRINES

For three weeks you have nailed and sawed, taped and sanded in Regina's third-floor apartment, splattering her verdant wall-to-wall shag with plaster dust and spackle, going goggle-eyed at the new pumpkin paintjob in the living room. Those orange walls! that green floor! and above the TV a strange framed photograph of a horse, with a jumble of vertical and horizontal runes as caption—meaningless when seen straight-on, but take two steps to the side, the lines converge, connect, to spell out the cryptic message JESUS. Christ in code, Jesus on the horsehead. . . . Before this you worked six days in a house where a woman had lived twenty years tacking every postcard sent her, every pretty magazine picture, every blessed Catholic newsclipping (*Pope Approves Grape Juice; Primate Blesses Pigs; Our Sister 3, Immaculate Word 2*) through four coats of wallpaper into her ninety-year-old plaster walls. Four red-headed thumbtacks per piece, a thousand holes per wall from waist-high to eye-level, and you fill them all with spackle. Six days it took, and it was so mindless, such desperately dull work, that you charged time-and-a-half and padded your materials double, a pretty penny but still not worth your trouble. Monkeys could have done it. And before that you and Breeze, your assistant, your high school dropout bandana'ed kid assistant, had spent a month re-wiring bathroom light fixtures in a highrise slum apartment building full of Cubans and Haitian refugees. By rights the job was too big for a freelance handyman and his boy go-fer, but you underbid and it helped that you speak *un poco de español*, however poor the grammar.

It is there you first find the shrines. They're all identical: a color Christ on cardboard backing, the kind churches hand out, propped in a corner and ringed by offerings: oil, lit candles, a pan of water, flower petals, a plate of limes. And not a single Cubano who'll look you in the eye. They sing calypso and chant and chatter, and ignore you as you rip from the walls their ancient wiring. You nudge Breeze in the ribs, mutter from the side of your mouth: See amigo, in voodoo is believed that Jesu, the Christ, he is a powerful spirit, probably the most powerful of all the others. This place is bad news, Breeze says, I can't wait to get outta here.

But you stay in the neighborhood, in this burned-out stretch of city which is too foreboding to support even a pawnshop. On one corner an abandoned grocery (*We Take Food Stamps; Hog Maws $1.09 lb; Hot Head Cheese*). Across the street, Eddie Soul's Marquis Lounge, "Disco Nightly—Up In Here," *Closed*. Next door is Artie's Liquors, brace of winos attached like suckerfish to sharks. A-1 Donuts—derelict. Laughing Sam's TV Repair—derelict. The derelict House of Beauty, whose sign you often misread from the corner of your eye, because of broken places in the letters, as "House of Reality." There is a chicken wing place and a chop suey joint, the Saigon Inn, and the rest is buck wild and edged as a razorblade, whores and pimps and tough boys and the mailman goes armed; the cops lock their prowl car doors. You're not afraid, as many whites would be, because you never carry money, not even a dollar, and because your face shows not fear or defiance but stoicism; it's a calm, any-age face and it looks in the eye anyone it meets. And because you know the neighborhood.

A ROOM

He is in a white room, wide white walls. You see him falling again, slow. You were yelling but now you cannot remember what. Scrabble, baby. Scrabble. You slouch on a shiny couch, smoking. Under *Patient's Name,* you printed Breeze, then drew a blank.

REGINA

Regina irons. She watches soaps, Sanford and Son, the Jeffersons, Family Feud. Here is how she laughs, a hundred times a day: Ah ha ha ha. Anticipating wrong answers, she yells at game show contestants, You're crazy, white man.

She bakes yams and ribs for supper. She vacuums up your plaster dust, daily. She watches Noon Report and says the President is too dumb to breathe, even.

She has a little girl, Doowanna, and a stepdaughter. Half-sisters, cousins. A dozen people drop in daily. Her father comes to bum whiskey money. You keep your eyes open, discern blood ties and allegiances. Claudette hates Jackie, Nadine's dad's in jail. But what is Bernard, nephew or lover?

Bernard, Regina says. She stands on tiptoe and kisses his cleft chin. Bernard my boy.

STORIES

One day you are sitting at a red light in the truck and two hookers slide up on either side. The windows are down, the heat shimmers off the street, and you look over, grinning, at Breeze. Both women wear one-piece jumpsuits with big gold zippers, and they giggle. Sweet whitemeat! Pull my string. Whatcha got for me today baby.

You send yours over to the kid's side, two of them leaning in his window, spilling out of their top-heavy suits. Breeze tries to laugh them off and keep their hands away from his crotch. Lemme sees what's in your pocket, sugar.

Nothing, Breeze says, smiling hard.

Well I sure feel *some*thing.

Let *me* feel, the other whore says.

You start to laugh. Breeze, you say, you're turning red. Breeze, you're blushing.

Drive, he yells. Just drive on!

One day you're interpreting for Feld, the owner of the voodoo shrine highrise. In the dark lobby you feel Breeze's bad vibes. Feld has collared one of his tenants, and he stands screaming to you: This greasy fucker's been lurking around the building, trying to get a look up some woman's dress, or worse. All day he rides up and down on the elevator and hassles people, all day he's in the halls. I've already had one family move out, living in fear of these Cubans. You speak spick, ask him what the hell he thinks he's up to.

The Cubano looks at you and shows his teeth.

El jefe dice, you say slowly, groping for words. You point to

Feld. El dice, porque es tu en el corridor? Siempre. Si? Todo el dia.

The Cubano puts his thumb in his nose and turns it.

The women are complaining, Feld says.

Los mujers, no le gustan.

No answer.

Don't you spit on my floor, Jack, Feld says.

The Cubano looks at the wall.

El jefe, no le gusta. Comprende? Si? I don't think I'm getting through, you say.

Then tell him this, Feld says. Tell him if I catch him molesting anybody again, or loitering out here, or even so much as *looking* at Mrs. Stovall's little girl again, he'll be out on his ear. He'll be out pronto, his ass'll be out on the street. Evictado, comprende, Jose? Tell him that.

But your Spanish has left you.

One day you are eating lunch on the second floor sunporch of an abandoned building and you see a black man detach himself from a group of street people and begin screaming: Stupid niggers! Goddamn apes! You all suck your granny's titties in the sewer water. With both hands he grasps his shirt at the neck and rips it down the front. He flings a broken plastic tricycle against a parked van. He staggers a few feet down the street to tear a young tree in half with a crack like gunshot. Hey, Conan the Barbarian, Breeze says. The people on the stoop are hooting and yelling taunts. One stands and hollers with simple eloquence, Your mama. He is laughing loudly, sarcastically. It's Bernard.

STREETS

These are the streets you work: Lowery, Spunt, Cooter, Hood. Skinker, which all the natives call Skink. Acme Avenue. Limit Avenue. Pitt Street. Gravois, pronounce the s. The place you live, miles west, is called Earth City. Streets there were named by NASA. Neptune Place. Alan Shepard Circle. Andromeda Court. You explain often that you're not making this up. Apollo Drive, Lunar Drive, Werner Von B Drive. Alpha Centuri Circle. Breeze lives further west, in Carondelet, do not pronounce the t, on a street named by his mother. It was a new development, he explains, and we were already living there when they paved the road and so they asked us to name it. The houses going up around him had lawns the size of football fields, garages big as barns, front porches garnished with pillars, soffits, fluting, fretwork. Breeze's mother wrote down the name for the city cartographers: Plum Nearly Lane.

LADDER

Breeze is going up with new shingles, he clutches at the gutter, you're bracing with both arms against the rungs, and there's something sharp suddenly at your throat.

This thing's honed fine, a voice says. You know where your carotid *artery* is?

You nod without looking. Breeze freezes on the ladder.

A different voice says, You ain't got to turn around or *nothing*.

They lift your wallet and go through it.

All the major credit cards. Two dimes in here for the phone. Stamps, a book of stamps. You loaded for bear, huh whiteman?

Ain't no money?

Hell no. Now what we gonna do with this fool?

Kill him.

What you come down here with no cash for? How you eat?

He got a charge account at Burger King. He scrounge garbage cans. He bring his lunch in a paper poke. Kill him.

Hear that, fool? We kill you for two dimes and a Sears card.

Take my truck, you say. There's a checkbook in the truck. Tools in the back you can hock.

Tools, shit. Truck, shit.

They back up a few steps, then turn to Breeze. Okay, our man on the ladder, one says.

Breeze still looks back over his shoulder. He throws down his wallet. Don't hurt him, you say. He's just a kid.

Shut up.

They kick the ladder out from under him. He's clawing at the roof, legs jerking, a rain of nails falling from his toolbelt, one torn black shingle flopping down like a broken bird. Scrabble, baby, one of the men cries gleefully.

They knock you down and run.

DOGHOUSE

Braced by bricks, rust-pitted, ragged-edged oil drum turned on its side. A skinny pup, tied up with swingset chain. A wilderness of glass, shards of brick and concrete, shambles. His muzzle forlornly protruding in the rain.

SPANISH

It is important to keep saying I did not see him fall. You keep telling yourself this. Look at the walls. But the doctor is shaking his head now and smiling. At Regina's you knocked out a wall with nothing but a 14-ounce hammer and a pry-bar; you built closets, a hall, cleverly added a bedroom, sculpting with sheetrock and two-by-fours, soffits, berms, arches. You lowered a ceiling to cover the new forced-air heating ducts. You laid new tile in the bathroom. Space is fluid, floorplan is, to be reapportioned and subdivided anew, so long as you never knock out load-bearing walls. When the kid hit the ground you could hear something snap. An ambulance. That is what you were yelling about. Blood was running into your eyes but you could see another man at the end of the alley, a dark, hispanic man listening to you call for help. He has recognized you. He sneers. He says, cuttingly, tough punk voice and spitting slow, as if talking to an idiot, Los mujers, no le gustan.

BERNARD

Months later you see him in a huge suburban mall, vast as a stadium, holding a pencil-thin microphone like a conductor's baton and speaking into it the words *stylish* and *variable speed,* slurring the second syllable of *variable.* Sun streams from the skylights two floors above. Women walk from display to display, caressing the sleek machines.

You wait for a break in the monologue and then you take his hand. Your name is Robinson, you say, and he smiles, puzzled, says that's right, glances down at his nametag: Mr. Robinson. He of course does not remember you. You're wearing a dark suit, you're bare-headed. On impulse you pull his hand, which you still grasp, up to your face, peer at the lines there, knit your brows. Your family calls you Bernard, you say.

That's right, Bernard says. How did you know that?

I see it in your hand. Your mother's name is Regina. Your sister is Claudette. You live uptown, on Ward Street.

Hey, Bernard says, confused.

Your apartment has three bedrooms. The livingroom walls are pumpkin, the shag rug's green. There's a picture of a horse over the TV and a bumpersticker on the bathroom mirror that says JESUS IS YOUR BEST SHOCK ABSORBER. Your mother smokes Winstons, your sister smokes Kools. The landlord's name is Kockle. You have new baseboards in your bedrooms.

Just who the hell are you, Bernard says, jerking his hand away.

When you have to talk in front of people you break out in a sweat. You've been like that all your life.

Bernard's mouth hangs open and you laugh. At first, when you started, you thought you'd explain, when the joke broke down and you could push it no further, that you'd been in the apartment, you'd put in the new baseboards. But now, on impulse, you turn and inexplicably walk away, with Bernard yelling, but only once, Hey, wait!

You don't bother looking back to see if he is following. You go deeper, into the heart of the mall. You know you can lose him, if you need to, in the press of people, in the miles of white floor and wide white wall.

Sylvia Wilkinson

CHICKEN SIMON

(from *The Chattahoochee Review*)

If you got behind a chicken truck going to the farmer's ex-change, it was like being in a snow storm. You could see the chickens huddled together in their cages and think they must be freezing to death, half-naked, their feathers blowing off. Then when the truck would stop at the one stoplight downtown, the snow storm would stop. That's where the loose chickens cackled and fluttered down to the pavement and took off running. They squeezed out through the broken bars or wiggled out of their slots between the cages where they had done like chickens do and hopped on the truck with the rest of their friends. The chickens ran down the alleys like old ladies with their skirts lifted, right into the arms of Summit's colored people, ending up in the cook pot faster than the ones on the way to the processing plant. They got their necks wrung instead of chopped, I guessed. The truck driver hardly turned his head when they squawked away. It wasn't his job to go off chasing loose chickens through the alleys of Summit.

When I was walking home from school one day—it was when I was a seventh grader—I saw a chicken marching around the dummies in the back-to-school window of Simon's Department Store which is the fanciest store in the whole town. I had decided to go past Simon's for the twentieth time at least to look at this red and green stitched-down pleated wool skirt with a kelly green sweater and a sweetheart blouse with the prettiest stick pin through the johnny collar I had ever seen. I figured it wouldn't be long before it was off that dummy and on somebody at school. The chicken reminded me of our head majorette the way she picked her feet up from the knee and held her head kind of high and snooty. She had to be smarter than your average chicken since she made it off the truck, across the intersection without getting squashed, and through the revolving door at Simon's. My mama quit going in Simon's when they put up that revolving door. I'm not saying that that chicken was smarter than my mama, but it was a little braver I think.

I figured the chicken liked the corn stalk–hay bale display because it looked like her long lost home on the farm. But Daddy told me they raised them on concrete floors. They turned the lights on and off three times a day so they would think the sun was rising and setting and lay three times as many eggs. He also told me how they did chickens at the farmer's exchange, tying them up by their feet to a wheel that turned them one by one to a pair of scissors that snipped off their heads. I told him he was making that up, but I wouldn't go with him to see him prove it.

I liked the looks of that chicken. I mean she acted like she owned Simon's window. Back before they put in the revolving door, Mama used to go "feeling" in Simon's; she never went shopping in there because she couldn't afford to buy anything. She always said if she got to be rich, she still wouldn't pay highway robbery in Simon's but she'd go feeling and make them be nice to her because they thought she might buy something. I saw the floor walker through the glass; he always followed me in there because he figured I was going to steal something. The chicken walked up and pressed the hay bale with feet fit for a rooster, like she was testing a feather bed, then she looked up and frowned. People were gathering around me and pointing and laughing. I went inside through the revolving door and almost got my booksack stuck. I can't see the point of those doors. Even the floor walker was laughing, watching her with his hands tucked under his arms like he was trying to keep them clean.

Then, right out of the blue, the hen went squirt-splat, a gray and white blop, plastered on the grade schooler's lunchbox behind her being reached for by a dummy hand. I couldn't believe the nerve of that chicken. I laughed too, the first thing I thought of being one of Daddy's unfunny jokes: "What's the white stuff in chicken shit? Answer: That's chicken shit too."

The people in front of the window were starting to walk away, one snotty old lady pinching her nose as if she could smell it through the glass anyway. I figured the chicken in the window display had outlived her welcome, as Mama would say. I also knew I was safe from another gray and white blop for a while, so I climbed into the display and picked her up. I knew how to hold a chicken properly, so it wouldn't scratch me. The janitor who was already there to clean the lunchbox glared at me so I hurried out before he told me the chicken wasn't mine and was going to be his supper.

I walked home with her, holding the yellow legs tightly that were cold as sticks, telling her about Summit.

"This is a pretty nice little town you picked, Miss Chicken, not too big, not too small. Over there is the grocery store where they sell all sorts of things—some of which I won't mention. You don't have to ever think about that again, ever. Nobody is going to pull out your feathers, at least over my dead body. The grocery does have a good supply of sunflower seeds and shelling corn and the feed supply can get you the mashed oyster shells you need for making eggs. Since chickens can't read, you don't know what's on at the movies. It's *The Yearling* which I sat through three times last Saturday.

"Now, Summit has its not-so-nice side too, I have to warn you, but mostly you can find that in there, the Rebel Bar. The one in the gray jacket whose hair needs cutting, or at least combing in the other direction over the bald spot, is my daddy which is why I'm whispering now. He used to be a farmer, but they took his land for taxes. The one with the pile of red dirt under his stool is Homer Crutchfield. He's still a farmer. You may have known him in your earlier life, so let's just slip on by so he doesn't see you.

"The library is in that old house. The roof leaks and has ruined some of the books, including the whole shelf of horse stories, which, thank goodness, I had already read. I was the first one to find out and tell the librarian about the water. Boy, to look so scrawny, you're getting mighty heavy, Miss Chicken. They must have fed you rocks or something. Those poles with boxes on them are the new parking meters. Turn your head towards the street, that's it, and you can see the place for the new library. The reason it has a faded sign on it now is because the bond issue didn't pass. That noise you hear is drums. Purp, purp, yourself. You like me pretty good, huh? That noise is the Summit High marching band, as I was saying before I was so rudely interrupted, just kidding, which is practicing for the first football game."

Miss Chicken hummed to me like she was interested in everything I said and never tried to get away. She came to be known as Chicken Simon after she moved in with us in the apartment. She got her exercise indoors running from my daddy who stayed about three sheets to the wind most of the time. She teased him, staying two steps ahead, cackling with the other two girls, until Daddy sprawled on the couch and passed out. Daddy said us hens had him outnumbered three to one and he just might bring home a weasel and a chicken hawk for his side. But Chicken Simon became a member of our family, making an egg a day in a shoebox nest as her present to us in exchange for a handful of corn. She was especially good at making eggs with two yolks. Once she left an egg in Daddy's shoe that he thought was a blister breaking on his toe. I thought it strange, that living with people and no other chickens, she still tossed her head back to swallow water and never seemed to think twice where she went to the bathroom.

That day after I found her at Simon's, when I climbed up the steps to our apartment, I had a funny feeling as if I was in a dream, taking home a chicken. All of a sudden the chicken felt so light I looked down to see if she was still there and of course she was. And the steps usually made me feel tired and my booksack heavy. I knew I was supposed to come straight home after school, but I felt a little dizzy. Not confused exactly, just swimmy-headed, as Mama would say.

When I reached the top step, Mama met me at the door. She clapped her hands together and they went "whoof" because they were still in her apron pockets. You'd have thought I had brought her home a bunch of flowers, not a bird that had been on its way to ending up on our table on Sunday after a trip through the Piggley Wiggley, a bird who had never felt dirt under her feet.

"Pearlie Sue," Mama said with a smile. "What a pretty chicken!"

BIOGRAPHICAL NOTES

Max Apple was born in Grand Rapids, Michigan, but has made his home, for the last 14 years, in Texas. Mr. Apple, who teaches at Rice University in Houston, is the author of several books of fiction, the most recent of which is *Free Agents*. A new novel, *Disneyad,* will be published in 1987.

Madison Smartt Bell was born and brought up on a farm just south of Nashville, Tennessee. He graduated from Princeton in 1979 and went on to get a master's degree from Hollins. He has published two novels and a third is due out from Ticknor and Fields this year. Mr. Bell now lives in Baltimore where he is teaching at Goucher College. His short stories have been anthologized in *Intro 9* and the *Best American Short Stories*.

Mary Ward Brown is a native Southerner. She was born and raised on a farm in the Black Belt of Alabama where she still lives, on the same farm, in the same house. Her collection of short stories, *Tongues of Flame,* was published by Seymour Lawrence/Dutton in June. One of her stories was included in the *Best American Short Stories 1984.* She has one son and two granddaughters.

Suzanne Brown was born in Fort Benning, Georgia, but grew up in Goldsboro, North Carolina. Her short stories have appeared in such journals as *Carolina Quarterly, The Southern Review,* and *Southwest Review.* She teaches at Dartmouth College where she co-directs the program in creative writing. She spent the 1985–86 academic year in West Germany as a Fulbright Professor, teaching at the University of Mannheim.

James Lee Burke grew up in Texas and Louisiana. His work history includes stints in the oil field, on the pipeline, as a social worker, land surveyor, and newspaper reporter. Now he teaches fiction writing in the

239

MFA program at Wichita State University. His short stories have appeared in many magazines, and he has published numerous books of fiction. The most recent is a collection of stories, *The Convict,* and two new novels are scheduled for publication in 1986.

Ron Carlson lives and writes in Salt Lake City. Norton has published his three books: two novels, *Betrayed by F. Scott Fitzgerald* and *Truants,* and a collection of stories out this year, *The News of the World.* His short work has appeared in *Carolina Quarterly, TriQuarterly, Sports Illustrated, McCall's,* and other magazines. He was the recipient of an NEA grant for fiction in 1985.

Doug Crowell teaches at Texas Tech University in Lubbock. His stories have appeared in *Mississippi Review, New Directions, Crazyhorse, Epoch, Florida Review,* and other journals. Work of his is to be included in an anthology of Texas writers to be published by the University of Texas Press, *South by Southwest: Stories of Modern Texas.* Mr. Crowell won an NEA grant in fiction in 1983.

Leon V. Driskell was born and raised in Athens, Georgia. For the last 22 years, he's lived in Kentucky, where he teaches English and writing at the University of Louisville. *Passing Through,* his collection of related short stories, is set in the northern Kentucky farmland. Mr. Driskell also writes criticism and poetry, and seven of his short stories have been listed as "distinguished" in the *Best American Short Stories* series.

Elizabeth Harris is a Southerner by "ancestry, birth, half-raising, and later choice." Born in Fort Worth, Texas, she was reared there and in Pennsylvania. She settled in Austin, Texas, in 1976 and teaches fiction writing and modern literature at the University of Texas at Austin. Her short stories have appeared in a number of literary periodicals.

Mary Hood lives near Woodstock, Georgia. She is the author of two collections of stories. The first, *How Far She Went,* is now available in Avon paperback, and the second, *Venus Is Blue,* has just been published by Ticknor and Fields.

David Huddle, from Ivanhoe, Virginia, has taught at the University of Vermont for the past 15 years. His most recent book, *Only the Little Bone* (David Godine, 1986), is a collection of short stories and includes "Summer of the Magic Show." Mr. Huddle is also a poet.

Gloria Norris was born and grew up in Holcombe, Mississippi, a small hamlet on the delta-hills border. Her great-grandparents were pioneer settlers of the region. Ms. Norris has had three short stories reprinted in the *O. Henry Prize Stories* volumes and is the author of *Looking for Bobby,* a novel.

Kurt Rheinheimer was born and raised in Baltimore and has lived in Roanoke, Virginia, since 1976. He is editor of *The Roanoker.* His stories have been published in many magazines, from *Black Warrior Review* to *Redbook,* and several of them have been cited on honor lists in the *Pushcart Prize* collections and the *Best American Short Stories* series.

W. A. Smith was born and raised in Charleston, South Carolina, and attended the University of Virginia. He lives now in San Francisco, where he is finishing up work for a master's degree in English at San Francisco State University. His stories have been published in *Calliope, FM Five, Transfer,* and *Cimarron Review.* "Delivery" was listed as an honor story in two annual prize story anthologies in 1986.

Wallace Whatley grew up in Alabama and still lives there. He was educated at Auburn University and the University of North Carolina at Greensboro and now teaches at Columbus College in Columbus, Georgia. His stories and poems have appeared in several quarterlies including *Descant, The Greensboro Review,* and *The Southern Review.* He is the recipient of a Book-of-the-Month Club College Writing Fellowship, a grant from the Alabama State Arts Council, and an award from the Ingram Merrill Foundation.

Luke Whisnant's fiction and poetry have appeared in *Esquire, Grand Street, Southern Poetry Review,* and other journals. A native North Carolinian, he teaches in the writing program at East Carolina University and is a co-editor of *Leaves of Greens,* an anthology of poems about collards.

Sylvia Wilkinson, a native of Durham, North Carolina, has lived for many years in California, near Los Angeles. A race-car enthusiast, she earns her living as a race-team timer and, in this capacity, travels the world. She is the author of five novels, numerous children's books, and two nonfiction works about car racing, the most recent, *Dirt Tracks to Glory,* having been published by Algonquin Books of Chapel Hill in 1984. Her short stories are rare and treasured.

Shannon Ravenel, the editor, was born and raised in the Carolinas—Charlotte, Greenville, Camden, and Charleston. She attended Hollins College in Virginia and worked as a fiction editor at Houghton Mifflin in the '60s and early '70s. Since 1977, she has served as Annual Editor of the *Best American Short Stories* series and has read thousands of short stories. She lives now with her family in St. Louis and is Senior Editor of Algonquin Books of Chapel Hill.